Timber Rose

J.L. Oakley

ISBN: 149370981X
ISBN-13:9781493709816
Library of Congress Control Number 2014905460

DEDICATION

Here's to the real Timber Roses, the women who climbed mountains in skirts, hiked with the early mountaineering clubs and pushed for the formation of national parks and trails in Washington State all while raising children, tending to home and fighting for the right to vote.

ACKNOWLEDGMENTS

Thanks to my wonderful Friday critique group of many years, especially Heidi, Sherry and Kari who started it all.

Thanks to Mary Gillilan and the Independent Writers' Studio for the comments and writing hints.

Thanks to Andrew Shattuck McBride for his editing and keen eye on those little details.

Thanks for Norman L. Green of Threshold Documents for formatting advice.

Thanks to Suzanne Bailey for being a Beta reader.

Thanks to those fabulous Starbucks E. Maple Street baristas Terri, Jess, Jen, Shalom and Holly for their friendship and good cups of coffee.

And Rolf, who always got his steelhead and forever, my heart.

We have seen the summit of the mountain. As I sit here in camp and consider our feat, I'm still moved by the experience. Of course, all want to know what it feels like to stand on the tip-top of "the" mountain. IT was a heavenly moment. Nothing was said. Such sensations can be known to only those who reach the heights.

Fay Fuller, first woman to ascend Mount Rainier, 1890

Book I
Kla-how-ya
1907

Chapter 1

Caroline Symington leaned against the sheer rock wall rising above her, her cheek flat against its cold stone face. She took the rope belayed down to her from the crest above and moved to her right. Her high top boot found a good spot and she stepped over to it.

"How is the weather up there, Miss Symington?" a male voice called from below.

Oh, bother, Caroline thought. *Martin Colton.* Of all the people to worm his way into the only society where she could be herself. She barely knew him, but wondered if his presence was a plot of her parents to keep her in tow. They always fretted about her belonging to a mountaineering club.

She knew she should feel grateful being a scion of a proper, influential family. She had prestige and money, a comfortable life amid proper and comfortable friends and an insured future if she took the opportunities sent along her way. But often being a scion felt like a twig grafted onto root stock and nurtured to grow a certain way. She felt forever foreign, a pear growing on an apple tree.

"Do I spy a flock of hens?" Colton called again.

Caroline considered the rock face above her. *Hens!* The

women in this mountaineering club were the most well-educated and adventurous people she had ever met. Women made up almost half of the club. She ignored him and pulled herself up to the next foothold, her long canvas skirt scraping the rock.

Below her were the five others still climbing the last part of the hike to the pinnacle. The climbers were on a wide ledge mottled with gray lichen and stunted alpine flowers. Underneath the ledge, the drop went down one hundred feet.

She continued up, taking the gloved hands of Peter Lim and Sissie Major for the final step to the top.

Peter smiled at her. He was an experienced hike leader.

"Welcome to our kingdom," Sissie said, sweeping her arms around. "Isn't it magnificent?"

"Truly." Caroline tied her floppy hat's chinstrap to keep it from blowing away in the steady breeze circling around the top and took a breath of the clean sharp air. The kingdom lay out in all directions, the sharp crags of the Oregon Cascades still snow-covered in summer, mountain meadows and great stands of evergreen forests. A lone homestead sent up a gasp of smoke through its chimney.

She joined the dozen climbers gathered at the center of the flat pinnacle and drank from her canteen. The men sported Filson packer hats and jackets while the women wore a diverse array of long skirts, knickerbockers, or bloomers and logger boots that went almost to the knee. Sturdy shirts, jackets and hats of all styles completed their attire. Except for her logger boots, her friend Sissie looked like a secretary from a Portland firm but looks deceived. She was an accomplished mountaineer, one of the first to climb Mount Hood in the 1890s. Caroline nodded her head at the next three climbers to arrive and raised her canteen to them.

"This is quite a success, don't you think, Caroline?" Sissie said. "Won't we have something for our next bulletin?"

"Oh, yes." She felt like she was on the top of the world for this adventure was her tenth time out on a vigorous hike that required a bit of rope work.

"Miss Sy-ming-ton," Colton's voice rose up clear and annoyingly possessive.

"Who is he?" Sissie asked under her breath. "Your beau?"

"Heavens, no. I barely know the man. I didn't even know he registered to go, let alone liked tramping."

Peter, still holding the line, called down from the edge. "You having difficulty?"

"Not at all. Not at all. Just wondering how Miss Symington is faring."

Not well, Caroline thought and blushed. The mountain air made everything so clear and embarrassing.

"I believe she's fine. Would you please get in line to take the belay so we can get everyone up here?"

"Indeed."

"Why don't you join the others over there, Caroline," Sissie said. "I'd like a group picture and Margaret has a Brownie camera."

Caroline was relieved to oblige. She started toward her friends then turned back sharply when Colton let out a loud. "Uh-oh."

"Colton. What are you doing?" Lim shouted. He strained back on the rope. "It's not your turn yet."

Before Caroline could register there was trouble, Sissie sprang into action along with two other hikers and seized the rope. Caroline ran to the edge and gasped in horror at Colton on the other end struggling to find a foothold. His legs dangled out in space, scissor kicking wildly at the rock face. His face was pale, his eyes wide with panic. Above him a young woman fought to keep her hold on the very place Caroline had been ten minutes before. To save herself, she let go the rope to keep Colton from pulling her off. He was about fifteen feet above the ledge, but each time he struggled, the rope bumped against her long skirt and caught on her knapsack.

"Hold on, Miss Finch. We'll get another rope," Lim said. "Caroline, Morrisy, give us a hand here."

Morrisy hurriedly passed a rope over to her and together they dropped it to the woman.

"I can't get my footing," Colton gasped.

"Stay calm. Can you lower yourself to the ledge?" Peter asked, straining against Colton's weight and wild actions. "We'll get someone down right away." He and his companions braced their heavy boots against the rim.

Caroline was relieved when Tabitha Finch got the new rope in her gloved hands and began to step over to the next foothold, but she couldn't take her eyes off of Colton. *What possessed him to come?* She was angry and she was afraid. When Colton's rope rolled along the rock and caught the young woman's boot, she began to shake.

"Oh, Mercy." Tabitha twisted away from Colton, her caulked boots dug into stone as she climbed higher.

Colton swung back.

He's going to fall, Caroline thought. Her heart jabbed into her throat, the strain of her shoulder building to agony as they pulled and lifted the young woman to safety.

"There you go, Miss Finch," Lim said. "You — Mr. Colton — quit twisting. Stay still. We'll get someone down." He motioned to another man in the party to go down.

"I can't seem to manage," Colton called up.

"Oh, for gosh sakes, Mr. Colton, stay still," Caroline said.

Colton stopped and hugged the gray wall of stone. He beamed up at her. "My lady. Oh —"

With that, the rope slipped through his bare hands. He fell to the ledge with a hard thud and a shriek. Miraculously, he doubled wrapped the rope around his left arm for dear life, but Caroline could see that one of his legs tucked under him at an odd angle. A second climber went over the side to aide him.

"Oh," Colton groaned. "I think I broke my ankle. Oh! It hurts like blazes."

"Is he all right?" Caroline shouted.

The climbers signaled yes.

Tabitha dusted off her skirt. She gave Caroline a sidelong glance. "That was close."

Caroline hugged her arms. "Should we bring him up or lower him?"

"We'll have him well in hand, Miss Symington," Peter Lim said as he checked the belaying ropes.

Caroline watched her friends gather around Colton with the calm dexterity she admired. She felt a swelling pride she was one of them.

"How is he?" she called down.

"Not too bad. Looks like a bad sprain, not a break."

"Thank goodness."

She flinched when Colton let out a cry that ricocheted across the peak and the forested valley below, but truth be told, the poor man would never understand she was beyond his reach.

Chapter 2

"Caroline, were you listening at all?"

"Of course, I was." Caroline sat immobilized at her chair in the dining car as she listened to her sister Sophie bemoan her prospects for marriage. Outside the long window, the massive white head of Mount Rainier kept pace alongside them. From a distance, Sophie probably thought it looked like a fancy upside down tea cup covered with thick, white icing, its wide slopes belittling the forested mountains and foothills that rolled beneath it. Caroline, however, thought it commanded its place and dominated the endless stream of fir and hemlock stands and mist-soaked valleys skimming past the window like images on a spinning top. She wished she could climb it.

"I'm very sorry that your prospects with Mr. Kinsley didn't work out, Sophie. Perhaps Cousin Raymond will have some offerings. Aunt Emma has promised a social at least once a week. You'll be forgetting him in no time."

"Oh, Dennis. He was such a bore."

"I thought you loved him."

"He was only trying to impress Father."

"How inconsiderate."

Caroline took a sip of her tea. At twenty-three, Sophie was

three years older than Caroline, a beauty who affected all the airs of their class. Everything about her was as graceful as a china doll: from her hour-glass figure to her oval face set on a long neck ensconced in a high lacy collar. Her thick chocolate colored hair, silky as a sable pelt, was swept up and piled on her head. A little teal-colored bowler held it all together, though it looked as though it would slip off as she sipped her tea with lacy gloved hands.

Sometimes, Caroline didn't understand her sister at all. Where Caroline was outspoken, Sophie was conventional in her thinking, still ascribing to the dictum of fashion that kept her corseted in the latest style and simpering female thinking. Caroline often wondered why their differences could even include underpinnings. She was grateful, however, that Sophie had agreed to come. Caroline would not have been allowed to travel alone.

Sophie startled her back to the moment. "Will you be seeing Martin Colton again?"

"Heavens, no."

"He seemed very determined."

"Determination is not a quality I desire in a suitor." Caroline sighed. "I prefer common sense. No, I won't be seeing him again." Caroline kept her eyes on the outside, crossing her fingers under the table. The whole affair not only embarrassed her but mortified her. *What was he thinking? What were her parents thinking?* Didn't they understand she was a New Woman of the new twentieth century? In living that creed, she had no intention of marrying someone like Colton just because they selected him. She wanted to fall in love first.

It was stifling in Portland where she had to be the accommodating daughter of an old and influential pioneer family, politely attending the affairs of the tight-knit society that made up life there. Her grandparents on both sides of the family had made the famous trek out across the prairies to the new Garden of Eden in the early 1840s.

The stories were thrilling, but they were only meant to be a moral that never changed: the Symingtons were the first —

always first — to do such and such a thing in the wilderness until the homesteads and settlements grew into proper facsimiles of New England towns. They were the pillars of society, their prestige grown up alongside the trappings that went with it. Caroline hated those trappings. She preferred tramping out in the mountains with the hiking clubs.

Sophie put down her teacup. The creamy pale liquid continued to shiver after the cup was settled on its little plate. The train was climbing as it rounded a steep forested bend. Caroline leaned against the window to see more clearly. The mountain had disappeared behind the huge grove of cedar and fir they were passing. The inside of the dining car darkened; the gas lanterns seemed to glow brighter.

"How much farther to Seattle, do you think sister?" Sophie wiped the edges of her mouth with her napkin as though she might mar her skin.

"I don't know. We should ask our waiter." Caroline hoped they would get there soon. The train trip had not been unpleasant, but another hour of Sophie chatting about her beaus! If they hadn't taken their tea here, Caroline would have gone mad.

Sophie folded her napkin by her plate, its tip pointing to Caroline. "I wonder how Seattle will really be? So crowded and uncouth. Nearly ninety thousand people!"

"Or less. Depending on the loggers coming into town. At least from what I've read."

Caroline's literary conception of Seattle, however, didn't match reality. They were met at the railroad station by their Uncle Harold, who quickly organized their trunks and suitcases and had them loaded onto the back of a hired cab. While her sister daintily held her skirt away from the thick mud around the wheels of the carriage and climbed up into her seat, Caroline patted the nose of the horse nearest her and took in all the sights.

There was new construction everywhere. Several hills closest to the station looked as though they were under attack as a regrading operation was underway. Many of the three-story and four-story buildings were in fine brick, clamoring for attention among the older wooden structures as they spread out to the newly filled tide flats several blocks away or climbed the steep hill rising behind the station. Caroline counted dozens of signs and awnings announcing all manner of undertakings as settlers old and Klondike new vied for their place in the bustling commerce: dentist, outfitter for the gold fields, lawyer or greengrocer. The streets were paved, crowded with people and all kinds of horse-drawn vehicles and bicycles, but in many places, they were not. Herding them along, their wires hanging like gigantic clotheslines, telephone poles marched across the raw city landscape like toothpicks on a tea sandwich tray. Her nose wrinkled at the dirt and the smell of horse manure and oiled rope mixed in the pungent mud of the tide flats. Caroline began to look for some trees.

"Will we be going over to *Kla-how-ya* tonight, Uncle?" she asked.

"I thought you should like dinner out, then spend the night in our town house. We'll take the ferry over in the morning. It's supposed to be fair tomorrow. The mountain puts on quite a show in the morning."

"Are Cousins Liza and Raymond there now?"

"Yes. They've been over for a week settling in. Your Aunt Agatha is here, though. She's anxious to see you girls." Harold Symington gave her a warm smile, then gave the leather straps that held the luggage at the back of the cab a final tug.

Caroline smiled back. She hadn't seen her uncle in several years and she couldn't help notice that at fifty, he was still a strong and powerful looking man. *Someone more at home in the country than behind a desk in a bank,* she thought. Uncle Harold smelled of cigars and a hint of whiskey and looked like a man who could take a big stick and walk into any labor line and cow it. Her father, Charles Symington, however, was a leaner and more refined version of the Symington line; someone who was cultured and spoke from the knowledge of books and the experience of privilege. Not like Uncle Harold.

9

"In you go, Caroline. And mind your good shoes. It rained last night as it's wont to do here." His dark brown eyes twinkled, spreading whispery crow lines across his cheekbones and under his dark beard.

She took his hand and settled in. As they lurched off, she held onto her hat. *The adventure has begun*, she thought, all the day's tedium brushed away. She could hardly wait to see *Kla-how-ya*.

It was the trees, Caroline thought. She had loved the pictures of the grounds there immediately, for it appeared to be barely pried out of the great forests around it. Behind the three-story home, there was a stand of fir trees — long, sorrowful giants stripped of their understory and their dignity, yet defiant to the end as roads and fields were hacked and cleared around them. They stood like guardians at the edge of the world that lay beyond the house where the forest came together again and continued east to the foothills of the North Cascades. It made her long for them.

First, she'd have to get there.

It was bright and crisp when they left for the eight o'clock ferry. Settling into their carriage, they headed east toward Lake Washington, passing new homes under construction among the farms and forested homesteads that told of an earlier, more rugged time. There were log piles a story high stacked for burning and big frame houses sitting in the cleared areas like lonely white frogs on lily pads.

"Do you see how Seattle is striking east from Elliot Bay?" Uncle Harold swept his hand about like he was riding through his own private domain.

Caroline sighed. She thought she was coming to a wilderness, but here all she saw was development spreading out with missionary zeal. Even the electric trolley lines came out this far, ending next to an amusement park. The only thing that gave her comfort was Mount Rainier coming into view as they came over the hill and down to the ferry dock. The mountain was in full view, a towering white pyramid that seemed to take up half of the sky. It stood at the southern end of the lake, dwarfing the forested hills and inlets that marked the eastern side of the water.

The mountain gave her hope. She read a schoolteacher wearing a bloomer suit and boy's shoes with caulks had climbed it in 1890, the first woman to reach the top. She felt confident she could at least hike the meadows around Mount Rainier and hoped her cousins would go with her. If not, she'd seek some hiking group similar to her group in Oregon, the Mazamas, one of oldest mountaineering clubs in the northwest.

"Come girls." Aunt Agatha swept past her with Mr. Train, their butler, sagging under overstuffed *portmanteaus* and a hatbox in his hands. Her aunt was a spare but pretty woman a few years younger than Harold Symington. Caroline had always liked her.

They crowded onto the little steam ferry and headed to the passenger cabin. Caroline had barely sat down when the boat began to move. As they set out on the water, the lake shimmered in the clear air. Ahead of them a large island loomed to their right. Beyond the island, cedar and Douglas fir rose high along the shore.

As they came past the half-cultivated island, the party went out onto the open observation deck. Uncle Harold pointed toward the mainland where several homes were visible along the shoreline.

"Is that *Kla-how-ya?*" Caroline asked over the sound of the little stern wheeler's paddle slapping the water. Some large homes in the new Craftsman style peeked out from under towering firs.

"Yes," Symington said. "The second from the right of the ferry dock. We'll be there in about twenty minutes after we land. Raymond will be at the dock with the wagon."

Caroline smiled at the thought, then hugged her arms. Her stomach fluttered since they left the dock and she was glad the ride would soon be over. The water was surprisingly rough for such a glorious day.

"How far away is Mount Rainier, uncle?"

"Fifty miles. It looks close, but that's because it's so huge. Highest in the forty-five states."

"Oh." Tramping there might not be as easily accessible as she thought. Disappointed, she stepped over to the railing and looked down. She was sorry she did. Below her the main deck seemed to sway. Her stomach took a decided lurch and she threw a hand over her mouth. Embarrassed, she groped along the rail to the back of the observation deck where the steep iron stairs went down to the deck. To her relief, her family didn't see her when the nausea seized her again. Groaning, she leaned against the rail.

"Don't look down," a man said next to her. "Look across the water to the shoreline and keep your eyes on that."

Instinctively, Caroline obeyed and stared as hard as she could at the only horizontal line that wasn't bobbing up and down. She fixed her eyes on the trees.

"Now take a deep breath. It'll bring cool air into your lungs."

Caroline obeyed again. The shore moved closer without churning her stomach and the nausea began to pass. Finally, she turned and looked at her adviser. She was surprised to see that he wasn't the gentleman who had boarded the ferry along with them earlier and had promised to call after they were settled in. He was a different sort, a laborer perhaps, returning to the logging camps somewhere deep beyond the shore.

He was a man in his early twenties and not especially tall, but lean and muscular. The kind of strength which comes from hard work and not a barbell that was the fad with some of the gentleman Caroline knew. He had dressed neatly for the day, wearing a dark Sunday jacket and pants, but they didn't cap the raw ruggedness underneath. He was fair, blonde hair — stuck out under his cap — with intelligent, light blue eyes filled with as much concern as masculine interest. She blushed and quickly turned back to the shore.

"Are you feeling better?" he asked.

Caroline nodded and hoped he'd go away. Or, at least, not

see her face. She stared desperately toward the looming shoreline.

"Will you be all right?"

Caroline was too mortified to answer.

"Then I'll be going."

He murmured something else behind her, but she couldn't hear it because the ferry's horn let out a grand blast as it drew closer to the shore. She stood stock still as he moved close behind her, a electrifying prickle running over her shoulders and arms, then it was gone. Feeling seasick again, she leaned weakly against the railing and willed the shore to her. She wondered if he was still there, but all she felt was an empty space. A cool breeze on her shoulders.

"Caroline? Are you unwell?" Aunt Agatha swooped down and placed a shawl over Caroline's shoulders. "Poor dear. You mustn't exert yourself."

"I'm all right, Aunt Agatha. It's just the movement of the waters."

Caroline turned around. The stranger wasn't there. Only passengers herding together as they got ready to descend to the deck below. Cautiously, she leaned over. At the bow of the ferry, a group of workers were congregating, in the throes of getting ready to disembark. They all seemed chums from the way they jostled each other and talked. In the middle, was her rescuer, his cap removed. He must have sensed her because he looked up and slowly bowed his head to her. Caroline was too mortified to look at him directly, but she did incline her head back before withdrawing to her aunt's side.

He was not there when they disembarked.

Chapter 3

"You mess with my gear one more time, I'll flatten you for good, Arntzen."

"*Ja*, sure. You just quit pinching my *tobac*."

The loud voices on the other side of the row of bunks boomed on top of each other for a few more seconds, then gave way to an explosion of blows. There was the sound of someone slamming into the beds, followed by swearing and a general shaking of floorboards. Bob Alford paid them no mind, though. Keeping his head low and out of target from flying projectiles — namely bodies shaking the wall of hand-hewn bed posts next to him — he closed his wooden chest for the final time and prepared to drag it over to the door.

"You taking off, Alford?" a voice behind him called out.

"If these ladies will calm down. When's the next stage leaving?"

"Within the hour. You should check in with the office before you go, though." A stout mustachioed man in his late thirties came into the bunkhouse and scowled. "You boys quit or by God, you'll buck or swamp for the next week."

McKinley stepped around the bunks and grabbed each of the big loggers by the collar and marched to the door. The camp foreman pushed them both as easily as if they were small boys and sent them tumbling out into the muddy path below the bunkhouse stoop. One of the men began to swear, but was careful to aim it at the giant cedar stump he had rolled against, not the foreman. Alford couldn't see much with McKinley in the door, but he knew the storm was over. The foreman didn't work on threats alone and the men knew it. He'd earned their respect because he was also a fair and decent man. Alford decided that it was all right to go.

Arntzen and Mueller were brushing off caked mud from their knees when McKinley let Alford through. They looked at him sourly, then backed off in the direction of the camp kitchen. A crew of men just coming into the center of camp with eight-foot long crosscut saws on their shoulders stopped to let them pass. A sandy-haired man whooped out a call to Alford.

"You really doing it?" he yelled.

"It's done," Alford said as he stepped down to the group. "My letter came in just a while ago. I'll spend time with the folks this summer, then report to the Forest Service this fall."

"Not without a send-off from us," another logger announced. "It ain't decent. Besides, what's Margie Gorham gonna say? You being a client and all."

"*Ja*, Margie. She send you away good, you betcha."

The others guffawed and made some crude remarks, but Alford took it all in stride. His friends never let up.

There was a time when visiting a cathouse had been a particular joy in his life as a logger. That was when he was quite young and still proving himself to an exceptionally rough crowd. He hadn't been interested in the past few years. Not since he lost his eldest brother Stein in a senseless logging accident. That single event sobered him as it opened his eyes to his own mortality and what he ought to do with his life.

It seemed an obscene joke that someone so full of life, so good and honest could be cut down at twenty-six. It made Alford's world collapse. For several days, he was unapproachable, but instead of going on a drinking and

15

whoring binge that others might well have done, he became quiet and withdrawn, spending time alone in the woods. When he finally rejoined his friends, the wildness was gone out of him. The girls and gaming meant nothing any longer. For the first time, he saw them as a dead end. He began to look for different answers.

Ribbing Alford about Margie Gorham was a joke. She ran a place on the east side of Lake Washington that served the logging camps, entertaining lonely men that couldn't make it over to Seattle. She was a generous woman who took pride in running a clean establishment and giving her "clients" a bit of home. He'd come once to retrieve a friend of his, waiting out in the red satin-walled parlor without female company. There he found that Mrs. Gorham kept a fine collection of books that wasn't available to the average man. A conversation ensued. He already knew she was the daughter of a doctor and the widow of an early homesteader to the area long before the wealthy denizens of Seattle looked eastward for fancy summer homes. But her background and taste in things that were more cultured than the general run of the camps intrigued him and he asked to return. To read and talk.

Alford grinned at the collection of six young men that were his friends. Two hadn't been speaking English any more than a year and though Swedish and Norwegian were spoken in his home, it took a bit of concentration to figure out their pidgin. The rest were from around the Seattle area and unlike him, had not gotten beyond the eighth grade. Billy Howell could barely read in any language. None of this, however, had any bearing on their friendship. They were all good chums, looking out for each other in the woods and out on the town on paydays

"When's the stage goin' in?" Billy Howell asked. He was a strapping young man with straight brown hair, high cheekbones and square jaw. A fairly handsome young man if he kept his mouth closed. His teeth were uneven.

"Not too far off. McKinley says I have to check out."

"Then check out. Dan'll get your locker and put it out for you, won't you Dan? Sven and I will hold the stage if you're late. We can be at Margie's in no time."

"Maybe his folks are expecting him," another of the chums allowed.

Alford shook his head no. "Not for a couple of days."

"Good," grinned Billy. "The night is ours."

But not necessarily the morning. Alford woke up in a back room at Margie Gorham's with a headache as piercing as the proverbial log in the eye. How he got there, he couldn't remember, but boa feathers on his chest weren't a good omen. Sitting up in the wrought iron bed, he brushed them off and began to look for his trousers and shirt. He had apparently fallen asleep in his union suit.

"Coffee?"

Alford looked up too fast and groaned. Mrs. Gorham was standing in the doorway on the other side of the beaded curtain. She wore her usual dark morning dress and watch chain around her neck. In her hands was a cup of coffee.

"What happened?" he grimaced. "Did *anything* happen?"

"Rosie was disappointed. The boys primed you too much. You were asleep before anything serious happened, though she did get to tuck you in. I'm surprised at you, Bob Alford. All this time coming here and you've never let on what a ladies'-man you could be. My girls are all going to quit because of you."

She swept into the room and put the coffee on the little side table by the bed, then went over to the window and tied back the drapes. An eye-piercing stream of light roared in, compounding his headache even more. When he grumbled behind her, the woman laughed.

"When you're decent, you can take breakfast with me."

"Don't think I can eat."

"Nonsense. I'll make something up for your stomach and you'll be fine."

"Where're the boys?"

"*Deshabille*, I'm sure. I thought I'd get you first."

"Thanks...." He gingerly tried on his trousers, careful not to move his head too much.

"Don't think of it." Mrs. Gorham left the room in a rustle of satin. Not necessarily a beautiful woman, she had a handsome figure and a fine complexion that belied years of hardship. Her large brown eyes were both perceptive and kind, framed by rich brunette hair that would make any of Gibson's girls envious.

He made his way over to the washstand and poured some water into the bowl. Outside beyond the lace curtains behind the drapes, he could see chickens pecking in the yard next to her roses. This place always intrigued him. It had been cut out of the wilderness twenty-three years earlier, the tall stumps that stood like accusing sentinels out in the pasture still bearing the spring board marks that helped to bring them down. For many years, the white clapboard house had been the only dwelling in the area. Then there was no road to speak of, only a trail over which an ox could pull a sled through the dense and endless woods. Even now, with the plank road in, the giant trees seemed to lean over the pasture and pathways, held at bay by some strange incantation. It took courage to homestead back then and perhaps more courage now as civilization felled its way across the land. Every day, it seemed that logging operations were increasing and after them, a society that didn't appreciate the Mrs. Gorhams of the world.

A light breakfast waited for him but her promised concoction helped him handle the fresh biscuits. He didn't say much, though, having a hard time with his aching eyes. So he let her talk.

"I'm going out this afternoon. What are your plans? Is it true you're entering the Forest Service? Going to be a guide or ranger?"

Alford nodded his head cautiously.

"Ah. Well, I'll hear more I'm sure — when you're able. I must attend to the other gentlemen."

He finished his biscuits, then went out onto the back porch. Out in the forest, some thrush was trilling its head off, but Alford wished it would sing elsewhere. He wasn't in the mood.

Funny how a few years could change your perception of things. He hadn't been so shellacked since before Stein died. That was two years ago. Since then, he had kept his drinking to a minimum. He still played cards with the boys, but he decided to better himself and enrolled in a correspondence course to improve his writing and math. Often that kept him in the bunkhouse working by lamplight until early in the morning. The rest of the time he went fishing, angling for trout and salmon with a pole he had made himself. It was a love acquired from his father and lately brought him the most peace. When logging season was over in the fall, he often took on jobs guiding city folks to the rivers and lakes that bounded on the east side. He also sought out the advice of old timers and honed his skills in packing, fishing and general woodcraft and when he heard that they might open a department of forestry at the University, he wrote and asked for information.

"There you are."

Behind Alford, the screen porch door screeched as Billy Howell — upright and cheerful after consuming unknown quantities of beer — came through the door. Alford flinched.

"Mornin'"

"My, my. The doldrums of life."

"Sorry. My head has an distinct undercurrent."

"Then the gentleman needs further rehabilitation." Billy picked at his suspenders and stretched, letting out a loud belch. "There's a dance over at Swede Hill tomorrow. We can get you to your folks, then check it out."

"I'm not sure if I'll be recovered."

Billy snorted. "You're not the hellion I've loved and admired."

"Those days are over."

"Then let's celebrate. Heck, Alford. Whatcom's too far away. Why'd you have to do some fool thing like that and get signed up? I'll probably never see you again."

"The welcome sign will always be out."

Alford smiled at his friend. He was, for all his rowdiness, a good one. They had known each other for seven years and during that time worked as a falling team among other jobs. That meant teamwork. It was dangerous being high up on a springboard working an undercut with only an ax and crosscut saw to take a thunderous cedar down. And the work was hard. You had to work closely with your partner to make things go right. Billy made things go right.

"Alford, Dan says it's the best dance of early summer. It's not a loose place. My own mother would like it. Sometimes some of the summer girls are around. Pretty too."

Alford made a face, then laughed. "All right."

Chapter 4

Which is why on the third of June, Alford found himself on the second floor of the local community hall staring across the wood floor at one of the most beautiful young ladies he had ever met. *Again.* The seasick girl from the ferry wore a soft, white dress so popular these days that tucked in her little waist before flowing down to the floor. Across her breasts up to her throat was a wide expanse of lace. Her cinnamon brown hair was piled up, sweeping away from her high forehead and lovely green eyes he could see even from where he stood. Never one to be shy, his mouth suddenly went dry as he agonized over whether she'd remember him or not. The encounter on the ferry had only been a few short minutes, but in those moments, he had known his place. She was from a different world and class, so he had to dismiss her even if her beauty had knocked him flat. Yet seeing her again brought an uncustomary longing and an overwhelming desire to talk to her. The problem was, would she want to talk to him?

"Where you want to sit?" Billy asked coming up behind him.

"Think I'll go over the bandstand. I know the fiddle player." Alford adjusted his stiff collar and brushed his jacket, then plunged into the long space that separated them. Not sure of what he'd say, he made it over to the band, which was finishing its tune up and about to begin the evening's program.

"Hey, Mackie," he called out and shook the fiddler's hand as the man leaned down to greet him, then wandered over to the refreshment table where the object of his interest was talking to a female companion her own age.

A matron behind the table was serving and he took the non-alcoholic cup of punch offered him. Beside him, the young woman chattered with her friend. He felt her turn and swish away to the chairs set up along the wall. He sensed her light perfume of lilac and wondered what in the hell was he doing? Indecisive, he put the punch back on the cloth-covered table and walked back to Howell.

"That was quick," Billy chuckled.

"That was murder. I think I'm going to go."

"Go? We just got here. I ain't going. Not with that blonde in the corner. What the hell's the matter with you?"

Alford couldn't answer. Besides, the band had struck up with a saucy little number that got some of the parties up and heading out to the floor. He looked to see if the girl had been picked up, but she was still with her friend. From behind her gloved hand, she appeared to be giggling.

Billy caught the direction of his look and whistled under his breath. "Now who's that?"

"I don't know, but I'd appreciate it if you would let *me* find out."

"Then I take it you want to stay."

"I want to stay."

The band finished its first number and went into an easy tune. Some of the couples left and rearranged, while a few stayed on the floor chatting. At the back door, a party of young men came in. The room seemed to fill up, squeezing the bulk of the crowd back to the girls' end of the wall. When Alford saw her again, someone was talking to her, but she apparently declined and sat back in her chair. Her female companion, however, was being led away by another.

"Why don't you make your move?"

"Why don't you mind your own business. This isn't the Third Avenue." Alford pulled away and made his way over to her as steady as he could. He felt ridiculously adolescent. When he drew alongside her, she was sitting erect, watching the couples swirl around the floor.

"I see you're feeling much better, miss. I hope the rest of your journey went well."

The girl slowly raised her head and looked up him, her face at first puzzled, then curious.

"Sir?"

Alford's stomach tightened. Not such a good start.

"The ferry... several weeks ago."

"Oh, but of course." Her face flooded with a vibrant and lively glow.

There is a strength in that beauty, he thought, and it pleased him. "You don't mind, do you? I was just surprised to see you here."

"No, not at all," she answered. "Do you live near here?"

"My parents do," he answered and then the pleasantries began. Normally, it would've been tedious for him, trying to remember the rules of what was correct and not correct. The pleasant little bantering the sexes engage in as each presented their cases so to speak and then work it out in the proper boundaries of propriety. He was relieved to know she wasn't married and that the girl with her was a friend, not a sister. A sister could make things a bit sticky. But most importantly, he was relieved to find she was a young lady with a good head on her shoulders.

"I'm just visiting with my friend," she said as they sat down on the creaky wooden folding chairs set around the hall. "We're going on an outing with a mountaineering club from Seattle. Somewhere up near Snoqualmie."

"You're from there?"

"Actually, I'm from Portland, Oregon."

"Oh," Alford said. "Afraid I haven't been there. I've climbed down near Mount St. Helens, though. The lake there is quite breathtaking. From the mountaintop I could see all the way into Portland. Have you been on many outings?"

"Whenever I can. Mostly, they are simple adventures. It's not always easy to get out to the mountains, but I've managed to climb up around Mount Hood twice."

"Really?"

"Yes." The young lady smiled at him. "And how is it with you? Do you get out often?"

Alford grinned. "All the time, though lately it's been on the business end. I've worked a few logging camps these past years, but when I can, I guide and fish. It's what I prefer." He paused, then apologized for being rude and asked if she'd like something to drink.

"Why, yes. That would be very nice."

Alford got up to get her a cup and was surprised when she got up too.

"You needn't wait on me."

"Maybe I'd like to, miss...."

"Henderson. Caroline Henderson."

She smiled at him. "That's very thoughtful, but if you don't mind, I'd like to walk around."

He didn't mind.

They found the punch, admired the paper decorations and eventually he asked her to dance, timing it with the band's choice of a folk tune so that he could show her the steps.

"It's Norwegian," he said. "Almost all the community's Scandinavian here — Norwegians, Finns, Swedes — but they like to mix their tunes. The band does ragtime too, if you're so inclined."

"This sounds fine. The fiddle is so plaintive." He guided her around, gently touching her waist and soon they were moving with the whole hall across the floor. There was a second dance after that and then another. When they were done, she put her hand to her breast to catch her breath.

"Do you mind? I need some air."

Now I've done it, he thought. He stepped back to let her go, waiting for one of twenty other young men to take his place.

"Will you come? You must think I'm silly. Always going for air or the side of a boat, but I do find it a bit stuffy."

"I don't think you're silly at all. It's a bit crowded, that's all, and unusually hot for a June night. It generally rains."

"Is it always so?"

"June tends to be wet here."

They stepped out on the long back porch of the building and looked down toward the waters of Lake Washington. The trees had been cleared, making a wide path down to the shoreline. It was bright out, as it always was this time of year. By the twenty-first, it would be light as late as ten-thirty, but for now the sun was slipping down into the west above the forested hills across the lake, causing the water to glow like molten gold.

"It's so beautiful," Caroline said.

"Like it?"

"Yes. I didn't realize how big the lake is."

"It's big, all right. The lake shore here is one of my favorite places in the evening."

They talked for a while about the forests and hiking clubs.

"I can't wait until tomorrow," she said. "I haven't done an outing here before and the group is so involved in conservation *and* recreation. The women too. Only I have to buy some equipment if I'm going to do any serious mountain tramping."

"What do you need?" Alford asked.

"Oh, I have my alpenstock and boots, but I didn't bring a proper knapsack. Is there any place that might outfit a lady?"

"I could ask around," he said. "I know a man who outfits the Alaska expeditions. C. C. Filson. Has a place in Seattle. We've used a lot of his stuff in the camps. One of my brothers swears by it for mining. Might have something."

"That's very kind of you, but I'm not sure if I'll be staying in the area much longer. I have to return to my uncle's home."

"A pity."

They leaned against the rail and watched the sun brush the treetops. Eventually, they went back inside where they danced some more. He felt a natural ease with her as though he had known her for a long time. She seemed at ease too and as the evening wore down, the dance music slowed and so did they. They talked less and became aware of the company they kept. He held her more firmly though keeping a proper distance and always polite and gentlemanly.

"Caroline?" A woman's voice interrupted.

"Oh, Emily."

Caroline let go of Alford's hand. Alford stepped back.

A young woman with a plain, but still pretty face and practical in appearance stood beside them. Alford took her for a librarian or preacher's daughter, but then she had eyes that twinkled with mischief.

'This is my friend, Miss Emily Drew," Caroline said. "She is a family friend from Seattle who was summering in the area."

"Emily, this is…oh, dear, I never got yours."

"Bob Alford." He bowed to Emily. That was as far as the conversation went.

"It's time to go," Emily said as she gave her friend's wrap to her.

Alford looked outside. On the water, the sun had slipped behind the hills and twilight was falling. Some lanterns were lit in the hall for those that were staying.

"Yes, we must go." Caroline set the shawl on her shoulders. "It's an early start, you know."

Ah, the walk. Alford bowed to her slightly. "I hope you enjoy yourself." He thanked her for the evening, then offered to escort her to her carriage.

Caroline laughed. "Oh, but we rode bikes!"

"And we better go before the dark crashes right down on us," Emily said.

"Then to the bikes." Alford would see her off. It might be his last chance.

"Good-bye, Mr. Alford," Caroline smiled softly as she mounted her bicycle. "It's been most pleasant." She smiled again and Alford's heart sunk. She adjusted her soft dress skirt, then pedaled off behind Miss Drew who was anxious to be away. They headed up the gravel road toward the center of the tiny community and were about to turn, when she suddenly peeled off and came back.

"I hope you won't think me forward if I were to invite you to come on the hike with us. I was thinking that we might talk more about how I could get those provisions...."

Alford tried hard not to look too anxious when he said yes. He'd been desperately thinking of a way to see her again. His voice was strong and confident when he said that she was kind to think of him. He would enjoy the walk very much. "And you needn't worry, Miss Henderson. It will be well chaperoned. At least forty people hike at a time on some of these outings, especially if food was involved at trail's end."

Caroline laughed. "That's probably true."

"Good-bye," she said sweetly and dared to look him in the eyes. He dared back and felt they both knew this evening was no ordinary meeting.

"Caroline, how could you!" Emily stepped out of her dress and hung it up in her armoire. "You don't know who he is."

Caroline laughed as she undid her own. "I know. I'm not sure what came over me, but it'll be all right. He's very nice. Besides, he knows some of the people in the group. He outfitted some of them." She folded her dress over her bedstead and looked out into the woods behind her friend's home. They were taller than this second story floor, but not old growth. The place had been logged out fifteen years before.

"Is he a guide?"

"Apparently." Caroline began to remove her waist cover.

"He might be like many of the young men around here. He does everything."

"He says it's the seasonal nature of the work."

He's not a Wobbly, is he? They're so disgusting."

"We didn't talk politics."

"But he's a logger. Maybe my uncle knows him. He's foreman at the Big Cedars camp."

"Emily, please... I want my stay to be — pleasant. When I

came for the summer at my uncle's, I thought I'd be free of having to kowtow to someone else's wishes, but I seem to have attended as many social gatherings as I have in Portland. I enjoy meeting people unhindered. And I so look forward to the hike tomorrow. What a lovely group of people. Mrs. Casper's letter sounded so nice."

"She is nice. She writes articles for their magazine. I'd say she represents the temperament of the club. Very egalitarian. Almost half of the membership is women."

"Then you must be. Give poor Mr. Alford a chance."

"Hmpf. I've noted that you have, but then…" Emily grinned as she let down her long brown hair for brushing. "He has quite a manly figure and dances so —"

In a peal of laughter, Caroline threw her beaded evening purse at Emily's back. The girl turned quickly and together they collapsed giggling on their beds.

"Poor Mr. Alford" had equal trouble settling down from the dance. After Miss Henderson left, he had gone back into the community hall to find Billy and ended up staying another hour. They got to their rooms around midnight. Billy went promptly to bed, but Alford couldn't sleep. Lying awake on the bed with his arms behind his head, he thought of the evening's events and oddly of his parents.

They had met at a dance. He had heard the story over and over how his mother Anna Lise had come to Kongsberg, Norway from Sweden to be a housekeeper and had met his father at some fete. They fell in love, married and moved down closer to Oslo where he could find work as a carpenter. There had been children —four boys —before the country fell on hard times and they made the momentous decision to immigrate to Minnesota where land was cheap and a man could work an honest day and become rich. They didn't become rich instead moving around until they finally took the train out to the Pacific Northwest and put down a claim in the wilderness.

Papa had to often seek work in the woods as well as in

Seattle, but he was an excellent finish carpenter and woodworker. It didn't hurt he could also work on boats and fish and soon the family did prosper. Alford and a sister who died in infancy had been born here, but during this time, the family's modest fortunes grew. An uncle came over from the old country and started a store catering to the growing population. Alford's father sold his furniture pieces there and was in demand for the new homes built by the rich on the east side. Eventually, Alford's grandparents came over from Norway and established their own farm, selling dairy products and eggs to the logging companies.

Alford smiled into the dark. They were from the old country. Sometimes they had been strict, but never harsh. He and his brothers had grown up under a loving roof. But it was his parents' love for each other that he thought about the most now. His mother, he'd been told, had come from a respectable old family in Sweden, which like many others in the mid-nineteenth century had fallen on bad times. She was different from his father, yet they had made a marriage that worked because of the many things they had in common. Papa had always said that she was the woman for him because she wasn't afraid to try something. She was hardworking, kept a good house and had good business sense. That made the marriage work. Mama said that it was because he helped her lift the heavy pots and sang a good tune. Alford only knew that whenever he left his parents' house, they were there when he returned, ready to give God's blessing.

He tried not to think about tomorrow, but one of the fiddle pieces from the dance got stuck in his head and then there was no getting away from it. Over and over again he saw himself and the girl twirling across the floor and he knew he not only wanted to see her tomorrow, he wanted to call on her. To be with her at all times. From the open window outside his room, a lilac tree was in its last bloom. He thought the scent would drive him wild. Pounding his pillow, he flopped on his side and groaned. This wasn't going to be easy.

Chapter 5

Early the morning, the hiking party left by train for the mountains. Caroline and Emily were already on board in the main car when Alford galloped up on a borrowed horse and tied it off next to a row of buggies. Wearing corduroy hiking knickers and shouldering a canvas rucksack, he walked alongside the train until he found the right car, then got on board.

"Caroline," nudged Emily. "It's him."

While she buried her face behind her guidebook depicting the flowers and birds of the area, Caroline swallowed and took sudden interest in the canvas split skirt she was wearing. *What have I gotten myself into this time?* She picked at a pocket seam and tried to get her heart back to a normal beat. She heard the door to their car open in front of them and imagined him coming toward her and bellowing, *"Good morning, Miss Henderson! My, you look fine today."*

Instead, there was nothing. When she looked up, she discovered he was talking to someone near the doorway. Apparently, they knew each other, for the gentleman shook his hand, then introduced him to a middle-aged woman. Alford inclined his head to her. Eventually, they broke off and he continued through the car.

"Miss Henderson," he said when he spotted her.

"Miss Henderson?" Emily said under her breath. "Who's Miss Henderson? You told him that?"

"Shh," Caroline whispered back. "I really don't know what came over me last night, but I was tired of being Miss Symington. Flusters people. I wanted to be myself." She gave her attention to Alford. "Good morning, Mr. Alford."

Alford looked at both women curiously. "Mind if I sit across the aisle from you?"

"Of course, you may," Emily said. Caroline's heart thumped.

Alford removed his rucksack, then taking the outside seat, made way for a club member dressed in tweed knickers and jacket. "Good day for a hike," the mustachioed man said as he unloaded his gear and sat down. Alford allowed that it was.

Caroline looked outside. It was already light, even though it was a quarter to five. She sensed it would be a beautiful day once the clouds burned off. Someone opened a window, letting in the train's whistle as it readied to pull out. The outing was on.

The train trip took about an hour and a half. While Emily chatted with Alford and the other hikers seated around them, Caroline sat by the window and watched the countryside go by as it changed from the light greens and caramel browns of farmland and woods wrapped in morning mist into deep forests of Douglas fir and hemlock, rich as the deepest jade. For the first time since she had arrived in the Seattle area, she felt a surge of purpose and peace.

From what Emily had told her over breakfast, this Seattle hiking group was very progressive with about half the membership of one hundred and fifty being women. But what she desired most was to be tramping in the woods. She had been told that the railroad was used normally for logging, with the occasional passenger train for sightseeing, following a tight path that rose higher and higher into the foothills of the Cascade Mountains. Twice it passed over narrow bridges high above craggy streams full of late spring runoff. Eventually they arrived at their destination, a lonely deserted platform in the wilderness. Caroline counted nearly thirty people when all disembarked.

A couple of wagons were there to take them out to the trailhead, a wide opening hacked out in a recently enhanced packhorse trail. By six-thirty, they were hiking. It was a motley group of hikers with an equally motley assortment of equipment. Many of the men wore "tramping" suits of good, stout material, finished off with hats and tennis shoes or high boots with caulks that appeared to have been salvaged from logging outfits. About a third of the hikers were women, but they looked experienced and well prepared. Most wore skirts made of rugged material such as khaki or denim, worn just below the knee. Underneath, they wore bloomers that topped off their tall boots. A durable "waist", an everyday hat, fresh from the millinery shop, and an alpenstock, a European-made walking stick, completed the attires. One brave soul dared to wear knickerbockers, but most of the women looked like they were going out for a stroll. Caroline checked the laces on her high boots and secured her practical wide brim hat before they were called to order.

As they gathered around the trailhead, the leader of the outing said a few words about the hike and what they should be looking for. "The trail was scouted out two weeks before. Water's adequate and there are places to stop and eat once we get to the top. You'll want to explore the meadow. It's lined with rhododendron. Some homesteader's claim abandoned a while ago, but still has handsome displays of colors every year.

The leader continued. "Those of you who have only taken our city walks might find it challenging, but we've provided for that."

The group was divided into smaller groups of Companies `A', `B,' `C' and `D'. When Alford was put into the same group as Caroline and Emily Drew, along with seven other people, she took a deep breath. *Now she would pay for it.* When everyone was introduced and settled in, the leader gave the signal to go and they were off.

Once the group started out, it took off fairly quickly, but after a mile or so, part of the group held back a bit as the trail went up. Alford and Caroline stayed in the middle with Emily where they were content to walk and talk. Passing up through thick stands of fir and cedar, they negotiated a trail recently cleared of winter blowdowns. In some cases, branches still lay across the path and Alford found himself out of habit tossing the limbs off to the side. At the top of the hill, the trail leveled off, giving some in the group an opportunity to stop and catch their breaths. One of them was the middle-aged woman she had seen Alford talk to earlier on the train. He stopped next to her to adjust his rucksack and introduced her to Caroline.

When he said Miss Henderson, Caroline held her tongue and hoped that the woman didn't know anyone in her uncle's circle. It was too late to make a correction now so she had to let it go. Mrs. Westford didn't appear to notice anything amiss. She was too busy collecting herself. She was a large woman and had overdressed. She sat down on a log and patted her neck with a bandana.

"Your first outing?" Alford asked.

"Oh, I've generally done the bird outings, but I so wanted to see the rhododendrons."

"From what your leader told us, it shouldn't be too much longer." He looked over the top of her head to Caroline and slowly shook his head. A group of hikers went around them and continued on. Caroline watched them go, then asked Alford to check a lace on her rucksack. She stepped away and when he came over to her, she asked what was wrong.

"She's overheated. If you would, have her remove some of her outer clothing. She can always put it back on if she gets chilled."

"Oh."

Caroline found a way to make the suggestion and when she was satisfied that the woman was more comfortable, she excused herself and joined the flow going across the flat forest floor. Alford walked slightly ahead of her and for the first time that day she was truly glad and not ashamed he had come.

A mile later they found the meadow with the rhododendrons in a natural prairie that sometimes occurs in Northwest forests. Full of grass dotted with ferns, the area covered several acres. At the edge closest to the abandoned cabin, there was a wild assembly of ten foot tall rhododendrons blooming in their fullest color. Huge reds and violet blossoms of the deepest kind and the size of tea saucers covered the bushes. The entire party stopped here to rest and admire the flowers. Some drank from army canteens, while others nibbled on raisins, hardtack and bits of chocolate.

"Want to go look at the homestead?" Alford asked Caroline.

"Sure."

It was an old shack, made out of split cedar, the ends carefully dovetailed. The glass in the windows had been punched out, exposing the interior. There was an old stove and ramshackle table. On the walls, newspaper had been used to cover up the cracks between the cedar slab boards.

"Quite a forlorn place, now isn't it?" A man from the 'A' group joined them with another man from their party who was dressed more like a lawyer than a hiker.

"Quite."

"Lost his shirt in a mining claim dispute," the other man said.

"In the Klondike?" Alford asked.

"No, here. Later shot himself."

Caroline gasped. Alford shook his head in disbelief.

"Heard you know something about the rivers around here," the stranger continued. "Do you like to fish?"

"I should think so," the friend exclaimed. "Alford helped guide a group I was in last fall. We did quite well. I understand he's going to leave us at summer's end."

"Oh?"

"I'm going to work for the Forest Service up in Whatcom County," Alford replied.

"Ranger?"

"It's not spelled out yet. Besides, the district has one. I'll just assist."

"What'll you do in the meantime?"

"I'm not sure. I just finished up a job with the Henshaw Logging Company outfit south of here. Thought I'd take some time off."

Some of the hikers got up and regrouped with their hiking teams. Caroline went back to join Emily who was up brushing off her skirts, but not far enough to not hear the men continue talking.

"Lovely girl with Miss Drew," the voice said.

"You know Miss Drew?" Alford asked.

"Yes, she's a new member of the club. Her father's a Presbyterian minister in Seattle and on the board of several civic commissions. I don't believe I know the young lady with her, but she certainly is a peach."

Caroline blushed. She slipped on her rucksack. "Time to go, Emily."

"Shall we collect Mr. Alford?"

"I think he'll have no trouble finding us."

The next lap of the journey was easy as it gently wound through the trees. Along the way, they crossed a stream by walking cautiously over a huge downed Douglas fir. The girls made it over easily with the others in the group, but Mrs. Westford in Company `C' had trouble. Though she didn't complain and was a good sport, she was increasingly having trouble keeping up. Alford's group bounded up the slight rise in the trail anxious to get to the promised set of falls at the next stop, but they weren't any more than a hundred yards beyond the log bridge when someone let out a screech, causing everyone to turn and look back. It was Mrs. Westford.

Instantly, people started back to investigate, Alford among them. Down on the side of the trail was the woman rubbing her ankle. A man from her group was talking to her. It turned out that he was a doctor. Alford went down to see if he could help. Caroline decided to follow.

"I think she's lightly turned her ankle," the doctor was

saying to the members of `B' and `C' gathered around the woman as he examined the foot. "It's not broken nor badly sprained as far as I can tell, but you understand, Mrs. Westford," he said addressing her, "that you can't go on any further. You should return to the train station and wait."

The woman groaned, not from the pain, but apparent disappointment. "However will I manage?"

"Well, you won't go alone. I'll see to that. The leading committee can send someone back with you."

"The leading committee," answered Alford wryly, "has gone on ahead. They are quite a ways ahead of us."

There was a general murmur of dismay about what to do now. No one in the group was really prepared for this. Their fieldcraft only went so far and they weren't sure about the trail.

"I could do it," Alford said.

"You wouldn't mind, would you?" one of the leaders from the group asked.

Alford said no.

The man from group 'C' turned to the others. "It's a capital idea. He's experienced in the woods. Another could go with him."

"All right. As soon as Mrs. Westford feels that she can stand, we'll go. What time do the trains come? No sense in waiting all day."

Caroline stood at the edge of the little group. As she listened to them express various opinions what to do next, she couldn't keep her eyes off of Alford. There was something about him so solid and strong. She had enjoyed dancing with him last night, but this was an unexpected quality — someone who cared about others, someone willing to give up whatever hopes he had for the day. Someone consulted a train timetable and noted that there was one at one o'clock they could make.

"What's been decided?" Caroline asked Alford.

"I afraid I'm going to have to leave you, Miss Henderson. I'm escorting Mrs. Westford back."

"Oh."

"You can always go on with Miss Drew. The rest in the

group is capable."

"Yes, I know, but...perhaps...perhaps Mrs. Westford would like some female company," she heard herself say. "I could be of some help, I'm sure—" Caroline's voice trailed off. *Here I go again.*

Her eyes met his and she blushed slightly, but Alford moved on to the immediate problem at hand which was getting Mrs. Westford upright. With assistance from the doctor, the woman was pulled up and her ankle tested.

"It does trouble me," the woman said. "It's very tender, though not like the ferocity of a sprain. Continuing on, however, will just tire me more."

"So we'll go back. You really want to come?" Alford asked Caroline.

"As soon as I talk to Miss Drew."

Funny how you see things differently, Caroline thought, when you walk back the same direction you've just come. The log bridge had to be conquered with new insight to its height over the hurried waters of the creek and entering from the east, the homestead with its palette of clashing rhododendron flowers was lost by the giant ring of hemlock and big leaf maple trees around the edges of the pasture. Only when they came alongside, did the colors jump out.

Caroline stopped with Mrs. Westford as Alford readjusted the additional load he was carrying — her rucksack had been tied onto his. She plucked a dark red head from one of the rhododendron bushes with the intent of putting it into a journal that she inconsistently kept. She watched Alford carefully attend to the woman and thought she was seeing him differently too. He was at ease here in the woods and very confident in himself, giving her a sense of security and peace. It was easy following him down the trail and when they finally reached the train station three hours later, chatting as they went, she felt she had known him all her life. Was this why she felt compelled to go with him? Why she invited him in the first place?

They arrived at the station ahead of schedule, so they had to wait. While Mrs. Westford put her foot up on one of the benches inside, the two young people stayed outside on the porch and talked. Caroline had made an awful mistake telling him her name was Henderson, but every time she got up enough courage to tell him, he was off talking about something else. Then she would think, what if he knew I was a Symington? Would that name mean anything to him? Would he treat her differently?

For the first time she felt free being someone else. She didn't have the family name hanging over her which in Portland carried considerable power. "Miss Henderson" was a new life of her own invention.

Across the single track was a bank covered with salmonberry bushes and twelve foot high alder trees. Hiding in the midst of them was an old growth stump with huckleberries growing on it.

"See that stump?" Alford pointed it out. "I betcha there's a stand of them in there. All cut down for this rail bed."

"How did they do it?"

"You've never seen?"

"No."

"I'll show you," he said. Crossing the tracks, they squeezed up through the scratchy green branches and came upon several large stumps scattered under the weedy alders behind the brush.

"Cedar, " he announced. "See those roots? They're like the arms of an octopus growing out of the ground, only loggers call them toes. They supported a tree ten times taller than anything you see here or as wide. Take seven men to hug that tree over there."

"Why are they cut so high?"

"Because of the roots. Faller doesn't want to cut through them so he's gets up on his springboard and cuts them off – there. See that axe notch in the stump a ways up there?"

Caroline looked up and saw several such cuts on all of the stumps, like little mouths.

"You put your springboard in that notch, then you stand on the board and you're ready to fell a tree."

"But you're so high up."

"Right..." He looked around and grunted when he found a bottle with a hook sticking out of the cork cap. "Oil can. For the saw."

"How do you get up?"

Alford laughed. He searched again, then whistled when he spied something in the brush. "With this." He came out with a wooden board with a curious metal tip. It was a round plate with a "lip," all of which had been bolted to the end of the board. Alford took the board and slammed it head first into the springboard notch, then pushed down on it. In an instant he was throwing himself on it and then to her surprise, standing on it. Carefully, he walked out to the edge where the board bounced up and down. The lip grabbed into the notch.

"You stand here," he said nearly six feet above her. "Quite a view."

"I can't imagine. I had no idea. It must be very hard work."

"And dangerous. It's a hard for a man. You can put a lot of time in and show nothing for it. Twelve hour day isn't uncommon. Eight would be more humane."

"That's Wobbly talk." Caroline had heard terrible things about the mad men who organized strikes against logging companies.

"Perhaps. I know a lot of old-timers say that when they cleared the land for their homesteads, they worked every hour. That's true. My own folks did that. But some of these outfits can work a man to death."

"You work for an outfit like that?"

"A couple of times. Last few years, the outfit's been good. Henshaw's all right."

"Are you going back?" Caroline hadn't asked that before.

No. Like I told the gentleman at the homestead, I'm going to be going north at the end of this summer. I've got a position up there." Alford sat down on the board. "Time to get on in life."

And on the train. From far off they could hear the whistle and they scrambled to get their gear ready.

Mrs. Westford called for a friend to get her at the station and after she left, Alford and Caroline stood in the station and watched her carriage go off.

Now what? thought Caroline. She suddenly felt tired, feeling the effects of the day and the dancing last night. How would she get back to the Drew's home? Alford must have caught her thoughts.

"Would you like to freshen up? My parents' home is not too far from here. I'll see about arranging a ride for you."

"Is it close by?"

"Yes," he answered. "But we'll have to walk. I had someone collect my horse after I boarded."

There was no one at home in the two story cedar slab house set back off the dirt road. Whitewashed and dovetailed at the corners, it sported a wide veranda cut across most of the front, giving it a finished look not often found in early homesteads. In the back, Caroline saw an addition. When they stepped into the house, they came immediately into a generous kitchen that not had only a large cookstove, a work station and a large, round dining table, but a sitting area as well. Alford led her down a hall to the addition and into a bright, cheerful bedroom with a washstand.

"I'll bring you some water," he said, then left her to survey the room. Although very simply furnished, the bed and dresser pieces were some of the finest Caroline had ever seen. Lace curtains hung in the single tall window. The whitewashed walls were accented by a painting of a mountain scene from some far-off country and a print of Christ tending his flock. Near the top by the high ceiling, a floral design had been painted all around.

She went to the window and pushing the curtain aside, looked out onto a flowerbed bordered by a river stone path. Beyond was a pasture, fenced in by the immutable forest. *How charming*, she thought

"Your water, Miss Henderson." Alford handed her a

pitcher. "I'll be in the parlor next to the kitchen."

Caroline finished up early. Alone in the parlor, she once again encountered exquisitely made furniture of rich maple and cherry. Family pictures and mementoes of family life scattered on the shelves and side tables. She drifted toward a collection on a small pump organ. The largest grouping showed five boys and two adults gathered outside the house on a summer's day. She found Bob's likeness: a young teenager with his hand resting lightly on a woman's shoulder sitting in front of the group. *His mother?*

"Are you comfortable?" Alford set down a tray on a sideboard. "I thought you might like something to drink."

"Thank you." She was definitely thirsty. Eventually, she asked about the picture.

"Oh, those are my brothers and my parents. Lars, Olav, Ake and Stein."

"Do they live nearby, Mr. Alford?"

"Yes, all except a brother who's in Alaska. My oldest brother, Stein, passed away a couple of years ago."

"I'm so sorry."

"I am too. We were very close. He was killed in a logging accident." He flashed his eyes at her. "It shouldn't have happened."

Caroline didn't know what to say, except that they all had just strong sounding names. "Isn't Alford an English name?"

"No. It used to be 'Alfjord.' Got changed to 'Alford' at Ellis Island when my folks emigrated from Norway."

"But your full name, Robert, is."

Alford laughed, his white teeth showing. "That's a fabrication too. It's just plain Bob. I was the first to be born here in America, so my parents wanted me to have an American name. They liked the sound of Bob and that's how it reads on the baptismal sheet." He seemed amused by their logic, but didn't question it.

"Well, it's a handsome family," she commented.

"Thank you." He looked at her curiously. "You haven't said much about yours."

"Would it matter?"

"I don't know. But I figure from knowing you, it must be a very nice one."

Caroline thought an icicle had struck her heart. She shouldn't let this pretense go on any longer, but she weakened again and only thanked him for his kind words.

He smiled at her gently, his eyes seeming to take her in. Caroline felt her skin prickle. It was as though he were standing right beside her, touching her, even though he was really quite a distance away. She almost didn't hear him say,

"I hope you won't think I'm too direct, but I wondered if I might be able to call on you after today. I've really enjoyed this day with you, complete with all the adventures. You're not leaving soon, are you?"

Caroline shook off her odd feeling. "No, actually, I shall be at Miss Drew's for another week."

"Then I may call?"

Unnaturally weak, she answered yes.

"Oh, Bob, how good you are here." Standing in the doorway was a small, prim woman with large, blue eyes , the same woman in the family photograph. She wore a simple, long dark dress, cut in the latest fashion with a silver cross on her bosom and could have been any lady in one of Caroline's mother's circles in Portland, except when she spoke, her English was accented and somewhat misspoken. The woman gave Alford her cheek for a kiss, then greeted Caroline warmly.

"And this is how I wait for you to come? You are having company?" She patted her son hard on the arm.

"I've been with Billy Howell. I'm a day early, Mama." He turned to Caroline. "Mama, this is Miss Caroline Henderson. My mother, Mrs. Alford." He explained why Caroline was there.

"Walking club?"

"Mountaineering," Alford corrected.

"I know. I am teasing." Her face lit up and she laughed. "Do you know Dr. Ellis?" she asked Caroline. "He is in this club."

"No, I'm afraid I don't."

"He has asked your *faren* to come, Bob, but first he wants another set of chairs."

"My father does some carpenter work," Alford explained.

"The best..." The older woman swept her hand around the room. "All the pieces he make."

"They're very beautiful" Caroline said.

"Where's Papa?" Alford asked.

"He is in Seattle. He has gone to see old friend of his who is here now. He was forester in Prussia. *Ja.* He knows his trees. Like Papa. Like my son."

Alford snorted softly, then changed the subject. "May I borrow the buggy so I can take Miss Henderson home?"

"*Ja*, sure, but first I think you should have fresh milk and berries. Good for hot day. Will you stay Miss Caroline?"

Caroline smiled. "That would lovely. A perfect end to the day."

"Good. If you not mind, we go to kitchen. Not so formal there for family friend."

Alford grinned wryly at Caroline. He looked like he wished it was true.

Chapter 6

"Letter from home?" Harold Symington asked David Harms as he came into his study. He unlocked a drawer in his desk and put some papers in. Behind him outside the window, he could hear Sophie laughing on the porch with her guest. She'd been quite taken with him. Symington supposed he should write his brother. At least the young man came from a respectable family and his prospects were good.

"No, from Caroline actually." David said. "She's having a good time and wonders if she could stay a little longer."

"Ah, my spirited niece. She likes the Drew girl. I find her quite plain, though her father is a man of some importance. I guess that's what a good companion's for. I'll grant that she's a respectable young lady although *that* mountaineering club she's joined. They impede progress."

"Which is probably to Caroline's liking."

Symington coughed in protest, then selected a cigar out of a box on his desk. "Would you like one, David?" David shook his head no, so Symington went on. "Caroline gets her spirit from the Lindsey side of the family. They were great New England radicals."

"I don't think Caroline's radical at all, although she does

agree the women in this state should never have had their voting privileges taken away. Twice."

Symington grimaced. That was one thing about this state he could never get used to. The Progressive movement had been very strong here since the 1890s, perhaps stronger than Oregon's. And now the agitation in the woods and lumber yards with the newly created International Workers of the World. The IWW or the Wobblys as they were known. Like hiking clubs that wanted to preserve things, they impeded progress.

"How's my niece spending her days?"

"Outings, apparently. You should read the letter for yourself. She invites everyone too. She sounds quite happy."

Symington clipped his cigar over a wastepaper basket and allowed that he was glad for that. "Her mother has been getting worried. Feels she'll be an old maid or worse lose herself to some cause with feminist trappings such as the vote or voluntary motherhood." He found a carafe on a side table and poured himself some port before he got his cigar going.

"Maybe she should just concentrate on Sophie," David drawled his words out. "Mr. Ford is about to pop the question."

"You don't approve."

David started to say something, then shrugged. "They'll make a good match."

"You've been quiet since Caroline left."

"Have I been so moody?"

"You're very fond of her."

"Oh, there's no doubt about that. She's very dear to me. Perhaps it was the kindness done to me as an orphaned child. She was forever making sure I was a part of the family."

"You are, David, and I think I speak for the others when I say we all wish you the best in your studies. Dr. Ellis from the university has mentioned you several times lately for your scholarship. Unlike my brother, I never went in for books, but I do admire you. In fact, I wish you would speak to Raymond about the university. School would do him good."

Maybe you too, thought David. Harold Symington needed to join the new century.

Chapter 7

Caroline *was* happy. She stayed another week, then another because of Alford. At first, she wasn't sure how public they should meet, so she asked Emily for assistance. The girls would take bicycles out on the dirt country roads and meet him at some prearranged location. From there, the three would go off on some walk exploring the countryside or, on some occasions, go to a stream where he liked to fish. Fishing, Caroline discovered, was something he not only indulged in as a hobby, but was something he'd been actually *paid* to do.

Each day was different. Swede Hill was a mix of dense forest and small farms through which several small creeks and a river ran. As the trees were cleared away, new homes sprang up on the claims and pastures created around the stumps. Emily's father had such a claim here and it was being proved up by her older brother and his wife. Often they liked to hike back on the skid roads no longer used by the logging companies. They had opened areas that were interesting to get to, although the countryside along the way had been devastated.

Once they were there, they would picnic or fish or both. She was glad Alford didn't mind Emily was along. It was a proper move and he said liked her. He seemed impressed she had hopes to go to the university and study biology next fall.

They were a good threesome, but one day Emily didn't show. Her sister-in-law was in the family way and not feeling well, and Emily had stayed behind to help. When Caroline arrived, she asked what they should do and Alford said he wanted to show her a place that he knew about.

They took bicycles out to a newly logged out road, then leaving them, walked back into a thick stand of trees. Locating the path at the edge of the clearing, they tramped along side by side. It was incredibly peaceful. The only sounds were their boots on the ground and the dizzy call of a tiny winter wren in the brush. Far-off in the woods came the glad song of a thrush. Maybe there would be rain soon. After a half-mile, the trail spread out as the trees thinned. Little rivulets crossed their path and soon they could hear the sound of a river.

"Just a few yards more," Alford said, gesturing with his pole.

Caroline smiled, then laughed at herself. She had forgotten she was alone with him. She hadn't felt self-conscious at all. Rather, she had that feeling of knowing him a long time again, like a dear friend who has come to stay after a long absence.

The trees stopped abruptly, flushing them onto the edge of a riverbank. Caroline stopped and gasped in astonishment. Across the clear-as-glass river which ran slow and wide through its stony bed, fir and big maple trees soared above a sandy bank. In their branches was a huge gathering of bald eagles. Never had Caroline seen so many or so close. They were magnificent, the white heads of the adults unmistakable. Laughing, she began to count, but some of the birds took off lazily and drifted over the river or simply played musical chairs in the branches.

"What do you think?" Alford asked.

"Oh, it's wonderful. Have you come here before?"

"Many times as a boy. It's a great place to fish too."

"Why didn't you show us before?"

He shrugged. "I guess it's special. Like you."

Caroline murmured her thanks, then slipped off her rucksack. Alford pointed down to the rocks. There were places to sit. If she didn't mind, he was going to fish.

The morning drifted peacefully by Alford wore tall, rubberized boots and waded in the water, casting his line out again and again. Several times, he was rewarded with a fish, which he put on a stringer and secured in an eddy near the bank. Caroline whiled away the time sketching in a little notepad that served as a journal. At noon he came and sat next to her.

"Not bored? We can walk upriver again."

"I'm fine," she said. She adjusted the hat pins in her straw hat, then asked if he was hungry. It was her turn to bring something to eat.

"Sure..." He beamed broadly at her. "Why don't we go up where it's softer ground?"

She set her picnic and a tablecloth out on the grassy sand. She had some meat, smoked salmon, pilot crackers and a bottle of cider.

"Cheers," he said when his tin cup was filled.

The cool of the morning burned off. The day turned hot, but the air was fresh with a hint of rain and before them the river ran. Alford pointed out a summer run of salmon, attracting the attention of the eagles. They watched the silvery backs of the fish as they plowed through while above the haughty big birds perched on every available branch of evergreen or alder tree to keep an eye. When she shifted her position and her sketchbook slid away, he asked to see it.

"These are wonderful, Miss Henderson. Worthy of any magazine for printing." Caroline thanked him for the compliment, but the dagger of deception cut deeper when he called her "Miss Henderson." Feeling ashamed, she changed the subject and asked about his fishing.

Alford explained a bit about the fish in the river and their habits, but after they ate, he showed her a little leather fly book he kept in his pocket. It was handsomely made with celluloid leaves and compartment pockets to which clips were attached, capable of holding up to several dozen fishing flies. "These felt pads can be moistened to keep the flies moist if I wish."

"Why they look like bugs!" exclaimed Caroline.

"Exactly their purpose. Fish love them. I tie most of them by hand myself, but there were a few imported ones come all the way from England in there." He flipped through the pages to show her the variety he made.

"Flyfishing is very popular back east," he went on, "but the flies here are different for the kinds of large fish we have. I study the English ones for ideas. I've known people to order theirs from the *Sears, Roebuck Catalog*, but it's better to make your own."

"Is that a feather?" Caroline peered closer. One of the tied flies bristled with something that looked like it came from a rooster.

"Yes, it is." When she asked how he did it, he went on to tell her about how he collected materials such as feathers, the hairs from deer tails or muskrat fur, then bound them onto steel spring hooks. Each fly had a purpose and name.

"Look. This is the Queen of Waters." He pointed to a large-bodied trout fly of silver with a dark ginger hackle and a light mottled black and white wing. "It's a dependable fly, though not my favorite." He pointed out some others. "These are the midges and these are Grizzly King, Royal Coachman, Brown Palmer..."

"And this?"

Alford gave her a wry smile. "Cow Dung."

Caroline clapped her hands and laughed. "What are they tied onto?"

"Gut. I make them in the winter months." He folded the pocket fly book closed. "Sometimes I sell them to city folks. My father taught me. He learned from an Englishman many years ago, but has adapted his own ideas to the waters here. I use bait as well and spoons and spinners too. Whatever works. I enjoy the flies the best, though." He looked down at the fish dangling on the chain stringer in the clear, cold water. "We could cook some now if you like..."

When Caroline hesitated, he said not to worry. There would be another time.

Caroline became quiet, though the thump of her heart was not cooperating. "There may not be another time. My uncle wishes that I return, so Emily and I will go to *Kla-how-ya* for a while. We're going the day after tomorrow."

Alford's face flushed with disappointment, but he seemed to find the right words to say as if leaving was all the part of a summer friendship. "Well, it's been wonderful, I grant you that. Little did Mrs. Westford know when she turned her ankle."

Without thinking, Caroline put a hand on his arm. "Nor I. It has been wonderful. The dance, the walks. If I could stay, I would."

He put a hand on top of hers and just so lightly stroked it. Caroline forgot to breathe. The kiss came almost dreamily, and then it was over. "Then don't go," he said, putting a hand on her shoulder. "Don't go."

"I have to. Uncle Harold is my guardian while I'm up here. I must do as he says."

Alford nodded. He put the pocket fly book back in with his fishing gear. Caroline cleaned up the food and loaded her rucksack. Neither said anything until they talked all at once.

"I won't be far away, Bob." Caroline said. He smiled when she spoke his Christian name. "We could arrange to meet. Emily will still help us."

"I'd like to be without Miss Drew."

Caroline clasped her hands in her lap. "Nothing has changed with my leaving. Really."

He loaded up his gear onto his back and helped her put on her rucksack. "This *Kla-how-ya*. Is it one of the new summer homes near the ferry?"

Caroline closed her eyes. *Oh, here it comes.* "Yes."

"Those people on the boat."

Her aunt, uncle and sister. He's beginning to get the picture. She came

50

from a well-to-do family.

"Perhaps... we shouldn't pursue this any further."

Caroline sighed audibly. At that moment she knew she didn't want that to happen. The thought made her miserable.

"I want to."

"Caroline." She was so glad he said her name at last and she was prepared for the kiss this time. He drew her to him, kissing her fully on the mouth. She kissed him back and let him put his arms around her and hold her closer than any man had before. He stroked her hair and kissed harder, then stopped and just held her.

"I love you," he said. "Maybe since the dance. I just wasn't sure what you thought." He nuzzled her ear.

Caroline giggled, then laid her head on his shoulder. "I love you too. For whatever that means. I couldn't bear not seeing you again."

"It means being together. It means going away with me at summer's end. It means... probably a hard life for you. I'm not a lawyer or doctor. Not a railroad baron. I work with what I know and I work hard at it. I can build our own home and furnish it myself. I can give you the best I have. Except...maybe that's not the best for you."

Caroline wiggled out of his arms and pulled her walking skirt down to her ankles. She knew what he was asking and considered what it would really mean. It *would* be hard. The thought both excited and terrified her.

"Why don't we just see," she said. "We have all summer. We can meet any time. I'll come here or we can find a place to meet down there."

From his look it wasn't the answer he wanted, but he took her hand and kissed it. And for now, it's what she wanted.

Chapter 8

Caroline returned to *Kla-how-ya* on the nineteenth of the month, taking Emily as a guest. They went by buckboard wagon, which could handle the rough road better than a carriage, taking three hours to make the fifteen-mile trip. The day had been overcast when they left and before they reached Uncle Harold's, it began to pour. The girls put on their water-proofed wraps and hunkered down behind the seat with a large piece of canvas while the hired man braved the onslaught. That's how David found them when they drove into the circular driveway behind the summerhouse.

He came rushing out with umbrellas and helped each girl down, staying to assist Raymond, Caroline's Symington cousin, with the trunks while Caroline scurried in with Emily. In the hallway, a maid came to help them with their wet outer clothes, then ushered them into the parlor where a crackling fire danced in a hand-painted tile fireplace and kerosene lamps burned. Aunt Agatha and her cousin Liza came not long after with hot drinks. Soon everything was in order.

"How sunburned your face is, Caroline," Aunt Agatha admonished. "You should be more careful and cover yourself when you go out."

"I didn't even think," she answered. Her aunt wouldn't understand her love of the sun on her face and the breeze in the woods.

"You must remember your place and what people think of you."

Caroline undid her wet hair and worked on its long stringy strands. "I don't think anyone thought anything of me except kindness. Emily's brother and wife were so nice." She smiled warmly at her friend, then gave her aunt a hug and kiss. "Thank you for letting me go, Aunt Agatha." She felt so happy, yet at the same time, completely out of place.

David poked his head in and gave her a quizzical look. When she met his eyes, she wondered if he guessed why she was so happy. *Did she look different to him?* She suddenly felt very self-conscious, afraid he knew everything about her stay. She gave him a quick smile, then immediately looked away. In that instant, she had seen Bob Alford there, not David. He was holding her in his arms and kissing her with a passion she hadn't yet experienced. She flushed.

"I think we ought to let the ladies get changed. All of you men, shoo." Aunt Agatha swept David and Raymond out with her hands, letting Sophie in before she closed the doors. "I've taken the liberty of getting your wrappers, girls. You can undress in front of the fire." She came and helped Caroline with her buttons, commenting on how wet the hem of her dress was. "You should take a hot bath, dear. Flora can arrange it."

"I'm all right, Aunt Agatha. As soon as the wagon stops moving."

Emily giggled. It had been a wild ride.

"It was kind of Mr. Johnson to get you. Of course, he was well paid."

Caroline let her dress and petticoat fall to the floor, leaving her in her light cotton knickers, corset and underwaist. Turning away, she removed her top underpinnings. She had full, high breasts and a slim waist. She didn't need to worry about fashion, but convention had her all bound up and she disliked it. More and more she preferred the "hygienic" clothing using a corded and boneless waist with shoulder straps or at least the lightest corset used for sports — unlike her sister who wore the fashionable corset that thrust the chest out, creating an "s" figure and back problems. She slipped into her wrapper and tied it up before sitting down on the chair to remove her stockings.

Oh, it feels good to be free of all the contraptions. She pressed on her breasts in relief.

Cousin Liza was full of questions. She was three years younger, a sweet, but sometimes empty-headed girl. *Maybe that's unkind*, thought Caroline. Liza's only fault was that she was young and very sheltered. She hadn't the advantage of working with the poor in a hospital as Caroline had done. She hadn't seen the real world. Liza offered to brush Caroline's hair and while she did, she asked about the outing they had gone on.

Caroline gave them a funny rendition of all the people that went on it.

Aunt Agatha looked up in surprise. "Why I know Dr. Ellis. I had no idea he was interested in such a thing as conservation. I believe I know Mrs. Westford, but I'm not sure if she's Mrs. Randall Westford or Mrs. John Westford."

"Were there any nice gentlemen our age?" Sophie asked from her seat by the fire. She stroked her aunt's tortoiseshell cat like she was only half interested, but Caroline knew she was hunting for some account not told.

Caroline flashed Emily a "please-don't-tell look" and the girl nodded her head slightly.

"I believe there was one unattached gentleman," Emily replied as she brushed her own hair out. "But he wasn't in our hiking group. There were quite a few unattached young ladies, wouldn't you say, Caroline?"

"Yes," Caroline said, emphatically wishing the fishing expedition for wedding prospects would end, but Sophie wasn't about to let that go.

"I heard there was a dance. Not a gala, of course, but a

respectable country affair put on by the local community club. Did you go?"

"Yes, of course." Caroline reminded her that Emily's sister-in-law was on that committee.

"Is the community all foreigners?"

"My brother is hardly a foreigner." Emily was the kind of person who never raised her voice, but she sounded almost cross to Caroline.

"Oh, you mustn't jest, Sophie," Aunt Agatha scolded. "Emily is our guest. But the name Swede Hill does suggest the nature of the population it is. A lovely place, nonetheless."

The conversation went all around Caroline. Tired, she leaned against the wing backed chair. The one occupied by Emily was made of plain wood and she wondered if Bob's father had made it.

Bob. She couldn't stop thinking of him. They had said good-bye yesterday evening. It had been a very formal good-bye, full of all the right conventions and procedures, but his eyes said something else. He had kissed her with restraint, then wished her a safe trip. He promised to contact her in a couple of weeks. *Weeks!* She was having trouble with half a day. She didn't think she could stand it.

Aunt Agatha excused herself and went out to talk to Uncle Harold who was just coming into the driveway. As soon as she was gone, Liza bounced up. "Oh, Caroline. Have you heard? Sophie is going to be engaged."

Caroline looked up and did her best to show interest. "Sophie, how wonderful. Who's the lucky man?"

"James Ford."

"Ah, the constant suitor. You've only known him a little more than a month, Sophie." *That's more than you've known Bob*, a voice nagged at Caroline. "Does Father know?"

Sophie leaned over the cat and spoke in a hushed voice. "James is writing a letter right now. You mustn't say anything to Aunt Agatha. It's still a secret."

"Oh, I won't." Lately, she felt detached from her older sister and almost didn't care. But she did care. She was worried

Sophie make a foolish decision. She wasn't sure she liked James. He was several years older than Sophie — nearly twenty-seven year s— and was much too worldly. He had a public facade that was very charming and urbane. Caroline found him coarse, yet couldn't explain why. He could be the type that took advantage of a young lady. Caroline already had an inkling when she discovered them alone in the boathouse. Or rather heard them. Caroline flushed remembering.

"He has given me a ring, but I've promised not to wear it yet. Not until Father knows." Emily and Liza leaned in for more details. Had he ever kissed her? How had he proposed?

But Caroline closed her eyes and listened to the fire popping and crackling like the bonfire she and Alford helped build with some people from the local church on the beach near the community hall. Caroline could see him now on the other side of the flames and his uncovered blonde head seemed to glow with a bright light. Little sparks shot up and dispersed like red fireflies in the dark, then a coal popped in the wood stove and the image was gone.

Chapter 9

"You decent?" Billy Howell's voice sounded muted on the other side of the window screen.

"Should I be? What is it, midnight?" Alford rolled to the edge of his bed and put on his drawers.

Billy rubbed his head against the screen. "It's two a.m."

"What the hell's going on?"

"Sorry. Didn't think this could wait. There was some action over at the Puget Sound Logging Camp Number 2 tonight. Some of Symington's thugs bashed in a few heads."

"Anyone hurt bad?" Alford was more awake now.

"Cal Sorenson. They had to get a doctor."

Alford didn't usually get involved with any organizational efforts in the camps and lumber mills, but he was sympathetic. If things had been done right in Stein's camp, he might still be alive.

"What do you want me to do?"

"I dunno. Go back to bed. I just wanted you to know before the rumors got out."

"You've got to be kidding. I can't sleep now. I'm coming out."

He dressed quickly and slipped out the addition's back

door. On the wall outside, he lit a lantern and brought it over to where Howell was waiting by the toolshed.

"Sorry," apologized Billy.

"Don't bother." Alford put the lamp on a wooden table his father kept outside. "I wasn't really all that asleep. What's the word on the strike?"

"They're talking about a slowdown. Symington must have gotten word of it. It was some of the key leaders that got hit."

"Didn't know Cal was involved."

"He isn't really. He was just in the wrong place at the right time."

"Symington's not an owner. I've always wondered why he gets involved."

"Probably the bank or some of his real estate deals. Get some of that land logged off and he can sell the parcels. People seem to want it, even if the soil's poor." Billy dug into his jacket pocket and brought out a bottle. He offered some to Alford, but he declined, so Billy took a sip himself. Alford blinked his eyes hard to get further awake and realized that his friend had been probably drinking all night.

"You should go slow, Billy."

"Nah, I'm all right. I'll stop. I haven't got the jimjams yet. It's just this damn Symington thing." He slammed the cork on and put the bottle away.

"The Hensaw outfit came around," Alford said. "They can still have ten hour days, but the bunkhouses are clean and they treat the men right. Pay more attention to safety."

"Symington won't. He thinks progress means profits. That can kill a man."

Alford grew quiet. *Stein had died because of that*, he thought. Working men hard 'til they made a mistake that killed someone. Stein's outfit had been working with a new donkey engine, pulling logs up a skid road with a cable instead of oxen. The man running the machine had been on the job all day without relief. A twelve hour day and he'd fallen asleep at the gear box. The cable had become snagged but he didn't wake up to stop it until it was too late. By then, it had snapped and flung itself like a whip across a hundred yards of logged off land and sliced off Stein's head as he was returning from cruising the woods.

Alford remembered the look on his mother's face when she got the news. Papa had tried to discourage her from going to view the box and he had to finally tell her why. *Stein!*

"You say something, Alford? Or are you going back to sleep on me?"

Alford rubbed his arms from the damp cool air and chuckled. Billy was like an irritating mosquito sometimes, other times a kid, but in the lantern light, his friend looked older than his twenty-three years. "Why don't you go into the barn, Howell? You can have the bed in the tack room."

Billy muttered he just might do that, then as afterthought asked about "the girl."

"Miss Henderson?"

"Would I be speaking about any other? She was some looker."

"She left."

"And...?"

"I intend to see her again."

Chapter 10

Caroline didn't see Alford for nearly three weeks, but when Emily's brother's new baby come a week early, Emily announced she would return to Swede Hill.

"I'll get in touch with Mr. Alford and send you any message he might have," Emily said as she prepared to leave, "but you must tell Mr. Alford your real name."

Caroline agreed, but she didn't know how. He already had some inkling they were well-off. She didn't want being too well-off something that got in the way of their happiness.

On the given day, Caroline took one of Liza's riding mares out on the excuse she would bring back some of the little wild blackberries for tarts. She intended to sketch. When Aunt Agatha protested and said Liza or Sophie should go with her, Caroline objected.

Sophie stuck her head into the parlor where the argument was going on, "Auntie, don't you know Caroline is a New Woman?

"Are you?" Their aunt's eyes were wide with horror. "You haven't been reading the Equal Suffrage literature, have you?"

Caroline patted her back. "Don't be silly." The stare she gave her sister was sharp as a wasp's sting. Caroline left on her own.

She met Alford at an abandoned homestead in a district a few miles northeast of *Kla-how-ya.* Set back off a grassy trail overgrown with alder saplings and salmonberries, she found its opening marked by a red scarf tied to a branch and made her way in. Back in the shade of a large old red cedar, she fell into his arms and thought, *I've arrived home.*

Beyond the initial "I missed you," neither said anything, except to hold onto each other and relish that feeling of complete oneness. Never had she felt so whole, so complete. Mother always pushed suitors her way, but as Caroline stood enfolded in this man's arms, she realized he was of her own choosing.

But how far could it go?

"Caroline?" Was it her imagination he was the first to call her by her Christian name and make it sound unique? Were his eyes really the mirror of his soul?

"How was your ride?" He pulled away and led her by her hand to some log rounds set up on the grass for chairs. They sat down still holding hands.

"Lovely. I had no trouble finding the place." She looked around the forlorn cabin. "What place is this?"

"I think they used it as a stopover for travelers. Got abandoned ten years ago with the railroad coming on this side of the lake. Probably had some refreshments, although I think it was of the rougher stock. The stove's still inside. So's the bar." He let go of her hand. "How have you been?"

"I'm fine, but I've thought of you every day."

They made small talk for a while, then changing the subject, Alford pulled an envelope out of his pocket and took out some pictures taken with a Brownie camera. "I got some views of the place I'm going to. It has more going for it than I thought. They just put in a transformer for a mill and the leftover electricity goes to the little hamlet there. Every building in the town has it." He handed the pictures to her, along with commentary.

"That's the main street of Frazier. They've got a hotel,

general store, plumber, barber. That's more than Swede Hill has."

"What do they do there?"

"Lumbering, of course. That's the mill. But mining's one of the leading industries. They can't really farm there on a wide scale. Too far back in the mountains. You grow your own things, but the season's short." He passed another picture to her. "That's a scene around the area. It's close to the new National Forest."

How beautiful, she thought. Nestled in a valley, high, sky-scratching mountains and towering Douglas fir, red cedar and hemlock surrounded the little settlement. A river ran close by.

Alford tapped the photograph. "Excellent river for fishing. Sea trout and strong salmon runs get all the way up past the town site." His eyes brightened at the prospect and she beamed at him. He was so passionate about fishing.

Alford leaned back against the tree. He was in his shirtsleeves, his suspenders draping over his broad shoulders like blue arrows going up and over. He was lean and tough looking, except for his face. It was open and friendly, reminding Caroline of their first encounter on the ferry.

"How many live there?" she asked.

"About one hundred and fifty, I guess. I don't think that includes kids. Just voting men."

"As well as non-voting women."

Alford shot her a glance and grinned. "Maybe."

She lifted up her chin in challenge.

He put up his hands. "Hey, I've got nothing against the vote. My mother voted once before the courts took the right away. And, the western rhododendron wouldn't be the state flower without the ladies voting. It was either that or clover. Washington State had a special election just for that so the women could vote."

When he saw she wasn't amused with this bit of history, he added that his mother had declined. "She'd already had a chance to vote for a governor." He reached across and squeezed her hand. "Just testing the waters."

"You're going to hit rocks."

Alford laughed, his eyes twinkling. "Want to walk around? My horse is in the back. Should probably put yours there too for appearance sake."

"I'm not worried about appearances. It's perfectly acceptable to go out with you alone."

"A New Woman."

Caroline grew serious. "I am myself. I've always been."

"For which I'm very thankful. I mean it."

Around back there was a stable, but they picketed the horses in a little pasture where the remains of an orchard stood. Some of cherry trees there had fruit.

"Want some?" Alford challenged.

"I'll race you."

They scrambled and pushed their way to the easiest climbing tree, Caroline beating him by an ankle. "I'm first," she breathed and grabbed onto one of the main branches. She wore a split riding skirt for comfort, but needed his help up anyway. When she was settled, he clambered up opposite her and began selecting cherries.

"Open wide."

"Like a bird," she laughed and took the first offering on her tongue. "Ugh. They're sour."

"Are they?" Alford looked disappointed until he saw she'd spit out the pit and swallowed the cherry. Smirking, she took another and another until he complained she got them all despite the fact he was doing all the work.

"Allow me," Caroline said and fed a cherry to him. Balancing on the little crotch in the tree they shared, she reached up above him for a choice cherry. When she started to lose her balance, he grabbed onto her legs to steady her.

"All right?"

Caroline giggled. "I'm fine." She gave him a smile, then felt it drift away as he became more serious. He leaned his face into her skirt so that it touched her near the top of her thighs and he squeezed her legs. Hesitating only for a moment, she reached down and touched his silky blonde hair.

That made him press his face harder into her, then without warning, kiss her through the firm cloth. Shocked, she gasped and clutched his hair. Alford shot his head up and immediately apologized. Caroline let go, surprised by her reaction. His face looked so funny, flipping from desire to propriety and back again. She laughed his apology off and slid down opposite him so that their knees touched. "Fresh."

"Not so New Woman." That remark set her off and she crawled over him and kissed him hard, pushing him into the tree branch. He put his hands on her waist and pressing her against his body, kissed her back. An odd ache went through her, but before she could reason it, they lost their leverage in the tree. For a second they scrambled for a hold, but at the last second Bob let go and took the brunt of his fall on his back, cushioning Caroline.

"Augh," he groaned. "I hit a rock." He arched his back at the pain, then sagged against the damp grass. Caroline started to roll off, but he caught her. "I'm not dead yet." He rolled her back on, so that she lay upon him.

"Does it hurt?"

"It resembles a mule kick." He flung his arms above his head and closed his eyes.

"I'll get water."

"No, you don't. You're doing fine." It was a jest, but Caroline was conscious of how close they were and where their bodies touched.

"You're indecent," she said, but made no attempt to move.

"Am I?" He opened his eyes. "You're so beautiful. Such a wonderful girl. I'm crazy about you."

"I thought the latest saying was spooney."

"OK. I'm spooney. Stay where you are. Don't..." He winced. Caroline got off him in alarm.

"Can you sit up?"

"Yeah... I think I can." Alford rolled gingerly into a sitting position. Caroline helped him, then without asking, pulled his shirt out of the back of his pants and examined the cut there. The impact had already caused some swelling and the area was beginning to bruise. She touched it with her fingers.

"Uhmm..." Alford stretched his back a little.

"A cold compress would help." Caroline pulled the shirt down.

"I won't object as long as you're administering."

She started to rise, then kissed him. "I'll be back." She dashed around to the pump she had spied by the stable. A few minutes she was back with a can full of water and a cloth. Alford had already dropped his suspenders and taken off his shirt.

For a moment, her heart skipped. Caroline remembered some admonishment in her mother's voice warning her about the base nature of men. She felt a queer longing in her breast as she stared at his bare chest and solid muscles. She had never seen her father nor brother without any undershirt. Here Bob Alford was almost in the raw. She had started this. She took a deep breath and went back to him, can and cloth in hand.

Trying not to look at him, she made a thick pad. She folded and dipped it into the can, then pressed it against his back. He sighed dramatically.

"Bob." She laughed.

Alford cleared his throat. "What are you doing in the next few days? I'll be down in this district as long as I can see you."

When Caroline was silent, he lifted up her chin. "Something happen?"

"I may not be here. Uncle Harold wants us to go to Seattle for the Fourth. We're supposed to stay at their home. He's bought a new motorcar and wants to tour around the city for the holiday."

"Why can't you stay here?"

"Because my parents may call." She lifted her head. "I'm sorry."

"I don't understand. Must they guard you all the time?"

"It's not guarding. They mean well. Besides my sister's getting married and she wants to look at some of the department stores."

"When are you leaving?"

"I think the third."

"Then we have three days and nights."

"No nights, Bob. Please. As much as I want it. I want to be married."

"OK. I'll marry you first."

"Are you asking me?"

"Yes."

She dipped the compress into the water again and applied it, but not before kissing him on the hurt.

They managed to meet a few more times at the old way station. Though they talked, made plans, picked blackberries for her aunt or sought out a stream he had discovered, they found it increasingly difficult not to want to be with each other more intimately. Alford kept his promise and they spent a lot of time just resting in each other's arms, billing and cooing as Caroline's aunt would say.

The time they spent together filled Caroline with excitement as she was sure about her love for him and what that would entail. She would go with him. But first she must tell him her real name, something she dreaded.

On their last day, she brought a small picnic in a rucksack and after picketing her horse, joined him behind the stable where he was gathering clover for his horse. He greeted her with a kiss then went back to feeding the horse. The dark bay bumped its big head against him and sucked the flowers out of his hand.

"I had to tell him that we were leaving. He wasn't looking forward to the ride alone."

"I won't be gone long."

"Tell that to the horse. He has to do all the work."

Caroline laughed, but she felt hollow. This parting made her very sad. She put an arm around Alford's waist and melted at his long, slow kiss. When he saw how sad she was, he stroked her cheek. "We'll manage."

"Are you going back to Swede Hill tonight?" she asked.

"No. There's been a change. Abe McKinley wants to see

me. He's the foreman from my logging camp. I'm taking the train tomorrow to see him."

"Where will you stay tonight?"

"Probably here. Look, let's talk down by the stream. I brought my pole."

On the bank's edge they visited while he fished, later stopping to eat what she had brought. The day wore on, but as each hour passed, she struggled with how she would tell him her secret. Finally, it was time to go. As agreed, he escorted her out to the main road. Leaving his horse behind, he led hers as they walked. At each step, she became more silent.

"You're awfully quiet all of a sudden. Is it going to rain?"

Caroline smiled at his attempt to prod her into a better mood, but she couldn't maintain it. He teased some more, but realizing that it wasn't doing any good, asked what was wrong.

Caroline swallowed. If only she had told him the truth in the beginning. She swayed slightly and he grabbed her quickly.

"Caroline..."

"I'm sorry. I need to sit down." She chose the first log she could find and sat down heavily.

"We won't be apart long."

She bit her lip, her stomach close to the seasick feeling she had on that first ferry ride over. "It isn't that. It's something else."

"What?" his eyes asked. He searched her face, but she knew she didn't have any more excuses, so she began to tell him by asking if he'd done anything he regretted.

Alford said yes, but didn't elaborate. "Are you worried about something?"

"Do you love me?"

Alford scoffed. "Isn't it obvious?"

Caroline's eyes started to fill up. "Yes. Yes, it is and I love you so much." She twisted her hands together. "Oh, I've done a terrible thing. But I've never meant to deceive you."

"What do you mean? How you could do that?"

"I lied. About myself."

"So you don't live in a summer house down by the ferry."

His smile was tender.

"But I do. But I didn't tell you honestly what my real name was. It was the dance. Emily asked me to come, but I didn't want anyone to recognize me or give me special favors. I was just going to come and leave. When I began to talk to you, I just blurted out Henderson."

Alford listened quietly, but his shoulders stiffened like the beginning of taking offense. "Was it the company you kept? The people I know?"

Caroline was horrified at his implication. "Oh, Bob, no. You mustn't think that. I just wanted to be myself without someone recognizing my family name." He was looking at her warily now and it made her uneasy.

"Who are you then? Do I call you Caroline or is it something else?"

"I *am* Caroline, but —" She was near tears, feeling like she was on a ledge near disaster, but it seemed he'd give her no support until she finished. "My name is Caroline Symington. My father's a banker in Portland."

Alford looked at her strangely, like he was wondering what the fuss was about. And then his lips parted and he began to stare. "Symington?" He twisted his head oddly, like he had a kink in his neck.

Caroline nodded. "I should have told you the truth right away. During the outing. I —"

"Uncle Harold. That's not Harold Symington, is it?" Alford interrupted.

"Yes. I should have told you." She was stunned to see how dark and hard his face had grown.

"Symington. All-the-money-in-the-world Symington." He spit the words out like they were hot nails. "You're damn right you should have told me! What kind of fool do you think I am?" He lit into her so hard she shrank back on the log. The horse spooked and tried to pull the reins out of Alford's hands. He calmed it down, but not once did his hard eyes leave her.

"Jes — Jiminey Christmas. Do you think I'm some game? Did I amuse you?"

"I don't know what you mean. Oh, sweetheart. I love you."

"You have a strange way of showing it. Maybe you Symingtons are all alike." He seemed to wince when he said that though his eyes remained hard. He looked away like he was trying to rein in his emotions.

It gave Caroline some hope. "Why are you so upset? Why am I so awful?" She wondered if it was better not to have said anything, but it would have been worse if someone else told him.

"You're not awful," he answered in a flat voice.

Tears streaming down her cheeks, Caroline felt around for a handkerchief in her skirt pocket. He finally offered a bandana, but said nothing more. He just set his jaw and worked the reins over and over in his work-hardened hands.

Caroline stopped crying, still shocked by what was happening. They were standing on the grassy trail in the middle of a meadow, but they might as well have been on the moon. It was eerily silent, like the hush before a storm. The air felt heavy, increasing the weight in her chest.

Finally, Alford spoke, but he gave no words of comfort. "Maybe it's better you go on over to Seattle. Maybe we should split up now. It might be the honest thing to do. I should have stopped it the first time you left weeks back."

"Why?"

"Because we're different after all."

"I told you I was monied. It didn't matter before."

"You didn't tell me you were a Symington." Again he gave her a haunted look that seemed both angry and guilt-ridden for hurting her with words.

"But you don't know my family."

"I know your uncle."

Caroline felt like crying again, but gathered her wits to salvage whatever was left between them. She had no idea what he was talking about nor could understand the depth of his animosity toward her uncle, but she tried.

"What has he done that's so terrible?"

"I hold him responsible for my brother's death." Alford

spit the words out like a bullet to her heart. When Caroline gasped he looked miserable again, but seemed determined to end the conversation. He drew the horse over toward her, suggesting she get on. It was getting late.

She complied with heavy, dead legs, almost missing a stirrup except that his hand was there for her. When she was seated, he gave the reins to her. The bay tossed its head, impatient to go, but the two just stood there unable to speak.

A breeze stirred the maples lining the trail. It flapped at Caroline's hat and knocked it off her head. Alford caught it on the horse's rump and gave it back to her.

Please, please, she thought, *don't let this end this way.*

"I love you, Caroline. You'll never know how much. But this won't work. We'll just pass it off as a nice thing."

Caroline looked straight ahead, not believing things had unraveled so fast. He squeezed her boot. "Don't forget to turn left down by the bridge," he said in a thick voice. "It'll get you back to your district more easily."

"I won't see you again?"

"No... I don't think so. Good-bye, Caroline." He pushed off from her, causing the horse to move forward. Caroline had just enough time to look back and she knew that in his stinging eyes, he didn't want it so.

Chapter 11

The Fourth came and went. The Symingtons celebrated in style at their Capitol Hill mansion, inviting friends for a picnic that was far from rustic. Later, they went touring in the new car, a dark green Stoddard-Dayton touring vehicle with three bench seats. They wore special clothes and goggles to ward off the mud they encountered on the roads and streets. They soon became the talk of the promenade at one of the city's new parks where they came to watch the fireworks.

Symington was proud to show off his car as well as his children and his lovely nieces. He used Sophie's recent public announcement for nuptials to his advantage. He was in fine form as he greeted friends and politicos, with Agatha at his side. As the twilight deepened, the family sat with some of Seattle's finest families, like the kings and queens they were.

The only person in the party who couldn't celebrate wholeheartedly was Caroline. She presented a brave front, but her mind kept playing over and over like revolving images in a kinetoscope her last words with Alford. She finally went out into the warm night air and took a deep breath, searching for the scent of something natural.

The Symingtons returned to their home after midnight and

after saying goodnight to Raymond, the girls went up to the room they shared together. With them was one of Sophie's new friends Jenny Larimore, a pretty young lady of twenty-two. She was the daughter of one of the leading investors in the Power and Light Company, someone Symington courted in his dealings.

While a maid laid out their nightclothes, all the girls except Caroline undressed and sat on their high post beds glued to a book Sophie's mother had sent her — *What Every Young Wife Ought to Know*. The author meant to enlighten the bride to be, but they weren't interested in the sections on how to set up a new home or avoiding the corset curse nor even those on childbirth and raising children. Their attention, instead, was on those parts about the aggressive nature of men in the marital relation and the sin of pandering to sexual indulgences without husband and wife both willing to have the child that came as the result.

"Romantic love in a marriage is giving into man's lower nature," Jenny summarized. "Motherhood and wifehood is to be placed on the highest altar."

"Humpf," Sophie said. "What wisdom is that? The woman writes that a good husband should simply stay away. That passion in marriage resulted in babies. But I shall have passion in mine."

Caroline ignored the talk as she changed into a light cotton nightie in the side bathroom, then washed her face at the porcelain sink. She pulled her hair back with a ribbon as hard she could, as though pain would make her feel better. The face she saw in the mirror was drawn, tired of maintaining smiles she didn't feel.

He was gone. She'd never see him again.

Jenny Larimore was talking about something her mother had said about making babies and how men must stay away certain times of the month.

Sophie laughed. "I'd be hard-pressed to keep James locked up in a separate bedroom for months and even years in order to limit children." In the mirror, Caroline could see behind her.

Sophie and her friend were leaning into each other and giggling.

What high secrets did they know? she wondered. She already had a clue about some of the secrets she had heard nurses whisper at the hospital in Portland. Young girls having babies without husbands or worse, sick from trying to get rid of them. More sobering the large numbers of married woman worn out from having too many children and being forbidden legally to ask how to prevent them in the first place, waiting in line to limit them after the fact.

Caroline wanted children, but intended to practice "family limitation." Unfortunately, not having received any advice from her own mother, she had only vague information about how she would accomplish it. *What does it matter now anyway?* she sighed. The only man she had cared enough for to weigh such important decisions over was gone and most likely not to be forthcoming.

"What are you doing in there, Caroline? Sophie called. "Did you drown?"

"I'm fine. You'd better put the light out soon. Aren't you and James receiving tomorrow at his mother's home?"

Sophie made a face, not knowing her sister could see her in the mirror. Caroline sighed. Sometimes she felt like the older sister. She put on her light cotton robe and turned off the electric light.

"Come and sit, cousin." Liza, the youngest of the girls, patted the bed and Caroline came over. "Jenny has been reading out of your mother's book."

"So I heard." Caroline sat on the plump bed and undid her hair for brushing. Jenny Latimore began to read:

"The sedentary life of many men renders them a prey to the gratification of their lower natures. To all such men exercise becomes a religious duty, and should be practiced most persistently until their physical natures are well tired, and the nature will not then dominate the finer and nobler instincts of their being."

Sophie whispered to Jenny that it would take more than exercise to get James tired. Overhearing, Liza gasped, but

Caroline ignored them. She stopped brushing and thought of the past weeks. She had thought she'd never been happier and if her feelings toward Alford were base, what then about the other aspects of their love? She vaguely heard the girls snickering behind her as she pictured him in the cherry tree. His thoughts hadn't been on some "higher plane" that day and she hugged the brush against her lap in remembering. Yet, he respected her and listened to her. He — it was unbelievable how it had all collapsed. How could he hate her uncle so?

Ever since she'd left Alford, she had watched Uncle Harold every moment she had with him. What had he done to cause the death of Alford's brother?

Tonight, her uncle had been expansive, the great host during one of the most festive times of the year. The whole city seemed to want to show itself off to its best advantage and Harold Symington was its leading booster for the growth of industry and commerce on the east and north side of Seattle. After the patriotic speeches had been made, Caroline thought that business was being conducted as usual as the men gathered together at the picnic. She wondered what deals were being made. She had no real idea about politics, but thought perhaps the more progressive ideas needed their time.

The girl went on:

"— there is a vast amount of vital force used in the production of the seminal fluid. Wasted as the incontinence of so many lives allow it to be, and prostituted to the simple gratification of fleshly desire it weakens and depraves. Conserved as legitimate control it demands it to be, it adds so much- to the mental and moral force of the man —"

"Where are you going?" Liza asked. Her face was flushed with excitement over the readings.

"I thought I'd get something light to drink."

"You could ring for Flora."

"I'd like to do it myself," Caroline answered, not saying she'd enough of Jenny and Sophie's prurient prattle. She tied her wrapper tight and slipping into some soft slippers, she went downstairs to the pantry.

The house was totally dark, but she knew her way around

enough to find the icebox and take out some milk. She turned on the kitchen light and filled her glass at the table. She wasn't settled in more than a minute when David came in.

"Mind if I join you? I'm having trouble getting to sleep too."

Caroline shook her head no.

He found a glass and scuffed over in his slippers. He was wearing a long smoking jacket over silk trousers. When he sat down next to her, he rolled up its large sleeves. "You've been awfully quiet all day."

"I'm tired." She sighed. "I've been thinking maybe I should go home."

"Portland?"

Caroline shrugged.

"ophie getting to you?"

Caroline ran a finger up and down the side of the glass. "No. Not really. It's probably a good thing that she's getting married."

"The Fords are certainly happy. All that Symington money."

Caroline shot a glance at him. She sometimes forgot how close they were in their thinking. It was often jarring to hear her same words spoken out loud.

"That why you're so sad?" he asked.

"I'm not so sad —"

"I had an interesting talk with one of my advisers at the university today — Dr. Ellis. He didn't realize you were on the club outing until afterward, but said you seemed to be having a delightful time. He was especially appreciative of your helping one of their female members who had injured herself. He also had kind words for the young man who helped as well. Said he's known the gentleman's family for quite a while."

Caroline stopped moving her fingers. It'd be so like David to guess at her inner thoughts, but she was astonished he would decipher exactly why.

"Said you left with him."

Carefully, she looked at her cousin, not sure how to

comment. It could be taken so many ways. "I thought she'd need female company."

David took a sip of his milk. "I'm glad. Very thoughtful. Well, it's not my affair, but I'm just worried that you're not yourself. You seemed happy after that."

Caroline thanked him for noticing and squeezed his arm. "Drink your milk, cousin. I've finished now and think I can sleep." She stood up, but he stayed her very gently.

"Remember, Caroline, that above all, I am your friend."

Caroline leaned over and kissed him on his head. "I know," she whispered, then went upstairs to bed.

David got up too, but after putting the glasses in the sink, he turned off the light and stayed there in the dark.

"Caroline," he murmured, but no one heard him.

Chapter 12

Alford felt as miserable as Caroline. The day after parting from Caroline, Billy Howell talked him into going out to the train and catching a ride on one of the boxcars. Normally, it would have been a lark, but Alford felt sour and beaten down.

"What'd you eat?" Billy asked.

"Huh?"

"You know what I'm talking about. It's that Henderson girl, ain't it? You act like you swallowed something hard to take."

Alford leaned back against the boxcar wall and rested his hands on his raised knees. They were going through the countryside at a good clip. Outside the opened door, the trees went by like fast targets at a midway shooting game. The steady, repetitive sound of the train going over the tracks came close to drowning out Billy's voice.

"What happened?" he yelled again.

"Ah, stop being a nag. We broke off."

"That bad? I thought you were stuck on her."

"It didn't work out." He slammed his head back against the wall and withdrew into himself.

"Well, maybe a trip to Margie's will cure all. Probably should go anyway. She's selling the place."

"What?" Alford sat up in surprise. "How's that?"

"Progress. She was getting some pressure from the sheriff, though I don't think he had his heart in it. Actually, I heard someone proposed to her. She's a great old gal."

"Where's she going?"

"Dunno. Rumor was she was going north. The Klondike."

"All right. We'll swing by after we see McKinley."

The foreman greeted them in his office, offering them coffee as they sat down.

"Good to see you again, Alford. How're your plans working out?"

Alford cradled his mug. "Things are going well. I'm supposed to report at the beginning of September. Gonna be sending what little I have by the middle of the next month. Working on housing now, but I don't think it'll be a problem. I'm willing to share. The border patrol agent got mighty lonely there and might want to double up."

"What'll you do in Frazier?"

"Whatever they tell me to. They're still organizing the office. Forest Service's only two years old under Pinchot, you know. Just started calling forest reserves national forests this year. If things should slack off during the winter months, I can guide or fish."

"Have enough money?"

"I saved some."

"Got work for you if you want it."

"There a slowdown?" Alford liked McKinley, was even sympathetic, but he was on the other side of the trail.

"Yes. I could use the manpower. There was an incident, you know. Cal Sorenson got hurt pretty bad. All the logging camps are being targeted."

"I'd like to help, but you know how I feel about things. Not going to go against what the workers feel. Not with Stein gone the way he did."

McKinley nodded somberly, making Alford feel bad. McKinley had known Stein, though he hadn't worked for

Henshaw Logging. Had even come to the funeral.

"I'm sorry there's talk against your outfit," said Alford. "I know you're small and it'll hurt. You're a fair man, McKinley. Made a real effort for conditions. Bet the bigger companies didn't like that."

"And how. The Puget Sound Logging Company in particular."

"Who backs that?"

"The Ford-Morris crowd. Symington's the chairman."

Suddenly, Alford's interest peaked. He drank his muddy coffee and mulled his thoughts while Billy had his say. He remembered how McKinley had treated him after Stein was killed. He'd been decent to him and his family. Even the owner had kind words and had given him leave.

"Maybe I could say something to the boys," Alford said. "Keep production going without raising the ire of the loggers or the companies. Symington will target you anyway, but the mills will be happy. I think the boys owe you something."

"Say, I'd appreciate that, Alford. Surely do."

Alford returned to Swede Hill a week later and threw himself into work around his parents' home. He had a successful meeting with some of the loggers working for Henshaw and a deal was worked out. There'd be a slight slowdown, so that the board feet McKinley would lose would be nil. No one would lose face. After that, he went with Howell over to Margie's where they spent the afternoon. Piles of neatly stacked boxes and trunks heralded an impeding move.

"Place don't look the same," Billy said. "It true you're getting married?"

The woman beamed. "Yes, it's true." She sighed. "I might be throwing caution to the wind, but he's a nice man. He's a prospector with good knowledge of ore. We're going to try our hand in the Klondike. Me, I might run an inn."

Billy and Alford exchanged glances about what that inn might look like.

"We'll miss you Margie," Alford said. "You're a good woman. Hope he knows that."

"Why Bob Alford, I didn't know you cared."

Alford worked like a silent ghost around his parent's place, mending fences for them and painting, occasionally taking delivery with his father on some of the goods from their store.

At lunch one day, he ate alone with his mother. For the past week, he'd been attentive to her and his brothers who came to visit with their numerous children, but some days he could barely get out of bed.

"You're not eating good, Bob," she said in English. "You work hard, so you should eat more."

"I'm all right, Mama."

"*Ja, sure.* And how is your young lady? I hear nothing."

Alford stirred his fried potatoes on his plate, hoping to avoid this conversation. When he realized he couldn't dodge her, he tried a different tack, but he couldn't fool Mama and soon he began to talk about their sudden break off.

"That is all? Family is all?"

"It's who the family is, Mama. Symington. Harold Symington is her uncle."

"Ah." She paused. "Do you love this girl?"

Alford put his fork down, his hand trembling.

"Good," she smiled. "She was nice young girl. I liked her."

Alford wiggled in his chair. Mama was working on something and he knew when that happened, to watch out. He wasn't sure if he'd like the results.

"How much?" Mama asked.

"I wanted to marry her."

"Then that is what you do."

Alford stared at her in amazement, wanting to protest, but she wouldn't let him.

"I know why you do this breakup. It's for Stein. But Miss Caroline she didn't kill Stein. She don't know Stein. Stein is problem with her uncle." She rapped the table smartly with her hands. "I think you should marry her. She is lovely girl. She is always welcome here."

"She's from a powerful family."

"This is America. Anything is possible."

Alford didn't want to get her started on that. He just took her hand and squeezed it.

"A little prayer help too," Mama said. "I do that for you. You see girl again."

Chapter 13

Caroline returned from Seattle on the eighteenth of July. It had been a difficult two weeks, but David made it easier by keeping her entertained. While Sophie tried on wedding dresses and made up lists, David squired Caroline to a concert at the university and showed her the sights of a city energized and alive.

Seattle had new public parks and ferry rides over to the newly-opened West Seattle recreational sites. Additionally, the Denny Regrade was on-going. The Regrade was an ambitious engineering feat literally washing away the hills around the center of the city to make a flatter area for commerce

The days were hot and bright, opening up spectacular views of Elliot Bay and Puget Sound waterways. To the west there were forested islands and beyond the islands the Olympic Mountains. To the south, mighty Mount Rainier lifted its head up above it all.

At the end of her stay, Caroline almost believed she'd be all right without Bob Alford, but as soon as she was back at *Kla-how-ya*, the misery returned. She was relieved to find Emily's calling card waiting in the silver tray near the entry door. Emily alone would understand.

Emily arrived that afternoon. Together they walked down to the boathouse arm in arm and sat on the dock. It was slightly overcast, but the air was warm and humid. Watching the boats out on the lake, they dangled their legs off the side and made small talk. Eventually, Emily cleared her throat. "I saw Mr. Alford."

Caroline tried not to show any emotion, but her voice squeaked. "How on earth did that happen?"

Emily gave her a wry smile. "He came calling at my brother's homestead. Said he heard I was returning to Seattle for a few weeks and would be passing by *Kla-how-ya*."

"Oh. What did he want?" It was hard to keep her voice calm.

"Well, he wanted me to give you something. And I think you should take it."

"Really?"

"Yes, very much. You see, we talked for a long time."

Caroline stared across the water to the large island that was situated between the east and west sides of the lake, but she was listening carefully.

"I'm glad you told him your real name, Caroline Symington. It was dishonest not to in the first place. Yes, even sinful."

"He doesn't want to have anything to do with me now. To have won my affections —" She sighed. "Maybe it was for the best."

"Ah, but he does. I believe he's truly grieved for hurting you. He's deeply sorry."

"Is that why he's sent a messenger?"

Emily put a letter into her hands. "You must read it."

Caroline would have been playacting if she refused and her friend knew it. She took it humbly and got up to read. She made no sound, but when she finished, she turned to Emily. Tears rolled down her cheeks, but she felt a stirring of a wide hope. "Where is he?"

"At the old place. I'll ride with you if you wish."

The meadow around the old way station was a garden of

foxglove that streaked the grass with spikes of lavender and white. Caroline found him in the back as usual. She had intended to be reserved, to punish him a little more, but when she saw him, she relented and went straight to him. Alford was wearing the suit he had worn at the dance and he had trimmed his hair. He smiled faintly when he saw her, then the wall between them shattered and they walked into each other's arms.

Satisfied, Emily took her horse and walked it further out on the trail.

They stayed for an hour or so. It was enough time to forgive and try for understanding. When she asked about what had happened to Stein, he told her simply and gave his reasons for his dislike for Harold Symington.

"I love you so much, Caroline. I'm sorry I hurt you." He took her hand. "I don't want to be without you, but beyond that I don't know what else to do. I suppose I should write to your father."

"Oh, Bob, that would be wonderful." *Maybe there was some hope*, she thought.

At the end of their time together, he walked her over to her horse. After greeting Emily who was already astride her horse, he turned to Caroline and promised to see her soon if she wanted. "We need to talk some more."

Caroline brushed against him as she prepared to mount. "Yes, we do. I think I can get away in a couple of days."

Alford turned her toward him and softly, kissed her on her lips. It made her cry, an emotion she wished she could control lately.

Alford pulled Caroline closer and they just held onto each other.

Emily coughed and it was time to go

Chapter 14

"And how's my new sister today?"

Caroline turned around sharply and gave James Ford a polite smile.

I'm not your sister, she thought. If he were someone else, his clean, dark looks and plastered-down hair might have appealed, but he was no gentleman. *I trust you like a bull in a pen with a red flag.*

She finished arranging the bouquet of roses brought in from the garden and dusted off the table the vase was set on. His eyes wandering all over her made her uncomfortable. Not paying attention, she accidentally poked herself on one of the rose thorns as her hand brushed by. She made a little noise in her throat as it bled. She popped it into her mouth and sucked on it, then backed right into Ford who'd come up behind her.

"Allow me," he said, taking her hand and supporting it like some treasure. He put his other hand on her shoulder. She could feel his hot, sweaty palm through the light cotton waist she wore. She tried to move her shoulder away, but he blocked her as he wrapped some silly bandage from his handkerchief around the injured finger one-handed. When he couldn't do it, he used both hands, but he had her bottled up against the table and to her horror his groin against her hip. He said nothing, the combination of liquor and cigars on his breath making her want to gag.

"Thank you," she said politely, attempting to remove her hand and body before he was done, but he was insistent.

"Finished," he crowed. Like he'd just netted his latest butterfly. He admired her hand, then kissed it. "Are all the Symington women so beautiful? Especially, Charles Symington's girls. I wonder why I didn't notice you earlier?"

"Probably because I was busy ignoring you."

"Come now, sister. That's a unkind thought. Since we are to be family."

"Family! You're disgusting. Let me pass. You're drunk."

Ford must have thought she was joking and increased his advances.

"Have you lost your senses? I'm not Sophie."

"Come, come." Ford leaned over too far and losing his balance, planted a hand on Caroline's breast. Disgusted, she twisted away, but Ford managed to kiss her hard.

"Stop!" Caroline slapped him as hard as she could and slipped out of his grasp, but not before she saw Sophie standing in the door, her poor delicate face aghast. Caroline dashed out of the room and left the couple behind closed doors alternately weeping and yelling at each other. Ford left a few minutes later, slamming the outside door as he passed. From the safety of her room upstairs Caroline watched him leave in his buggy for his mother's summer home.

"How could you?" Sophie stormed in and banged the door shut. Her back against it, she gasped until she got her breath, then tore into Caroline. "How could you! He's my fiancé."

"It's not my fault. James Ford's a crude, uncouth man."

"He's from one of the city's most influential families."

"I've met better cowherds! They at least know where to put their feet in a barnyard. He grabbed me, Sophie."

Sophie flushed. "You're one to talk. You tramp around mountains with strange men and women who wear pants. Why did you turn Martin Colton down?"

"None of your business."

"You expect too much. All that New Woman talk." She crossed her arms in a huff. "Wait until Uncle Harold hears."

"He probably has already. Stop making such a scene."

Sophie burst into tears. It was a complete flip-flop so Caroline was wary. "I love him so," her sister sniffed.

"I'm sure you do."

Caroline sighed. She didn't want to have another scene. She had enough worries of her own. Since the middle of July, she had met with Alford regularly and he had recently composed a letter to her father. Waiting for the response had been nerve-racking. She had to mend things. She sat down on her simple box bed set under a large paned window.

"Ford just had too much to drink. How old is he? Twenty-seven? He has been a bachelor for quite some time. He's as skittish as you are." She patted the mattress. "Let's be friends, Sophie. Look, I'll help sew some things for your trunk."

Sophie stopped crying. "Do you think Uncle Harold really heard everything?"

Caroline wasn't sure, but she *was* sure James Ford would be back with hat in hand to apologize. She didn't add it was also for the money.

Ford did come back and all was mended, but he avoided Caroline. Sophie began to take this as sign of some doings between her fiancé and her sister. She watched for any loaded words or absences. When she began to notice that Caroline went riding every couple of days, she became suspicious. Then one day, about a ten days after the incident in the parlor, she followed Caroline.

The meadow was deep in summer. It had been dry, so the trees showed their thirst by turning a little red at their tips and the grass with its grainy heads was yellowing. Alford met Caroline at their usual spot near Danville, a few miles north of *Kla-how-ya*. He folded her into his arms.

"Get away all right?" he asked.

"My usual excuse. Out to sketch. Really, I'm running out of room on my wall where I've pinned some of my work up." They walked their horses down to the stream where he fished and she sat on a blanket and read a book. It was a custom now and she cherished it. She loved to watch his back as he cast out. It was almost sensual in its form, his strong shoulders and arms leaning out toward the water, the water rippling endlessly by his feet.

She sat on the bank in a dark blue swimming suit with the legs rolled up and her hose off. The sleeveless top was loose and she had removed her corset. *Ah, such freedom.*

For past weeks, they had spent this time making plans. He had secured a place for them to live together in Frazier, but hadn't told his employer yet that he'd be getting married. The house had electricity, something his own parents didn't have and several acres of recently cut land that could be cleared further for pasture. They could rent for five dollars a month.

The hardest thing he had to do was to write a letter and ask her father for permission to marry because that is what Caroline wished. In the letter, they asked only for a private wedding. No fuss. After the wedding, they'd go to an inn he knew for their honeymoon. Alford hadn't heard back yet, but he hoped it would be soon. They had about three weeks before he had to be in Frazier.

Alford made a final cast, then came up on the sandy bank next to Caroline. He hadn't done well today, but had enough for supper. He put his gear into a new creel he had bought in Seattle, washed his hands in the stream, then sat down by her. She put her book down and gave him her attention.

"Ready to go back?" he asked.

"Unfortunately. I can't stand this waiting."

"Me too. I want you wed for obvious reasons. Maybe there'll be a letter or even a telegram this time at my parent's. It should be any time. I'll check when I get there tonight." He drew her to his lap and she nestled against him, but he seemed occupied, so she put her arms around his neck and gave him a kiss. She let out a whoop when he rolled and pushed her onto the blanket.

"Gotcha!"

"Bob..." she fingered his lips. He sucked her fingers into his mouth. She laughed at him and pulled them out. He found the hollow of her throat and kissed it slowly, giving her a strange tingling in her breasts, then lay down close to her. He laid an arm across her chest and closed his eyes, his breathing becoming slow and regular. She closed her eyes too and they slept.

They didn't see or hear the intruder who discovered them nor heard her slip away.

Alford received a hastily posted note about four days later. It was an invitation to come to *Kla-how-ya*. When he read the note, he waved it at his parents and brother Olav who was visiting.

"It's come. I'm to meet her family."

"Didn't I say things work out all right after all?" Mama said, beaming.

"It's a start."

"When do you go?" his oldest brother Olav asked.

"Tomorrow. Caroline's father apparently arrived already."

"I will brush your best suit and iron a shirt for you, Bob. Papa can trim your hair," said his mother.

"I don't have much time."

"We can ask Ake if he can take you down in his boat. It will be faster," his father volunteered. A good family cause.

Chapter 15

It was early evening when Alford found the grounds of *Kla-how-ya*. Ake had put in at the ferry dock where Bob was able to rent a smart-looking buggy at a livery. It had delicate Savern hubs and spindly spokes, but it made it over the half-corduroyed road in good time. As he gazed across the summer home's grounds carved out of the forest around it, he wondered what kind of world the woman he loved really lived in. It was a charming, very beautiful home, but to him it also looked artificial. *What if she belonged only here?*

A butler greeted him at the door and led him down the hall to an office that overlooked a wide veranda. There was no one on the wide lawn nor on the lake beyond. Inside, the house felt equally empty and locked up. He was invited to help himself to the cognac on the table. "Mr. Symington will be in shortly."

Alford declined and went to the window. Outside the dark, grey water reflected the overcast day. Rain threatened. The hemlocks and cedar lining the edge of the lawn leaned in dark and foreboding; their tops whipped noticeably in the wind off the lake. A crow tried the air and was swept back. The wind didn't bother the ducks down by the boat house, however. They greedily nibbled slugs in the grass. Inside, the eerie silence of the house weighed down like the approaching storm, the room lit only by a single lantern. *Where is everyone?* Somewhere in the house a door closed and then another. Footsteps came close.

A powerfully built man entered the room. He closed the door like a conspirator and faced Alford. "Bob Alford, I presume. A common enough name."

Inwardly Alford groaned. Though he had only seen him in newspaper photographs, he knew the man could only be Harold Symington. "Where is Caroline's father?"

"He should be here in four days. He's been detained. His son Samuel broke his leg in a riding accident. The lad had to be hospitalized."

"When will I meet him?"

"Hopefully, never. Let me get to the point. The only reason you are here is so I could meet the bastard that had the nerve to spunk up my niece."

Alford's face flushed in anger at the insult, but he kept his tongue in control. "You've been misinformed. My intentions are honorable."

"Your intentions are cause for arrest. You're out of your league."

"Did Caroline's father get my letter?"

"I believe he did, but no matter. Because of the advantage you've been taking of my niece, you have violated a trust."

"Where *is* Caroline?" He still wasn't sure what he was up against, but his skills in surviving brawls in the rough and tumble camps he'd worked in since a boy began to kick in.

"Miss Symington is confined to her room until her father arrives," Symington was saying. "Until that time, you will have no contact with her. If you are seen with her, I'll have you beaten."

Alford scoffed at him in disbelief. This was the twentieth century, not the Dark Ages. "I'll see her anyway."

"James," called out Symington. A door next to the office opened and James Ford stepped in. Symington came over to his desk and took out a cigar. He prepared it while he talked. "I

91

think you should reconsider. Believe me, you're outnumbered. I have more acquaintances in the hall. Not so gentlemanly as Mr. Ford. Why upset the girl any further? Just let it go." He lit the cigar and taking a puff, shot a circle out into the air. "I suppose you want money."

"Don't insult me any further."

"How noble. James, why don't you escort our friend to the door."

"I'm not finished."

Symington smiled wickedly as he liked a challenge. "So?"

"This isn't over yet. I'll be coming back for her. You can't hold her against her will." He watched both men carefully and backed to the door. "You should talk to Ford about his own manners. Caroline's father will not appreciate his prospective son-in-law's roving hands."

"That's a goddamn lie!"

Ford reached out to strike Alford, but he wasn't fast enough. Bob laid him flat with one solid punch. Ford bounced on his backside then slid back across the polished wood floor to a round table. "Stay away from her. And you. Don't bother to call the police."

Symington's face flushed a deep red. "Insolence!"

"No. Law of averages. The center won't hold forever."

Alford opened the door. There were several toughs in the hall, but even with heat he felt coming from behind him, he suspected Symington would let him go. He made his way outside into the wind-slashed evening. As he untied the horse he searched the windows upstairs and saw in the fading light what he desired most: Caroline, her hands and face pressed up against the windowpane. She was trying to say something to him, but he couldn't figure it out nor had the time. Several of Symington's men came out and threatened him. He got into the buggy and miserably left her behind.

Chapter 16

Caroline watched Alford go with strained eyes. At least she had seen him. At least he didn't appear hurt. As he disappeared at the end of the driveway, she vowed not to cry any more. She needed all the strength she had for the battle that was coming. She would not give up the fight now in its horrible fourth day.

Upon returning to *Kla-how-ya*, she felt a silent chill in the household, though Sophie was overly friendly. When Aunt Agatha asked how her ride had been, Caroline felt her sister's eyes on her as she answered.

"More pictures for my sketchbook. Where's Uncle?" Caroline asked.

Aunt Agatha exchanged a glance with Sophie. "He's been called away unexpectedly." The two women let it hang at that.

When Symington returned the following morning, Caroline was called down to his office. He greeted her warmly over his brunch, then invited her to sit next to him. Aunt Agatha sat on the veranda outside. When Caroline raised her hand to her, her aunt quickly left the veranda.

"What's wrong with Aunt Agatha?" Caroline asked. "She looks like she was crying."

"I believe she was." And then he struck. "Where were you

yesterday?"

"I went riding."

"You're lying. You went up to Danfield and you weren't alone." He pulled his napkin from his neck. "How long have you been seeing this young man?"

Caroline couldn't answer. She was struck dumb.

"It doesn't matter. Whatever liaison you've had with him is over." When Caroline protested that Alford had written to her father for her hand in marriage, Symington ridiculed her. "You've been acting like a whore."

Caroline reeled, her hand on her lacey breast.

"I have been in touch with your father. That's why I went to Seattle so unexpectedly. It appears your lover has written, but all contact with him is forbidden. Your father is coming, but not until young Samuel is back in the family home. Your little brother broke his leg."

"Sammy? Is he —?"

"— When *my* brother is able, he will come and take you home. Until that time you will stay in this house and if necessary, your room."

Caroline was shocked. "You're not my father!"

"You are my responsibility!" he shouted. "Have you lost your senses? A common man! You're a Symington!"

Caroline shot up. "I wish I wasn't." She started to the door.

"Where are you going?"

"Don't worry. I'm going to my room." *Maybe I'll find some peace there.* But she didn't count on being locked in.

Not long after Alford left, there was a knock on the door, then someone unlocked it.

"David!" Never was she so glad to see him.

"I brought you a tray, Caroline."

"I wish it was my freedom."

"You're too stubborn. If you want to win this you must be compliant." He set the tray down on the cushioned window next to her. The rain poured outside, the last of the light fading. He watched for a few minutes in silence, then said that the whole affair disturbed him. "Tell me more about this man. Is he the same one Dr. Ellis mentioned from the outing?"

Yes." Caroline sighed. "He's wonderful. He comes from a good family, just not monied. His father owns a store and has other income. And Bob *has* secured employmen."

"How long have you been meeting him in secret? Three weeks ago you were miserable. Then you were happy again. Don't give me the sordid details, just the facts."

"There is nothing sordid, David. We're perfectly chaste. We just wish to marry."

"Did he really write your father?"

"Yes. We've been waiting for word for over a week."

"How will you live, if you marry?"

"He has employment for the fall with the new Forest Service. He's experienced in timber cruising, falling trees, guiding people in fishing and outdoor activities."

"Where will you live?"

"In Frazier."

"Frazier? Do you have any idea how isolated that place is? So different from this life."

"I've lived differently already these past two years."

David made a face. "Well, your father could certainly attest to that. You have a courageous soul, Caroline. Seriously, though, if you were to marry, what do you think you each will bring to it? Is he going to let you vote?"

Caroline laughed and curled up her legs at the window "Yes." Her face flushed.

David bit his lip as he mulled something over in his head. Finally, he looked straight at her. "Do you want to see him?"

"How?" Caroline's heart skipped two beats.

"I'll try to locate him. Uncle Harold knows I have to go out. I'm picking up a package from the ferry."

"In this weather?"

"I'll find him. At least I'll try."

"And?"

"We'll manage a way for you to meet."

"He might be found out. How will I get out?"

"We'll manage. For now, be nice. In fact, give into Uncle Harold. Say you've made a mistake and that you've come to your senses. Tell him you'll give up your lover." He cupped her chin between his hands. "Be compliant."

Caroline smiled wryly. "Okay. I'll be a good little girl. But first tell me about my brother."

Symington was waiting at the bottom of the stairs when David came down.

"What does she say?" he demanded.

"She has come to her senses." He walked heavily over to the hall tree and got his long cloak. "Perhaps, if she behaves, she could come down?"

"I think that can be arranged." Symington pounded a fist into his hand. "Damnation. My brother's daughters. He's too undisciplined with them. I love that girl, truly. I just can't tolerate her willfulness. Are you still planning on going? The ferry may not run."

"Hopefully, it started before the storm broke. I don't mind waiting." David put on his hat, then went out into the wind.

David found Alford on the road about two miles up, stuck in the mud. The thin wheels of the buggy were all the way up to the hubs. David got off his rain-soaked horse to assist, excited luck should go his way, so soon. Now if Alford didn't recognize him. He didn't.

"Can I give you a hand?"

Alford didn't object.

Once the buggy was pulled out, both men were soaked. They decided to go on to the hotel near the ferry to dry off. And get something warm to drink.

Bailey's was a simple two-story clapboard building with a tiny restaurant. Standing by the roaring open fire, Alford thanked him again for his help.

"I was afraid one of the spokes would finally go and then the whole wheel would have been lost. Damn rentals. You never know."

"I know what you mean. I've had few disasters of my own. And now they're talking about renting automobiles back East. Isn't that something?"

When their meals came, they stayed at a table near the fire and continued talking. David decided he liked Alford. There was a slight tense undercurrent to him, but understandable after his interview with Uncle Harold which David had overheard part of. Alford seemed strong, sensible and intelligent, and even with the strain he must have been under, had a sense of humor.

"Where are you staying?"

"On my brother's boat."

"Good," David said. "Keep a low profile for a while." Then he told him who he was.

"Hell's Bells," Alford snapped, pushing back from the table. "Who sent you?"

"Please," soothed David, not wanting to destroy the good feelings between them. "Caroline. I volunteered to find you."

"Why? Why couldn't you be one of Symington's thugs?"

"A point well taken, but I assure you that I'm here to help you — and Caroline. I think I can arrange a way for you to meet."

"Why would you want to do that?"

"Because Caroline desires it. Look, I know my Uncle Charles. He's a good, decent man. Not so forceful as Harold Symington, but he *will* oppose you. He's particularly fond of his daughter and will do what he feels is right for her well-being. You, sir, are not in his plans. He would consider it a disastrous marriage for her. Sorry. If Uncle Harold says he's coming to take her back, then he's coming to take her back."

Alford eased back down on his chair, but he seemed to grow harder. "Then I'll take him on. We'll elope."

David parted his lips and sighed. "I suppose that's the only way." He rearranged the silverware on his plate, then changed their direction again. "What will you give her?"

"Everything that I possibly can. A home, a freedom to be herself." Alford laughed. "I know my gal. New Woman."

David felt Alford studying him carefully, his eyes as hard as flint. David hoped Alford didn't see what he really felt about this whole mess, but he cared for Caroline and her happiness. The best he could do was help her. He breathed a sigh of relief when Alford softened. Alford was going to trust him.

David cleared his throat. "Can you get a marriage license? It might be difficult around here."

"I got one just days ago."

"Cheeky."

"Being prepared. I have to leave for the north in about four weeks."

"Then it's agreed. I'll help."

"Thank you. I'm still not sure why."

"I swore I would."

Chapter 17

Caroline was compliant *and* obedient. She confessed to her uncle she'd been misled by the young man's affections. She was sorry to have caused trouble with those she loved. She would accept her father's displeasure. After another night in her room, she was allowed to come down and join her family in the warm parlor. Once she had free run of the house again, she continued to be obedient and helpful, careful not to arouse anyone's suspicions.

On the day before her father was to arrive in Seattle by train, Harold Symington left early in the morning for a weekly meeting to the south. He asked Aunt Agatha to oversee the filling of Caroline's trunks and other effects for the ferry ride over the next day, but his wife announced she could only do so much. She and Liza both suffered stomach troubles and needed to rest. He promised he could help her on the morrow. He would be back too late.

He found David Harms at the dining table. David was getting ready to go to Seattle on an afternoon ferry. Symington asked him to keep a watch on things until then.

"No one's seen Alford," Symington said as he put on his calfskin gloves, "but I don't trust him. He seemed a persistent sort. Caroline's composing a letter to the bastard. It'll be delivered when she goes. If you see Alford on the premises, inform Mr. Jenkins. He knows how to deal with riffraff. We'll see you over there when Charles comes in?"

"Yes. Have a pleasant day, Uncle."

David found Caroline in their aunt's room reading to Aunt Agatha. He beckoned for her to come out into the hallway, then told her he'd taken the liberty of acquiring one of the maid's uniforms. At four she was to put it on and then leave by the back door. She was to cut to the north of the stump house and take the first trail she saw. Alford would be waiting for her.

"What shall I take?"

"I can't advise you, but nothing suspicious a maid shouldn't carry."

"When do you leave?"

"Just before you do. I must be on that ferry, but I'll meet you in the woods."

The rest of the day was tension-filled. At every opening of a door, Caroline imagined her uncle had come back early. It was hard to appear natural, but none of the women seemed to notice anything strange. They were too busy with their ailments. That left no one watching her because Sophie had gone to Seattle to stay with her friend Jenny, an easy solution to the strain between her and Caroline. Caroline didn't know how, but somehow Sophie had discovered her meetings with Alford and had told someone in the family. Why else her haunted, guilty look whenever she brought a tray to her sister?

At four, David poked his head in to say good-bye to Aunt Agatha. She was propped up in her bed on a fortress of pillows, a satin bed jacket on her shoulders.

"Safe trip, dear," she said to him.

"Thank you, Aunt. I hope you'll feel better. "

After he left, Aunt Agatha announced she was going to follow Liza's suggestion and sleep for a while as she was feeling a little feverish. "That sounds like a good idea. Shall I bring you some water?" Caroline knew her aunt might want to take one of her sleeping draughts, but this time she declined. "Auntie, the house is so quiet that I think I'll lie down too. It won't do to be sick with Father coming."

"There's a good girl," murmured Aunt Agatha, then drifted off to sleep

In the hall, Caroline checked on Liza who had been already sleeping for an hour. Liza looked flushed and would probably sleep hard for a while longer. In her own bedroom, she changed quickly into the uniform and threw an old cloak over her shoulders, then stuffed all the things she could carry into a small travel valise. Taking all the pillows and clothes remaining, she formed a figure on the bed that looked like someone sleeping, then drawing the drapes, she plunged the room into darkness.

All was clear in the hallway and she made it safely down the backstairs to the kitchen. At a side door, she slipped out, avoiding the arrival of one of the maids to check on the evening's meal, then walked briskly down through the garden to the stump house. There was no sign of Mr. Jenkins, an ex-policeman who sometimes did favors for her uncle. She had always thought him a congenial man, but she was afraid of him now.

She stared into the mix of brush and trees next to the lawn and spotted the trail she discovered once while looking for a badminton birdie. It had drizzled earlier and the leaves and branches of the salmonberry were wet, but she squeezed through with her valise and began to walk hurriedly. No one followed her, but as soon as she was away from the edge of the woods, she began to run.

"Whoa." Strong arms grabbed her and then she was in Alford's arms. She grasped his neck and held on, but he said that they must hurry. Taking her luggage, he led the way through the forest to a clearing about a half mile from *Kla-how-ya*. Standing there were two men: a man dressed like a boatman and David.

"Hurry," David said. "I spoke to Mr. Jenkins at the gate not long ago. He doesn't suspect anything, but I must make the ferry. Take care, Caroline. I hope you will be happy." He gave her a kiss then shook Alford's hand. "Be good to her."

"I promise." Alford nodded to the other man and they took off down to the water. There a rowboat was waiting for them. Out in the lake a thirty-foot boat bobbed up and down at its anchor. As they climbed into the rowboat Alford made introductions.

"Caroline, this is my brother, Ake. This is Caroline, Brother."

"Where do you want to go?"

"North. We're eloping."

"What?"

"Never mind, just get us there."

Chapter 18

Several miles up the lake shore, Alford and Caroline debarked near a settlement where he had arranged for horses and more importantly, a parson. By then she had changed out of the maid's outfit into a green travel suit. As they made their way along the muddy forested trail to the parson's home, Alford gathered ferns and foxglove to make a bouquet for her and she had found a sprig of huckleberries for his lapel. They found the parsonage easily — it had the only picket fence in the place — and with the Reverend Kvistad officiating and Mrs. Kvistad as witness they were married. When the pastor called for rings, Alford slipped a gold ring with a small moss agate in its center onto her finger. He had thought to bring a ring for himself and let Caroline put the band on him. After signing the marriage certificate, they sipped some claret to celebrate, then excused themselves. Collecting the horses at the livery, they headed north.

By now, it was getting well into the evening. Alford kept a steady pace. "I want to get as far away as possible. It's too hard to push for Swede Hill and the nearby railroad," he explained, "so I've made arrangements to stay at an inn I know. We can rest for the night before going on. I want to get out of the area

103

without much notice as quickly as possible."

Caroline looked around her. The elation of the marriage ceremony filled her with such joy, but as she looked around her surroundings, she saw the seriousness of the situation. People would be looking for her. They would have to work hard to ride fast. In Seattle at her uncle's house, the century was new and modern with telephones and electricity, but here people were still homesteading in the immense forests of King County where the roads were awful and amenities few.

"When can we contact my parents?"

"Let's give it a week. It'll be suitable enough by then."

At eight, it began to pour. They put on rain slickers, but after a half hour of enduring the onslaught Alford said they had to stop and rest. "We're about an hour shy of the inn, but I know of a cabin close by. I just don't want to push you too much."

"Where are we?" Caroline shouted from under her hood. The road they were on wasn't more than a trail enlarged to accommodate wagons going through the woods.

"About three quarters of the way to Swede Hill. We're going to float before this stops, so we're going to dry out," he yelled back. "Gonna get you warm."

They found the cabin off the trail in a clearing. The front porch sagged badly, but the rest of the building looked sound. Bob helped her down to the porch, then put the horses in a lean-to next to the cabin. Caroline went inside and took off her slicker.

"Sorry, love," he said as he came in. "I didn't count on the rain holding us up."

"I'm all right." She smiled at him, but the strain of the last six days was taking its toll.

He built a roaring fire for her and pulled a straw mattress over in front of it. He took out hardtack and cheese and a bottle of wine to wash it down.

"Hang up your skirt and waist by the fire, Caroline. We'll get them reasonably dry before moving on again. If you have dry stockings..."

For the first time, she felt self-conscious. She complied quietly, slipping out of her clothes so she wore only her lace-edged cotton underwaist, light corset and knickers. After removing her dark cotton stockings, she knelt on the mattress and began to comb her wet hair. Alford rustled behind her then came over and hung up his pants and coat. She tried not to look at him in his union suit. He sat down beside her and offered her some cheese. On the roof above them, the rain began to roar like a train.

"Some hotel," Caroline grinned.

"Only the best," he laughed. "You all right?"

She nodded yes.

"Not sorry?"

"No. It was very lovely. My ring is lovely." She stroked his cheek. "I love you." She kissed him and he kissed her back. They ate and drank some wine. The rain continued to come down in droves, so he put on his slicker and went out to check on the horses.

Caroline didn't hear him come back in, but she was aware of him as he knelt behind her. There was an electrifying pause, then very gently, he brushed aside her thick hair and began kissing her on the back of her neck. He stroked her bare arm with his fingertips.

"Caroline," he whispered into her ear. She couldn't hear him very well with the rain, but his hot breath sent a strange feeling through her. The skin on her arm twitched like that of a thoroughbred horse when something alights on it. She closed her eyes, tensing slightly.

Reaching around her, his hands moved down her thighs and back across her flat belly. He had touched her before, but this felt different now. A touch of wanting. He clasped her breasts firmly and pulled her to his lap, kissing now her ear, now her shoulder. She began to breathe deeply, her heart thumping at the unknown.

This is my wedding night come early, she thought. She began to wonder if she should have read *What Every Young Wife Ought to Know.* , but then again it had said nothing about this. Her brush dropped into her lap. She was still bound up by her light corset. Kissing her on the shoulder, he reached around and began to unhook it. Weakly she helped him and soon it was undone. He put his hands beneath the underwaist and squeezed her freed breasts. She made a little noise in her throat and arched away from him. Gently he pulled her back, his hands not once leaving her.

"Don't be afraid," she thought she heard him say. He leaned around and began to kiss her on the mouth and throat with a mounting hunger as insistent as his hands on her breasts. She felt powerless against the gentle onslaught, bewildered by her own growing feelings of desire. When a hand slid down into her cotton drawers, to her own surprise, she moaned.

"... wife — love — you." She was only vaguely aware he had removed his drawers before he was slipping off her top and exposing her slim figure and full breasts to him for the first time. The fire was making strange visions on the rock fireplace and behind the logs. She felt hot and short of breath as he touched her again and pushed her gently down on the mattress. He seemed unearthly, the fire making strange golden shadows on the strong muscles of his bare chest, arms and thighs. No one, and certainly not her mother, ever told her what a man would look like in arousal and if someone had, she wouldn't have known what that meant. Her heart began to pound with fear and anticipation, her mouth went dry. Kissing and caressing her with hands and words, he removed the last of her underclothes and lay on her.

"Oh," she gasped. She flung her arms about his neck as he began to push apart her thighs and thrust gently. The shadows on the wood slab ceiling danced wildly above her. She saw his face, the look of love. She gave into him, then cried out at the sharp pain when he took away her maidenhead.

He became still, not moving inside her and stroked her hair. "Are you all right?"

She smiled weakly. "Yes." She didn't want to say otherwise but she throbbed and ached.

He looked into her eyes. "Caroline, sweet, beautiful Caroline. I love you so much." He began to move again, thrusting more firmly.

A strange rush of feeling came over her. She dug her fingers into his back, then dared to touch the round muscular curve of his backside and sought his mouth on her own. She felt his moist flesh against hers as they moved together, golden shadows in the dark. He was breathing hard, and though it hurt, she was no longer afraid. They moved faster and faster, greedy for each other and then it was over. He lay as he had that day at the stream, his arm flung across her breasts. But now his leg was flung across her thighs as well, the weight pushing her into the straw mattress. She kissed the fine hairs of his forearm and tasted salt. He squeezed her shoulder and breast. Tenderly nuzzling her neck, he asked again if she was all right. When she said she was, he relaxed and lay still.

Caroline stared at the ceiling. The reflected light was softer and so was the rain. And here she was on her wedding night on the floor of a falling down cabin dripping water in the corner. Hundreds of miles from her mother. Not what she imagined. She looked at the naked man resting facedown next to her. Married to him. He'd just made love to her and taken away her maidenhead. *What came next?* The author of *What Every Young Wife Ought to Know.* never mentioned the bridal bed and what to expect and had gone straight to the next chapter, "The Layette."

Suddenly, he was turning and pulling her to him, spooning his hard body against hers. He kissed the moist hair on the back of her neck and enveloped her in his arms. His rough hands cupped her breasts.

"You sure I didn't hurt you?" he whispered. "I tried to be gentle."

"I'm fine. It was lovely." When he tickled her nipple, she giggled, feeling very naughty. The warmth of his body comforted her. He pulled something soft over them. She began to drift with sleep and closed her eyes.

"Caroline."

She opened her eyes. The fire in the fireplace had gone to coals.

"I think we should go now. The rain has stopped and we'll make good time to the inn now." Alford was already up and dressed. He waited with her petticoat draped over his arm. "I'll get you something to drink and heat water for us to wash up. Then we'll go. I'll do whatever you want. Anything."

It took another hour to get to the inn, set at the edge of a one street town. Caroline felt weary and sore, but their smartly furnished room with a high post bed and dresser pleased her. Set at the end of a long hall for privacy, its tall laced-covered window looked outside over what she thought was a garden hidden in the dark. Bob came behind her and put his arms around her.

"How're you doing? Ride tire you out?"

"Uh-huh." She put her arms over his and rocked him, feeling safe.

"We can sleep in. Then we should move on."

He checked the fire in the little parlor stove. Caroline slipped behind a screen and put on her nightgown. She laughed when he whistled at her as she came out. Made of the finest white lawn cotton material with delicate lace, the low-necked gown dropped from her shoulders to her ankles. She knew the translucent cloth revealed the swell of her breasts and slender thighs. She hopped across the cold floor and into bed. He turned down the lantern by his side and removed his clothes. Crawling into bed, the old-fashioned rope bed sagged, causing him to slide into her. Caroline giggled.

"Go to sleep, sweetheart," he said. "It's been a long day." He spooned up against her and held her in his arms, but did not make love to her and went to sleep.

Sometime before dawn, they woke again. In the predawn light, they could see outside to the tops of great woods behind the inn. Somewhere a rooster crowed. They talked for a while about the coming day and fears about what might be happening back at *Kla-how-ya*. They lay with their heads together on their downy pillows, sometimes touching, sometimes not. It was like courting again, Alford going very slow, but soon one thing led to another and they were making love. It was different from the cabin. There was no urgency, just a gentle expression of tenderness in an over-stuffed, sagging-in-the-center bed. They were both laughing softly when they were finished. Eventually, Caroline put on her nightgown and went to the washstand. Alford lay staring at a framed picture taken from some magazine. The ascent of Mount Rainier.

"Did you ever hear anything about the unfortunate Mrs. Westford and her ankle?"

"Oh, my aunt thought she knew her, but then she claims she knows everyone. No, I haven't. Emily would know."

Outside a dog began to bark wildly. "Why don't they shut it up?" Alford said. "It must be only five thirty."

There was pounding downstairs and suddenly he sat up. Caroline went over to the window and gasped. Too late Alford started to rise. The inn shook as a horde appeared to roar through the building and then it was at their door.

The attack was carefully orchestrated. Piling in through the busted down door, three heavyset men assailed Bob with billy clubs and fists while two other men grabbed Caroline at the window and rushed her to the door. She screamed and screamed as Alford rose stark naked to defend her and was knocked viciously back across the bed. He rolled off on the other side and began to stand, but two of the men seized him by the arms and held him while the third punched him with a set of brass knuckles.

"Get your cloak, miss," said a large man with a handlebar mustache. It was Mr. Jenkins. "Get the rest of her things," he ordered to another.

"What the hell is going on?" the owner of the inn shouted from out in the hall.

"Nothing to concern yourself with. Just taking care of a Wobbly. We'll pay for any loss."

Caroline screamed, twisting and pulling away from Jenkins,

kicking his ankles, but he was too strong. For a moment she thought they might be saved when Alford broke free and landed a few good punches on his attackers. But he was subdued again.

"Caroline!"

As she was pushed out, she turned to see him collapsing on the floor where he was viciously kicked. Blood dripped from his head. Then he lost his dinner. It was the last thing she saw. Hustled outside to an awaiting carriage, she fainted and remembered nothing at all.

Chapter 19

Charles Symington arrived at *Kla-how-ya* late in the evening of the day of the attack and found Caroline in her room, distraught and in a state of exhaustion. Her face pale and swollen from crying, she received him in a nightgown and her wrapper.

"Oh, Father, please speak to Uncle Harold and find out what has happened to Bob. Why did he do it? Why?" She pounded the questions out on his chest.

Her father took her in his arms. "Hush. Everything will be all right. I promise."

For a moment she believed he wasn't like her uncle. That he couldn't be cruel. But as he calmed her, she began to realize he was just as bent on getting the whole affair behind her.

"We'll rest a few days here," he went on, "then we'll return to Seattle and take the train for home. I'll arrange for a quiet annulment."

"No." Caroline wiggled out of his arms and stared at him, her heart pounding as she gained courage to oppose him. "No. Never. I won't go, Father. Only to see my husband. We're legally married."

"Caroline..."

"I love him, Father. There will be no annulment."

"This marriage will ruin you."

"I think Uncle Harold has already done that." Caroline shook as she looked into her father's eyes, for she loved him so much. It went against her grain and training to oppose him, but she loved Alford more. "Have you no shame? They broke down our door! They dragged me away like some pillager's prize! They beat him horribly. I don't even know if he's alive." She sagged down on the window seat.

"He was alive this morning. I suppose that I could have someone find out — "

"No! You'll send David — then you'll tell my husband I'll be coming." She leaned her head against the window, fighting back the urge to start crying again. She felt positively drained, her resistance to further trauma just about nil. Her father's shoulders slumped. He sat down on a chair by the dresser, resting his hands on his walking cane. Caroline felt a momentary pang of remorse for him.

"Caroline.... What will your mother think? She's already at wit's end about Alford's letter. And as for David, I'm very disappointed in him. Your uncle suspects he may have had a hand in all this. My favorite nephew conspiring behind my back! He has the gall to tell me he even likes the damn seducer." He pounded the fir wood floor with his cane. "What of your sister? Her wedding plans may be in jeopardy. If this gets out..."

"I hardly think James Ford will be willing to give up Sophie's hand." Caroline leaned forward. "I want nothing, Father. Just your blessing or if not that... then..." She was hesitant to say it, but she did. "Then... I'll go without." She bit her lip. "I love him. There'll be no fuss. We'll leave when he is able to travel. But first... first, I must know how he is. Please, Father."

Charles Symington scowled. He seemed surprised at her explosion of emotion. He leaned heavily on his cane. Eventually, he sighed.

"I'll have Harold send one of his men and find out what has

happened with Alford. I did understand he was vacated from the inn sometime this morning. When we're able to locate him, I'll send David. In the meantime, Caroline, my dear, please let your aunt draw a bath for you. Then eat some food and rest. It's unhealthy to be so distraught."

Caroline agreed to that, but beyond that was firm in her desire to be with Alford.

Alford woke to the sound of a skirt rustling next to him, a terrible dream of lying in an open wagon wrapped up in a blanket still vivid. In it, above him the tops of trees ticked over and over him like an Edison Kinetoscope show, flickering shadows as painful as the jarring lurch of the wagon. Shadows seemed to be all about him, especially in his left eye that saw only red. From time to time someone would look over the seat and talk to him, but he didn't recognize the shadow. He didn't recognize anything, only the pain.

Someone lifted his head and pressed a cup to his lips. He must have groaned because the shadow spoke to him. He opened his one good eye and saw the concerned face of his mother. He sipped the water carefully through his swollen lips, then let her lay him back on his pillows. He didn't think he could manage it alone, he was so sore.

She smiled at him. "*Ja.* You are not dead yet, though I think the cat has never brought home something as ugly as you."

He gave her a half-smile and made a sound in his throat before closing his eye again. *I'm so tired* he thought.

"Bob."

He opened his eye again. "How... long here?" he managed to say.

"It is three days. Someone put you in freight wagon and headed you north. Billy Howell see you and bring you here. He was very angry and has been making talk."

The door to his old room opened. It was Papa asking if he was awake. Alford raised an arm in response and quickly regretted it. A terrible pain sliced through his left side, as though something separated and rejoined into a whole. It made

113

him nauseated.

"Shh. Don't move, dear. You have one, maybe two bruised ribs. Dr. Ellis was kind. He was here to see Papa and when he heard what has happened to you, he helped. He has bound you, but you have been out of your head, so nothing gets better." Her cool hand wiped his brow.

Einar Alford came behind his wife's shoulder and looked down at him. He was an older reflection of Bob, a handsome white-haired gentleman in his late fifties. He looked at his face and grumped, "Some job they do on you. What did you do, Bob, to make them so angry?"

"We e-loped." The words got out despite his swollen jaw.

Both his parents gasped. "And where is wife?" his father exploded.

"I don't know... I...don't know." Alford laid his head back deep into the pillow. Almost instantly, he was asleep.

A day later, David Harms arrived by carriage at the Alford homestead. Ake and Olav Alford were on the porch with their mother, Astrid Lise Alford. They greeted him warily and invited him into the yard.

"Is Bob Alford here?"

"Who wants to know?" Ake asked.

"Caroline. His wife."

Anna Lise sighed and sat up in her chair to meet him. He removed his derby and offered his hand. "I'm David Harms, her cousin. She's asked me to talk to him."

"And why she not here to talk to husband?"

"It's a delicate thing, ma'am. There has been opposition to the marriage."

"That why they beat him so hard?" Olav's face was dark and sour like he'd eaten a pickle.

"Nothing relieved me more than to learn he'd survived this awful business."

"Business? You call this business? Dead, more like," Ake spat.

Seeing the level of hostility from the Alford men he

appealed to the mother.

"Caroline's been frantic with worry. It was a very ugly scene, I'm afraid."

"You are not here to accuse him?"

"No, ma'am. I'm his friend and I think he knows that."

David found Alford resting in a room off the back. There was a slight breeze stirring the lace curtains at the window, adding further to the sense of well-being in this cool refuge from the hot day outside. Propped up on pillows, he appeared to be asleep until David stepped further into the room. Then his eye snapped open in the bruised and swollen face. Alford looked ghastly. What was he going to tell Caroline?

"You! What are you doing here, you bastard?" Alford croaked.

David hesitated. He didn't understand.

"You told them," Alford struggled to sit up better, holding his left side around his bandage, but it appeared too much for him and he fell back into the pillows. The only thing the effort had produced was sweat on his bare chest and shoulders and cotton wrapping.

"Believe me, Alford, I didn't. I went over to Seattle as planned. I just heard about your beating and came as soon as I could. I'm here because Caroline wishes it. She wanted to make sure you were all right." David shook his head. "Good Lord, I hope a doctor has seen you. You look awful. I'm not sure I want to tell her that."

"Tell her the truth." Alford eyed him carefully, his voice bitter, but he toned it down when he asked about Caroline. "How is she? They didn't hurt her, did they?"

"No, but she's quite beside herself."

"God dammit! Wouldn't you be? I'd like to kill Harold Symington for what he's done. Treating her like common baggage. He ought to be horsewhipped."

"That won't serve anyone," David murmured.

"What?"

"I said Caroline's father wants an annulment."

"He can't force her!"

David snorted. "He'll try. Both sides are digging in." He sighed, cautiously turning his hat in his hands. "It may not be resolved for some time. How long do you think you'll be here?"

"I don't know. I have to get permanently vertical first. I apparently have some sort of concussion." He touched the stitches on the side of his head. "There isn't any danger in the meantime to her father's threat to take her home?"

"Caroline has dug in her heels and Uncle Harold doesn't want a public scene, so I think for now, she'll be at *Kla-how-ya*. Still, I wouldn't underestimate my Uncle Harold's dislike for you and in family matters, he holds sway over Caroline's father too often."

Alford looked at David curiously. "I still don't know where you are in all this. It bothers me."

"I can understand that. Let's just say that I care about her."

"You're in love with her..."

"It's quite impossible. I'm her cousin. Caroline is, however, very special to me. Don't make it any more than that." He saw Alford was tiring and suggested he go. "I'm to return to *Kla-how-ya*. Caroline's father has requested this meeting as much as Caroline, but he begs you reconsider and not stay in the way of Caroline's future. He wants you not to fight an annulment."

"And kindly beg him not to interfere in what is done. He forgets that Caroline can legally make her own decisions. Tell him, above all else, I will be a good husband to her. And remind him also that I can press charges for kidnap and battery."

David shook his head. "There was some Wobbly action at one of the mills the day before you eloped. Several people were injured, including the foreman. It has given the local authorities powers to do whatever they feel is necessary. Even though J. J. Jenkins was there at the inn, he has claimed no connection to Symington. He was part of a group acting on orders to clear out a Wobbly."

"I'm no Wobbly," Alford snapped. Angrily he worked his jaw as his frustration grew. "What about the police?"

"I gather they acted rather quickly," he continued. "Caroline was discovered missing at seven. My uncle was back at eight. By then, Jenkins had already wired a couple of places, using the story they were looking for an agitator traveling with a young woman. No mention was officially made of Caroline to avoid a scandal. I suspect there were some payoffs."

"As for the sheriff, he was there. He received notification about your whereabouts about ten. Jenkins rode all night to get to you. He was the one who had you thrown into a wagon and taken north — with the sheriff's blessing. I'm afraid that Uncle Harold will come out clean."

At that, Alford turned away, his face showing complete humiliation.

The standoff lasted another three days, then much to Harold Symington's chagrin, his brother gave in and said he wouldn't contest the marriage. Caroline had permission to go with her new husband. He would wire her mother and let her know. Then, if she'd wait, he'd go with her to Swede Hill to see her young man. Caroline was elated, but her happiness was short lived.

On the way to the settlement, her father told her that she'd always been his favorite. "I've had such high hopes for you, Caroline. This liaison with Alford, however, is a great disappointment. I'm fighting the notion you've acted immorally, throwing yourself at him before marriage" — he ground his teeth — "meeting secretly as you have with him. But you've made your own choice and now will have to live with it."

"Father... " She stiffened at his icy tone.

He clutched his cane so tight his fingers grew pale. "You're very young and don't know a great deal about men. I just hope you won't be disappointed. I know you believe in the new social mores and attitudes currently in vogue, but your husband has the legal and moral authority over your life no matter how you wish it otherwise. Whatever he has promised to you, you've chosen a rougher life because Alford can offer only that. It will be difficult. And difficulties bring out the worst in some men."

Caroline looked down at her hands and eventually out into the cleared woods and farmland passing by. Her heart felt sick. She had never meant to hurt her parents. When a wheel hit a stone in the rough road, she felt a hard realization that worse was to come.

"Harold believes that I'm too lenient with you. That you have disgraced the family with your unladylike behavior. Since you've made your choice to go with him, you cannot consider yourself a part of this family any longer." Caroline gasped in disbelief. Her father looked straight ahead. "After today, since you insist that you must have him, we'll see no more of each other."

Alford was standing on the porch when the carriage pulled up. He gave Caroline a wide smile when he saw her. Gingerly, he made his way down the path to the gate while the driver unloaded her trunks and other possessions. Charles Symington stayed seated in the carriage, but he watched Alford with intense interest. Caroline got down by herself and ran to him, shouting his name. He looked bruised and battered, but when he put his good arm around her, she felt comfort and safety.

"Won't you come in Mr. Symington?" Alford asked. "There are refreshments and you're most welcome."

"No. I'm returning this evening. There's no time."

Caroline felt a tremor go through Alford then resignation. He drew her closer and nodded soberly in agreement that it would be futile to persist.

"I'll take good care of her," Alford promised.

The older man glanced at Caroline. He betrayed no emotion, but his eyes seemed to want to say *something*. Then he looked away. He tapped the side of the carriage with his cane and told the driver to go, but he didn't say good-bye.

Chapter 20

Three weeks later, Alford and Caroline boarded a train for Frazier, Washington. Given a warm send-off by her in-laws, Caroline was grateful they had accepted her with the love and understanding as they had during her stay with them. Mother Alford had been especially kind, involving her in the daily chores around the house, but also sharing her own stories of her marriage. It made Caroline's abrupt separation from her family both tolerable and poignant. There was a change of trains on the coast, so the newlyweds caught the excursion train at six in the morning the next day and headed east into the foothills of the North Cascades.

Arriving just before nine, they were met at Frazier's tiny depot by a Forest Service employee.

"Name's George Fuller. The boss sent me down to take you to our local hotel. You'll be staying there for the night. We had to scramble to locate housing suitable for you and your bride, but we found a vacant house just outside of the town."

"Is it far?" Alford asked.

"It's about a half mile away, but has electricity as the rest of the town does, thanks to the generator at the local mill." The man finished loading their pitiful belongings into the back of the buckboard, then got in the driver's seat. "You can have it for a very small monthly rent with an option to buy. Jack Vernell, the district ranger, will give you directions. Once Mrs. Alford is settled at the hotel, you're to meet him at headquarters."

"Thanks," Alford said as he helped Caroline into the buckboard. Smoothing down her traveling suit, she arranged herself on the seat while Alford stood behind her in the wagon box. Already she was feeling lost and overwhelmed. She have half-listened to the colorful commentary as they were taken down the main street of the tiny town.

" — Frazier was carved out in 1902 when an enterprising homesteader seeing a need for a closer jumping off point for the miners working in the mining district near the Washington National Forest, decided to put down a claim and call it a store —"

Caroline's eyes strayed to what passed as a hotel with a saloon and tobacco shop next to it. They seemed to establish a pattern that continued up and down the street on both sides. Saloon, tobacco. Saloon, tobacco.

" — When the train came in three years later, it seemed to bring along with it the electric light and city folk wishing to heal their lungs with the pure, clear air. The area had begun to boom — "

Boom? It looked like the ragtag frontier towns she had seen only in pictures. Its impertinent wood buildings with their illusory false fronts and cheerful hand-painted signs displayed a courage she didn't feel at the moment. Its "main street" seemed to be directing Caroline to the other end of town where enormous firs stood like a giant wall waiting to absorb her. Beyond them, dwarfing them to insignificance, were the mountains that surrounded the valley. The scene was both breathtaking and awe-inspiring, but it was the town that struck her the most. There were stumps still left in part of the road and though she could see signs for a lawyer, a butcher and a surveyor, she wondered what society was kept here and how she would manage.

After Alford left with Fuller for headquarters, Caroline went down and spent part of the morning shyly talking to the hotel proprietor's wife. It had taken about five minutes before most of the town knew she was in the restaurant drinking coffee. Consisting of only three tables and what appeared to be an equal amount of chairs, she was joined by several other women who had come out of nowhere to pay their respects. She found them to be cordial, friendly and very curious about her. She was glad when Alford showed up at noon to take her to look at their future home. He must have made an impression. Having never been around him in the company of others outside of his family, she was surprised how disarming he could be to other women. Polite and self-effacing, he fended off any other questions about her and announced he was stealing his bride away. Outside, he loaded her in a buggy and thanked everyone standing on the porch for their kindness. Everyone allowed back it was their pleasure and winking at each other, wished them a nice ride.

"Now what was that for?" Caroline asked when they were out of earshot.

"I'm not sure, but Vernell warned me that the last time they had a shivaree here was over a year ago."

She turned sharply to him. "They wouldn't dare. I mean, people don't still do that, do they? Bang pans and scare newlyweds out of their beds?"

"We're not dealing with the society page of Portland." Alford clucked at the horse. "However, you do cut a handsome figure, Mrs. Alford, in your traveling suit. I must say you've made an impression on them. As for me, I just might marry you all over again."

About a half mile out of town as they'd been told, they found their rental. Built on a small, natural prairie, the two story house stood between a river and a road recently widened to accommodate wagons. Skirting it on three sides was the ever present forest mix of alder, maple, fir and cedar. Next to it on the left was an especially old cedar perhaps two hundred years old. Its graceful dark green branches swept down next to the long front porch and like an ancient sentinel, guarded the main way to the water.

At the dirt path to the door, Alford stopped the buggy and helped Caroline down. He stood alongside and gazed across the yard.

"Too many alders for comfort. They'll need to come down. Looks like I'll have to rebuild the stable too."

Caroline stared at the house and thought that the whole place needed to be rebuilt. She couldn't believe it was only six years old. The moss covered shake roof needed repair and the porch was sagging.

"It has an inside pump, sweetheart. And a good cook stove. We'll have to set up a wet drip outside for cold things, though." He took her hand eagerly and led her up to the front door. Through the screen door, she could see into the hall. To the left was a large dining room. To the right, a living room. Both rooms boasted large windows looking out onto the porch, but all she could see was the dirt and clutter on the floor.

"Who built this?"

"A miner who made a killing, then lost it all three years later. It hasn't been lived in since. His heirs..."

"His heirs?"

"He mysteriously disappeared and left his debts to his family."

"Oh, Bob. Like the place on our first hike."

"It isn't a bad luck place, Caroline. Someone got the local medicine man to bless it. It just needs some people." With that, he swooped her up in his arms and gave her a kiss. "I think we should bless it too, seeing we're going to be staying for a while. Mind if I waltz you across the threshold?"

"Bob, your ribs!"

"I'm all right." He opened the door and stepped in. The house had a hollow sound, like the occupants had scurried out of the house through the roof. It smelled uninviting.

"Where do we sleep?"

"Downstairs," he said, putting her down lovingly. "The

upstairs isn't finished." Caroline looked at the door leading up and shivered. She stayed close to him, unsure of the place, but he was very excited. "It won't be difficult to finish. When I'm here, I can work on it."

"When you're here?"

He smiled guiltily. "It appears Vernell's going to show me the neighborhood. I'll be riding out with him and Fuller tomorrow to the mining district to inspect a road and then learn the location of some of the buildings in the forest reserve. I'm going to be gone three days and then will be in and out until this weekend."

Caroline was taken aback. This wasn't what she had envisioned. She thought she'd be with him every day. That he wouldn't have to work full time at first, partly because she didn't think that he'd fully recovered from his beating. Alford tried to reassure her that things would be fine. His ribs only moderately bothered him and he would be careful. She would stay at the hotel for a few more days and when he was free on the weekend, they would come out and clean.

"Look, let's check out the kitchen. We'll find out what we need." He headed out down the long hall. From the far end, he opened a swinging door and a shaft of light shot out.

"Caroline! Come here, honey. You should see the view."

But Caroline couldn't see anything. Only the dirt, mold and broken dreams of some poor sojourner going through life before her. She stared at the busted up rooms and then outside to the trees that rose like a fortress around her. She suddenly felt isolated and closed in, completely overwhelmed by all the events of the past four weeks. She was far away from anything she'd ever known and in a moment of weakness, her father's words of doom came roaring back in her head.

"Oh, dear Lord," Caroline murmured in a small, weak voice. "What have I gotten myself into?"

Book II
Frazier
1907

Chapter 21

S*o this is what forest rangering is*, Alford thought as he sat up on a boulder eating his cold lunch of sandwich and dried fruit. His new boss, Ranger Jack Vernell and the other half-time man, George Fuller, sat nearby. He could see in every direction, including south to the adjoining mountain peaks and glaciers and west to Puget Sound. It was a spectacular view, a steep bare perch looking down into deep valleys carved out by ancient ice and now holding threads of icy blue water at their feet several thousand feet below. Somewhere among the forests of cedar and Douglas fir covering the hills and lowlands, he spied a thin line leading away southwest to Frazier.

"What's that trail?" he asked Vernell. "I didn't think we had any to speak of back here." He squinted against the sun and a light breeze that caressed his face.

"Oh that. A Seattle hiking club put it in just for their annual outing, but now other groups use it too. We plan to enlarge it and make it into a wagon road, but funds aren't forthcoming. I think private monies will have to be raised again. This whole Washington National Forest thing is new and being in the northern district of it sometimes forgotten. We're a little out of the way."

Alford found that true. The Frazier Creek District of the reserve was a mountainous wilderness with only one wagon road and a few trails devoted to getting supplies back to the miners in the mining district. The rest were more suitable for game. There were creeks, lakes and high mountain meadows while down in the lower environs, jungles of stinging nettle, Devil's club and brambles clogged the land beneath the big leaf and vine maples and forest giants. The mountains were rugged and high, including the white-headed Mount Kulshan just under eleven thousand feet high. Alford loved every bit of it.

"So what do you think?" Vernell was an older man in his mid-forties. A tall, wire-thin man with drooping gray mustaches and long legs, he looked like a gust of wind could blow him over, but Alford already knew he was incredibly strong. In addition to prospecting and homesteading, he'd been one of the first to climb Mount Kulshan in the 1880s and had been in on some of the earliest surveying. Vernell had climbed and ranged every inch of his domain and he was as flinty as the mountains.

Alford took a swig from his canteen, then capped it. "No fire lookouts, no shelter for visitors. Looks like we have a lot of work cut out for us."

"Well, I'd like to get some trails, but it isn't the job of the Forest Service to build roads. Trail making's for practical use, mainly for pack trains. But as I see it, I'd like to make it a priority to cruise for trail building. Good goal for this second year of the Forest Service's existence in the area. "

"What about the Mazamas Mountaineering Club? Heard they were active up here." *At least from what Caroline told me.*

George Fuller leaned in. He was a local man who had spent most of his life in the area. Fuller's father had been a miner, working on one of the first gold claims in the area, later working on copper claims as well. "They're an enthusiastic bunch. Can't figure out why a group from Oregon likes this place so much when they have their own mountains, but they seem to think the area should become a national park."

"That's true," Vernell said "And really there's nothing wrong working with the hiking clubs. Local chambers of commerce are interested in opening up Frazier and the national forest for recreation. It's a way of preservation." He smoothed down his mustache. "As yet there's no logging in the national forest, but with the changes in technology and the butting up of private property against the forests of the Frazier Creek District, it's a matter of time before pressure gonna be put on them to open the area up. That's why I hired you Alford. I wanted someone who knew not only about timber cruising, but had experience in harvesting the big trees. And I also like you for your appreciation of this place for recreation. It's a coming thing, you know."

Alford looked down at the river in front of him. "Does it have fish?"

"Dolly Vardens," Fuller spat. "Voracious little critters. There's brown trout in the lake, though. I was thinking of hauling up rainbows."

"How'd you do that?"

"Milk cans and river water, packed in by horse. It works, too."

"You've had time to check out the river for salmon?" Vernell asked Alford.

"Not really. Too much to do about getting settled in."

"Well, I hope that things are working well for you. Mrs. Alford's sure a pretty little thing. Being newlywed and all, I'm surprised you're here talking about fish. Now I'd be thinking about my wife. She gonna be all right up here?"

"I think so." But after Alford left her at the hotel, he wasn't so sure. He'd been excited about the house. Being a carpenter's son, he was used to seeing possibilities in wood and buildings where others might not. It really wouldn't be difficult to finish the house. In fact, he was planning on having his father and brothers come up and help him before the snows came.

But Caroline had surprised him by her quietness. The house seemed to depress her and when he said good-bye, for the first time since their elopement, her eyes betrayed a fear and unsettled sorrow. Though he had tried not to think of it during these last absorbing days, he was worried that she'd been left alone.

"There's some nice gals in Frazier," Vernell said, "in addition to Mrs. Vernell. Ellie Turner, for one. She's got a young 'un about six months. She taught school for a while. There's Miss Jensen who teaches school now and Mrs. Black whose husband is an assayer. Berta Olsen's a nice gal. There's a women's tea club that meets once a month. I'd say they keep the community up to standard."

"What about Mrs. Bladstad?" Fuller chimed in.

Vernell laughed. "Now that's a woman. Charlie Bladstad didn't know what he was getting into when he married her, but I must say if it weren't for the fact she's one of the prettiest gals to ever grace our little village — beg pardon, Alford — and grudgingly, the nicest, I think the majority of the male population would have put her on a train and sent her home to be spanked."

Alford raised an eyebrow. "Who is this woman? Did she try to break up the saloons with an axe?"

"Nope, but she has some interesting notions about men."

Fuller laughed. "She's the damnedest female I ever met, but every time I see her, I always get tongue-tied. Her husband, Charlie, is head over heels in love with her and doesn't give a damn as long as the house is clean and food's on the table. Hate to admit it, but I don't blame him. That woman's packing some cargo."

Vernell cleared his throat to show his disapproval of Fuller's description of Mrs. Bladstad, but Fuller said he meant no disrespect, her being Charlie's wife and all. "Charlie's one of my best friends." When he realized his real blunder in his description, he turned beet red.

"Does she cook?" Alford asked.

"He ain't starving and he has the nicest kids," mumbled Fuller.

"She going to that ladies convention in the fall?" Vernell asked Fuller as he put away his food.

"Probably, though I heard Charlie say he wished she reconsider since she was in the family way again." Fuller got embarrassed again and looked away.

Alford listened to the talk, but it began to drift off behind him, like the clouds settling on the mountains to the east of him as the day shifted to a hazy afternoon. They conjured up a picture of Caroline stepping over billowy hills in her light night shift. He guessed he was a newlywed. He suddenly ached to see her.

"...and take some time off, Alford," Vernell was saying. When we get back, I won't be needing you until Tuesday, so you can work on your place. If you need to haul anything down, George here, can loan you the freight wagon."

Fuller chuckled. "Don't hurry about it, Alford. I suppose after this time away, you'll want to get reacquainted with the Mrs."

"I do miss her. That I do." Alford grinned. He took a swig of water and capping the canteen, wondered why the world thought being newly married was so damned comical when it was serious business. There was certainly considerable community attention. It made him all the more anxious to get home. Increasingly, he was feeling guilty about leaving her alone.

Chapter 22

When the sun burst through the early morning mist of her third day without Bob, Caroline finally decided it was time to stop feeling sorry for herself and get to work. Hers wasn't the first husband to go off and work away from the family home (even though theirs at the moment was a hotel room). She was luckier than most, she figured, except she hadn't known anyone with a kind of life like this.

It had been romantic at first. Once the shock of her father's words stung less, she looked forward to their move north. She was, after all, with the man she loved, the man she'd stood up for and won. If she'd have to be on her own, so be it. He was young, handsome and clever with his hands. It would be an adventure to go so far away and start a totally new life. She loved the mountains and forests. She'd be a part of it, hiking the hills and ridges with Bob right beside her. Together, they would tame it. Except Frazier was more isolated and primitive than she had expected, even if it was electrified.

She had braved their first night in the hotel under the guise of adventure, but she felt as though she had a letter "N" in the middle of her forehead, signifying newlywed as they went up to retire. It didn't help that the bedsprings creaked. Bob said what-the-hell, but she put him off. "No one's going to burst in on us again," he tried to soothe jokingly, but Caroline said they wouldn't need to with the whole hotel on alert. Alford had to settle for a quick kiss.

He's been patient, though, thought Caroline as she looked out of her hotel window. On the other side of the main street, a deer darted between one of the saloons, another sign of how this place wasn't Portland. The maples behind the one story buildings were starting to turn, reminding her that the summer of her youth was nearly over. She turned and gazed at the picture taken in Swede Hill just before they boarded the train for here. His mother-in-law had insisted on it, so they had put on their wedding clothes, Bob gathering ferns and foxglove once again for her bouquet. It seemed like an eternity since she'd made the decision to run away and ages since her father turned and told her on she couldn't come home until she came to her senses.

Caroline opened her trunk and searched for some clothes she had neglected to hang up: her tramping outfit from the hike. She dressed quickly into the skirt and waist, lacing the tall boots quickly. She piled up her rich cinnamon brown hair, then pinned on a saucy straw hat.

"Mrs. Alford," greeted the proprietor's wife when Caroline came into the dining room. "Good morning."

Caroline took her seat at the table and welcomed the cup of coffee set before her. After three days on her own, she was beginning to understand the interest of everyone. *They look out for each other here,* she thought, *and because Bob's gone, they feel responsible for me.* The women weren't really nosy, just concerned.

"And what will you do today?" Mrs. Wilson asked as she put down a little pitcher of cream .

"I'm going to clean my house."

Caroline found it just as they'd left it, with a pile of trash swept up in the center of the living room. The house felt just as forlorn, almost haunted as a crow cried outside behind her, but maybe it's just waiting for me. Bob had been right about the kitchen. When she finally entered it, she stumbled into the most incredible view that filled the tall south windows of the kitchen over the sink. Across the river, the forested hills of maple and alder rose high until they were taken over by the firs and cedars. Behind the hills were mountains still covered with snow this late in the summer. Even as the house weighed down on her now, the window gave her expansive hope and a feeling of incredible longing.

I belong here. Suddenly, she felt a surge of action, like her days at the Portland hospital when her supervisor would say, "Miss Symington, these are your charges today. Bring them home by five." Caroline checked her watch pin on her canvas waist. She had five hours of work ahead of her.

She started in the kitchen, because despite its charm, it was a dusty, greasy mess. Though her family had a housekeeper back in Oregon, she had learned to tackle such untidy jobs at her tramping club's annual clean up at their cabin and various outings. Everyone pitched in and what she had only seen Mabel the housekeeper perform, she inquired and was duly taught. How she loved the women in the club. They were educated and strong, but still pursued household tasks with aplomb. Her volunteer work at the hospital helped too.

She fired up the cookstove, secure in the knowledge Bob had checked the stove pipe on their first visit and deemed it clear and soon had water boiling in an old washer tub. She scrubbed down the enameled counter of the kitchen pantry then did the sink, table and cupboards. She swept the floor, then carted out all the junk she could find to a burning place outside. Coming back in she cleaned the handsome cook stove and scrubbed down walls and cupboards. At noon, she took a short break and wandered down to the water where she ate the lunch packed for her at the hotel and some hot tea in the newfangled Thermos bottle Emily had given her for a wedding present. After surveying the outhouse and using it despite its strong nose-twitching stench — *It needs a new dump of lime,* she thought — she returned to take on the rooms in the front. She worked until three-thirty, then cleaned up her equipment and got ready to go back to the hotel. She almost didn't hear the buggy come up as she came out onto the front porch.

"So the stories are true. Old Finster's place is being occupied."

Caroline turned sharply to face a pretty young woman in her mid-twenties perched on her seat as if she was reviewing the troops. She had beautiful dark brown hair, bright blue eyes and a glowing complexion. Her sturdy cotton waist and skirt were dark and practical, but something about her didn't convey such an equally austere personality. She had a friendly, pleasing face. She was the picture of health and vitality. When she dismounted, it shocked Caroline to see that she was pregnant. Caroline watched in fascination as the woman brushed off her skirt, and then extend her hand.

"I'm Cathy Bladstad. Welcome to Frazier."

Caroline came down to meet her and took her hand, shaking it more out of surprise than anything else. She'd been welcomed by the women in town informally, but somehow this visit felt official.

"I'm Caroline Alford," she volunteered. "Very nice to meet you, Mrs. Bladstad."

"Oh, bother. Just Cathy, if you please. May I call you Caroline?"

"Yes, please do."

Cathy secured her horse, then pressed her hands on her back to ease some twinge. Caroline wondered how far she was along. She was showing quite a bit under her skirt and loose waist.

"Would you like to sit?" Caroline asked.

"Just for a moment. I wanted to see if I could help."

Taken aback again, Caroline said, "Actually, I'm done for the day, but I may come back tomorrow and finish the front rooms."

"Then I'll come tomorrow. If you don't mind."

"Oh." Caroline wasn't sure what to think. "Are you sure it's all right?" All her intentions of being a forthright, New Woman were suddenly collapsing under her mother's dictum of never speaking publicly about pregnancy.

"It never bothered the others. If I didn't have a funny leg this time, I'd go climbing as well. It doesn't do to just sit around and wait for the little darling." She said the last sentence with a touch of humor, then suddenly aware that Caroline was unduly quiet, she apologized.

"Oh, you mustn't mind me. I heard you were dropped as soon as you got here and I thought — well, it doesn't do to be alone. Women should stick up for each other with or without invitation." She lowered herself to the porch step and laughed. "It's getting longer and longer to the floor. In fact, this is the last time I ride a horse."

"When is the baby due?"

"Not until late November, but I feel as big as next week."

Caroline asked after the "others."

"Two boys, one's a five-year-old and the other's two. My home is full of snakes, rocks and toy soldiers. Lovely dears." She talked with such affection Caroline couldn't help but smile. Eventually, Cathy took off her hat and laid it on top of her swelling abdomen. "Three's it, though."

She took a deep breath and sighed. "You want children?"

"Oh, yes, but I believe in voluntary motherhood."

"I volunteered all right," replied Cathy.

Caroline gasped. She'd never met someone as outspoken as this. At first, she was shocked, but when she saw the look of total merriment on the other young woman's face, she laughed nervously.

"You mustn't take offense, Caroline. A good sense of humor is such an antidote to life." Cathy frowned. "I do apologize. Forgive me." She struggled to get herself positioned to get up, but Caroline stayed her.

"Would you like some tea? It's not fancy. I have some left in my Thermos bottle. We can sit outside in the back. I'm afraid the kitchen's not quite ready for company."

"Why that would be lovely."

They walked around to the back and sat on the "lawn"

going down to the river. Caroline found a decent ladder-back chair for her new friend, while she sat in a precarious canvas chair she had discovered while cleaning. While she drank out of the cap on the bottle, she gave a tin cup she had brought along for Cathy. They watched the river as it flowed by, exchanging bits of information about each other.

"My Charlie is head foreman in a logging camp south of here. We met on an outing to the mountains — we had a common interest in hiking and exploring the area, you see." Cathy rubbed her belly and giggled. "Which eventually led to courtship and marriage." From the way she spoke, Caroline could see she was quite happy.

"My father was an Englishman who had surveyed the area many years before," Cathy went on. "He stayed on to homestead, but loved books so I am quite well read. My mother — my mother died in childbirth when I was just eleven. Being the oldest, I was put in charge of my many siblings left motherless after the tragedy."

When Cathy got a far-off look in her eyes, Caroline gathered this had made an enormous impression on her. Perhaps it was why she was so outspoken.

"I'm so sorry."

Cathy shrugged. "Didn't keep me from finishing school despite the responsibility of looking after my brothers and sister. And when I had the opportunity, I moved into the city so I could go to the high school there. My brothers and sisters were well looked after, but I wasn't going to deny myself a life. I continued my schooling at the normal school over my father's objections. When I met Charlie, I was glad to go, but first I had to educate him."

Caroline didn't know what that meant, but thought she'd find out soon enough. Cathy's natural curiosity led her to ask questions about Caroline's family, but other than mentioning she was the second eldest daughter in a family from Portland, she managed to ward off any further questions. Caroline felt like a cheat, but she was afraid of saying anything, fearing further scandal over her elopement. In less than two weeks her sister would be married and she dreaded reading the announcement, as she was sure it would be posted in the local city paper. She didn't underestimate her uncle's importance. Instead, she talked about herself and Bob's family.

As the afternoon slowed down and shifted to the cool of the approaching evening, they gathered up their things. Cathy Bladstad intrigued her — *shouldn't she be getting supper ready?* — but it wasn't just the ideas coming out of her mouth. It was the feeling of complete trust and comfort with someone female. Though they had just met, she sensed the surge of understanding that comes when true friends meet for first time. As Cathy left, Caroline said, "Thank you for the lovely visit. I look forward to tomorrow."

"Me too." Cathy said as she accepted Caroline's help onto the horse. "Til tomorrow then. I can hardly wait."

Back at the hotel, Caroline ate alone again but buoyed by her day's adventures she felt bright and cheerful. Mrs. Wilson, the hotel's proprietress, took note and came over with her coffee pot and refilled Caroline's cup.

"Did you have a good day? I hope so. It's just like the men to go off and just think that because the honeymoon's over, everything was all right." She picked up Caroline's empty plate. How are your housecleaning efforts?"

"Oh, I got quite a lot done today. Almost suitable to move in." Caroline wiped the edge of her mouth delicately with her napkin. She may not tell people who she was, but she hadn't forgotten her manners. She put aside her napkin and looked up at the pictures on the wall near the stone fireplace. In one, to Caroline's amusement, Cathy Bladstad stood beside a young man in wool pants, high boots and suspenders. He was holding a tall alpenstock, the long walking staff favored by the mountaineering clubs. Cathy carried one too and was decked out in bloomers, waist and straw hat. She was at once confident and fiercely beautiful against the steep white line of the glacier.

"Those are the Bladstad's," Mrs. Wilson said. "They were a

part of a climb in 1900. It caused a stir. She was one of the first women from our area to reach the summit."

"Do you know Mrs. Bladstad quite well?" Caroline asked, proud of her new friend.

Mrs. Wilson sniffed. "Everyone knows Mrs. Bladstad quite well."

Caroline sensed it was better not to say more and changed the subject.

Cathy and Caroline met at the house the following day. Caroline came again on horseback, bringing in tow a wagon load of furniture that had just arrived by train. She had hired two men to help unload and while Caroline directed the placement of the dining table and bedroom set, Cathy unwrapped plates and cups in the kitchen. When everything was in place and the men paid, she was joined at the kitchen table by Caroline who flopped down in the only other chair and groaned.

"I never thought I'd get done."

"I've never seen such nice pieces of furniture."

"A wedding gift from my father-in-law. Do you think they look all right where they are?"

"Oh, yes. Makes the house come alive. Old Finster would be pleased. I remember when the house was built. It was outrageous. He used mill siding from the start and it was his pride and joy, but he came into money so fast. In two years' time it was gone."

"What happened to him?"

"Well, first, Finster disappeared. Some folks think he committed suicide, but there's another camp that thinks he made another strike and was murdered for it. Funny thing. All those debts were taken care of a few months after his disappearance and the family eventually was able to leave and go back to Ireland. Mysteriously, the monies were deposited before he disappeared, but no one notified his wife until he'd been gone a while."

"Didn't someone want the house?"

"No. A city attorney finally put it up for rent about the time

Jack Vernell started looking for a place for you."

Caroline shook her head. "You all seem to know a great deal about everyone's affairs."

"You're living in Frazier. Gossip has been around before clay tablets."

Caroline laughed. Cathy stretched back in her chair and cradling her stomach, sighed. "It's often the source of much amusement. Anything else I can do?"

"Else? You've done more than enough. I can't thank you enough. I haven't felt more welcomed."

Cathy seemed to like that, but when Caroline wasn't looking, gazed at the younger woman with large, sorrowful eyes.

Chapter 23

Alford got back the next afternoon. As Vernell's party passed the hotel, he got permission to leave. As soon as he tied his horse up, he sprang into the front room looking for Caroline. Suppressing a smile, Mrs. Wilson was only too happy to tell him that his wife was upstairs. He tipped his hat and bounded up the creaky stairs two steps at a time. He came down a few minutes later with Caroline on his arm and ordered an early supper in the little dining room.

"She's watching us," Caroline said leaning in.

"And how." As they ate, Alford held her hand from time to time, his booted feet restless behind the curtain of the tablecloth. "As soon as we're done, let's get our bedrolls and get out of here."

It was a fair, warm evening when they left. He helped Caroline up into a buggy borrowed from Fuller and slapped the horse into a fast trot. Once safe into the dark trees crowding the narrow dirt road going south, he stopped the horse under the high roof of Douglas firs and took Caroline into his arms.

"Now without the entire town listening — " He gave her a long kiss, liking the way her breasts and slim figure felt against him. He squeezed her tight. "God, I missed you."

They decided to get out of the buggy and walk. Buoyed by her loving response, the stories of what he'd seen burst out, his hands moving with excitement about the views he'd seen and stories of his boss and co-worker as he led the horse along. Caroline wrapped a hand around his free arm and sparkled with her own story of meeting Cathy Bladstad and how she came to help. By the time they reached the house, they had regained much of what they had and then lost after the violence after their elopement: the peace of the easy summer walks together, the solid times of talking and visiting with one another at the old way station. Those feelings returned, with a love as deep as Alford's favorite fishing pools.

It was different going into the darkened house this time. The lights had been connected and when he turned on the hall light, Alford could already see the changes. He put down their bedrolls and knapsack at the bedroom door and looked into the room. The furniture was all there, with an old kerosene lantern by the bed.

"I didn't have the heart to put it away," Caroline apologized. "I love its light. It's not so harsh as electric lights."

Alford smiled. It was like her to say something like that. She led him by the hand through the rest of the house and he saw all the hard work she'd done. "How did you manage to place the furniture?"

"I hired some men. It was no great expense."

Alford was relieved. They had to be careful about money, but it had to be done.

He set a fire in the stove for her and she made some tea. They sat outside on the back kitchen stairs and watched a full moon come over the mountains. It was so bright that it lit up the water rushing and gurgling over stones in the middle of the river. In the woods next to them, an owl settled into a tree and began its eerie night vigil, its call loud in the dark. Alford moved down in front of her and while she began to rub his aching shoulders, he talked more about the mountains.

"I've got a couple of days off. Why don't we finish cleaning the house and make it as presentable as possible to live in, then just get out of here?" He nodded toward the mountains. "I want to get you up there. Fuller told me of large waterfall not far from town we can check out, or we could take to one of the high meadows and camp for a day or two."

"Can we see one of the glaciers?"

"Maybe. I was told it's not wise to cross them when it's been so hot, but we could certainly go up to one. I believe that it'd be safe. I'll find what clothes I can for you. You should have a good pair of boots. I — "

Caroline leaned around and covered his mouth with a kiss. He instantly put his cup down and he kissed her fervently and deep. Then, without warning, he pulled her down to his lap. She came with a sudden swoop and squealed as she nearly slid out of his reach.

"Not the cherry tree again," she scolded as she looked up at him. "That's an old trick."

"But a pretty good trick." He pulled her skirt up above her knees and put a hand on her thigh. He picked at the top of the black stocking where it met her cotton drawers, picking and smoothing over and over.

"Caroline," he whispered. "I thought about you all week." Then with a strength that made her gasp, he rolled her against him, stood up and carried her inside.

Caroline decided Mrs. Emma Drake, M.D., author of *What Every Young Wife Ought to Know,* ought not to write books for young wives. What was marriage without passion? What was wrong about marital love on a baser plane? And how could she have been afraid? By lantern light, Bob had made love to her and for the first time, she responded with the deepest feelings. They were lovers in the truest sense and for the rest of the night kept each other awake. The sun was already pushing through the cedar boughs outside their room's curtained window when they finally dozed off.

Later, they rose and took turns bathing at the washstand. Alford was a terrible tease watching her, but she didn't mind.

She felt unusually naughty. She put on a thin wrapper she had made for their wedding night and went into the kitchen to make coffee. He shaved and washed his hair with spring water she pumped at the sink and then ate the simple breakfast she prepared for him. Once the dishes were cleaned and the kitchen straightened up, Bob said it was time to stop and close up shop. "We'll go to town to get supplies, then head into the hills. Where's our hiking gear stashed?"

As soon as they secured canvas for a makeshift shelter and supplies for several days, they dressed in their tramping clothes and headed into the mountains.

It took an hour to reach the trailhead, but they soon followed the trail cut out by the hiking club. It was wide enough for both of them to pass comfortably, its bed cut and pulled out from a bank that lined one side. Salmonberry, vine maples and spindly alder rose above them. When Caroline stopped to adjust the hard wooden frame that supported her rucksack, a little bird flitted out of the bushes in front of her.

"Oh, the dear thing. Was that a winter wren?"

"I think so." Alford helped her adjust the straps, then kissed her. He was so close against her that his felt hat knocked back against the bedroll and canvas tent on his back.

"You want something, Mr. Alford?"

"You betcha." He tucked her hand under his arm. "But not here."

Caroline giggled. He had been so randy over the past day. She felt unexpectedly flushed and alive. *Was this what wedding bliss was all about?* The man beside her, *her husband,* pulsed with energy, humor and good looks and a nature she knew she could trust anywhere.

"If only you let me lead. After all, I'm the experienced one here."

Alford bowed. "Lead on, Mrs. Alford." He gave her a pat on her backside as she went ahead, causing her to stab the alpenstock into the damp ground.

"Mr. Alford."

The trail took them across several creeks lined with ripe

snowberries and alder and hemlock trees dappled by the September sun. Once they stopped to drink water from their canteens and eat the smoked salmon jerky Bob purchased at the general store. Then they moved on, climbing higher. Now the trail became steep and narrow, the roots of trees making risers as they snaked across the pebbly soil.

When Caroline's skirt got caught beneath her boot she faltered for just a moment and grabbed onto the fir sapling next to her.

"Steady," Alford said behind her.

"Oh, pshaw." Caroline pulled herself up to the next plateau where the trail flattened out. When Alford joined her, he took out a sketch showing a trail and oval lake.

"How you doing, sweetheart?"

Caroline wiped her forehead with a sleeve and saw damp circles under her arms. "Fine. It climbs fast doesn't it?"

Alford looked up. "Sure does. Shall we rest for a spell or keep tramping?"

Caroline shook her head. "Only for a bit. I was taught not to tarry too long as not to cool down."

"Well, it's not far to the lake according to this map Vernell sketched for me. Saw it from way on top the other day. Thought we'd camp there for the night. He's been putting in trout there for the past year. Might get some for dinner."

"Always the fisherman," Caroline chuckled.

"Um-hm." He brushed a hand across her breast, lingering at the top of her corded corset under her canvas shirt. She turned away and smiled when he kissed her there.

"I let you lead," Alford muffled into the cloth.

Caroline lifted up his head and laughed. "You did indeed, Mr. Alford."

They set up camp in a place called Darcy Meadows where an alpine lake settled in under a backdrop of craggy mountains. In its center was an island approachable only by a sliver of a pathway made of large stepping stones. A few trees stood watch over it, just enough to hang a rope and canvas between them. Beyond it, a large trout leaped into the air.

"Ha! I told you." Alford swung Caroline around.

"I'll get out the pan."

Alford never caught it, but he got enough smaller ones for a decent meal with potatoes and onions thrown in the butter Caroline brought in her rucksack. Later, after they washed out their pan and tinware in the lake, they snuggled under their half-faced camp shelter, watching the sun go down behind the trees and crags until the stars came out. When he made love to her by the light of their camp fire, a shooting star streaked across the purple night sky, followed by a meteor shower. The stars seemed so close that there was no way to count them.

Perched up on their open knoll the second night, the stars seemed to be especially dense around them, their twinkling points like red and yellow gems. They became a part of Caroline's dreams like the field of stars that blanketed them when they made love together. Sophie had talked of her planned honeymoon to the Oregon coast at some mansion, but Caroline wouldn't change their mansion of stars for anything.

Chapter 24

Rain caught up with Alford and Caroline as they came down from the mountains. Unable to get into Frazier without freezing, they stopped at Vernell's place where his wife fixed up a room in the ranger station. The place started out as a homestead in the area before the claim became part of the national forest. It was about a mile and half from the creek. While Caroline changed into some dry clothes Mrs. Vernell offered, Alford warmed himself at the fire, satisfied with a tin cup of hot coffee with a shot of whiskey in it and a change of shirt.

"Pleasant time?"

Alford grinned. "Yup. Mrs. Alford has sand. Also got some trout out of that lake of yours."

"Well, it's a good time of year, for sure. Colors starting some show. I'm glad you had some time with your bride. But now — " He wiped his moustache with a bandana and put it away in a back pocket. "— the corral needs to be rebuilt up at Cedar Bottom. You and Fuller go tomorrow. Pete Hansen's a hire-on."

"All right. I'll be there." Alford toyed with his cup. Vernell made him feel right at home but he was his boss. Alford needed to make a good impression.

"In the meantime, if Mrs. Alford needs assistance, my wife, Mary, can give your bride a hand." Vernell went over to a writing desk set. "There was some mail for you and Mrs. Alford." He handed over two letters. "You had a visitor too."

"Visitor?"

"A man named Howell came by looking for you. He wanted you to know he's relocated up south of here at one of the logging camps."

"Really?" Alford thought Billy would stay with their old boss McKinley. He was a good foreman and the company decent. "When?"

"Yesterday. He said he'd get in touch with you again in the next few days. One other thing," Vernell said, " — and I want you to come clean on this — you know a man named J. J. Jenkins?"

Alford shook his head, then stopped. *Not Symington's lackey?* "Might."

"One of my friends down near Brandon — that's about ten miles west of here if you take the wagon road — said this man came up here to cruise some land for a possible logging camp. He asked about you and your wife. He was particularly interested in your wife."

Alford swallowed, stung by his memory of Jenkins and his humiliation at the inn. It had been over five weeks since the incident, but suddenly he felt threatened again. He dug his nails into his fists. He was blind to think there wouldn't be further trouble, even though he and Caroline had left discreetly without any embarrassment touching the Symington family publicly. *It was all hushed up.*

"Is there something I need to know?"

Alford chose his words carefully. "When I wrote you about this job, I was always square with my plans and intentions. Only I didn't count on falling in love and getting married. It was the furthest thing from my mind. My wife's a good young lady from a respectable family in Portland, but I was also the furthest from *their* minds. There was some opposition."

"I'll have no scandal."

"There won't be. We're properly married." Alford worked his jaw, his face growing dark. "I know Jenkins. He's a thug and a bully. Him showing up here's disturbing. He likes to stir up trouble in the camps where honest men work."

"Do you know who pays him?"

Alford shot Vernell a flinty glance. "Occasionally, Harold Symington. Caroline's his niece."

Vernell downed a straight shot of whiskey. He placed his tin cup on the mantle of the fireplace and stroked his moustache thoughtfully. Alford stared at the fire. *Jenkins. How long could he keep the news from Caroline?*

"What you do want me to do?" Vernell asked.

"Take my word on it. No scandal. I plan to make a good go of it and — I love her deeply."

"Hmmp. What'll you do about Symington? He could be cruising for himself. Which means he'll be up in this area eventually."

"Do my job. Make my reputation here for myself. I care more about the local folk's opinion than all of Harold Symington's stack of gold or perceived importance."

"Well, on some levels, he *is* important. Frankly, other things count up here." Vernell put a new log on the fire, then straightened up. "You're a good man, Alford. I like you. You're mature for your age. You're a quick learner and you don't mind the load. Get that fence corral fixed and we'll see about hitting some holes around here. I want to see some of those flies you've been talking about. Steelhead flies. I never —"

The women came back into the room.

"Dry now?" Alford asked.

"Much better." Caroline tugged at the borrowed sweater. She moved stiffly to the wood bench by the fire.

The ranger cleared his throat. "Mary, may I speak with you alone?" He took his tin cup and following his wife out, closed the main room door.

After they left, Alford came over and rubbed Caroline's shoulders. "Tired?"

"Oh, that. I'm fine. I had a wonderful time. We must tramp again soon."

Alford gave her a peck on her cheek, then handed a letter with "Mrs. Bob Alford" on it.

"Why, it's from Emily. I've been so hoping for news." All the weariness in her face disappeared like sunshine showing up in a shady glen as she tore the envelope open.

"Nice." That was about all the enthusiasm Alford could show, without betraying worry over whatever contents the letter might contain. He opened up his own letter from home.

Caroline read hungrily. When she was done, she patted the bench. "Come and read for yourself."

"You sure?"

"Of course, I'm sure. We'll have no secrets between us. Besides, Emily gives a favorable account of you." Her voice was light, a playful tease.

So Bob read.

My Dear Caroline,

I hope this letter finds you well and basking in the glow of marital bliss. So much has happened since I saw you last. Although, nothing has been published abroad about it, I just recently learned of your difficulties last month and I pray that all is well, as it should be. I am very fond of Bob Alford and think he has the qualities my father wishes all young men should have. That he has clean habits (my father would approve!), we both know is true, but I equally like his sense of humor, his industry and his love of the outdoors.

Alford harrumphed, then read on:

I have been re-invited to your sister's wedding, although I had no idea I had been invited in the first place to such a grand affair, but your cousin David, who came to call on me not long ago, says that he objected and so the secret invitation stands. I have not seen your sister Sophie in several weeks, in fact, have not returned to Kla-how-ya *since you went away, but the news about the coming nuptials of Sophie and James Ford are widely followed. There was even a picture in the* Seattle Times.

The wedding will be quite costly, but David says it is your uncle's

148

doing, so eager is he to bring the Fords into the family fold. My father thinks that money would better serve the poor, but I think he worries about my own future, struggling daily with heavenly principles and the reality of an unmarried woman.

Alford glanced quickly over the next pages, his thoughts a jumble of emotions. Anything about Ford rankled him, but in an odd way, he felt sorry for both women. Miss Emily for her material poverty; Caroline's sister for her poverty of empathy and spirit.

Emily's letter showed a talent for story, one page recounting the girls' adventures this past summer, others full of news about the city. And family.

"I'm sorry to write of this," Emily wrote, "when it must pain you so. Your mother is well but as to what she has to say about your leaving, David is not forthcoming."

Emily also mentioned her father had come back to Seattle for business. According to David, he wasn't so angry any more with him for helping her, but he wouldn't speak of it any more. There was news of her brother who was doing much better:

The leg is mending nicely and he should be out of the cast by Halloween. Be brave, dear friend. Time will heal all things.

Alford closed the letter up. "She is a good friend, isn't she?"

"The best. And you? What does your letter say?"

Alford grinned as he handed it over to her. "It's short and sweet. My family is coming next week to help on the house. The offer we made to buy it has been accepted." "

Caroline gasped, putting her hands in prayerful thanks to her lips. "Oh, darling. That is wonderful. Wonderful." She leaped up and came into his arms. He rocked her for a moment, then said,

"We're going to have a houseful, but they're coming to do some repairs and build us a stable." He kissed her lightly on her lips. Jenkins was banished from his mind.

The Alfords arrived by train that Friday evening. They filled nearly two wagons for the drive to the house. Alford forgot to explain to Caroline what family meant. It not only included his father (whose carpentry skills were welcomed) and his mother, but his brothers, Ake and Olav, a cousin and their families. Everyone came to help, but it was a house raising of a different sort. They brought food and shelter as well, camping out around the grounds. Having two days off for the weekend, Alford organized the troops into various groups, giving Ake the task of repairing the front porch, Olav a new stable of cedar posts and boards to raise. He assigned his father and cousin to finish work upstairs. Offspring old enough to help, did so, the younger children played in the prairie and trees next to the house and stayed out of the way.

The women helped Caroline lay shelf paper in the kitchen and clean out the root cellar, then prepare the dinner for the hungry horde. They took a moment to give her housewarming presents over cups of coffee and *kake,* chattering in English with a smattering of Norwegian. Caroline was struck again by her in-laws' generosity and unconditional acceptance.

She told about her trip into the mountains, but by their comments, the women only partially understood why *she'd* want to do something like that. Just when she felt this was something they would never accept, Mother Alford put down her coffee cup and looked straight at one of the women.

"Ingabor, why so hard? What think I do when I girl? In the old country, I go every summer to the mountains and live with our cows and goats making butter and cheese for the long winter. This I loved and you know why? I was free. No Papa. No Mama. And the air. The beautiful mountains." The older woman smiled at Caroline.

Caroline's heart felt full. She wished her mother here, but would she want to be?

Boards and sawhorses were set outside on the lawn and the food laid out. When a bell rang, all came and stood for grace, then spread out along the river shore to eat. Above the stir of the river's run voices in English, Norwegian, and Swedish could be heard, telling stories of the day.

Alford sat with Caroline. He was very expansive about the

stable. After four hours, five eight inch thick cedar posts had been cut down, hauled and spudded. They would have them sized and put in place sometime in the afternoon, the beams and support pieces ready mid-day tomorrow. He invited her to come and look after the meal was over. Not feeling well, Caroline took little bites of her food, but his boyish enthusiasm was catching and she followed him to the stable when she was done.

The men made progress upstairs as well, some of the space framed off into four rooms with lumber purchased long ago by Finster and never used. Caroline followed Alford upstairs to see the direction the construction was going. A room was planned for them, complete with closets for their clothing and a window that looked out to the river in the back.

"What'd you think?" Alford asked.

"I'm overwhelmed." She took his hand. "Can they really finish?"

"The walls will be up by this evening. We can finish the painting ourselves or if you wish, paper it. It's yours to decide." He gave her hand a squeeze and said he had to get back. Releasing her slowly, he started down ahead of her. When she began to descend, a dizzy spell came upon her. She grabbed the railing as she stumbled over her skirt and caught herself. Alford called back up to see if she was all right, but she waved him on. Only when he went away, did she sit down, disturbed by her clumsiness.

The afternoon project continued as before, but around one-thirty Jack Vernell, George Fuller and another man pulled up to offer a hand. With them were Cathy Bladstad and Mary Vernell.

"This is Charlie Bladstad," Vernell said to Alford. "He's been wondering what all the hammering was all about at the old Finster place. I told him it's yours now."

Alford shook Charlie's strong, rough hand. He was a dark blonde and lean man in his late twenties. His smile indicated that he didn't take himself seriously.

"My wife, Cathy," Charlie said proudly.

"And mine," Alford said, stepping back. "Caroline. It seems they are both ahead of us in the social department."

"Well, it's about time the two of you showed off their other half," Cathy said. "My pleasure, Mr. Alford. Caroline has been all aglow about you." Cathy shook his hand, then turned to Caroline. "Where's the senior Mrs. Alford?"

"In the kitchen working on tonight's dinner."

"Love to meet her." She winked at Charlie and nodded to Alford.

The kitchen was busy again as the Alford women worked on the next meal. A ham was in the oven and something brewed on the stove. The smell of fresh baked bread mingled with cinnamon and anise. Caroline quickly introduced her in-laws around. There was clucking over Cathy's expanding girth and good wishes for her future confinement.

"I heard you went hiking," Cathy said as she eased down into the chair.

Caroline brightened. "It was wonderful." She went on to talk about the lake, the climb higher up above it. The clarity of the nights under the stars.

"You should make the climb on the mountain itself. Isn't Mount Kulshan wonderful up close?" Cathy said.

"Oh, yes. Powerful. Those glaciers... Someday. I need to hike more. I feel quite tired."

"A good tired. How I envy you for going. I have missed most of the summer." Cathy sighed. "Since I can't go into the mountains, I'll have to seek loftier heights elsewhere. I'm leaving for the women's convention in Seattle on Monday."

Dead silence fell. All activity ceased. Cathy ignored it. "I shall be gone two days, then come home and resume *my responsibilities*." She put emphasis on the last two words, but her voice a mocking lilt to it.

"You won't exhaust yourself?"

Cathy rubbed her stomach. "My daughter has much to learn."

Caroline laughed. "I wish I had such confidence."

"You will."

The women served dinner at six with an invitation for the new helpers to stay. Then after the tables were cleared and the dishes washed, Olav took out a fiddle and began to play. At the front of the house, young and old gathered to dance. Clapping their hands in approval, the family called Caroline and Alford out to start it. This was their housewarming and celebration of their new life together.

"I guess we have to perform," he whispered in her ear. "If I could only remember what to do." Caroline took his hand. "If you stick to your half, I'll take care of the other." The joke, of course, was that he was a very good dancer. She felt light as a feather about to swirl up into the air so happy she was. She was all grin when he led her out and began moving smoothly across the yard. It reminded her of their first dance together and then the next and the next, because by then both had been so taken by each other, but not yet comprehending the impact. She caught the smiles of his parents and brothers, of Ranger Vernell and the others. That they accepted her filled her with joy. After a time, the others joined in and they danced until the sun went down.

Then, as a group they began to clap. Someone banged a pan.

"What's happening, Bob?" Caroline asked.

"It's an old way. While we were dancing, some of the men took our bed upstairs. Now we're to retire there." He squeezed her hand and leaning in, whispered, "I love you."

"Will they come too?"

He laughed. "Good heavens, no. But they'll make a ruckus. As soon as we are alone, we can just fall into bed." He brushed a curl off her forehead. "And sleep, if you don't mind. I'm drained."

The "ruckus" went until midnight and neither could sleep, snuggling and giggling in each other's arms to last bang on a pot. At one point, Alford said they had to get up and go out to the little window in front of the house.

"In my nightgown?"

"They just want to wish us well."

So holding hands, they went to the window and opened it, Bob in his nightshirt, Caroline with a hastily thrown shawl over her shoulders. The family greeted them with a song in Norwegian, followed by applause. Alford gave Caroline a peck on her lip, then said "goodnight."

Caroline woke the next day dizzy and sick when she sat up.

"You look unwell, Caroline." Alford lifted up her chin. "Did you catch a chill coming down the mountain? Or all the ruckus last night? "

"No," she said. "I'm all right."

"Then good morning." He kissed her, cupping a breast in his hand. She winced when the cloth brushed against her nipple.

"Caroline... Perhaps my mother..." Alford's face deepened with concern.

"No," she said seizing his hand. "No, please." She looked at him with growing uneasiness as she began to ferret out the truth. "I'm all right. Just don't want anyone to know. "

"Know what?"

"That I'm going to have a baby. At least, I think I am." As soon as the words were out, she felt it must be true, though she didn't know why. Her mother had never spoken of it. Even her progressive Oregon hiking friends didn't speak of the signs of pregnancy. An image of Cathy Bladstad on her horse the first time she met her flashed before her. *Cathy surely knows.*

Alford's eyes searched her face as he took her hand and held it. He looked as stunned as she felt.

"I'll get dressed now." She stood up and standing away from him, slipped off her shift. She knew he was studying her. She was as slim as ever, but she noticed now that her breasts hung heavier and dark. She put on drawers and an under-blouse, then searched for her corset. She sniffed, her face away from him.

"Caroline?"

"Yes?" She answered thickly. Tears started to roll down. He

154

got off the bed and took her into his arms.

"We'll be okay, sweetheart. We'll get by. A little one's fine. But first, let's get a doctor's opinion."

But I didn't volunteer, she thought. Maybe Mrs. Drake, M.D. was right. Passion and marriage don't mix.

Chapter 25

Two days after Alford's family left, he took Caroline down to Twin Forks on the train. It had been an incredible weekend, but Alford sensed Caroline's exhaustion and worried that it had been too much for her. All he wanted now was the best care for her. *A baby!* If it were true, the baby might be coming earlier than they intended, but the thought made him feel virile and strong.

While Dr. Gates examined her, he went for a walk along the muddy street of the settlement even smaller than Frazier. Barely cut out of the trees six years earlier, it boasted itself as the gateway to the new farmlands in the surrounding countryside, even though half of it was still full of stumps and forests. At the only saloon, he stopped for a moment and considered going in, then turned around and started for the opposite end of the five building town. He only got a few feet when someone yelled at him.

"Hey, Alford! Where you think you're going?"

"Billy Howell. What the hell you doing up here? My boss said you were in Frazier looking for me."

"My health and the pursuit of happiness. What brings *you* here?"

"Caroline and I are down for the day." He grinned at his old friend. Billy had worn his good suit jacket over his working pants and had combed his hair down sharply. It always gave him mixed results.

"You want a drink?" Billy asked.

Alford shrugged. "I could stand for a beer."

Inside the saloon, they found seats by the cafe-curtained window. Looking around, Alford was amazed to see a magnificent bar and counter against the far wall. A handsome piece of wood and glass, a large collection of hunting trophies mounted on the wall further complimented it. In one corner, stood a full blown specimen of a bull elk. In the other, a black bear attempting, it seemed, to glower over the room and remind customers they had better pay.

"Holy Cow," Alford said. "Where'd that come from?"

"Settler's homestead. Tried to run off with a pig. Ever see a bear run with a pig? They stand up and hug them, then amble off like this." Billy gave a rolling interpretation at his seat, hugging his imaginary pig in front of him. "This bear run off with the farmwife's favorite sow. She got so mad, she went out and hit the bear with the butt of her shotgun."

"And?"

"It dropped the pig and backed off."

Alford chuckled. They talked in general for a while, then taking a sip of his Olympia beer, he changed the subject. "What sort of health problems were you having exactly?"

Billy pulled his mug toward him. "After you left, I got some mysterious notes suggesting I leave. I can stand my own ground, but there was some other stuff I didn't like, so I decided to come up here and look around."

"Why would anyone threaten you?"

Billy gave him a twisted smile. "Now you were in no shape to remember, but while you were ramblin' out of your head and spitting up blood at your mother's, I got wind of something and asked around. That led me to Jenkins and more importantly, Piles."

"Who's Piles?"

"The sheriff in the Danville district. He was a part of that crowd that jumped you. He not only stood by and watched you get beat to a pulp, but threw you on the wagon and sent you north." Billy surveyed Alford's face. "Looks like you healed fast." He swallowed hard, gripping his mug firmly, as he collected his thoughts.

"Heard Symington paid him and a few others to make it all end quiet-like, only they didn't reckon any push back from your bride. They just thought cuz she was a Symington, she'd just give you up. 'Cuz I stuck my nose out, Piles remembered me. The hints started coming."

Alford slumped back in his chair. He became so quiet Billy finally prodded him with his boot.

"Hey, don't get thoughtful on me. Ain't nobody's fault but my own. What I don't like is Symington putting his screws on anyone he pleases. There's been more agitation in the camps, but when someone like a good boss like McKinley tries to be fair to his men, the big companies squeeze."

Alford's head shot up. "McKinley still having trouble?"

"Oh, the boys came to an agreement, but the company's having trouble with contracts. Railroad all of a sudden wasn't going to deliver the logs."

"Symington, that bastard." Alford leaned over the table and clenched his fists on its battered surface.

"You all right?"

Alford downed his beer in one long pull. "Don't pay me any mind, Billy. Got a lot on my mind."

"Wouldn't be the young lady out there, would it now?"

Alford looked out the window. Caroline stood on the rough planked sidewalk, a stunning vision in her traveling suit and wide brim hat, but he saw no sign of distress.

"Uh, yes. My wife, Caroline." Alford stood up and put a coin on the table. "Do you mind? I'd like you to meet her. Can't remember if you ever did."

"Just at a distance at the dance."

So long ago. "Give us ten minutes."

"Almost seven weeks? That for sure?" Alford took the news calmly. Taking Caroline's arm, he began walking her down to the narrow two story hotel. Outside, the proprietor was sweeping, so he stopped and turned away.

Caroline smiled faintly. "Uh-huh. The baby's due in May."

He squeezed her arm. "Wow. That's some news, Mrs. Alford. A little one. That just makes me proud somehow. Did the doctor say you're okay? You want to write something to your folks?"

"Doctor Gates says I'm fit as a horse. She patted Alford's arm. "I'll wait writing until after Sophie's wedding. Maybe Emily can deliver the note or David."

"David? Why him?" Alford felt an odd sensation worm its way through him.

"Because he's the one member of my family who does care about me."

They returned to Frazier by boxcar late that evening after an enjoyable meal at the hotel with Billy. Alford loved Caroline even more in the way she warmly greeted his friend.

Alford put his coat down on the hard, dusty floor. Caroline sat between his legs, nestled in his arms. As he leaned against the wall, they were silent for a while as the train moved out into the woods.

"You'll love me when I'm fat as a butterball?" asked Caroline in the dark.

"Always." He rubbed her stomach, trying to imagine. All he could feel was her slenderness. "I suppose we should think of names. If it's a boy, I'd like to name him for my brother Stein. Maybe someone else. Something — Stein."

"All right," Caroline said "If it's a girl, I'd like to have a daughter named Katherine or Kate. It's such a strong name."

"Kate Alford sounds good together. To let young men know where she stood."

"No junior for the boy?"

Alford winced. "I don't think Bob Jr. carries the same story as my naming. We'll just let that one lie."

Caroline laughed and settled deeper against him, becoming

quiet as the train began to pick up speed. He squeezed her hard, kissing her on her ear. "I love you, Caroline."

"I know."

Chapter 26

Vernell got on Alford as soon as they were back, sending him around the district with various projects as the days hardened into fall. The nights were crisper now as the leaves of the maples and alders began to turn into russets and golds. The mornings broke foggy with smoky clouds settling on the lower hills like gossamer.

These days he loved the most, when the mountains lost their shape and blended into the hills of color down below. Birdcalls sharpened; the water in the river and streams crisped up and ran clear as they carried their little boats of golden leaves westward. Sometimes during the early morning hours, when mist cloaked the meadows, the shrill sound of elk bugling jabbed the air as they finished their rut.

Equally frenzied, came the sound of gunfire as the search for elk and deer began. Although it was national forest land, hunting was unlimited. It wasn't uncommon to see many animals bagged and trussed up for loading on the evening train for the city. Alford wondered how long it could last, but held his tongue when he was sent to mend some of the simple shelters set up for hunters in the area.

One day, Vernell joined him on one of his assignments

down near the valley and showed Alford one of his favorite places to fish. Without ceremony the ranger undid a pole from his saddle and set to fixing it up. For the next hour, they took turns at it, Vernell pressing Alford for his philosophy on fishing and other important things. They managed to land a few trout, but when Alford got a good strike from a steelhead hen on an early fall run, Vernell watched in awe as the younger man maneuvered the fish to shore.

The ranger whistled. "That's some beauty. Must be some twelve pounds."

Alford sliced open the steelhead's belly and took out its skeins of eggs, promising to share them when he had them cured. The rest of the fish, they would split.

"Damn, Alford," Vernell said. "You sure know your stuff and then some. Tomorrow, I'm going to take you down to the new hatchery."

Alford was in and out the rest of September and early October, sometimes leaving for days at a time. Caroline stayed behind. She continued to be tired and feel nauseated in the mornings, but generally by noon had enough energy to take on household activities that included sewing curtains for the rooms and planning a layette for the baby. Having a baby was no longer a foreign idea but it sometimes seemed unreal and far off.

Cathy Bladstad often came to help. They were on a solid first name basis now and as their friendship grew, they felt more confident about intimate things and Cathy came to know Caroline's fears. Though Caroline now confessed an excitement about the new life in her, she didn't want to have a child this way again. She wanted to choose the time. In talking with Cathy, she discovered that it was against the law for some to possess information about such things, even if she was married. The subject made Cathy alternately angry or so still in her thoughts that Caroline grew concerned.

"Did you want your new baby?" Caroline asked timidly one day as they sat in the living room winding yarn. Outside in the yard the little Bladstad boys played in the dirt, building forts and roads for their lead soldiers, much to Caroline's amusement.

"Wholeheartedly," Cathy said as she finished up her second ball of yarn and put it into a large cedar basket next to them. "I volunteered for it. I've always wanted a daughter." She paused for a moment over her next skein. "I don't believe my life can't have passion, Carrie. My Charlie's a randy man and I'm his match. There isn't any mountain I wouldn't climb or trail I wouldn't go on with him. So it is with love, too." Cathy sighed. "But I won't have a child I don't want. This may seem to be a paradox to some, but they wouldn't think to break the law." She spoke candidly, without a thread of wickedness. Caroline wondered if some might think Cathy possessed wickedness. "There are ways not to have a baby without putting your husband in the root cellar for a year."

"Did they talk of this at the women's convention in Seattle?" Caroline wondered.

"A few did, but too many others feel the political need for the vote and the freedom it'll bring." Cathy lumbered up and went to the screen door. "Sometimes, I think our freedom should begin in the bedroom. I've got to go to your facility. Be back soon." She got to the porch stairs then stopped suddenly and clutched her side. Caroline jumped up and went out to her.

"Are you all right?" Caroline's heart began to pound. *Is this what's it like? Does it hurt?*

"Just a twinge. I get them now and then. It'll pass." She smiled at Caroline looking at her wide-eyed. "It's all right, little sister. It's just life practicing for the real thing." She eased down the stairs and after waving to her boys, waddled off to the outhouse.

Around the tenth of October, Alford worked a few days in Frazier. In the evenings, he took the time to put on a few touches in the little room they had set aside upstairs for a nursery. The room off the kitchen became his place for fishing tackle and supplies for making flies. He'd shown some to Bergstrom at the general store who exclaimed over the flies:

163

"I'll give six dollars if you make a dozen at fifty cents apiece. Same price in *Sears, Roebuck and Co.'s Catalog*, but yours are better than their best."

With his first Forest Service paycheck, Alford bought an electric lamp for his work table and built some shelves for storage. Caroline gave him a watercolor of a fish for the wall.

"Some fish," he said with his arms around her. "It looks like a bass with a spawning salmon's hooked nose."

"It's the thought that counts."

"The artist obviously wasn't thinking. Still, it's the first piece of artwork anyone's ever given me, so we'll keep it there." He gave her a hug, then rested his cheek against hers. A hand strayed to one of her swollen breasts and brushed her lightly. She hadn't felt well, so it had been weeks since they made love. Now as they stood in the dying yellow light of the October evening, she sensed his tension. She laid a hand on his. Gently they rocked to some secret tune they could only hear, then stopped. He nuzzled her softly, then said under his breath,

"Will you come upstairs, Caroline and lie with me? Just take off your shift and lie with me. It's all I'll ask of you."

Caroline thought of what Cathy had said in their earlier conversation and after pausing, said yes.

Chapter 27

On October 16, six weeks after they arrived in Frazier, Alford left for what Vernell said would be a four day ride around the back country before the first snows came.

As he stood in the lobby of the hotel dressed in his rain slicker and ranger's hat, Alford took Caroline's hand. "Fuller told me it's always unpredictable in October as the rains down below get more frequent, but weather permitting, I'll get back as soon as we're done."

"I'll be fine," she said. Caroline was so proud of him. He looked like someone who knew how to take on anything Mother Nature threw at him. "Besides, I'll be busy enough today and tomorrow with some of the things my friends have planned. They'll take care of me — and ours." Caroline flushed. The whole town had known for several weeks now about the pregnancy and followed her progress with both interest and helpful concern.

"Take care then." He gave her a peck on the cheek despite the amused audience just inside the dining room entrance. "Love you."

Caroline joined her new friends Ellie Turner and Berta Olsen inside at one of the tables decorated for Halloween with black cats cut out of paper and stuck to little pumpkins with toothpicks.

"So glad you could come," Berta said. "Our October tea is always entertaining. You'll see many of the ladies from Frazier, but some come from the surrounding district too."

"Where's Mrs. Bladstad?"

"She's gone down to see down to see Dr. Gates. Her time is coming soon," Ellie said, then passed around the little basket of rolls.

After lunch, there was a dramatic Halloween reading of "The Legend of Sleepy Hollow" and a piano piece by Ellie Turner. Even though the holiday was nearly two weeks away, they had chosen it for their theme. After the entertainment, refreshments were served. The women all gathered around Caroline and asked about her.

"I feel fine, though some days, I am little tired," she admitted. For which Caroline received all sorts of advice she wasn't sure how to use.

Afterwards, Ellie leaned in and cautioned Caroline not to take the others too much to heart. "Though I'm the newest mother in the bunch, I've heard no one's the same. In fact, I'd say after dissecting frogs for several years, I'd say it's true for anything."

"Oh? What do you teach?"

"High school biology and science. I'm crazy about it. Course now I can't teach since I've married, but I go in anyway and help."

Caroline smiled. She hadn't really talked to Ellie before, but felt a kindred heart.

"I heard you went up to the meadows," Ellie continued.

"Yes, it was beautiful," Caroline answered wistfully.

"Don't worry, you'll go again soon. I'm going to put Jack junior into a rucksack this spring and take him up. He'll be a year old." She stole a piece of cake and made a mock gasp as she saw a tall man walk past the window to the front door of the hotel.

"What?" Caroline laughed.

"What a handsome man. I suppose he's coming for you."

"No, not today," Caroline giggled. They were both shocked when Mrs. Wilson announced that a gentleman *had* come to see her. She put an emphasis on gentleman to denote his character as well as his bearing.

"David!" Caroline shouted when she saw her cousin, forgetting all decorum. She flew to his arms, laughing at the puzzled looks of the tea club matrons. The shock of scandal made her dizzy, because it'd be delicious to pop their misconceptions. David gave her a big grin and then a hug to go with it.

"Ladies, this is my cousin, Mr. David Harms, of Seattle. He's been very naughty not to let me know he was coming. What shall I do with him?"

"You can have him join us," Ellie said, pulling out a chair for him.

There was some oohing and ahhing over him as facts about his university affiliation were pried out of him as well as several other tidbits that made him the most interesting object of their universe at the moment. Tea was offered, but he asked for coffee. He seemed to be enjoying the attention, his eyes twinkling, his laughter spontaneous, like he didn't have a care in the world. *But why on earth did he really come?* Caroline wondered. Eventually he asked to be excused and politely removed her from the hotel.

"Can we go somewhere?"

"We were somewhere. The hotel has the only respectable restaurant."

"Then the train depot. There are some seats there."

They walked over with his arm gently linked through Caroline's and she felt a surge of happiness. It had been nearly ten weeks since she'd seen him or anyone from her family. Emily had only written once since the last letter and only then to send her a clipping about Sophie's wedding.

"I suppose you want to hear all about the wedding," David said as he stepped around a pile of horse manure.

"Oh, yes. The only news I got was a newspaper clipping

and a note from Emily."

I know this will pain you, but then again I know you enough to know that you'll think I'm coddling you if you didn't receive any news from me about the wedding. Affectionately, Emily.

"Well, it was grand, as you might expect. An impressive list of guests and a reception bordering on gluttony."

Caroline felt a strange pang that bordered on envy and sadness. Sophie in her elegant gown. Sophie on Father's arm. *Sophie, Sophie.* "You were not moved by its elegance?" Caroline asked.

"I know your parents wanted to make her happy, but sometimes Ford and Uncle Harold seemed to be in charge."

Caroline's vision of regret vanished. *Of course, that was probably true.* David always had a nose for what was really going on in their world. For once she felt sad for her sister. She sighed. "It would be terrible if the wedding was more important to them than to Sophie."

David shrugged. "That would be sad, indeed."

The depot was closed and empty as the train had turned around and gone back to the city on the bay. They sat outside on a platform bench. David took a pipe out of his jacket pocket while Caroline inquired about his trip. "Why didn't you write you were coming?"

"I wanted to surprise you. I also promised your mother I'd do it this way. She doesn't want your father to know. At leastways not yet."

"Mother?"

He waved in the direction of a large pile of wooden boxes and a trunk stacked against the depot wall. "She's sent things she feels are yours and not right for them to keep. In the same breath, she's still hoping you'll come to your senses and leave this man while there's still a respectable amount of time." He scowled, then gave her a letter. While she read, he worked on his pipe.

The letter was in her mother's handwriting. By its scattered thoughts, it seemed hastily written. She prayed that Caroline was well. *I'm well enough, but I need you mother,* thought Caroline.

The letter went on:

I had hoped that you would have come home to the bosom of family affection, where you could have thought through your feelings of passion that the young man must have inflamed in you, but since you have disobeyed and eloped, this is no longer possible.

I have consulted our pastor and he says that it is still within your means to come and set this all right. All shall be forgiven. If you cannot do this, then I pray, dear daughter that you will remember who you are and where you came from. I will always love you and keep you in my thoughts even as you have disobeyed.

Be well and most of all, be wary, for a man's profession of love can lead to a young wife's downfall and ruin.

When Caroline finished, David cleared his throat. "She keeps bending either way. She doesn't want to be harsh, but she does want you to understand that her displeasure's based on her concern. They give the marriage a little less than a year."

"They could be grandparents by then," Caroline said quietly as she folded up the letter and put it away in her skirt pocket.

"Oh."

She watched him mentally count back the months. "Don't, David. Not to me. Tell my mother my baby will not be a six month child when it's born. His father and I were properly married and have nothing to be ashamed of."

"When does it come?" Her answer made him quiet for a moment as she watched him. "Jesus," he murmured. She didn't hear him, but she knew what he was thinking. *The inn.*

"My mother doesn't know anything about the inn, does she?"

"No. Not even Sophie, although Ford knows. The women all think you slipped away with Alford and then were later returned by Jenkins. They know nothing of the attack nor of Alford's beating. That fact in particular has been completely covered up. What they do know and speculate on is that you were found in bed with him."

Caroline cringed. *How crude.* She closed her eyes and gently touched her rounding abdomen. Sweet baby. She vowed that the baby would never know either.

She leaned against the wall. "What else do they speculate about me?"

David's voice softened, as if he sensed her pain. "Uncle Harold doesn't know, but his own daughter Liza has expressed admiration for your running off with someone who sounds like a cross between Cooper's Hawkeye and Wister's Virginian cowboy."

Caroline sat up and laughed. "And you? What do you speculate, cousin?"

He shrugged. "I think you're strong. And despite some misgivings I might have, the man's crazy about you." He finally got the pipe going. "He's also resourceful. It's either an extremely small community around here or he's already made a good name for himself in this entire district. On the train, I mentioned I was going to see Alford and his wife up here and several said they knew him as one of the rangers. Had kind words as well."

"An assistant ranger. He's out rangering right now."

"He's left you alone?"

"Not alone as you can see. I can't go anywhere without someone knowing my whereabouts. It's become everyone's civic duty to ensure that when Assistant Ranger Alford is out, someone will be in with his wife. Someone female, that is."

"Until today." For the first time David genuinely smiled at her. He shook his head. "I was going to ask something, but I see that I don't need to."

"What was it?"

"Are you happy?"

Caroline's smile went ear to ear.

The boxes and trunk were delivered to the house that afternoon. David helped drive out one of the wagons and along with a man hired from the hotel, unloaded the boxes where Caroline wished them to go. As David stepped into the kitchen, he stared in astonishment at the view and nearly dropped a box of china. When everything was done, she led him on a tour of the house and stable where they had two horses and a buggy now — on loan from Vernell. He was impressed by her account of how Alford's family had come to fix the house up for them and had helped make the down payment. Each room had special character, to them even with the lack of furniture. He found Alford's tackle room especially intriguing as it revealed more of the man than any other place, but it was the view of the mountains and forests that moved him the most. It was spectacular.

"Can I come back another time and bring a friend?"

"Of course. I'd love to have you stay. You are going to stay, aren't you?"

"I can for a couple of days. But not here. I'll stay at the hotel. It's more proper with your husband away."

Caroline nodded her head in agreement. It wouldn't do to inflate already curious minds.

She prepared a cold plate of salmon that Alford had smoked a week earlier and other sandwich makings, then joined him at the kitchen table. Even though she had a more formal dining area, the kitchen always seemed just right to her. It was natural to look up and see the mountains and trees through the window. She loved how each day the scene changed, depending on the weather or the light. Soon October would gone and winter coming in. What would her mountains look like then?

Caroline visited with David quietly, asking about his studies and present interests. Somehow, he let slip that he'd begun to call on Emily.

"We found we were co-conspirators. I had wanted to find out what had transpired while the two of you were visiting in Swede Hill. Your father had requested it. He was very angry with me, you know, for my part in your elopement, though I'm still hopeful he may come around to your side. Miss Drew was very forthright. We began to see we had other common interests." He grinned at her. "Since several professors at the university belong to the mountaineering club, I have joined."

"Is Miss Drew the 'friend' you want to bring?"

"Yes. And perhaps the whole club. They're talking about meeting with the local club here for a spring outing. Several business organizations are interested."

Caroline smiled. "I'm interested too. I hope I can go after the baby comes." She cut her sandwich in half and took a bite.

She was excited about the hiking club coming, but something nagged her since he'd talked about the inn.

"You said my father was angry with you, but did he ever say anything about the inn and what happened there? I truly don't know how he feels about what happened, other than his displeasure in me."

David frowned, concentrating on the sandwich he was assembling.

"David?"

David sighed and looked at her. "He was upset, of course, with the method of your return — it could've easily been fodder for the radical papers — but he didn't really learn of the extent of Alford's injuries until later. He had assumed there might have been a struggle to take you away, but not an outright assault. That, I know, upset him the most and he did protest quite strongly. Especially after Jenkins's lurid account. That's why he sent me to look in on Alford in Swede Hill."

"But he never said anything to me afterwards. In fact, he disowned me."

"I know. I'm so sorry, Caroline. It's so wrong, but your parents still hope you'll come to your senses and come home."

Caroline folded her arms on her stomach. "Too late. It's far too late," she murmured. She pursed her lips, then sighed. "But I can't be sad. I'm here. I've made my choice and that's that." She leaned across the table and pinched her cousin's cheek. "And what a choice! At least be happy for me. I am. I've the most wonderful friends and for now life's very good."

Alford arrived home a day early and heard laughter in the kitchen. It was wonderful to hear her so bright and cheerful. The pregnancy seemed to have worn her out so early on, although he was told that often women improved once the initial sickness passed. Assuming it was Cathy Bladstad in there with her, he delayed going in and hung up his coat in his tackle room. He was shocked to find David Harms sitting at the table playing cribbage. He hadn't expected it at all.

"Bob!" Caroline laughed. "Look who has come to visit. Isn't it wonderful?"

"Nice. Good to see you, Harms."

David stood up and offered his hand. "Awfully good to see you too, Alford."

I'm sure it is. He shook David's hand in a firm grip, surprised it wasn't as kid glove smooth as he thought it was going to be. He gave an extra pump, then let go.

"Coffee, sweetheart?" Alford meant to assert himself, even if it was in the kitchen, a male ceremony only he and Harms could understand.

This is my territory and this is my wife.

He poured himself a cup of coffee, then stopped to kiss Caroline.

Mine alone.

Alford made sure Harms saw his hand stay a little longer on her shoulder and kneaded it lightly before moving away. He sat down next to Caroline and inquired how she'd been, leaving room for David to put in something if he wanted. To his surprise, David seemed totally buoyed seeing him with Caroline.

"Well, here's a belated toast to the charming couple. You've carved out quite a place," David said at one point with his coffee cup raised. This made Alford feel more distrustful.

He watched David with hidden suspicion and hurt. He shouldn't grudge Caroline her one family friend, but he was wary of Harms's mixed feelings. Unable to read them, Alford could only assume some romantic interest, despite Harms's protestations he hadn't any. And Alford still wasn't sure where Harms stood with Harold Symington.

"Any word on Caroline's parents? Are they well?" He tried to be pleasant for her sake.

David said that they were. When he began to talk about Miss Drew and the mountaineering clubs, Alford started to warm up to him.

The rains came the next day and filled the forests with a cold mantle of gloom. Alford saw Harms off at the depot, then took Caroline to the hotel to meet with her friends Ellie Turner and Berta Olsen. He had questioned bringing her in to say good-bye, when she complained of being tired and achy. It wouldn't do to catch cold, but she had insisted. The meeting was a little respite and a chance to sit by the fire with friends. While she visited, Alford went over to the general store to check on the batch of flies he had dropped off recently. Tom Bergstrom, the storekeep, greeted him with the usual nod of his round blonde head.

The store was a fairly new structure, built just the year before. It was set on the main street, with its entrance diagonal to the street, giving it a grander facade than most structures in the settlement. It stood two stories high and its sides were planked and painted white.

Inside, like the rest of the buildings in town, it had electricity making it a passable imitation to any city store. The wood floor was stained with dark oil and cluttered throughout by large cases of dry goods, tools and equipment for sale. Canned food and other items appealing to the mining population was also in evidence. In the back, Bergstrom had made a rough counter for the display of sporting equipment. He favored hunting equipment right now as it was the season, but there was ample space for fishing tackle as well.

"Any bites?" asked Alford.

"Matter of fact, a fellow from Rockport down Skagit way was asking about your flies. Bought two, I believe." He went to the cash drawer and took out a notebook. He flipped through a couple of pages until he came across the item he wanted. "Yeah, here they are. I owe you one dollar."

"He complain about the price?"

"No. Think he was too interested in those little wings you put on. Size too."

"He knew they were for steelhead?"

"Yeah. That's what intrigued him." Bergstrom counted out the change. "If you have more, just drop them by. We get folks up this far, but you might talk to Reed Culley. He fishes a lot down toward Twin Forks. Might make some sales for you." He closed the cash drawer and came out around the counter. "How much longer you working for the Forest Service?"

"Hopefully until Thanksgiving. Vernell's working on an angle for money."

"Well, you run out, you come see me. Steelhead comes this far up around November and there are some January-February runs as well. I got a proposition."

Alford thanked him and pocketed his change. As he started down one of the aisles behind Bergstrom, George Fuller hailed him at the front door.

"Hey, Alford! Get your gear. Some fool's gone over the falls. Vernell wants us there at once. It'll take about an hour to get up there, then who knows." Fuller closed the door and went out. From his slicker, it looked like it was still drizzling.

Alford found his horse, then went into the hotel to inform Caroline he'd be going.

"I'll go with her, Ranger Alford," Ellie said. "Probably leave soon. It looks like the weather's going to get worse."

"Thanks. Much appreciated." He gave Caroline a kiss. "I'll be back as soon as I can. Get some rest, sweetheart. Too much company the last few days."

Caroline pouted at him. "Oh, bother. Everyone's hovering over me."

Alford leaned in. "I'd love to hover over you."

She batted him out of the hotel sitting room.

The rain hit the women about halfway to the house, sending down sheets of water that disturbed the horse and made it hard to handle. It didn't help that Ellie's horse was tied on the back. Trying to avoid puddles and keep the horses under control was difficult, but they managed to get back. Ellie helped secure the animals in the new stable, then went up the front porch with Caroline and shook out her umbrella and rain gear. Caroline attempted to remove her travel wrap as well, but lethargy overcame her, making her feel faint. Her back ached from the jarring of the buggy on the road. She tried shaking out her umbrella, then cried out in pain as a strange pulling sensation grabbed at her groin. Sharp and urgent, it seemed to gain momentum as the pulling expanded, causing her to drop the umbrella and grab her stomach.

"Caroline?"

She reached out to the wall. *I must get inside and lie down, but how weak I am.* Her legs didn't seemed to want to go. She must have begun to slide down too. *The pain!* She didn't seem to have control of herself or her bladder and when the pain finally ceased she crouched up against the wall, panting in relief.

"Caroline?"

"Oh, Ellie"

Her friend knelt beside her, her face calm and practical as an ex-biology teacher ought to be. "What's wrong?" Ellie asked, but Caroline thought she must have already known something by the way her eyes fought to hide her fear, by the way Ellie wiped back her wet hair.

"I have a pain. Just came on like a banshee."

"Well, sometimes you get something like that. Let's get you inside."

Ellie helped her upstairs to the bedroom and out of her clothes and onto the bed in her shift.

"You're a dear, Ellie. I'm just tired. I'll be al — " Another spasm of pain hit her. Frightened, she grabbed the edge of the mattress for support, trying not to cry out. She pulled her legs up to her chest, but they felt weak and wet.

"Oh. What's wrong with me?"

Ellie looked distraught and swallowed. "The baby is coming," she said in a quiet voice.

"But it's too soon," Caroline murmured.

"I know." Ellie sat down next to her. "Look, I'm going to cover you and make sure you're all right, then I'm going to get Cathy Bladstad. She's your closest neighbor. She can send one of her boys for help."

"What kind of hel — p" She cried out again as the pain returned without barely receding the first time. Sweat broke out on her brow as the pulling deepened across her abdomen. She hadn't expected anything like this. Suddenly, she began to panic. "Bob! He's gone. He won't know."

"He'll know," Ellie said. "Where's your toweling and monthly sheets?"

"In the dresser." Caroline could barely get the words out. "Ellie."

Ellie lifted up Caroline's legs and set a pillow under her, then pulled the blanket over her. "I won't be gone long. I'll bring you tea."

"Bring me Bob, please. I need my husband."

Alford didn't get word for several hours as he'd gone down into the canyon below the falls to look for a body. When a messenger reached him, all he heard was that Mrs. Alford took ill. Could he come as soon as he was able? He left the search party not long after, taking the trail as quickly as his horse could handle the slick grade. In the settlement, several people poked their heads out and told him to go on down. Mrs. Vernell and some other women were already there.

It was dark enough for the lights to be on and in the drizzle the house had a strange, sad presence under the trees. Berta Olsen met him at the door and took his coat.

"What is wrong with her? Is she all right?" On the stairs, Mrs. Vernell wiped her hands on her apron. "I'm so sorry, dear. The baby's coming."

"God!" he groaned in disbelief, then pushed his way past Ellie. "I've got to see her."

Mrs. Vernell stopped him. "Not until you're calm. She needs to see you calm."

Upstairs he heard someone cry out, then rustling as a door was closed. It was hard to imagine it Caroline's cry. Tears of hurt sprang into his eyes, but he fought them. "All right, I'm calm. I'm ready to go up."

The older woman smiled at him. "She's young and very strong. If she doesn't get the fever..."

Mrs. Vernell led the way, her steps heavy on the stairs,

announcing that this was women's work and sorrow was the duty of the day. Upstairs, Cathy Bladstad met them at the door. She was very heavy with child.

"Mrs. Bladstad," Alford said. He didn't know if he should resent her for reminding him what they could have had, but he was glad she was here. He'd heard enough talk from Caroline to know there was more to Mrs. Bladstad than suffrage and volunteer motherhood. He hoped she knew the most recent knowledge in this kind of matter.

"We're waiting for Dr. Gates, but Mrs. Bladstad is with her for now."

"Thank you, Mary," Cathy said. "You can come in, but you mustn't excite her."

"When did this start?" Alford's voice sounded too loud and foreign.

"Several hours ago, but most likely it started earlier, but she just wasn't aware. It happens with these things."

He stood at the low footboard, his heart sinking at the figure on the bed. They had only a kerosene lantern burning by her head. All the bed covers had been stripped off. She wore only her shift and from where he stood, he could see that it had been rolled up above her hips. A blanket was laid across the top of her legs. She was drenched in sweat, the light cotton clinging to her slim body so tightly that he could see the pink of her skin underneath and every curve of her heavy breasts. She looked frail, a wisp of the girl he knew intimately and he thought with dread, *I'm going to lose her.* She was awake, staring at the ceiling, her beautiful hair plastered on her forehead and neck, but she didn't seem to know anyone else was there. When a pain seized her, she grabbed onto the side of the bed and blanched, but she didn't cry out this time.

Cathy directed him over to the side of the bed. He sat down gently and took Caroline's hand. She turned her head and stared at him, not seeing at first, but something must have stirred in her mind and she slowly began to recognize him.

"Bob," she said weakly. "You've come."

"I'm here, darling," he answered, leaning over to kiss her

softly on her forehead. "I love you so much." He gently squeezed her hand. It felt clammy to him and he worried his fingers over hers.

Mrs. Vernell came over and put a hand on his shoulder. "We're looking after her. I promise. Stay with her a little bit, then you should go. Just a while longer and it will be done."

He nodded miserably, then smiled back at Caroline who hadn't stopped gazing at him with strange, glazed eyes.

"I'm sorry," she murmured. "I couldn't keep it."

He swallowed. He didn't know what to say. *Only I'm terrified of losing you and if I have to choose, I choose your life first.*

"It's all right, Caroline," he said awkwardly. "We can try again. I just want you well." Whether that was the right thing to say or not, he couldn't tell. A spasm seized her and she dug her fingers into the palm of his hand, biting deeper as the pain bore down on her. He was aware of the women behind him and wondered what they were thinking. Who knew what common female thoughts they shared toward him, being the lone male here and catalyst to the pain his wife was going through now. He was glad when Mrs. Vernell suggested he leave.

Downstairs, he was surprised to find Vernell. "Found the body," Vernell volunteered. "Couldn't wait, so I had Fuller finish up. How's she doing?"

"She's losing the baby." He choked, stepping away on the verge of tears. When he heard her cry out again, he rushed to the stairs. Vernell stopped him from going back up.

"Wilson got a wire. Gates will be here as soon as possible. My Mary and the others know more about this than anyone else. You go out to the porch and get some of that cool rainy air. I'll go up and talk to them."

Alford went out and stood near the porch steps. It rained lightly, filling the woods with the fresh smell of cedar and fir. It was still light out, but he felt like darkness had come early. Leaning against the post, he began to sob.

A few minutes later, Vernell came out with a creel and two poles. By then, Alford had composed himself.

"Don't mean to sound callous," Vernell said, "but let's go fishing. There's nothing we can do. Mary says Caroline's signs are fine. She just needs rest."

"But I want to stay."

"Nothing here for menfolk." He gave Bob a pole and slicker, then pushed him down the steps. "You show me that hole of yours near here."

They returned several hours and a flask of whiskey later to find Dr. Gates in the kitchen drinking coffee. Cathy had gone home at his urging, so close she was to her own time. Ellie sat upstairs with Caroline. Mary slept on the couch in the living room.

"Your wife's resting now," Gates said to Alford in an authoritative tone. "I've done everything I can for her, but it was, fortunately, a clean and complete miscarriage. She's out of danger now."

Alford looked at him dully, his head aching from sorrow and too much liquor, but he understood.

"She needs complete bed rest for at least a week. Then have her go slow with her activities for a few weeks more." He wrote out something, then handed a sheet over to him with a box of pills. "Give this to her for any fever. See that she stays quiet. And" — Gates made a particular point about it — "no marital relations for at least six weeks."

He closed up his bag. "You mustn't fret about this. Oddly, it's quite natural. Problems with carrying babies often occur about the tenth week. I like to think that it's nature's way of looking after things. Baby probably wouldn't have been healthy or even whole. Your wife's young and will have plenty more."

"Can I see her?"

"Sure. She's asleep, but stay as long as you like. Mrs. Turner's going home to her family, but Mrs. Vernell wants to stay. I think that this is sensible. I assume you have your duties to return to. Will you be informing your wife's family?"

"I'll get word to them somehow," Alford muttered, not wanting to go into details how hard that would be. "More likely my mother will come and stay for a few weeks. That all I need to know?"

"Yup" Gates wished them both well.

Alford said good-bye to Vernell and thanked him for his assistance. "You can stay as long as you wish, but *I'm* going to go up and sit with Caroline until she wakes up."

Shoulders sagging, he slowly climbed the stairs to their bedroom. The door was opened. Caroline was asleep on the bed, pale hands folded on top of the covers. Someone had dressed her in a fresh shift, her hair dried and combed so that it spread out behind her head on the pillow like a fan. The room had been cleaned and smelled fresh from a slightly raised window that brought in the clean forest air of the night. He found a chair and slumped down beside her. It didn't take long for the tears to come.

"Caroline," he croaked. "Will you ever find the heart to forgive me?"

Chapter 28

Caroline sat up the following day, drinking the light broths made for her and listening dully as Mary Vernell saw to her wants and encouraged her. The rains continued to fall, making it as gloomy outside as it was inside in the room and in her heart. Nothing cheered her. She felt like a deep well of sorrow. When Alford told her Charlie Bladstad and he were going to move the bed downstairs by the parlor stove, she nodded with no comment. She wasn't herself any more, unable to grasp the depth of empathy around her. When her mother-in-law arrived that evening, she only felt worse that her own mother wasn't there to comfort her.

She stayed in bed for several days, occasionally receiving friends like Ellie and Berta. They were true friends, she had discovered, formed by this female rite of passage and she'd never forget how they helped her, but she missed Cathy. Somehow seeing her, she thought that she could get past this gloom she felt, but it was too close to her confinement to hope she could come.

"Gates has been on her to stay put," Berta said, explaining Cathy's absence. "She's due any time, but she still insists on looking after the boys and doing some chores."

Caroline smiled, wondered aloud where she found the energy.

"Because it's unhealthy sitting around bemoaning the inevitable when there are things to be done," a sultry voice boomed.

Berta and Caroline both gasped, then broke into peals of laughter. "Catherine Bladstad!" they said together. She was as big and unwieldy as a cedar stump, but she managed to walk into the room with certain amount of grace and dignity. She took one look at Caroline and clucked.

"I was afraid of this. Old Gates would have you lie in bed a month of Sundays if he could find one. You should be up, little sister. You're strong enough now. Two days is enough rest. What you must do is walk, even if it's just short trips around the room."

She came over immediately and drawing back the covers, coaxed Caroline to the edge of the bed. When Caroline dangled her feet, she said she hurt.

"Of course, it hurts. You feel tender too. It's all life, dear. You can face it." She helped her to stand.

After three days in bed, Caroline *was* weak. Berta came to help and together they walked her to the living room window. The rain had stopped for a bit, leaving the front yard a sea of mud and ferns. The meadow across the dirt road looked yellow and forlorn next to the wall of great trees. Fall was firmly entrenched. Winter would be coming on just as fast. Soon it would snow.

"See what you're missing? I have to chain my boys down to keep them from going out twice every *hour*. Why do boys love mud?" She didn't wait for an answer. "Now for the kitchen. This'll be the test." Berta protested a little, but Caroline was beginning to see her friend's train of thought.

Don't take it sitting down. Stand up. Join life.

It took a bit to get there. Out in the hallway, Mother Alford greeted her, wiping her hands on her apron.

"Didn't I tell that doctor man that in that old country, we get up and milk the goats as soon as baby is settled? You listen to your friend. I think she knows a thing or two." She smiled at Cathy and gave Caroline a warm nod of encouragement. "Isn't she beautiful, my *datter*-in-law?"

Caroline bit her lips as she passed, trying not to burst into tears again, but let her hands slipped through the older woman's and squeezed them.

The kitchen doorway loomed. She hurt and ached all over, but as soon as she saw the view from the kitchen, something close to release came over her, flooding her with a new strength. Her mountains were shrouded in clouds this morning and the alder and maple trees across the water were losing their leaves rapidly, but everything was bright and clear to her as the day she first saw them. She began to weep and misunderstanding her, Berta urged her to sit, but Cathy understood.

"They're pretty, aren't they?" Cathy let go of her. "You think of them often and you come here often on your own." She pulled her shawl around her tighter. "I have to go. Charlie will kill me if I don't listen to him at least once. I won't be coming over for a while, Carrie, but maybe you could come see me."

Cathy gave birth to a baby girl the following day, but no one told Caroline for several days so as not to "upset her female sensibilities."

Alford finally said something about it. "To be honest, I wasn't happy at first when I learned that Mrs. Bladstad was here in her advanced state. I thought it would only make you feel bad. But I see my error. She really wants to help you."

Caroline's eyes filled up. When she began to weep, he put his arm around her. It only made her more miserable. She felt so useless.

Caroline grew stronger and finally, three days before Halloween, went outside for the first time. Alford had been given time off, but there'd been such a sadness in the house, that often he left and went fishing alone further down river. In the evenings, while she slept, he worked into the night tying flies or tinkering with a new spinner design.

A strain grew between them and as the days turned into a week and then another, it grew worse. He was loving and attentive, but to Caroline increasingly he seemed awkward when he talked about anything to do with her health. And because they never talked about the night she lost the baby, she never guessed the depth of his guilt and fear. He seemed sensitive and withdrawn in his thoughts, cautious about his words even when they talked about mundane things. Most of all he acted like he was afraid to touch her.

The bed had been moved back upstairs, but they slept in it like strangers, her back to him as far as she could go. She wondered if he was glad to be called away to work at Big Fir and stay a couple of days to repair a bridge and some shelters.

Fuller and Alford packed in enough materials for several days' work. Snow had already come in the very highest reaches on the last day of October, but rain was most likely where they would be. Expecting the nights would be chilly, one of their first tasks was to buck up a supply of wood for one of the shelters and their cook fire. When this was done and the pack train horses secured, they set to work on the bridge, spending the rest of the day falling small trees for posts.

Around late afternoon, Alford took out his pole and went fishing for supper while Fuller set up a cook fire. Coming back forty minutes later with several trout, they prepared a simple meal augmented by a strong pot of coffee. By the time they finished and cleaned up, the sun was close to setting. With only their firelight and a small lantern for light, they prepared for the dark, then sat by the crackling fire reading year-old copies of *Outing* and *Outdoor Life*.

"I like them hunting articles and ads," Fuller said. "You looking at that fishing gear?"

"That and some pretty good tales here." Alford chose a worn copy with a large trout jumping out of a stream on the cover and shaking sand out, sat on a log.

The camp set next to the river running through the area

wide and low. Only further down from them was it fast and prone to snags. The men visited quietly for a while, then with the sun just about to go behind the hills, Alford got up and said he needed to find a bush. His warm cheeks tingling as he encountered the chilly, damp air of the river away from the fire, he walked upstream to where the river broke into two gravelly islands. The air smelled of pungent fir and musky earth and faintly ahead of him, another wood fire and then the snort of a horse.

Coming from two different directions, sound and smoke seem to converge at the river's edge two hundred feet further up. Out in the failing light, Alford made out a rider on a horseback coming down on the opposite side of the water. Behind him, the man coaxed along a packhorse carrying a body of some sort. As the rider began fording the river, the fickle light changed and for the first time, Alford saw that the "corpse" in the blanket was sporting the large antlers of an elk. The water was deep and slippery, but the rider made it to the first island with no trouble. He stopped only briefly at the water's edge to cluck at the horse behind him, then shortening up the line between them, went into the second portion of the river and started across.

The horse and rider stepped in with ease, but as the second horse was poised to enter a sudden explosion of gunfire from the woods erupted in front of them. Hit, the packhorse panicked, pulling back and then crazily, bolting into the water. Screaming in pain, it lost its footing on the stones underneath its hooves and slammed into the other horse and its rider. Like an awful comedy of errors, the other horse lurched as the elk's antlers jabbed into its side, striking below the saddle blanket. One of the prongs raked a shallow mark across the animal's coat, but a second and third found its mark in the leg of the unfortunate rider.

"*Auwe*. You bugger," the man cried out.

Realizing the peril the rider was in, Alford clattered across the stony edge of the river, watching in horror as the horses became entangled and start to slide down with the rider between them. He heard the man curse and then in the dying light, saw him bring his reins down on the packhorse's nose. It was enough to get the struggling animal to pull back briefly and enable the rider to free his leg and throw himself down into the water away from them. Gasping and in pain, the stranger propelled himself down river from them, and onto the shore where Bob helped him up. The horses floundered and then fell sideways into the water. This time, the lead horse couldn't avoid the antlers and, kicking and squealing, sought to get the load off of it.

"Damn!" the man roared futilely. "Kimo!"

Alford shot away and unsheathing his knife, slogged through the chilly water toward the floundering packhorse. Thrashing its legs as it tried to rise with the uneven weight, he avoided its hooves and cut the ropes. As the elk carcass fell into the water, Alford grabbed the bridle and pulled the horse up into a sitting position. Soon he had it on the shore.

He started back to help the stranger's other horse, but before he could reach it, three riders burst onto the river bed from the woods' edge.

"Did you get the nigger?" one of the riders shouted.

The riders pulled their horses up sharp when they saw Alford, banging into each other in the process. They were a picture of thuggery Alford sometimes saw in the logging camps used for security. One of them carried his rifle carelessly in his hands, The other two dressed like men with money out on holiday. A very strange mix of hunters and all drunk.

"You boys looking for something?" Alford bellowed, wondering where Fuller got to.

"We thought we heard something snooping around. There've been bears, you know." The speaker was a skinny man, with a Filson canvas coat and leather-gloved hands on reins that pulled too hard on his horse's bit.

"The hell you say," Alford spat. "You could have killed that man. Who the hell are you?"

"Who the hell are you?"

"Forest ranger. This is public land."

Alford looked over to the stranger he'd just rescued and realized he wasn't white. *Too tall and much bigger than a local Indian*, he thought. "You OK?"

"I'll live. Can you help my horse?" The stranger pressed big hands down on his injuries. He had deep, rich baritone voice that cut right through the river's rush.

"I'll get it." The buckskin was up now and though shaken, limped over on its own.

The hunters began to fidget. One of their horses pawed the ground.

"Can we go?"

"No. You stay put." Alford reached for the limping horse as it came on shore. "I asked you what the hell you were doing up here."

"Hunting. We were startled, that's all," one of the hunters continued. *The clerk type.* Behind him the third man snickered.

"You!" Alford shouted, "Since you find it all so damn funny, clear out. Tonight."

"Says who?"

"The law," Fuller walked up toward the riders, his shotgun aimed at the group. As he passed by the wounded stranger, he nodded his head and said, "How-do, Micah. Where you been? Vernell's been getting itchy to see you." Fuller kept the shotgun casually pointed at the bunched party. "You're on public lands, gentlemen. Harassing a Forest Service officer could get you in trouble. Besides, I don't think you know what you're up against."

"Him?" the leader sneered at Alford.

"No, him." Fuller swept his hand back to Micah. The man had wrapped his bandanna around the worst of his wounds. "You might just consider yourselves lucky we came along. No telling what he'd do to you for ruining his favorite horse. Micah's known to get cranky."

The hunters didn't look convinced until Micah finally was upright. They grew quiet.

I don't blame them, Alford thought. What he mistook for bulk, was sheer muscle. Micah was a very big man.

"Shall I give them a head start, Micah?" Fuller's boots crunched as he walked on the stony river bank.

"Please do. It's going to take a moment to get reorganized." He limped over to his horse and gave Alford a look of gratitude, then checked his horse's leg and flank. When he was done, he glared at the men setting on their horses. "Who spooked my packhorse?"

The group stayed silent. Fuller kept the shotgun on them, but looked down like he was suddenly bashful. The hunters, not anticipating anything, relaxed, then tensed in astonishment as Micah took three steps and lifted the thug with the rifle out of his saddle like a sack of potatoes and deposited him on his feet on the ground. He tore away the gun, then grabbed the man by his shirt front and lifted him up to eye level. His face looked like an old Coast Salish mask.

"Hey," the clerk hollered. "You can't let him do that."

Fuller shrugged. "I told you he gets cranky. Someone going to fess up?" The remaining riders stirred. In the deepening gloom, they shot glances at each other, but no one talked.

"Why don't you just comply, boys." Everyone turned as one as a smartly dressed man in hunting clothes emerged from the black shadowed woods.

Jenkins. Symington's thug. Alford flushed from neck to his face with sudden anger.

Jenkins gave Fuller and Micah a nod. "An honest mistake, gentlemen. I'm sure the injured party will be compensated." His boots crunched across the stony edge of the river as he came up. The newcomer must have impressed Fuller, but he froze Alford in his tracks. Though it had been over nearly three months since he'd seen him, he'd never forget the face of J. J. Jenkins. Black haired with drooping moustaches, his dress belied the hidden cold eyes. Urbane and polished, Jenkins sounded as smooth as Alford knew he was ruthless. The others in Jenkins's party must have concurred for it wasn't long before one of them volunteered he'd spooked the horse.

Micah let the other man drop, and turned his attention to Jenkins. Fuller decided it was a good time to take everyone's names, assess a fine and if possible, collect damages. The hunters at first hesitated, then complied. Names were called out. Jenkins, Howard, Jackson and Piles.

Piles. Alford's head shot up the name. He stared at the young man's hatchet features. Although Alford hadn't seen the sheriff during the attack at the inn, from Billy Howell's description, Piles was supposed to be an older man in his fifties. *His son?*

Alford's head swam with turmoil, a mix of humiliation and anger as he recalled the swift movements against him at the inn.

"Let's go down to the fire where there's light," Fuller announced. "Alford, why don't you take Jackson there and give Micah a hand and get his horse and gear. I want to look at those leg wounds when I can."

Taking a deep breath, Alford stepped out into view, hoping he looked the opposite he felt — vulnerable. He caught up the reins of the packhorse and led it down to the fire. The gloom had deepened substantially in the last few minutes, but not enough to hide him. He was certain the gasp he heard behind him came from Jenkins.

The party limped its way down and gathered around the sharp light of the fire. Micah's horse favored its back leg, but seemed to be getting over its shock. Perhaps there might be hope. It was a handsome buckskin and it would have been a shame to put it down. While Fuller gave his final judgement, Micah removed the saddle, then taking some leaves from a leather pouch he carried around his neck, spit into them and mashed them into a pulp in his hands. He rolled them around and then patted the concoction into the wounds of his horse. It seemed to bring relief.

"You ought to boil some of that up and put it on yourself." Fuller didn't even look up, as he demanded a fine of ten dollars for recklessly discharging a rifle from the hunting party. When Piles grumbled, Jenkins stepped in and paid.

Alford put aside Micah's saddlebags and set up a place for him to sit. He heard Jenkins's soothing voice behind him, placating all the wrongs done that evening. Finally, the party began to withdraw, admonished by Fuller to leave in the morning. By the sounds of creaking leather and clattering hooves on the river stones, they seemed eager to disappear into the black woods. All except Jenkins. Alford wasn't surprised when he came by the fire.

"Wondered where you were, Alford. Symington hasn't forgotten," Jenkins sneered.

"The hell you say," Alford shot back, rising on the other side of the fire. "Tell Symington I haven't forgotten him either and how he treated his brother's daughter." He could barely contain his anger. Instinct warned him not to press.

At least not now.

Across the fire Jenkins waited, coiled like a snake, his gloating features reddened by the flickering flames, but before he could offer any retort, Alford nodded in the direction of the big mountain of a man caring tenderly for his horse.

"Why don't you go quietly now? It'd be for your own good."

"That a threat?"

"An observation. You made a big mistake crossing that man."

"That a fact. Who is he anyway?"

"I don't know, but I figure he's respected around here."

Jenkins flicked his eyes to Fuller, as if wary of possible eavesdropping. "Have a pleasant evening, Alford. I'll tell Symington you said hello." With that, he disappeared beyond the circle of the firelight and toward the woods above the riverbed.

"Who the hell was that unpleasant character?" Fuller exclaimed.

"J. J. Jenkins. He's a bully for some of the owners in the logging crowd."

"Acquaintance of yours?"

Alford gave him a sour look. "He bothers anyone up here, I'll slap whatever federal law I can find on him."

Fuller chuckled. "I take it you're not on good terms."

"The man's a menace," Alford spat. Upset, he drew away from the fire and out into the dark. As his eyes became accustomed to the gloom beyond, he thought he saw the salmonberry bushes rustling as something passed through to the murky shadows of maple and cedar trees beyond. He wondered if Jenkins had looked back.

"Let's take a look at your injuries, Micah," Fuller said behind him. "The horse can wait. See, it's settling down already." Alford heard Micah respond, his deep voice grumbling, but he couldn't make the words out. There was a pause, then the sound of clothing being undone. When Alford turned the man was in his union suit sitting on a log.

"Damn. Cut my good drawers." Micah took out a bottle of whiskey out of his rucksack. Aiming over the tears in the bloodstained cloth, he poured it over the wounds on his thigh, then took out more herbs from his pouch and made up a paste for himself. He said not a word, though Alford suspected the whiskey had made his cuts smart. When he was finished, Micah peeled off the union suit and put on a new pair. The cold didn't seem to bother him.

"Why you hanging around out there?" the big man called to Alford. "They won't get far without my knowing."

Alford shrugged. He came back into the firelight and sat down on a stump. Micah greeted him with the bottle of whiskey.

"Take the edge of whatever's eating you. It's medicinal, of course."

"Thanks."

"This here is Micah Thompson," Fuller announced. "One of our leading citizens and a prominent pioneer."

When Micah's eyes twinkled at the introduction, Alford thought the man could care less about titles. Alford took another swig, then handed the bottle back. Micah shot back one of his own before putting the cork in.

"You're the new man Alford, aren't you? Glad to make your acquaintance." He held out a meaty hand. "'Preciate your help."

Alford was amazed at the strength in the callused grip. "My pleasure. Don't like to see a dirty trick put a man down." He smiled at Micah, already liking him.

Micah groped for his pants, grunting for the first time.

"Vernell said to look you up. Said you had something I should see — flies for winter steelhead."

Alford nodded at Fuller. "Well, I've been experimenting with them for a couple of years. A lot of the better tackle comes from abroad or is sold in low quality catalogs, but few of them offer anything that suits local waters, especially the bigger fish. I've tried adjusting some of the tying techniques with a bigger hook with a few ideas of my own. Fish are supposed to only be attracted to shape and size, but steelhead seem to like color as well. They like a flash."

"Know a good hole. Just might take you there." Micah stood up and turning away, buttoned up his pants, then sat down again.

"That coffee I smell, George?"

Fuller didn't bother to ask if Micah wanted any. He poured a tin cup for him and passed it over. There was an easy rapport between them that intrigued Alford, but especially he was curious about Micah Thompson. He was pleased when the two men settled into an easy banter that led to stories over coffee.

"Show him your bead, Micah. See if he can guess." The mountain man pulled out a leather thong from around his neck. In its center was a large round stone shined to a laquered brown black. Ridges marked its sides like those on a pumpkin.

"What is it?"

"Take a look," Micah said, handing it over.

Alford rubbed his fingers over it. "Why it's wood."

"Guess again. It's a seed. Kukui nut."

"Ain't it something?" George seemed tickled with himself. "Micah's got some interesting family history. Grandfather was a Hawaiian worker for Hudson Bay Company, his grandmother a Coast Salish woman."

"Got some Scots thrown in too, though I never truck with haggis." Micah chuckled, his big shoulders shaking.

Fuller laughed. Alford didn't know what to say. He remembered his father telling him once that Kanakas — as he called Hawaiians — often worked down on the Seattle waterfront. Some mistook them for Indians. But he had never met someone like Micah Thompson. He was the frontier past, personified.

"How did you come up this way?" Alford asked.

"My pa. He was a miner. Homesteaded with my ma down in the valley but took to the mountains after she passed."

"How'd you two meet?" Alford asked Fuller.

Fuller laughed. "Packed my horse wrong. Micah found me on the trail way back up by Copper Mine with the load hanging belly under. I sure was green. That was '91, wasn't it?"

"Something like that." Micah grinned at his friend. "Making a national forest ain't easy, 'specially a mountainous one like this. They needed all the help they could get."

Both men laughed together.

"Do you have family?" Alford wondered.

"Naw. I tend to scare the ladies off."

" 'Cept one," commented Fuller.

"*Ah-ha.* 'Cept one..." Micah's voice trailed off, but neither man came forth with any details.

The fire cracked and popped from the cedar branches thrown on it. The men watched the red-orange sparks dance up to the black sky, then mingle with the field of stars overhead. All around them the woods felt cold and close, making the men want to hug the fire more. Wordlessly, they withdrew into the silence of the night and the continual babble of the river, each lost in his thoughts. From the black curtain of woods behind him, Alford thought he heard something in the direction of the hunters' camp, but the river flushed it away. Still, he couldn't shake the image of Jenkins there, and as it grew upon his mind, he felt a profound loneliness and sense of loss of love and home.

Micah could talk of scaring off a woman, but Alford questioned whether he'd done the same with Caroline.

Alford woke the next day to find the fire out and Micah gone. Climbing out of his bedroll, he walked to the river's edge and washed his face in the cold water. All around him, a heavy mist skirted the trees and stony shore, muffling the river's sound. There was a damp, sharp bite to the air, a sure sign of a weather change. Walking alongside the water, he looked upstream in the direction where the horses had crossed the night before, but there were no signs of smoke coming from any fire further back.

"Micah gone?" Fuller called from his bedroll.

"It appears so."

"Not surprised. You never know about him. He's as silent as death if he wants to be. You don't know how to read his sign yet, but he was pretty riled last night by the way he was treated. He won't forget that crowd. Probably got up and spooked them early this morning, then followed them out."

"Spooked them?"

"He's wily. Knows the woods and nature like they were family. Probably got them believing they were under attack from a bear."

"I heard nothing."

Fuller chuckled as he put on his caulk boots. "It wasn't for your benefit. Probably got their horses unsettled."

"How you know they're gone?"

"He's gone and there's no smoke. Just a hunch. Why don't we just go and see for ourselves?"

They found the camp deserted, so hastily pulled up that the hunters left their empty tin cans behind. Fuller picked one up in disgust. "Bastards. I oughta fine that crowd."

"If you catch them."

Using his boot, Fuller brushed away some leaves on a slim trail slipping between a clump of brown and dead stinging nettles and salmonberries.

"They won't be coming back here for a while. They may not want to. Micah's been here." He nodded at the ground, then looked off thoughtfully into the cedar grove still caressed by ground level mist. "Serves them right," he muttered. He clapped Alford on his shoulder. "We oughta go and get to work. We've got a least another half day, then onto Jimmy Creek if we can. Vernell will want us to finish before the snow flies."

"That going to be soon?"

"I'd say today or tomorrow."

They made a quick breakfast with coffee, eager to work, for the air continued to be cold and dank. A sharp wind stirred the trees, cutting through their clothing. Made of forestry cloth, an olive drab wool material, it was generally warm, but Alford wished he had put on an extra flannel shirt over his union suit. They worked until noon when the weather turned sour. Looking up at the heavy, grey sky, Fuller called it quits. "It'll catch us going down, if we don't hurry. Fall's officially over. Time to get out the skis."

"There you are! I was beginning to think you'd never come!" Cathy Bladstad swung open her front door. "Where have you been hiding?"

Coming into the entryway, Caroline murmured that she regretted not coming earlier. "I'm so sorry. This is my first time out. I just wasn't ready to go into the rainy autumn weather until now." She gave Cathy a kiss on the cheek and presented her with a gift-wrapped package. "For Baby Marianne," the tag read.

"Thank you, Carrie."

Caroline smiled. Cathy was the only one who'd ever called her that and it created a familiarity that was closer than her own sister's.

Cathy took her coat and invited her into the main room of the house where a warm fire snapped in the parlor stove. Her oldest boy was reading in a chair, but he obeyed when his mother asked him to join his father in the kitchen where he was making elk sausage.

"Has Bob's mother gone home?"

"Yes, just a day ago. She was so kind to me."

Cathy put away some of the papers on the sofa and

motioned her to sit, but Caroline had seen the bassinet by the wood stove and walked over to it. Inside, a tiny baby slept under a bundle of pink and white covers. "She's so small," Caroline said.

"Oh, she's grown considerably these three weeks." She gently tucked the covers around her little girl then straightened up. "She looks like Charlie. They all do, I think." Her beautiful face was still full, her breasts heavy, but her figure was no longer distorted and awkward. Caroline thought motherhood seemed to agree with her, flushing her complexion with a healthy glow. Still, there was an underlying tension about her, like a spirited filly dying to test her confinement. Even as the days became shorter and darker, she looked like someone about to embrace spring. Ready to bolt.

"You're looking well, Carrie," Cathy said.

"I'm well enough. Not so tired."

"And Bob? Still gone?"

Caroline laughed. The Frazier pipeline was still active. "Yes. I expect him back soon." She ended her sentence in a whisper.

"And things are fine." Cathy gave her a close look.

"Yes, things are fine."

When Cathy offered her tea, she gladly accepted. Later they went to the kitchen to taste a sample of the sausage fried up. It was delicious, not too gamey. While Cathy joked with them, sons and father cheerfully bantered over their clutter of bowls and meat grinder, a happy scene that haunted Caroline later.

On the way home under the snow-laden sky, she cried over what she had lost, but when she arrived to find the porch light on and Bob back, she felt a burst of comfort and joy. She had a home too, just like Cathy, with a wonderful man and a promise for the future. But why did her heart begin to pound when she remembered the look of longing in Bob's eyes for her? Why did she have to be so anxious?

Alford got back just ahead of the first snow whispering down from the flat gray sky. Finding the house cold and a note from Caroline on the kitchen table explaining where she was,

197

he set to work bringing the parlor and kitchen stoves to life.
Soon the house filled with a sleepy warmth. He was in the
kitchen putting on a kettle for tea when he heard Caroline
come in the front door. Wiping his hands on a towel, he went
to greet her, not knowing what mood he'd find her in.

"Bob, you're back early." She hung her hat and coat up on
the hall coatrack. She brushed snowflakes from her hair. "Did
you have trouble at Big Fir?"

"We caught some heavy snow coming down. Didn't have
too much trouble with the horses, fortunately. How's Cathy?"

"Fine." She kissed him on his cheek. Her lips were cold, but
they warmed him. "I'm sorry there's nothing for you, Bob. I
didn't expect you until tomorrow."

"I'll consult our supply of cans. You hungry?"

"Oh, yes, but we are in luck. Charlie Bladstad gave us some
elk sausage."

They worked quietly around the stove. While she worked
on the sausage, he made some hash browns and onions,
pouring eggs over them when they were done. Such close
quarters led to talk. At first it was strained, as they were out of
practice, but Bob's colorful story of Micah Thompson seemed
to captivate her. He told her about the hunters, leaving out the
part about Jenkins. They were laughing and teasing when they
sat down to eat.

"Picked up some mail. The *Filson Catalog* came. I thought
you might like to see it. Has outing clothes for women."

"It's too late now."

"The clothes are warm and practical, though. Especially
with weather like this. There's going to be a winter run of
steelhead any time and I'd like to take you. They have an
excellent Norfolk jacket and skirts. You could get
knickerbockers if you wish. So long as you're warm." He slid
the catalog over and while she looked at it, he ate.

"The sweaters are nice," she noted.

"You want one?" He scooted his chair closer to her.

"The expense."

"I can handle five dollars. A skirt too."

Caroline said it would be nice. "Do you really want me to come? Actually, I've never fished in winter. I'd love it."

"If you think you can stand it. Sometimes the fishing lines can freeze."

While she played with her potatoes, he flipped through the catalog looking for an order form. "Thanksgiving's not far off," he said out of the blue. "Would you like to do something? Are you up to it?"

"I am."

"Vernell's invited us to stay at their home. He says the community does something too. We haven't been out together since— "He cut off his words, regretting them instantly. He swallowed and looked away. *Damn.*

"Bob." Her touch was so gentle, making him feel worse. "Bob, it wasn't your fault. Dr. Gates told me things like that happen. Cathy said that too." She squeezed his hand and didn't let go.

"But I took you away. Exposed you to that bastard. If I hadn't been so determined to marry you...Maybe you wouldn't have...gotten sick."

"What are you talking about? My uncle?"

"No, Jenkins." He blew his nose on his bandana. "And the inn. All I wanted was to show you how much I cared for you." He hung his head in shame.

"You did. You always have. Besides, *I* ran away too." She hesitated only briefly, then kissed him lightly on his lips.

He grinned wryly, snorting softly at the gesture. *Were things so easily mended? A touch. A gentle word.* He looked up into her eyes, testing the depth of her forgiveness.

"How much do you like turkey?" she asked gently.

Chapter 29

Thanksgiving, Frazier style, proved quite an affair. There was a morning service in the Frazier Hotel followed by a community meal at one. The building was jammed to its gills, the company overflowing onto the front and side porches where the weather had turned mild again after a week of snow. All the employees of the Forest Service and the permanent residents of Frazier were there. A second dinner was set up in a saloon across the street where a group of displaced miners and vagabonds were treated to a feast of hand-raised turkey and wild Canadian goose, elk steak, potatoes, corn and whatever else harvested from the garden.

Alford and Caroline found their place among friends. Fuller and the Vernells were there along with the Bladstads, Olsens and Turners. Their various broods ate on the stairs, balancing plates on their knees while the babies slept in baskets in a hotel room on the first floor. The young couples gathered at one of the overloaded tables and shared their stories of the wild week in the snow. For three days, no one had been able to get out while the early, fierce storm raged.

"It's the earliest I recall," Vernell said. "Cold too."

Everyone talked of trees cracking under the weight of the

snow or troubles in keeping their animals warm. Strained provisions caused some worry, yet they also talked of the time their families had together, playing games and visiting between the chores.

Alford looked across the table at Caroline and thought the snow hadn't brought cold; instead, it created a thaw. Locked inside their house, they attended to its needs and those of their own. They built some shelves, repaired a chair and then in the evening, read to each other by the fire. Showing her how he tied a fly, he created a new one for her made of gaudy red rooster feathers, wool and gold filament. The *Caroline Practitioner* he called it.

"I'll work on the phrasing" he added.

Then, with frost on the windows and the snow resuming its onslaught and, they retired to bed, sleeping close to each other for the first time in weeks.

Alford came out of his thoughts when Berta Olsen's mother came into the hotel's cramped dining room and nodded at Cathy Bladstad. The baby was hungry. Cathy slipped out discretely and joined the gaggle of women in the temporary nursery. Caroline excused herself and followed.

Vernell broke out a cigar and prepared it. Taking a puff, he eyed Alford and Fuller carefully.

"Had some news on your visitor up at Big Fir," he said under his breath. "Appears that Jenkins fellow left for Seattle. Won't be coming back for a while. Negotiations on the land fell through for now." He crushed his match into his saucer. "Strong-arm tactics didn't work with Peterson." Vernell frowned. "Still, he got some options down near Twin Forks."

"Heard about that," Charlie Bladstad said. "A friend of his asked about mill operations."

"Anyone see Micah Thompson?" Alford asked.

Vernell snorted. "He doesn't like crowds. Provided the elk for this group, though. Mary's going to make him a steak pie." When Caroline came into the room to take a load of dirty plates, he lowered his voice further. "You needn't fear about her and Jenkins. Logging up here's a dead issue for at least another year or two. After what his party did to Micah, he's not welcome. He won't get a permit."

Alford nodded his appreciation. Jenkins would always be a sore point with him, but he'd rather work on his marriage and get it back on an even keel. He watched Caroline out in the crowded lobby talking to one of the townswomen. Her coloring was back and she held herself well. He loved the way her cinnamon hair swept up, exposing her slim neck and shoulders. How her eyes and face lit up when Cathy Bladstad joined her, her laughter ringing like a silver bell. Sometimes, he forgot she was still only twenty, for she had faced so many challenges and sorrow all in a matter of weeks many other women might never face. His love and admiration for her increased along with his desire. He would show Jenkins, Symington and their crowd.

December arrived two days later with sloggy rain that slicked up the few roads and trails in the area. Being Sunday, Alford stayed home and worked on some orders for flies from the general store. He knew it would be a more permanent arrangement soon. His contract with the Forest Service was ending. He'd be on his own until Vernell could hustle up some funding.

"I'm trying to impress on the powers that be that the district needs to have more permanent employees, but that might not be possible until spring," Jack warned him earlier. "In the meantime, I'll send work your way."

Alford flipped the calendar over to December and marked at the bottom of the page a potential date for a guided trip in January. 1908. It was hard to believe a new year was nearly upon them. He would be an assistant while he learned the local waters. Sitting back down at the table, he tapped his pencil in his hand. If he was careful with his money, they would get by.

"I brought you some coffee," Caroline announced, setting the cup on Alford's work table. "You'll freeze in here. Why don't you bring those squiggly things to the kitchen where it's warm?"

"I dunno. Didn't want to interfere with goings on there."

"What goings on? I'm afraid it's corned beef and potatoes for dinner again."

"Fit for a king." He put a hand on her hip. She stopped short and looked down at him.

"Come here," he said, pulling her closer. His fingers caught the wool flannel fabric of her skirt and held onto it. He didn't notice how quiet she'd become, not even when she sat down on his lap. She put an arm around his shoulders for balance, her breath slowing. "Caroline." He gave her a long and passionate kiss, his first in six weeks. Feeling a terrible longing, he stole a hand to her breast. She began to breathe more deeply, her fingers digging into his shoulders. He took it for her consent and pulled at her waist and its buttons. She seemed to fall into him, then just as easily pull away.

"Bob...." Her voice was so soft he didn't hear the intensity. "Bob! Please!"

"Caroline. I'm sorry. I thought —."He immediately released her, his face flushed with embarrassment.

"Not yet. I'm not quite ready." She slipped away, reassuring him with a kiss. "Soon," she promised.

Soon. Alford felt a flash of irritation. *Caroline should be getting over this.* It had been six weeks and Dr. Gates said that would be safe to be with her again and just now he knew how much he wanted her, needed her. He thought of his parents, his father and wondered what would he do? It was hard to be patient, yet in the end that was what he decided to do.

It continued to rain most of December, but the constant drizzle did not dampen preparations for a community sing on Christmas Day. Caroline went in and out of the house with friends as the Ladies' Tea geared up for the annual holiday event. As Alford feared, his contract came to an end on the fifteenth, leaving him with one final paycheck.

Putting the money away in a tin box, he reviewed his plans for budgeting the little resources they had available. He had already sent for Caroline's presents: a split skirt made of forestry cloth and designed for both hiking and riding and a

Shaker knit sweater in red. In exchange for some flies and a pole he had assembled, he had secured a secondhand gramophone and cylinders to play on it. It would be easy to cut a tree and he wondered about entertaining some friends, since Caroline was skilled in doing that. With January so far off, he might as well make the best of this month. He especially looked forward to a promised visit from his parents at New Year's.

On December seventeenth, Alford took the train down to Twin Forks to talk to a sportsman interested in some of his tackle. Caroline stayed home and made ornaments out of the inner bark from a cedar tree. She bent the pliable, golden brown ribbons into star shapes and tied them off with red yarn as Ellie had taught her to do. Cathy joined her for a couple of hours, then went home when the baby became too fussy. Left alone, Caroline cleaned, wrote letters and read.

It got dark early in the afternoon so the lights were on. She kept the living room stove banked, but in the kitchen where she lived a great deal these days, the fire crackled in the wood stove, filling the room with vibrant warmth. The windows steamed up above the sink and in the door. Taking a linen towel, she wiped away the steam on the center pane in the door and through the gloom outside, thought she saw a buckskin horse on the bank above the river. Curious, she enlarged the circle with her hand and saw the horse wasn't alone. Standing next to it was a tall, ragged-looking man of incredible size working on something at the back of the saddle. Dressed in a jacket made of a heavy wool blanket and tin cloth pants favored by miners and loggers. His face was a light mahogany, but she wasn't sure if he was a local Indian. To her surprise, he started up with a large bundle over his shoulder. He was going to come to the house.

Timidly, Caroline opened the door. "Yes?"

"Bob Alford in? I'm Micah Thompson. Heard he was out of a job."

Caroline felt a sense of relief when she heard his name. She cleared her throat. "Mr. Alford's away," she answered, then wondered if she should tell him that. Micah Thompson was even more impressive than Bob had described him, an exotic creature from the district's past. People like him had disappeared from Oregon some time ago, showing up occasionally at old pioneer get-togethers. But here — she had never met a pioneer with Hawaiian and Salish ancestry before.

Micah didn't seem to notice her confusion. "I brought you some meat for your table." He proceeded to unwrap a haunch of elk from its flour sack cover. "It's fresh. Thought you might like it."

Caroline stepped down, admired it, then closing it up, and wrapped her arms around the package. "You're very kind. I don't know what to say."

"No need," he answered.

The smile he gave her was very sincere. Instantly, any trepidation that Caroline might have had, melted away. "Please. Please do come in for some coffee. It's cold and damp outside."

"Are you sure, ma'am? That would be kindly, but with Mr. Alford gone..."

"I don't think Mr. Alford would object. He spoke very well of you. Village wags can just stay still."

"Well, *mahsie*. Don't mind if I do. Let me secure Kimo."

Inside, she had a cup of steaming coffee for him and a fresh baked roll she had made up that morning. "Sorry for eating in the kitchen, but it's the warmest place."

"Now, don't you mind. It's the heart of a good home," Micah said. "I remember this place. Before Finster built this house, there was a cabin here. An early homestead." He looked toward the windows. The dark had fallen completely now, invisible behind the misty panes of glass. "They were from Ohio. Tried to make a go until the family all came down with the grippe during their first winter. They all survived, but they decided to move to the city and find work there. Doctor too far away. Eventually, they went down to Seattle."

"When was this?" Caroline asked.

" '81, '82. I was still learning how to grow a beard then."

Caroline smiled, warming to the way he talked. "Ranger Vernell told me you were here long before anyone else."

He sipped his coffee, nodding as he did so. "Me and my father. Climbed every peak and valley there was around here. Seen just about every kind of character, four legged and two." He sat back philosopher-like. "You've got a good man. Decent. Quick learner. He'll do here. Not like some folks."

Caroline thanked him. "I heard about your troubles with the hunters. How's your horse?"

"He's coming along. I've worked out the tenderness and the cuts are healing. That was him outside. Best mountain horse I ever had. Better personality than some folks."

"Bob never said, but had you seen them before? The hunters?"

"No, miss. But I'm not likely to forget them. Now that Jenkins. I looked into him and he's trouble. Heard rumors about him strong-arming men in the logging camps near Twin Forks. He..."

Caroline gasped. "Excuse me, you said Jenkins. Not Jim Jenkins? Was he dark-haired with a big mustache?"

"The same. He's not local."

"Oh."

"Do you know him?"

Caroline lowered her eyes and looked away.

"You're afraid of him."

She hugged her arms.

"He won't hurt you, Mrs. Alford." It was just a statement, but she had an odd feeling he meant it. Micah got up, his big frame dwarfing the table. He paused. "Thank you for your kindness. Not many of the new folks would bother. Tell your husband I said hello and that I'll look him up when the steelhead run in January. It's the greatest of them all." He put on his weather-beaten hat and she was amused to see a dark plaid ribbon around it.

"My grandmother's Scottish clan on my father's side," he explained. "All my grandmothers would appreciate it. A family line is a powerful thing. For good or bad."

Alford returned home after midnight, tired and disgruntled. It had been a long, not very productive day. He got to Twin Forks only to find it had been a wasted trip. His contact was gone — out helping to repair a bridge damaged in last week's rain. There wasn't a train going up to Frazier until six in the evening, so he tried to find Billy Howell and spend time with him, but he was gone too, looking for work further down the valley. With the rain threatening on and off, Alford sought shelter down at the saloon and eventually at the hotel where he tried to stay dry in more ways than one.

Bad news turned to worse news when a tree fell across the tracks in front of the train on his ride home. He spent several hours removing it with other volunteers from the train. When he got back, the house was dark, but the fires lit. Trying not to wake up Caroline, he went into the kitchen and took off his wet slicker and undressed. He was in his stocking feet and union suit when she came in.

"Look at you," she said. "You're soaked." She took a towel from the drying rack and rubbed his wet hair vigorously until his hair stood up in spikes. She was wearing only a white flannel nightgown and a shawl. The faint scent of lavender soap on her skin enveloped him, but he was so weary he took her administrations quietly, closing his eyes to the strokes.

"There," she announced. Laying the towel back on the rack, she put a tea kettle on the stove. Alford sat down at the table.

"Hard day?" she asked as she prepared the teapot.

"Oh, brother. You don't want to know." He told her of his troubles anyway. When he finished, she came behind him and rubbed his shoulders until the tea kettle sang. She darted to the stove and poured the boiling water into the teapot by the sink. He watched her with half-closed eyes, the soft flannel cloth sensuously floating around her bare ankles. Sleepily, he followed the line of the gown up her back to where her hair caressed the lace collar peeking above the shawl. He didn't know why he stared at it, but when she turned and brought the pot to the table with a cup, he was still focused on the way lace and hair framed her neck. For a moment, the hot tea distracted him. He felt quite worn-out and he listened half-awake to her news.

"You had a visitor today. Micah Thompson."

"Here?"

"Yes." She went on to tell of his visit. "The meat is in the cooler. I wasn't sure how to preserve it."

"I'll look at it in the morning."

"There was something else."

Alford looked up. Something in Caroline's voice warned him of trouble. "Mr. Thompson said Jenkins was in that hunting party. Is that true?"

"Yes."

"Why didn't you tell me?"

Alford didn't know how to answer. "I guess I didn't want to alarm you."

"Alarm me?"

"You'd been through enough already, sweetheart. It would have been one more worry." When he saw his answer wasn't quite the answer she wanted to hear, he elaborated. "He'd been asking questions about you down in Twin Forks, just poking around, trying to find you. Billy Howell warned me that time we were down there. Jenkins hasn't changed nor apparently your uncle."

Caroline blanched. "You had words with him?"

"Don't worry. Vernell said he's not welcome around here after what he did to Micah Thompson. I understand Jenkins went back to Seattle."

"I wish you'd told me."

Alford made a face. "You're right. I should have. I'm sorry."

Caroline went to the sink and primed the pump. Her slim shoulders slumped. "I guess he'll say something to my uncle."

"We'll be all right, Caroline. We're among friends. Come on, Honey, let's go up. I tired and I'm cold." He got up and put his cup into the sink. "We'll look at that meat after breakfast." He checked on the firebox in the stove and banked the coals.

Caroline went ahead and turned off the kitchen light. Alford followed behind down the darkened hall. At the door they stopped to listen to the rain falling outside beyond the porch, the sound rattling on the steps.

"Don't think it's going to let up tonight," he said.

"No. Don't think so either. Oh, the parlor stove." Caroline slipped into the living room and stirred the coals in the stove with a poker. He could see the tiny points of glowing light in the ashes. Suddenly the rain began to rush down the roof, overwhelming the cedar plank gutter. She rushed to the window, her nightgown swinging against her slim body.

"Guess I'll have to look at that in the morning too," Alford said coming up beside her. He sighed lightly in the gloom, his weariness pressing down on him. Caroline turned and rubbed his arm.

"Not until you get a good rest."

Wordlessly, he took her in his arms and holding her close, rocked her gently. They were like two stranded dancers on a pie plate.

"I'm spooney about you," he said in a loud voice above the rain.

"I noticed," she answered back just as loud.

"You want to hike in the spring, Caroline?" He shouted as the rain increased. "Your friend seems determined."

"Emily?"

"Yes."

"Then we'll work on how you'll not do it with child. A couple of kids will do, but we can wait a while. I'll see to that. I love you so much. You're what I've always desired, Caroline. Always..." He hugged her hard, rocking her against his chest. "I need you, sweetheart. It's hard not to think about you all the time." He pulled back, his hands still resting on her shoulders and looked through the gloom at her. "I want to sleep with you, but I don't want you always afraid. Do you understand?"

Caroline nodded.

"Good." He kissed her slowly, his fingers skimming her jaw line, then pulled away.

"Let's go up before I fall down. That rain's clatter is making me cold. I think I can sleep a month of Sundays."

Chapter 30

"You haven't put him in the root cellar, have you?" Cathy asked from the sofa where she stretched out on the sofa to nurse her baby. They made a pretty picture in pink and white, she in her nursing gown, the baby in the folds of the gown and a soft wool blanket. Her noisy grunts of pleasure as she nursed made it easy to pinpoint her location.

"No." Caroline wasn't sure whether to laugh or cry. After they went upstairs to bed last night, Bob stripped out of his damp union suit and scrambling under the covers of the cold bed, pulled her to him for warmth. She was apparently still very much on his mind and for a moment he nuzzled her neck, then fell sound asleep on her shoulder, leaving her to wonder what he'd really meant downstairs. In a flux, she sought out her friend as soon as she could and told her of her fear.

"I'm happy to hear that," Cathy said. "Contrary to some books, it's not necessary. And Bob's such a wonderful man. Voluntary motherhood means just that — withholding marital affection or just plain abstinence. I assume you don't really want that."

"No, no, I don't. I'm just so confused. I love him so much, but I'm afraid of getting —" She bit her lip. "— in the family way again. I'm just not ready."

Cathy sighed loudly. "Look, if you need some advice..."

"Oh, no... We... I mean..." Caroline flushed, embarrassed, but truth was, she wanted to know.

"Well, I'll give it anyway. Men more or less have notions about avoiding pregnancy. Women, unfortunately, tend to be left in the dark, so must be educated. Did your mother ever say anything about the monthies?"

"No, she didn't..."

"Ah, you had to fend for yourself. Like me. I thought I was bleeding to death." Cathy sighed. "It's just about the same with the marriage bed and after."

"Well, I know a little bit. I — I'd just like to learn more, to hear what you know."

Cathy smiled. "Good. There's literature, but since it's forbidden to send it in the mail, you must instead ask it of someone like me. It's unfortunate that while many see the value of less children as better for the health for the mother and better for the welfare for her children, the subject's considered obscene, especially with means other than couples living in separate rooms for two decades."

"Cathy..." Caroline sat down on an ottoman, feeling like a silly school girl about to take a dare. Warming up to her topic, Cathy leaned back against her stack of pillows and seeing that Marianne was engaged, continued.

"Isn't it odd? At one of our meetings in Seattle, someone dared to point out that the birthrate since the Civil War had gone down even among the less fortunate. But that is largely due to husbands and wives going off separately on long trips or being completely celibate throughout most of their married life. Separate rooms indeed. I had an aunt and uncle like that, sour-as lemon candy. And then there was my own father and mother, loving each so very much, but because of too many pregnancies and most likely other drastic means, put her into an early grave."

Cathy made a face and looked away. "So unnecessary," she murmured before collecting herself and going on. She looked down at her little daughter. "I hope things change for her," she said quietly. "I shall be her example." Cupping the baby's head against her breast, she leaned down to the floor and took out a worn little pamphlet from her knitting bag.

"Here, you may take it."

"What is it?" Caroline turned it over in her hands.

"A little booklet on the prevention of motherhood. It explains so many things. Some methods are suspect, but by and large they work well. There was a time, I am told, when many devices and tonics were advertised openly in the magazines, but some were promoted by quackery. Did you know that potions even appeared in church bulletins?"

Caroline gasped. "No!"

"Well, times changed after the Comstock Law. The medical community back then objected about such implements of family limitation, though I suspect they used some of the methods with their own wives. Such hypocrites. It doesn't help now that in some even sympathetic circles, it's considered sinful or unhealthy for a man to spill his seed upon the ground or sheath himself up. A womb veil receives the very same scorn from that hostile camp."

Caroline blushed. Only her friend could dare say such things out loud. She opened the pamphlet. Cathy sat up. The baby had stopped nursing when Cathy leaned over, but now she resumed vigorously.

When Cathy saw Caroline biting her lips to express her unease, she laughed. "Carrie, it is so like you to be so modern, yet blush at the slightest idea of action. That's why I love you. You'll be my greatest student, only you'll do it with grace and no public pronouncement."

The baby stopped nursing. Cathy put Marianne up on her shoulder and gave her a pat. "Now, tell me. What are you doing about Christmas? And did I hear you say that hiking club is coming this spring? How wonderful. We both must go. We'll begin to train at once .I so miss my morning walks."

The subject, to Caroline's relief, was closed, but her friend's words stayed with her for a long time. As the morning went on, a sense of peace came over her and she knew she was passing another crisis in her marriage. Bob said he didn't want her to be afraid about having another child so soon. She sensed he would be a willing partner. She was now as sure of it as the mountains outside her kitchen window.

While the days to Christmas came fast, Caroline thought the world around Frazier slowed down as the landscape succumbed to deep cold. Even the river moved slow within its traces, sliding over frozen stones like mint-green ice. Then just before Christmas, the temperature rose and a terrific wind came up, knocking down trees and for half a day the electric power to the town. Still, its citizens persevered and on Christmas Eve by lantern light, Caroline and Alford joined their friends for supper and carols at the hotel. At midnight, they started for home in their wagon.

Coming into the house, they found the electricity back on. While Caroline put water on the kitchen stove for cocoa, Alford stoked the parlor stove. When she joined him there, she caught him poking around their Christmas tree where cards were stuck in between the branches of the Douglas fir.

"Sneak," she teased. "Just like a kid." She went over to the window and lit a candle on a little table set there. Its light glanced off the window pane, illuminating her face. When she turned around, Alford gazed at her. He still wore his heavy forestry coat, the front unbuttoned. It made him look both disheveled and rakish.

"It's Christmas morning," he rationalized. "Our first Christmas together."

"So it is, but we always opened after breakfast."

"My brothers and I usually came down before three to check the packages." He glanced at the wall clock. "The late hour we're at — "

"It's sinful to want." She went over to the window and began to draw the drapes.

"Can't I open at least one thing?"

Caroline laughed. "I suppose so, but please let me pick."

She reached for a small package in its pungent branches. Alford touched her wrist lightly in his hand.

"Not that. I can wait." When he searched her eyes, she became very quiet. "There's only one thing I want, Caroline. Only one thing you alone can give."

Caroline swallowed. She trembled head to toe. He brought her hand to his lips and kissed it softly. He didn't take his eyes off of her.

"Say yes," he whispered.

Caroline swallowed again. She thought back to what Cathy had said a few days ago. *"You don't have to put a man in the root cellar, you know."*

"Yes..." Her voice was so soft, she wondered if he heard it.

He drew her to him, holding her just in front of him. "I promised, you know. And I promise you again. I love you, sweetheart. I want to be a good husband to you in every way and I'll be careful." He kissed her on her forehead, then gave her just the barest kiss on her lips. She smiled weakly, making a little noise when he kissed her on the side of her mouth. Why she looked at the angel hanging on the tree, she didn't know, but she continued to stare at it as his fingers stroked the space above her high, lacy collar. He kissed her again and she knew his hunger. It'd been so long.

He reached behind and worked on her shirt waist's many buttons, his passion rising. When he removed the waist leaving her only in her corset and under-waist, her heart pounded. Her mouth came dry when the waist dropped to the floor.

"Lord, you're so beautiful." His words gave her goose bumps. He pulled her to him, then working on the hooks one-handed, began to kiss and caress her on the mouth and throat. He walked her to the wall, his passion rising.

"Bob..." Caroline grabbed his hair. Feelings she hadn't felt in a long time overwhelmed her. Her breasts tingled at the same time as her back stiffened in his arms.

"Caroline? Are you all right?"

Caroline hadn't even been aware he had stopped. From out in the kitchen, the tea kettle whistled its shrill song. Alford's hands left her shoulders as he pulled away and looked. She saw the desire in his eyes grow, then die down to nothing.

"I suppose I should go." His voice filled with regret and disappointment. "We'll burn the house down."

Maybe it already was.

He gave her a platonic kiss on her cheek and went out into the dim hall. For a moment, Caroline hesitated, straightening out the under-waist around her breasts. Down in the kitchen she heard him cluttering around. The light was artificially bright. She looked back where the candlelight winked and bloomed like a flower in the dark. Beyond, the ornaments on the tree glittered like the stars of her honeymoon hike. Her choice was so obvious.

Alford was still in his coat as he listlessly poured hot water into the cups on the sideboard. His face told his resignation about the state of affairs in their marriage. When she turned the light off, he looked up instantly where Caroline stood with a candle. She had removed her corset and skirt, leaving her in her translucent, white underthings and dark stockings. A maroon satin ribbon was tied hastily around her waist. The shocked look on his face was so comical, that Caroline burst out laughing. She never felt so forward, so bold in her life. Cathy would approve. It made it much easier for her to do what she'd set her mind to do.

"Merry Christmas, love," she said, her voice as light as the candle's glow.

At ten that morning, banging on the front door aroused them from the daybed in Alford's tackle room. Hastily, Caroline wrapped a sheet around her and giggling, fled upstairs, while Bob put his clothes back on. He was feeling especially buoyant after Caroline's kitchen surprise and equally confident that she was happy too. Thinking of her now made him ache. Showing her that Mr. Goodyear made more than tires, such reassurances put her at ease. They had made a night of it and Caroline responding beyond what he thought he could hope for under the circumstances. Sublime passion restored marital harmony between them in that moment.

The door banged again.

"Coming," shouted Alford as he pulled up his suspenders. "Come down when you're able," he called up to Caroline at the bottom of the stairs. "The Christmas crowds are coming."

The crowd was Billy. He brought with him gifts, food and greetings from McKinley and other old friends in the logging camp east of Lake Washington from where he had recently received letters. While Caroline dressed, Alford groggily mastered the stove in the kitchen for coffee.

"How's the bride?"

Alford grinned broadly. "Things are just fine."

"Heard Jenkins was here — and gone."

"Yup. The bastard."

Billy stayed for breakfast, then after making his presentations, left for the train. "Gotta go. Having dinner in Twin Forks with a family I've met."

"Aren't we family?" Alford asked.

"Yeah, but you ain't wearing no bow."

"Girl anyone I know?"

"Nah, but she's nice. Nice family too. Got an invite."

"Congratulations. I wish you the best."

After Billy left, Alford and Caroline opened their presents to each other. She was pleased with hers, but seemed anxious about his. When he unwrapped the box, he found materials to tie flies and a used, but very fine reel.

"Sweetheart, where did you find this? It's wonderful."

"I won't tell. It's a secret. Do you really like it?"

He pulled her to him and kissed her hard. She beamed and wriggled away to the tree.

"Oh, look, here's a card from Emily." She opened the letter and read quickly, her eyes full of happiness. "Oh, the most amazing news."

Alford raised an eyebrow.

"She's getting engaged — to David. Oh, my dear. David. How wonderful." Her head shot up, looking for his approval.

He gave it to her, wondering at the same time if it would

really happen. He was sure of Harms's feelings for her. While she read on, he looked for any signs from her about Harms, but found none except joy over the news. He felt a stitch of jealousy as her eyes roved over the pages. These were people from her old life, representing something he couldn't give her.

"Anything interesting?" he asked.

"Oh, she's talking about a Christmas party she went to."

"I suppose you miss the dances and things you did with your family."

Caroline looked up. She thought for a moment, then gave him an honest answer. "I suppose I do sometimes. Christmas was always important, with lots of visiting, but this is a parish party for the poor. It's just like her to do that. She writes that David came and helped."

Rebuffed however gently, Alford felt momentarily left out, but his good humor from their early morning together made him still expansive. He went to work opening a card made out to him. Taking it out of its envelope, he encountered a dark and somber card usually associated with funerals. He turned it over to the back.

GREETINGS. MAY YOU REST IN PIECES. SYMINGTON SAYS HELLO.

It was signed by Jenkins. Flushing, Alford got up and opened the door to the stove. He tossed the envelope in and almost put in the card, then stuffed it into his pants pocket. He watched Caroline from the corner of her eye, but she hadn't seen anything amiss.

"Bob?"

He turned back, hoping his face looked normal.

"May I ask a favor? David wants to come."

"Why?" He felt a spit of anger and tightened his jaw. He couldn't think of anything worse, since the last time Harms came, she had the miscarriage. And now the card. They were all alike.

"Bob." Caroline dropped her arms to her lap, holding the ivory pages in her hands. "He wants to bring Emily. For the New Year. They also want to talk about the club's hike in the spring and their summer outing later. Their plans are definite."

"My parents are coming."

Caroline looked askance at him. "We have enough room."

Alford wanted nothing more than to say, "No!" but her eyes were so full of joy that he squashed his feelings down. Loving her, he said yes.

There wasn't enough room, but it turned out better than expected thanks in large to Anna Lise, Alford's mother. Always the diplomat, she welcomed Emily and David into the house as if it were her own. Bemused, Alford stayed back as she orchestrated grandchildren and adults (for Olav had come with his family) and the newly engaged couple in the confines of the house. If there was any animosity toward Harms, Anna Lise showed none, only reminding Alford how he'd come to bring Caroline's concern for him after he'd been assaulted. The house soon filled with laughter and the sound of children running on the stairs. Alford cleared the tackle room table for board games such as Parcheesi and checkers while Caroline saw to the food served on the dining room table, augmented with traditional Scandinavian sausages, baked goods and dishes.

For Caroline, it was a happy time. Nothing pleased her more than to see two people she cared for deeply so devoted to each other.

"It's a good match too," she told David. *And I pray you'll have a better start than mine.*

"I'm quite content, cousin," he answered. "I never expected to find a lifetime companion so unexpectedly. We just posted the banns. We plan to marry in June, but we want to come in the spring for the planned hike and come back for the major outing our club plans in August."

"We want you to stand with us," Emily said later. "You can be my matron of honor."

"Oh, Emily, I'd love to," Caroline said, not thinking that it would entail a trip to Seattle and possible trouble with family there. All she could think of was her delight in David finding someone so nice and perfect for him.

They celebrated New Year's Eve in grand style, with the older children staying up as long as they could stand so that they could bang pots when the new year came. At midnight, someone blew the whistle on the train stationed in Frazier, sending its shrill message through the woods as far as the Alford and Bladstad homes. Standing outside their house with their families, Caroline and Bob answered with noise of their own that bounced off the cedars and the fir surrounding them before fleeing into the deeper shadows of the forest.

When the racket died down, Alford gave Caroline a hug and a kiss. "It's 1908, Honey. It's going to be a good year. You'll see."

At one, those that were still awake retired to their mattresses and cots scattered throughout the house. At the last minute, Alford remembered that one of his horses needed proper covering out in the stable. It had been in the weather earlier that day. In the stall, he set the lantern up on its hook and spent a few moments caring for the animal before he took up the lantern again and started for the door. A sound outside made him stop. There was a crunching noise on the frozen ground. A shape came by the entryway.

David Harms.

With a jaundiced eye, Alford watched him step in, but it was too early in the morning to guess his reasons.

"Hello, Alford," Harms said. "Thought I saw a light and came down to check. I thought everyone else was in bed."

"Had a horse to tend to."

"Ah. Well, I'll go back then."

"Good idea. It's cold out." Alford patted the horse nearest him and motioned for David to go forward. Outside, they followed the path through the cedar trees to the side of the house. Alford turned and headed down around to the river. Behind him, David followed. A full moon had worked its way over the tall mountains and was making its descent. It splashed the lawn behind the house with an eerie light. At the steps they stopped to look at the river, where the bright moonlight was reflecting on its water and stones.

"That was a grand celebration tonight," David said. "Frazier certainly played its part. That train whistle sounded like it was right next to us." His voice sounded loud in the cold air. "Thank you for having us."

Alford said nothing. Putting down the lantern, he jammed his hands into the pockets of his Forest Service-issued coat. His fingers touched his billfold where the card from Jenkins smoldered. At the moment he felt anger toward all Symingtons, including David Harms.

David cleared his throat. "We look forward to returning in the spring when the club comes for the weekend. The city chamber of commerce expressed interest in assisting us in our club's goals for recreation in your area."

Alford stamped his feet in the cold. "Caroline said something to that effect. I'm not sure about my participation. It depends on my duties." It wasn't an angry response, but it came out grumpy. Harms stiffened.

Silence. Even the river seemed muffled.

"You don't think much of me, do you?" David finally said.

"No," Alford answered.

"Why? What have I done to you?"

Alford's head shot up. "You can't guess?"

"No. Certainly, it can't be about last summer. I thought all that had been settled. What my uncle did to you was uncalled for. I got the two of you away."

Alford couldn't see his face very well, but it looked dark.

"My God, man. If you'd been crippled or worse — killed — what could I have said to Caroline to ever rectify my part?" David moved away.

Alford followed. "You said once you cared about her. It's more than that. It's deeper and you know it, even if you are engaged and deny it."

"Good God, do you think I'm going to take her away from you?" He shook his head. "You're wrong about that. Caroline adores you and thinks the world of you. And I have Emily."

"You didn't answer. Do you love her?"

David swallowed. He had moved toward the lantern. The light was bright enough to pick out his features and Alford saw the pain flick briefly across his face before changing to something else that was tenderly elusive. "When I was young, we were great companions and yes, there was a time when I thought... that... perhaps I wouldn't be the orphaned cousin to her and I could ask for her hand. That time passed."

"Why?" Alford's voice was harsh, his breath came out in short puffs of fog.

David shrugged. "I won't say. But, I *will* say that I love her for her own sake and would do anything to see her happy. She's been a childhood friend beyond friend when I was lost and alone. That means the success of her marriage."

Alford scowled and looked away. *What a pretty little speech.*

"Listen, Alford, I really hope that we can be friends. I'm crazy about Emily and love her very much. I hope you see that. She's kind, resourceful and has an adventurous soul that sparks my own. I know it'll be a happy marriage." David's voice grew soft, his words swirling puffs of steam. "I'm sorry for all the grief you have gone through the past few months. I keep telling my family that Caroline is happy and her marriage is sound. There's no reason to continue the quarrel."

"Someone wants to." Alford reached into his pocket and took out the funeral card Jenkins sent. "Know who might be behind it? Can't be Jenkins alone."

David brought the card up into the lantern's light. "Good God." He dropped his hand like the note weighed a ton. "It can't be Uncle Charles. I can't imagine him doing that."

"He disowned Caroline."

David frowned. "I know. I think it's just awful." He handed the card back.

Alford grabbed it and put it into his coat pocket. "Jenkins was here, you know. Made unspoken threats."

"Really? Wonder why he's up here? I heard Uncle Harold was interested in logging concerns in the area, but right now, he's dealing with labor problems in some of his own camps down in Seattle. It might be a while before he comes up." He blew on his hands.

Good, Alford thought. "Maybe he shouldn't overwork them. Wouldn't have those problems."

David stepped down toward the river. Alford reluctantly followed. It was cold on the river, but with a house full of people it was the only private place.

"I will speak frankly," David went on. "Sophie's marriage hasn't turned out as everyone thought it would. Uncle Harold's been pleased, of course. It suits his political and business ambitions in the Seattle area, but James Ford's a brute. On the surface, things appear happy. They're well received into society there and are to the public a charming couple. Privately, Ford drinks too much and is much too worldly for marriage. He is, my Uncle Charles now suspects, a wife abuser. Sophie has phoned several times of troubles."

"What does this have to do with me? These are your problems, not mine."

"True, but it has intensified their feelings toward Caroline and *her* welfare. My aunt — Caroline's mother — particularly. She was sorry about the baby, but found it difficult to write when she hasn't come to grips with the elopement. Yet any good news about you... She was very interested in our trip up here and your forestry work."

"How'd she hear that?"

"I told her. Like I've always told her." David removed the glove from his hand. "Look, let us shake and for once be friends. If not for our sakes, then for Caroline and Emily. They're such dear girls and they intend to see more of each other. It's a happy friendship I rather not break up. As for Harold Symington, I don't want to be caught in this. I'll find out what I can. He begrudgingly accepts me because of my university connections and what those might do for his son. Funny, they both are rather nice people, my cousins, despite their father. Maybe it's *their* form of rebellion." He looked at Alford's pocket where the funeral card lay smoldering. "I apologize about the card. I had no idea you were still having problems."

The cold seeped into Alford's muscles. *It must be after two in the morning. Why am I standing out here?* He turned to go in.

"Alford. Your handshake."

"All right. Peace...for now. As long as Jenkins and his filthy employer stays off my back."

The two men shook hands.

David didn't flinch at the insult. "How about in spite of. I promise to be your advocate."

"If I needed one, I'd go myself."

With that he went up into the house. The matter was closed.

The holidays ended with goodbyes at the station. As quickly as they had arrived, the parties left, promising to return in the spring. Alford's parents took him aside to wish him well and tell him how wonderfully he was doing.

Papa leaned in. "I see the frost is melting between you and David Harms. That is a good thing, *sonn*. He's a very fine man."

"Harms?"

"*Ja*, for sure," Mama echoed. "When he comes to see Emily..."

"Really? They've been at the house?" Alford couldn't believe it.

Mama patted his arm. "*Ja*. When Emily she comes to see her brother in Swede Hill, he comes too. She's a nice young lady."

Alford frowned. His mother was as happy about the engagement as if it were one of their own offspring getting married.

"It is new year, my son," Mama said, caressing him on the cheek. "Let there be peace between friends and near friends."

"Let it pass," his father advised as well. "Don't step on stones you don't need when crossing river. Life, I think, is too short. Let the river wear them down."

"We will come again and again," Mama said as she climbed on board the train. "And it will always be good news. Have a good new year."

"Now what was that about?" Caroline asked as the train pulled away. She waved to Emily who had found a window seat and was pushing down the window.

"Parting wisdom on life. I'm supposed to embrace it." He put an arm around her. "I think I'll start now." And with that gave her a heartfelt hug.

Chapter 31

"Look at you, Carrie" Cathy said while she and Caroline's other best friends, Ellie and Berta, sat in the Alford parlor making *papier-mâché* table pieces shaped like snow-capped mountains.

Caroline spun around in the doorway and pulled on the collar of the new plaid flannel shirt Bob gave her as soon as he was back on the government payroll in March. Up to then he made do with felling trees with Billy Howell and guiding a fishing party from Seattle. The first few months of 1908 proved tight.

"It goes with your split skirt," Berta commented as she applied white paint to the top of her form. "That's very nice. You'll be ready for the Seattle club when they come."

"Won't the esteemed members of the Frazier Women's Club be surprised." Cathy, as usual, had a wry smile on her face.

Caroline sat back down at her place and wired a green painted pine cone to the base of her mountain. "I suspect they are more interested in my family connections. Why else ask me to lead their tea? All Emily wants to do is prepare for the summer outing and to share her Seattle mountaineering club's interest in a national park here."

"Why shouldn't they? You are, after all, experienced with such important social matters and can climb those trails to boot."

Caroline giggled, then couldn't stop. Tea was the last thing on her mind. *Hadn't she run away from that?*

"Caroline, whatever is the matter?" Ellie asked.

"Oh, nothing," she said and then burst out giggling again.

"Well, we *are* a bunch of silly gooses sitting around making mountains," Cathy laughed. "We might as well take advantage and talk about the funds for the library. Berta pass me the glue pot."

Caroline bent her head down and smiled. This was something she always dreamed of. To be active outdoors and to know women like this. *It's my dream, not my mother's*, she thought.

She chuckled under her breath. She adored her friends, all young and somewhat unconventional compared with the other women in Frazier. Over the mercurial winter days of rain or snow or both, they often met to discuss women's affairs as well as concerns for the community and from their talks sought ways to improve it. A lending library was formulated and funds raised to improve the wagon road up from Twin Forks once it dried up. As a group, they enjoyed the outdoors and with intentions to promote the district's beauty to anyone interested, formed their own mountaineering association.

There were other good things too. Last week Bob paid off the last of her medical bills and put aside some money for a drift boat he hoped to buy. And they started to hike again. They relished the days when the sun would burst through the morning grey and it felt warm as summer. Once in a while, Caroline would come out on her own by horseback to where he was working and bring him lunch. Or they would take their wagon and fishing gear and go to one of his favorite fishing streams. While he fished, she read or wrote. Amongst the trees, they found solitude and love.

"Oh, Carrie. You look quite lost."

"Never mind me. I'm thinking about our event and I'm just happy."

"Well, something's going on. You just pinned a pine cone on top of your glacier."

With that, they all burst into laughter.

As it turned out, the tea was far from boring. From the moment they got off the train and hiked down to the Frazier Hotel, the most energetic bunch of forest and mountain enthusiasts enveloped Caroline with their excited chatter. Some were total strangers, but others were from her first hike, including Mrs. Westford who greeted her like a long lost niece. She looked much more fit than the day she turned her ankle, sporting knickerbockers and jacket and an elaborate wide brim hat with trailing black rooster feathers.

"I've taken up indoor tennis," she said. "All that running around has enabled me to be more surefooted. I went on my first climb this past April."

Caroline smiled at Emily. *Dear Mrs. Westford.* If it hadn't been for her, Caroline would never have gotten to know Bob, become his wife.

After a delicious luncheon of salmon mousse, coleslaw and pickle chips in the hotel dining room, Caroline pulled down the shades. One of the Mountaineers club members presented a magic lantern show of a previous club outing in the Olympic Mountains. Jack Vernell came down from the park ranger headquarters and gave a speech about the Forest Service and his plans for improvements so that groups like theirs could enjoy the beauty of the backcounty.

When the program finished, the Seattle club members discussed their plans for the summer outing and formed committees. Then en masse they walked down to the river running behind the mercantile. There Bob demonstrated a new pole and his flies. By the time the train blasted its horn for the return trip to the city, it seemed the settlement of Frazier had grown in size and prestige.

"Good-bye, good-bye," one especially enthusiastic member

shouted as the mountaineering party boarded.

"And good-bye, dear Caroline." Emily kissed her on each cheek. "I love being around you and Bob. You're so happy. It reminds me of our walks around Swede Hill when you first met." She took Caroline's hand. "I hope that when I marry, David and I will have such a marriage. As for today, it's been a great success."

Success, indeed. Things were turning in the right direction in her marriage to Bob. As for the tea, Caroline did so well that the chairwoman of Frazier Women's Club asked her if she could continue to consult with her on how to put on other events.

In August, fifty people from the Seattle club came to the mountains to hike and camp in the primitive backcountry. In order to prepare for the visit, a local hiking club from the county seat cut some new trails for them, while others were simply cleaned up. Generally, though, the party picked and worked its way around the high mountains, setting up camps complete with commissary and cooks at some of the high mountain lakes.

The braver of the bunch — about a dozen, including Bob and Caroline and newly married David and Emily — mounted a climb to the top of Mount Kulshan. Rising in the dark to avoid any melting when they crossed the glacier field, the merry gaggle of men and women took off. They all wore long, laced-up logger boots with hobnails and knapsacks with extra gear. Caroline wore her split skirt and a heavy layer of sweaters and waxed canvas jacket over her plaid flannel shirt. Emily wore a boy's baggy knickerbockers while the rest of the women wore long skirts rolled up over bloomers. Their long alpenstocks grabbed the crusty snow as they ascended.

As they stood on the summit roped up to their leader, a professor from the biology department at the University of Washington, Caroline looked down upon the deep valleys and mountains below. Low mist stirred in some of them, but generally the view fanned out bright and clear. Caroline thought she could see Frazier, tucked in behind a mass of dark green trees and mountainous hills, by the amount of smoke rising up in gray columns. The air was cool with a gentle summer bite, but she never saw anything so clear about her life. She belonged here.

She squeezed Alford's gloved hand. "Beautiful," was all she could say.

He squeezed her hand back and nodded at their leader. "I think we should head down. Glacier's going to wake up soon. Don't want a crevasse to open up."

The climbing party headed down, flushed by their achievement. Down at the glacier's edge by the tree line, they joined the rest of the party and camped for the night. In the late, unusually hot afternoon, Alford showed them all how to make ice cream from the snow and malted milk they carried in cans. Alford and Caroline hiked out the next day with David and Emily to do several more days of exploring on their own. When the club members finally returned to Frazier, the quartet greeted their friends at the ranger station. They had been gone for ten days.

Caroline and Alford's first year of marriage ended happy and secure. Thanks largely to Vernell's letter writing campaign, Alford's employment became more permanent. They secured a place in the community with friends and neighbors who cared about them and could truly call their house a home.

But no one, except for Bob, knows my secret heartache, Caroline thought, as the year ended and another passed by. The snubs her family persisted in perpetuating continued despite her desire to be reconciled. It kept her in limbo, a disconnectedness that most times she weathered except when she read some item in the newspaper about her Uncle Harold or some society event in Portland. Such news compelled her to write to Emily and David to learn the truth without giving away her hurt and anxiety. Caroline began to believe that despite their successes and growth as a couple, she'd never hear from her parents again, much less gain their blessing.

Why did choices have to be so hard?

Chapter 32

Caroline looked down at the infant tugging at her breast. Born on July 10, 1909, just three weeks earlier, it continued to amaze her how such a little bundle generated so much love. Named Kaare Stein, but called Cory, she hoped he would fit right into her activities as he grew. She didn't plan to be home alone. Bob agreed and devised a sling she wore when she went outside to walk on the rough road and trails near their home.

Bob, how on earth were we on that ferry at the same time? My love, my dearest heart. Life, admittedly, wasn't easy sometimes, but he had saved her from a duller one.

She put her baby on her shoulder and burped him. What would he think of his mother in high laced boots and split skirt leaping around boulders like a mountain goat? She laughed, startling him. For that matter, what would her estranged family think?

Caroline put him down in his bassinet in the living room and went out on the front porch. It was a hot August day and somewhat stifling in the house. Outside, the cool breeze stirred through the cedars next to the dwelling. In front, a newly poured cement walkway led to the wagon road passing in front of the house. Along the walkway on each side, they had recently planted little rhododendron bushes. Initially, she had wanted roses. After Alford gave her one from Portland, Oregon the previous spring and it died, they planted rhodies instead.

"They're better suited to the woods, anyway honey," Alford told her. "My mother always had trouble saying their name, so she started calling them 'timber roses.' I think that's true. They're like the roses of the woods — like you."

"Well, I get to choose the colors then, because apparently it's the only thing women in the last century could vote on in this state — making it our state flower."

Looking at them now, Caroline thought of their first hike together and the lonely pioneer cabin with all its rhododendrons. Maybe that's why Bob wanted them. As a reminder.

"Oh, Caroline! It *is* you. How you've blossomed!"

Caroline's head shot up, her expression going from disbelief to shock. Out the road, Hans Bornstein, the train agent, sat in his small buggy. Like a specter from the past, her sister Sophie perched next to him, as usual elegantly dressed in the latest fashion with her high waisted narrow skirt and jacket. Gone was the coy, fragile girl Caroline had known. *But at what cost?* Caroline thought when she detected a hardness around her sister's mouth. *And why on earth are you here?* She felt the old gnaw of irritation as she grappled with the idea she was not imagining Sophie.

"You'll not greet me? After such a train ride? You *are* a cruel sister."

No more than you are, thought Caroline, wiping her hands on her apron. Sophie's sudden appearance unnerved her. *Was Mother or Father ill? Dying?* Sophie was the last person Caroline expected to see here. She mustered all the good feelings of a lifetime ago and went out.

"Sophie, what a surprise." Caroline opened the new gate still smelling of fresh cut cedar and came out to the buggy. "Do you have baggage?"

"Just a small valise. I wasn't sure...."

"Of course, you are welcome," Caroline assured her, though she felt like she was playacting. "You must come in." She nodded to Bornstein and thanked him.

"When do you think you'll be returning ma'am?" he asked Sophie.

Sophie looked at Caroline. "Tomorrow. I'll call you."

"I don't have a telephone, Sophie," Caroline said. "I'm sure Mr. Alford can bring her in, Mr. Bornstein. Thank you again." With that she led the way to the house.

On the porch, Sophie stopped and looked around. Caroline followed her line of sight. The cedar trees next to the house and across the prairie were tall and graceful, ancient sentinels that didn't seem to mind the house and its outbuildings' intrusion. She knew it wasn't nearly as elegant as *Kla-how-ya*, but Caroline felt pride in Bob's craftsmanship of the planters on the porch rails spilling over with geraniums and the wooden fish sign over the steps that read "THE ALFORDS." The roof was new and porch's boards recently painted. Caroline loved every little bit. *But what does she see?*

"It's very nice. Are you renting?"

"Why do you think that?" Caroline gripped the handle of the screen door, suppressing the urge to yank it off its hinges. "It's nearly ours, thanks to Bob's family."

She led Sophie into the hallway. In both rooms on either side, there were the fine pieces of furniture made by her father-in-law. Pictures of outdoor scenes covered the walls. Her sister ran a hand over the back of the bench against the wall. "Lovely," she said out loud.

"Excuse me, Sophie. I need to check on the baby."

"May I see?"

"Of course." Caroline led her to the bassinet. Cory slept under a cotton coverlet, his yellow wisps of hair sticking out from it like down.

"He's so tiny. It's a boy, isn't it?"

"Yes, this is Cory." Caroline tucked him in. "Did you know about it?"

Sophie shrugged. "Not really. Maybe a rumor."

"Rumor? Is that how it is? My life the past two years a rumor?" Caroline balled her hands into fists. "Really, is this why you've come? After all the time? To confirm the rumor as fact?"

She brushed past her sister and headed for the safety of the hall, but for once, Sophie showed some feeling of consideration. She raised her hands.

"Caroline, I'm so sorry. Believe me, I wish you no ill will. It's just — it's just that this is so awkward." She was imploring now, something unlike the Sophie Caroline knew and it made her pay attention. "Sister... I've...come... to ask for your forgiveness."

Caroline's shoulders sagged, her back becoming straight and rigid before she took off down the hall. Tears threatened. "I'll get us some tea." Quickly, Sophie followed, practically falling into the kitchen and its wonderful view. It made her stop and gasp. Caroline continued on to the sink, but the view, as always, soothed her. The long afternoon sun was pouring in, flashing gold lights off the glass panes on the cupboards. The mountains outside were close, a palette of blues and heather green. Sniffling, Caroline slid the kettle over the firebox on the stove and laid out cups. Sophie stood silent at doorway.

Finally, Sophie spoke. "I didn't come all the way here to hurt you, Caroline. I really came because I wanted to see how you were doing for myself. David speaks candidly of you and the life you've made for yourself. Did you really climb a mountain with him and his wife?"

Caroline nodded, but didn't turn around. Maybe there was going to be a truce.

"Well. The closest I've come to anything of such height are the hills around Seattle with all their mansions. Was it like the mountains across this river?"

"It was higher." Caroline sighed audibly, then turned around. "Does anyone know you've come here?"

"No. They think I'm with friends at the Alaska-Yukon-Pacific Exposition in Seattle. It's quite a sensation, you know. They have Eskimos and South Sea Islanders."

"So you sneaked a hundred miles north," Caroline commented dryly.

"Rather. Oh, you needn't worry. I'm expected to be away." Sophie slipped over to the kitchen table and sat down.

Caroline cleared her throat. "How's Father?"

"His usual self. Holding court amid his books and philanthropic societies. He's in good health."

"And Mother?"

"Not so well. She's had some female troubles. I fear there will be surgery."

Mother. Caroline turned around. "I should go see her."

"Yes, you should, but I don't know. I just don't know."

Caroline flushed, the heat going from her face down to her heart. "Am I still such a pariah?"

"Father was hurt by your disobedience, Caroline. He can't understand why you chose to stay with — Mr. Alford."

When Sophie sniffed, Caroline wondered what she was thinking. She had so many of the prejudices of her class.

Sophie shifted uneasily in her chair. "Are you happy?"

"Yes. I'm very happy here." Caroline stared out through the window panes. Out on the grass a raven had landed and was pecking at some litter from the garbage pit.

"Are you, Caroline? I suppose that's what I came to see."

"Well, you can tell them that I *am* happy and I'm fine."

"Is he... affectionate?"

"What? Bob? Yes. We're very much in love. All we ever wanted was to be married and have that marriage acknowledged."

"But is he good to you and gentle?" Sophie became quiet and played with her hands, finally taking off her gloves. "Is he considerate of you?"

"Yes," Caroline said, feeling a bit exasperated with her sister's questions. "He's considerate and never demanding." When the kettle began to whistle, she thought it was a good time to bring it to the table and steep the tea. She filled the teapot quickly and put the lid on.

"I heard what happened on your wedding night. How Mr.

Alford was dragged out and beaten by some of Uncle Harold's men."

Caroline's hands shook so much that she nearly dropped the kettle on the table. "How long have you known?"

"Just a few months. I overheard James talking. Is it true?"

"Yes." Caroline felt her face redden, once again humiliated.

"And Father knew?" Sophie's voice came out like a squeak.

"Yes, but I promised no scandal if I could go back to my husband. We were legally wed."

"Oh," Sophie said, then such a long silence that the only sound Caroline could hear the raven outside having some sort of argument in the trees with a Steller's jay. Finally, Sophie said, "It must have been awful for you."

Caroline went back to the stove and set the kettle down. At the sink, she braced her arms. "Sophie... where is this all leading?"

"To the truth. I told Uncle Harold I saw you together. Up near Danville at that old place."

Caroline sucked in her breath, her sister's confession like a knife in her heart. She always wondered how her uncle found out about them.

"I never expected him to be so angry. He was livid, threatening all sorts of terrible things against Mr. Alford. I always thought they were only threats. Until I heard James talking — "

Caroline grabbed a kitchen towel from its hanger, but her hands shook. The room began to feel hot and closed in. This conversation wasn't real. Sophie wasn't real, but she had to know. "Why did you do it?"

"For the most stupid reason in the world — I was jealous." Sophie laughed bitterly. "I thought you were seeing James after that incident in the study. I suspected him of dalliances before, but seeing you together..." She leaned over her cup. "I followed you when you rode out to that rambled down place. I thought you were going to meet James. Instead, I found you sleeping next to Mr. Alford. Oh, I could see that it was very innocent. My proper sister. But I told anyway. I wanted to hurt you."

"You did. They very nearly killed my husband."

Sophie bowed her head. When she looked up, there were tears in her eyes.

"And I am so very sorry. You were right about James. He's a womanizer and a brute. A common stablehand does have more class."

"I thought you had a lovely wedding and honeymoon. The papers talk of you a good deal. You live in the best part of the city."

"He had his way with me." Sophie's voice was so low that Caroline could barely hear her, but she understood the words and they cut straight to her heart.

"Sophie?"

"On our wedding night, he got me drunk, then had his way with me in our private train car. When I wouldn't do the disgusting things he wanted me to do, he beat me."

"Oh, dear Lord. Sophie." Caroline sprang from the sink and clasped her sister's hand. "That's horrible. That's rape. You know that, don't you?"

Sophie pulled her hand away, her voice swollen with emotion. "Yes. He thinks he can do what he wants. Still does. Even when I know he sees other women. The last time he did it, I told him I'd shoot him if he ever did it again."

"Have you told Mother?"

"No."

"Does Father know?"

"Oh, no." Sophie's eyes lit up with fear. "I'm afraid to drop any notion of James's peculiarities to Father. I don't know how he'd react. I *am* going to divorce James. As soon as I'm able."

"As well you should. Then what? Are you prepared for the stir in Seattle circles? Will James agree?"

"James will let me go. Unknowingly, Father made some provisions where the bulk of my money would go when I had a child. I think that quite unlikely. I think James is sterile. I'll be able to settle with him on my own terms. After that, I plan to go to California. I met the most wonderful man last month on a trip to the Oregon coast. He has invited me to stay at his parent's ranch this Christmas. I'll go whether James agrees or not to divorce." She stopped talking, her voice choking.

"Oh, Caroline, will you forgive me? Please?" Sophie let out a sob, then began to cry.

Caroline felt choked up too. Tears rolled down her cheeks. *Oh, what was the point?* She took her sister's hand. "I accept your apology." *But you'll have to prove true.*

Down the hall, Cory cried softly. Caroline got up quickly and left. She was gone for some time, leaving Sophie to mull over her tea. Cory was hungry, so she nursed him, then brought him back to the kitchen.

She joined her sister at the table, patting the baby on his back. When he let out a good burp, she chuckled. Sophie looked at him for the first time more closely.

"He's quite blonde."

"Like his father."

Sophie stroked his soft head. "He smells sweet too. May I hold him? I am, after all, his aunt."

Caroline handed him over, showing her how to hold his head on her shoulder. She laid a diaper on Sophie's shoulder. "He needs one more good burp."

Sophie got up carefully. "He's so light. Oh, look at you. Hello, sweetie."

When her sister kissed Cory's head, something inside Caroline softened. She turned away. *Was this not what she had always wanted? Family acceptance?*

Sophie patted Cory on his back then holding him in her arms, gently bounced him over to the door. Caroline followed. Outside the raven was long gone, but on the shore, a boat had been pulled up.

"Is that Mr. Alford?"

"Yes."

"He's rather good looking. Would it help to know David quietly defended him, even to our father's face?"

"Really?" The news that her cousin continued to support her gave Caroline some comfort.

Cory let out a burp. He opened his blue eyes and peered

over Sophie's shoulder, trying his best to keep his head from wobbling.

Caroline laughed. "Perhaps I should take him back." She came over and taking the infant away noticed Sophie's line of sight. She was still looking at Bob outside.

"What's he been doing?" Sophie asked.

"Fishing. It's his day off." She smiled when he advanced with a large steelhead in his net. "Excuse me, Sophie."

Caroline pushed open the screen door with her left shoulder and letting it close behind her with a whine, stood on the steps to greet him. He stank of sweat and fish. Grinning, he came up to her and gingerly leaning over Cory, kissed her lovingly on the mouth.

"Evening. Want steelhead steaks for dinner?" He whispered something more suggestive in her ear when he noticed Sophie was standing at the door. He jerked back in surprise. "Beg pardon, I didn't know we had company. Is this secret women's stuff? I hear the vote is near."

"She's not from the Women's League."

"The hiking club then."

"I'm not from any organization, Mr. Alford. I'm Sophie Ford, Caroline's sister."

For a moment, he seemed incapable of speech, but Caroline could see that he was seething.

"Let me help you, dear," she said taking his fishing pole. Cory's head cuddled in the hollow of her shoulder.

"What is she doing here?" he whispered.

"She has come to ask for forgiveness," she whispered back. "I have given it."

"Why?"

"Because she has good reasons to ask and then earn it."

Alford gave Caroline a look of defeat. "All right. But she *will* earn it." He cleared his throat. "So you're Sophie." He gave a stiff smile. "You're a little long in coming, but you're welcome. Forgive me, if I don't give my hand. It's a bit slimey."

Caroline went back in with Alford following. Inside, he deposited net and fish in the sink, then hung his canvas coat up on the coat rack before returning to the fish to clean it. Caroline made small talk, cuddling the baby while she asked after his day. Sophie sipped her tea.

"Did you come by train?" Alford finally asked.

"Yes, though I originally hoped to come by automobile. I had a touring car brought up on the train from Seattle, but was informed that there wasn't a road that went all the way from the city to Frazier."

"That's true. They're enlarging the road between Twin Forks and here, but I doubt you'll see any road that goes all the way in within the next four years. There're mostly logging camps right now and few settlements. Stump farming is a hard go." He cut into the fish and gutted it, rinsing off the cavity with water he pumped into the sink.

"Cory's asleep, Bob. I'm going to put him down," Caroline said. She slipped away to the hallway, but worried, went back to the door out of view. Alford was still at the sink, chopping off the fish's head on the wood cutting board. The blood spilled against the sink and reddened his hands and the porcelain. He pumped up some more water and cleaned up.

"Are you a fisherman by trade, Mr. Alford?" Sophie asked from her seat at the table.

"No, I'm with the Forest Service. I work for the district ranger." He dried his hands and faced her. "Didn't David Harms tell you that or don't you speak to each other?"

"We speak quite frequently. I see him both in Seattle and at home in Portland during the holidays."

"Then you should know. I'll be frank, Mrs. Ford. Your welcome here's very thin. Unless, of course, I see that it's something Caroline wishes. Then I won't stand in her way. Until then, I ask that you not upset her. She has endured quite enough."

Caroline heard Sophie sniff, but couldn't see her. She stepped further back so *he* wouldn't see *her*.

"I know your kind," he went on. "You may fool Caroline with your halfhearted forgiveness, but you won't fool me."

"Why do you think it's halfhearted?"

"Because it's come too late."

Sophie sighed softly. "I'm sorry. I know you've been personally hurt and you've reason to distrust me. I know you must think me shallow and unkind, but I do mean to make amends to my sister. The family hostilities have gone on too long. And no matter what my part has been in it in the past, I'll no longer participate willingly. I had no idea what I set in motion."

"Did Ford know?" Bob's voice was so unnatural.

"Yes, apparently he did," Sophie said. "From the very start. He may have even participated in Caroline's abduction from the inn. He's very close to my uncle. He's more a son than his own son, my cousin Raymond — and is privy to many of my uncle's business transactions and social connections."

"You suddenly find this distasteful?"

"It's a hard awakening to realize your love for someone has been used to advance someone else's career and fortune. Oh, you mustn't look at me that way, Mr. Alford. I know I have done a terrible thing and may never have your forgiveness, but Caroline loves you and I can see that you love her. That's more than I have. It's more than many people have."

Caroline heard Sophie stand up. "I've had quite a long train ride. I'd like very much to clean up and rest. I only ask for a small space. I won't bother you and I promise to leave in the morning."

Caroline backed up and tiptoed down the hall. Sometime later Bob came into the parlor.

"What happened?" she asked. "Is Sophie staying?"

"Yes. We called a truce. I showed her our new washroom and tub. I punched up the wood stove for hot water. Seems we have a member of your family in our corner, though I wasn't expecting her."

Sophie stayed for three days. Awkward together at first, the two sisters made great strides in understanding one another. There was much to iron out, but to achieve that they vowed to speak frankly. It especially touched Caroline that Sophie paid so much attention to Cory, wanting to learn how to change and dress him, carry him around in her arms. That first afternoon, Caroline hitched up the buggy and drove her over to meet Cathy. Nervous about her friend's frank opinion of things and knowledge of Caroline's past with Sophie, she was relieved that Cathy greeted her sister with cordiality and interest.

"So this is Sophie? I see a resemblance here. How do you do?"

The Bladstad home pulsed, as usual, with the energy of small boys and signs of recent suffragette activity. As the women sat on the front porch drinking lemonade, they exchanged niceties. When Sophie mentioned that she had just come from the Alaska-Yukon-Pacific Exposition in Seattle, Cathy took special interest.

"Did you know," Cathy said, "members of the Mountaineers and delegates from the Annual National American Woman Suffrage Association climbed Mount Rainier in July? They planted a A-Y-P pennant along with one with "Votes for Women" on it. Our own Dr. Cora Eaton was there. She is working hard with Washington Equal Suffrage Association to get us the vote."

When Sophie said that she didn't know that, Caroline thought with a smile, *Now the education begins. Next family limitation.* She wondered if she should tell Cathy about her sister's marital plight, then decided that Sophie would have to do that.

"Carrie, you're all smiles," Cathy said over her glass of lemonade.

"Just happy to have you and my sister together here."

Cathy gave a tea for them and as the news leaked out about Mrs. Ford's background, a certain buzz grew around Caroline. No wonder she had such poise. Her father was a millionaire with shake mills and banks in Portland and back east and would soon grace their district with lumber enterprises of his own. Caroline would have to get the facts straight with the women outside of her circle of friends.

On their last day together, the sisters took horses and rode up to the falls above Frazier.

"You're so fearless, Caroline, taking the baby with us."

Caroline grinned. Slung in a canvas contraption in front of her, Cory rested against her breast. It was a device that Bob had come up with.

When they arrived at the falls, Caroline led them up to a cabin a ways from them and dismounted. Sophie tied up her horse and started down.

"Oh, goodness," she said. "They're enormous"

"Sophie, stop. We don't go near them from this side. Too dangerous. Come, let's set up here on the steps. We'll look later."

As they ate their picnic, Caroline told her about the history of the place. She nodded at the cabin. "This used to be a homestead. Our friend, Micah Thompson, owns it with the Forest Service's blessing. He takes care of this area."

"Is he here now?"

"No, he's gone east over the mountains to do some mapping. He lets us use the place when we want. He's become a dear friend."

Sophie shook her head. "Though your friends are absolutely lovely, I think I shall prefer cultivating friends in California instead of here. All these trees and the endless damp. A slug came into the bathroom last night. I had to sprinkle it with salt." She stared at the falls roaring not far from them.

"Has anyone ever gone over them?"

"I know of at least two in the two years I've been here," Caroline said. "The community's talking about putting up a sign warning city folks about the dangers of getting too close, but sometimes I think it applies to the loggers that come up too."

Sophie looked at Cory nursing under a blanket thrown over Caroline's shoulder. "What life will he have here? There are no schools, no church."

"We have a school and a traveling minister. When he grows

244

up he can work in the city, go to college at the normal school or schools in Seattle."

"What if he just stays?"

Caroline sighed, becoming pensive. "It's a good life here."

"And if you have a daughter?"

Sophie struck a chord. Caroline had wrestled with the thought. At the moment, there wasn't much for a girl, but all her friends were trying to change that. "I guess I'll have to deal with that if and when it happens. The world is coming here all the time. There are more automobiles than there have ever been, electric lights are in some parts of the county now and pretty soon I'll be able to have a telephone in my own home. The women *will* get the vote in our state. It's any time now. The progressive movement's very strong. Any daughter of mine will see a better future."

"Even here?"

"Even here."

Alford took Sophie to the station. It was raining. Alford and Caroline decided that Cory shouldn't go out. Caroline stayed home. The sisters said good-bye on the porch, not really knowing when they'd see each other again. Sophie did promise she'd try to see David as soon as she could. He and Emily lived near the new university campus. It wasn't too far from where she lived with James Ford.

At the station, Alford handed Sophie's valise to the conductor for safekeeping, then led her to her coach. There were only two connected to the locomotive and it was easy to find it. Miners and loggers going into town for the weekend off filled the other. Some were already drunk. The rain continued, turning the late August day into a dreary portent of fall, but Sophie Ford seemed unfazed. She dressed elegantly in a fawn silk dress trimmed with rich blue satin with the latest slimming lines at the hip and hem. Her wide hat soared over her delicate shoulders, her black button shoes completing the outfit. It caught the attention of several of the miners in the next coach, some of whom Alford knew. It was time to get on.

Sophie extended her small, gloved hand to him and let him take it. "Good-bye, Mr. Alford," she said softly. "I thank you for being so gracious to me. It was more than I expected."

Alford nodded. "It was more than I hoped," he said, surprised he meant it. "I can tell you that your visit has meant a good deal to Caroline."

Sophie studied him. "Well, Father is wrong. You're a decent man and you care about Caroline. I think he would secretly commend you. You'll let her visit me? If Caroline hasn't told you already, I may be living a long ways away."

"If she wants to."

"Thank you." She squeezed his hand and gave him a warm smile. With that, she stepped up the metal stairs to the coach, lifting her skirt carefully. At the top, she stopped.

"Oh, I almost forgot. It didn't seem important when I first heard it, but now I think it is." She gave him a serious look. "My uncle's going to be opening a lumber mill up here in the next year. He's planning to send some of his agents to acquire permits in or near the national forest. I understand that logging permits are now legal in the Frazier Creek District."

"When did you hear this?"

"Only last week. He came to speak to James of it — to arrange the monies."

"He was unsuccessful last time in Twin Forks."

"Oh, but he *was* successful. He's a silent partner, I understand, at the B & E Lumber Mill. He is actively looking for claims right by Frazier and is negotiating for possible claims in the forest. He doesn't always announce his part."

Alford's jaw tensed at the news. "He won't be able to get logging permits from Vernell, the ranger."

"He doesn't need too. He has friends in Washington, D.C."

Alford scowled. "One of his agents isn't J. J. Jenkins?"

Sophie paled. "I don't believe Mr. Jenkins is involved with this. That doesn't mean that he doesn't work for my uncle. I've seen him with my uncle on several occasions in Seattle. They weren't social occasions." She paused. "I'm sorry. I see that this disturbs you. Perhaps I shouldn't —"

"No, thank you. I —" The train whistle let out a loud blast the made them both jump.

"I guess this is good-bye for good," Sophie laughed. "Take care." She waved her gloved hand at him, then went inside the coach.

He watched Sophie find her seat as the train pulled out and waved. She smiled back. When she was gone, Alford went back to the wagon, his head full of the conversations of the past two days and what she had just told him about Symington. He got the sense from her that no one opposed her uncle and came out alive.

Book III
Kulshan
1916

Chapter 33

Dear Daughter,
How wonderful it is to learn of the birth of your little girl,
Katriana Louise. I'm am very pleased that you thought to name
her after my Aunt Louise who was a wonderful inspiration to me
when I was young. Of course, she was from the wild side of our
New England roots. I understand that your little Kate is very
fair, but where did that auburn hair come from? I hope that you
are well and being looked after. Minding two children can be
quite a burden despite the gains on the domestic front. I recently
acquired a new vacuum cleaner that works very well on rugs.
Mabel says it is much easier to clean.

Sophie is well, although she's still with that dreadful Californian,
Rex Porter. Sometimes I think her head's still full of fairy tales.
Now she writes of making motion pictures. The moviemakers used
his ranch to do two already. The company she keeps is most
disagreeable.

Caroline put the letter back into its envelope, then
looked up sharply at the sound of children playing outside
on the porch.

249

You urchins. Kate, Cory, you're harrying your uncle.

She turned the letter over in her hands; it was postmarked 1911. She treasured every line of it and often reread it. It was the first letter she had received from her mother since their first winter in Frazier four years after her elopement. It had been warm and friendly.

The letter contained news about Father, her brother, and several cousins, aunts and uncles as well as news of Portland society. Caroline cherished this letter especially for it marked the beginning of a series of several such letters sent back and forth through Emily or David, an arrangement she suspected her father knew nothing about. The letters opened up conversations about children, family recipes and local Portland happenings as well as giving Caroline an opportunity to give her mother glimpses of life in Frazier.

She set the letter in a basket full of them on the opened rolltop desk and brushed her fingers across another letter also written in 1911. She chuckled. Mother had been so worried about the mountain races city promoters had put on that year, pitting runners against each other on the two best trails to the top of Mount Kulshan. It ran for three years until a runner fell in a crevasse and nearly died.

In one letter, her mother wrote, *"Did Mr. Alford run in that frightening race?"*

Caroline remembered her reply, *"No, Mother, He did not, but we know some men from the teams."*

Now, nearly eight years after she had fled with Bob through the woods to the fateful inn, Caroline could look back in amazement in how far they'd come. The Forest Service employed Bob through all the seasons now. Increasingly, he worked with the fisheries as well. Since logging had been permitted in the national forest since 1909, Bob often had to deal with men from Ford and her uncle Harold Symington's crowd who immediately took advantage of the new rules. He also dealt with those who wanted the forest to be made into a national monument if not a national park.

Caroline retied the scarlet silk ribbon around her mother's letters and set the bundle next to the batch from Sophie. Her sister had been good about writing and had kept Caroline informed of the family and her own exploits. Sophie had obtained a divorce from Ford in January of 1910, four months after moving out of the house. There was a titillating ripple of scandal in the local Seattle society, but quite properly, Sophie moved in with their parents in Portland after a discreet announcement in the papers. The announcement didn't mention her trip at Christmas to California where she stayed at the Porter ranch north of Los Angeles nor her intent to return once the scandal receded. Sophie kept herself occupied with charitable parties for the children's hospital and public rose gardens. Then in June, 1911, the month Kate was born, she left for California for good.

The noise on the porch grew louder, so Caroline went to investigate. There she found six-year-old Cory and four-year old Kate climbing onto the broad back of Micah Thompson as he rose off the porch steps. Howls of delight came as he galloped down in a game of horse, firmly grasping each little body in his big arms. Around and around they spun until he pretended to stop bucking them off and fell gently to the ground. They showed no mercy as he tried to rise in a sitting position and finally gave up to their squeals. It was a good time to come to the rescue.

"Children!" scolded Caroline, trying to keep a smile off her face. "Is this how you treat your Uncle Micah?" She clapped her hands and shushed them off. Like street urchins, they tumbled away and lined up in front of her. Caroline groaned at the dirt. Cory's coveralls were dusty and Kate's cotton dress and knees were smudged. "Look at you! Rolling around like chickens."

"Uncle Micah's not a chicken," Cory said.

"No, he's not, dear." She gave the big man a wry look, then burst out laughing. Kate began to giggle and soon they all were laughing. Micah reached down and scooped up the little girl and put her on his shoulders. She didn't flinch at the movement, displaying a poise remarkable for her age.

What an angel, Caroline thought. Kate's curly auburn hair framed a serious oval face of rosy cheeks and green eyes that promised much beyond her little girl's chubby body.

"Isn't she heavy?" Caroline wondered out loud to Micah.

"Naw. She's lighter than a jug of air."

She turned her attention to, Cory. He was a graduate of Frazier's first kindergarten and a skilled student of the rugged mountain terrain. Fortunately, innate common sense had kept him from falling into the river or adventuring too far into the woods. When he turned five, his hair had gone dark blonde, mirroring his father and Alford uncles, but as she predicted, at two, he'd been a handful. *That stubborn Symington chin,* she thought.

"I have soup and sandwiches for you all. Why don't we go in and get them."

In the kitchen the two adults talked while the children ate their lunches and bantered.

"Any more news of the war in Europe?" Caroline asked anxiously. Micah had brought the city paper with him.

Since the previous August, England and France had been at war with Germany. America tried to stay out of it, but it was becoming increasingly difficult after the torpedoing of the *Lusitania* in May. One hundred and twenty-eight Americans had been among the over one thousand killed. Her brother Sammy was now draft age and that terrified her.

Micah rattled the newspaper. On the front page was what Caroline thought a sensational drawing of a woman representing Belgium being trampled by a German soldier wearing a spiked helmet.

"They're still talkin' war preparations. There's a practice meeting out in Ferndale," Micah said.

Caroline sighed. "I hope we stay neutral. The war's coming too close."

Micah caught the concern in her voice. "Things are going to be all right, Miz Caroline."

In the years since they'd first met, Micah Thompson became a regular member of the Alford family. From a friendship that developed since the incident at the river with the Jenkins hunting party, Micah often sought out Bob in the field. Finding an eager student in the younger man, the old pioneer taught Alford the art of woodcraft, mountaineering, and survival in the often unpredictable high mountain environment.

At first elusive around the Alford home — Caroline could have sworn she saw the big man in the forests around the house and hills during their first winter — Micah eventually began to show up more frequently, bringing smoked salmon and game for the family and staying to chat and "talk story" as he put it. Charming and old fashioned in his deference to Caroline — he always called her Miz Caroline, even though he long ago earned the right to call her by her first name —he soon became her friend too and over time, a confidante. As he assimilated deeper into their daily lives, he became her silent protector as well.

After Cory's birth, he took the little boy under his wing when Alford wasn't around. After Kate was born, he looked after Cory constantly while Caroline got her strength back. When she was older and walking, Kate joined her brother in his field lessons.

With lunch finished, everyone went outside. Caroline joined Micah on the steps. While they talked, the children took a pail and scavenged along the bank and woods for items from a list he made up for them. The afternoon was cool and full of the sweet, crisp air of the mountains after a rain, though none was forthcoming. The forest across the river was deep and thick, going all the way up to the mountains' edge.

"Pretty, ain't it?" Micah said. Like Caroline, he used a dry cedar shake for a mat on the stair.

"Yes. It's my favorite view in the whole wide world."

"Better get your Brownie camera out and take a picture. It's going to get cut."

Caroline was shocked. "I didn't know it was earmarked for logging."

"'Cording to Fuller, it's going. Nothing can be done about it."

"Who got the permit?" Caroline clenched her apron still disbelieving. Those were her mountains and forests.

"Now that's interesting. The permit says Randall Childs, but I think that it's a little closer to home. Harold Symington, most likely."

Caroline froze.

"No offense, Miz Caroline."

Caroline looked away, stunned for words. Though Bob had shared Sophie's concern about her uncle's interests, all those years ago, the warnings seemed distant. There had been projects down near Twin Forks and east to the border of the National Forest along the river, but never here. It was a personal affront to think that someone would log across the river so close. It was so unnecessary. But to also think that it might be her uncle gave her the chills. Did he know the land was close to their house? Or was it a coincidence?

"How do you know?"

"Man came making inquiries about the rails. James Ford, I believe. He's related, ain't he?"

Caroline wriggled her nose. "My sister's first husband. They've been divorced for some time."

"Humph. It's not forestry land, but somehow they got permission to cut," Micah said.

"When's this supposed to happen?"

"They'll cut a road in pretty soon. They're bringing a donkey engine up on the train. Maybe in the next week."

Caroline became silent. She couldn't imagine the trees gone even when whole stands of trees around them were being cut down. "Surely, they won't cut the woods down by the smokehouse."

"I dunno. Thought I might talk to Vernell about that. Long time ago there used to be boxes with remains in them up in the trees around there. They were put into the ground

Boston-style — white man's custom — about thirty years ago. Those graves are still there, though the markers are gone."

"Does Bob know?"

When Micah said yes, Caroline felt a strange pull in her chest. *Why does Bob keep things from me?*

"Bob's been looking into the whole permit process. Says something's funny. Vernell don't like it either, but then he's only an employee, not some high muckety-muck in a bowler hat working deals."

Caroline swallowed her pride. "You think my uncle is working deals?"

"Harold Symington's all deal. He's not afraid of showing muscle too."

Caroline bowed her head. "I'm sorry."

"Don't be. You can't help being blood to someone. Ain't your fault." He gave her a soft smile and eyes that said not to worry, he'd take care of things.

Caroline swallowed and smiled back. "You're incredibly generous, Micah. I don't deserve you."

"Don't talk that way, Miz Caroline. You deserve everything you got, including me." He gave her wink. "Think I'll go now. Got some work to tend to." He picked up his blanket jacket from the coatrack and put it on, slinging his leather haversack over his head. "Take care, now. Give that little lady a peck for me when she gets out. Tell Cory to keep looking for a rock with a leaf in it. We'll add it to our collection." He put on his hat and stepped outside. Standing on the step he looked up at the sky. "Better get some rain. Forest's dry."

After Micah left, Caroline sent the children upstairs to take a bath and then nap. After they were down, she stole an hour of rest in the parlor. She rose sometime later to the sound of machinery. Going to the window, she saw to her surprise, a black Ford touring car converted into a truck come rattling up to the gate. Alford, wearing goggles over his eyes, perched in the driver's side. Dust smudged his face.

"Bob!" Caroline laughed as she came through the door. "What on earth?"

"Ain't she a beaut? This is government property. Now if only we can get the roads to behave." He took off the goggles and grinned at her. "It's for going to Twin Forks. Won't be stuck to just the train."

"Is there road enough?" She tried not to giggle as there were wide circles of dust around his eyes. He looked like a raccoon.

"I think so. It's still a plank road, though the piece between Twin Forks and Hawley Creek has been graveled. Vernell warned me, though, that a trip of fifteen miles can mean around two flat tires and I'm not that sure I understand the principle. Kind of looks like a Sarvern wagon wheel, but the tire — " He pulled up a lever by his right leg and then got down. "Vernell heard that two of these were available, so he took them and added them to his fleet of one. Now we have two for hauling and one for business. Probably not much use up past his place though. We'll still keep the horses." He came over and gave her kiss.

"How're the kids?"

She laughed. "They were napping, but you made such a racket, who knows?" She squeezed his hand. "You missed Micah. He dropped by to say hi and played with the children."

"He's sweet on them."

"Uh-huh." She smiled when he put his arm around her waist and gave her a good squeeze.

"And I'm sweet on you," he said. "What's for lunch?"

"Soup and bread hot out of the oven," she answered and they went inside.

Bob Alford, at thirty-one, was in his prime. The years had been good to him and Caroline was grateful for those years, sparing him injury that often caught those who worked in the woods or mountains. The only thing that seemed to have changed him was the wind which had sharpened his cheekbones and added lines around his eyes.

While she set a place for him, he toyed with his bucket of leaders by the stove. Made of Spanish gut, silkworms that had been cut and stretched, he kept them soaking for use when he wanted to fish, which was nearly every day. Caroline long ago gave up trying to move the bucket elsewhere because Bob made part of his living tying his flies for the steelhead and trout summer runs and his fishing put food on the table. Since last January, he had been making ties for winter fishing, something not generally attempted. Working inside, he designed ties that would attract a sluggish fish in freezing water. Caroline was proud that other fishermen took notice of his skill. But as she recalled her conversation with Micah about her uncle and James Ford, she felt a touch of annoyance again that Bob hadn't said a word about them.

"Bob. You should eat before your soup gets cold."

He grinned, then complied. Caroline sat down next to him, staying quiet while he ate. "You eat already?" he asked.

"Micah."

"Ah." He looked at her curiously. "You're kinda quiet. Kids wearing you out?"

"I think it's Micah who should be worn-out. No, it something Micah said." She took a deep breath. "Is it true about James Ford being around here? That they're going to cut the trees across the river?"

"I haven't seen him, but George Fuller said he came up to headquarters a few days ago. Ford had a permit all right."

"Why didn't you tell me?"

Alford leaned over his soup bowl, spoon suspended in air. "I guess because, sweetheart, I thought one of your ladies might have mentioned it, Cathy in particular being married to a mill manager. Your uncle's been in this county for some time, working through his agents. Billy's seen him around the B & E Shake Mill down at Twin Forks. There are a lot of opportunities in logging now they've got the machinery to get it out. War preparations make things even more profitable. There's a big demand for spruce and fir.

Those airplanes Boeing builds."

"But James Ford's coming here to Frazier and you didn't tell me." Caroline hated to repeat herself, but the more she thought about it, the more annoyed she became.

Alford sighed. "No, I didn't. I'm sorry, love. After all these years, I still don't know how to bring up anything that has to do with your family. Sometimes, I just want to shield you and pretend that it's all right. Other times, I just want to flail them all. 'Cepting your sister and mother, of course." He shrugged his shoulders, like he was physically pushing something away.

"And David."

"Yes, of course David." When he looked at her guiltily for speaking his mind, she covered up her hurt.

"Go on," she said.

He played with his spoon before resuming. "I'm sorry, Caroline. Sorry for the slight and sorry that nothing's been resolved between you and your father. It burns me that he can't see his way to at least let your mother meet you and the children in Seattle without having to deal with me. It was sweet of Sophie to take you and the kids to Snoqualmie Falls last fall, but it was unspeakable that your aunt and uncle didn't invite you all to *Kla-how-ya* or their home in Seattle while you were down there."

Caroline played with a napkin, folding and unfolding it. "Micah says you can't help being blood to someone. That it wasn't your fault."

Alford reached for her hand. "He's right. They're family. I respect that. Just hate to see you hurt. Hurts me too." He let go after giving her hand a squeeze. She saw the glint of remorse there. "That doesn't mean," he continued, his voice growing harder, "that Ford'll have free run here. Vernell's looking into his and Symington's motives here."

"What have you heard about Ford?"

"Doesn't cut the fine form he peacocked around before. Fuller said he was bearded and filled out his britches pretty good. That's a translation, of course. He's obese." Alford grew more serious. "Down in the Seattle area, I know that Ford runs with that Employers' Association that's putting a lot of pressure on the unions. Now that the Republicans got the state legislature they've wanted this spring, the members of the association feel they can run over any workingman just by calling him a socialist. Mention the eight hour day and they're crying sedition."

"Some of the organizers *are* socialists."

Alford scowled. "I know and I don't approve of all of their tactics. But the press is pro-business and some of their printed stories are just flat-out lies. There *are* some real crying needs out here, but they get covered up by talk about agitators being under the bed and or behind every stick in the woods. Anyone wanting a better wage is immediately lumped in with the Wobblys. The very name incites riots."

"I know." Caroline chose a piece of bread and buttered it. "I'm afraid some of the ladies at the Frazier Women's Club support the owners. They are quite frightened that the Wobblys will tighten their hold here. Of course, Cathy just laughs and says they're all silly rabbits. Good wages mean happier families and more opportunities."

Alford chuckled softly in his throat. Caroline smiled. After eight years, Cathy was as fiery as ever. Even after the women in Washington State got the vote in 1910, she found other issues to champion, the latest being prohibition and family limitation.

He poked at his soup and got a potato on his spoon. "I know you and your little circle of ladies try to be informed, but there's more going on than what's written or said. Your uncle and all his cronies, including Ford, are out to smash all the unions."

"But the reforms —"

"I know. The women have *their* eight hour day and the vote, but they still have to work twelve hours if they work at a cannery. Our state's got workmen's compensation, one of the few states in the nation to have it. Wonderful. But a man still has to pay a dollar a month to some hospital fund that the doctors and the employers split among themselves. The camp conditions are often atrocious. And the hours — they're hideous. Asking for an eight hour day is humane, but anything less than twelve hours the association won't buy. There's no recourse but to organize and strike, even if the workers have to die for it."

Caroline bit her lip. She hadn't heard him so wound up before. Union talk made her uneasy, even when, in spirit, she could sympathize. She had to remind herself that Bob would be thinking of Stein who had died so senselessly. All because of a man working too many hours around dangerous equipment.

"You don't complain about the hours."

"My job's different. I know what I'm supposed to do and have the leeway to do it proper without a factory whistle and a man with a stick to prod me along. The pay won't make us rich, but at least I'm a free man." He put his spoon down.

"We're pretty much immune here although the shingle weavers in Twin Forks have struck before for better conditions and the logging camps have had their share of unrest. But that might change. The Employers' Association has its hands in everything around the state. The shingle mills and other lumber owners have recently organized in our county. How many shingle mills are there here? Sixty-five?"

"Seventy. Cathy said that the last time we were together."

"There you go. There's a move to shut out so-called troublemakers, especially with war talk. Logging operations are going to get bigger around here from now on. If your uncle is coming openly, then he's coming to stay. The best Douglas fir in the Pacific Northwest is here and down around the lake."

"How will that affect things?"

Alford sighed. "I don't know, but it doesn't bode well for the national forest. You ought to ask your hiking friends about that. I know they want at least a national monument made out of this place, but with all the valuable timber and still viable mining, that's going to take some doing. 1916 is going to be a hard year for anyone who loves this place.

"That isn't all, Caroline. There's a mean spirit abroad these days and war talk doesn't make it any kinder. The Association and other groups want to kick all the Italians and Japanese out of the Pike Place Market in Seattle and destroy the municipal utilities. Anyone they don't like, the Association calls a socialist or worse, a traitor. Without the initiative and referendum, the Republican-controlled legislature would just roll on its merry way."

He leaned back and stared up at the ceiling. "Sorry, love. Didn't mean to get so carried away. There are times when I just want to go off into the hills and get lost. I don't want to be bothered by all the politics and maneuvering, but I can't help it when conservation seems to be losing its appeal in the Forest Service and giving way to the lumbermen." He looked out the window toward the mountains. "Micah tell you how big a cut over there?"

"He just said the smokehouse and across the water."

"More than that. It'll go up to the Robber's Bowl."

Caroline gasped. That was clear up to where a rock slide cut a "V" in the mountain face nearest them. The bowl it brushed against was named for the large population of robber jays that congregated there.

"When?"

"As soon as they get the donkey engine up." He folded his arms on the table, then suddenly remembered something. He took a rumpled envelope out of his pocket. "Sorry. There was some mail. Looks like Emily's written."

From out in the hall, the patter of feet sounded on the stairs as Kate and Cory came down. They looked clean and rested after their baths and naps. They aimed straight for their father who pulled them up onto his lap. There was barely room for them both and they talked to him at the same time, but Caroline knew Bob enjoyed the attention. Just like his own father, he was dedicated to his little brood, loving each in a special way.

Caroline smiled at them, then opened her letter. Halfway through the first paragraph she stopped.

"Anything going on?"

"Emily wants to come." Caroline paused for a long time, then lowered her voice. "She's in the family way, only she hasn't told David yet."

Alford gave Kate and Cory each a kiss on their foreheads. "Cory, why don't you and your sister go outside and look for eggs in the chicken coop. Mommy and I need to talk." He waited until they were outside before speaking again.

"It's not good, is it?"

"It could kill her. You know how much trouble she's had conceiving. David was really frightened after her last miscarriage."

"Why don't you wire as soon as you can. We can make a room up for them both, if he should want to come."

"Thank you, dear. I so want to see her." She felt her eyes prickle with tears. It saddened her that Bob and David had never really developed a warm relationship, but they were at least civil. And she could tell that Bob loved Emily. Who wouldn't?

"I'll telegram Emily right away," Caroline said.

Chapter 34

Emily Harms arrived alone in Frazier on the 10th of July with enough baggage to stay several days. Alford and Caroline picked her up in the Forest Service truck and took her up to the ranger station. It was a hot afternoon and the road going to headquarters was dusty. Alford had been busy most of the week keeping an eye on potential fires.

"Is it that bad?" Emily asked as they bounced along the rutted street.

"Well, I keep telling tourists coming up here not to build fires in the logged out areas or next to trees. Sometimes, my words sinks in."

At the Vernell's they sat on the wide veranda of the log building and visited for some time over lunch, enjoying the beauty of the cedar trees that framed the house. Emily was interested in news of the local hiking club's outings for the summer and their new guide service for those coming to climb the mountains.

"Has the new trail been cut?" Emily asked. "It's supposed to take hikers further into the backcountry."

"Got done about a week ago," Alford said. "They're working on some shelters now."

"I hope they built them like the warming huts back in New Hampshire," Emily said. "One of our Seattle members took a trip there and was impressed with their huts and lean-tos. I think they'll be suitable for here."

Caroline leaned around Alford. "Did you know about the new registry for hikers in the backcountry?"

"I did. That's wonderful. And now you can get ropes and proper mountaineering gear for going to the summit. How times have grown. I'd love to go up again."

But not now, thought Caroline.

After lunch, Alford drove the women back to their house where one of the Olsen girls had been watching Kate and Cory. When they came up to the steps, the girl said that there'd been a phone call for Mr. Alford. Immediately, he went inside to the hallway where he made a call through the operator. Abandoned for the moment, Caroline showed Emily the guest room upstairs. Setting her bags down on the bed, Emily held her side and took a deep breath.

"Are you unwell, Emily?" Caroline asked. Worried, her heart took a little leap.

"Oh, I'm fine. Just a little winded." She smiled at Caroline. "I'm quite happy, though."

Caroline offered her a chair by the lace-curtained window, the only one in the room. The ceiling in the room was slanted, so she had to stay away from the wall. Caroline found a spot on the bed. "Why on earth did you take such a chance? What will David say?"

"Oh, he'll be all right. We've been so careful, then this — " Emily turned to Caroline, her hand caressing her stomach. "It wasn't supposed to happen, but I really want this baby. I've always wanted one." She sat up. "I'm only missing a very few weeks. I wanted to see you first before David came. I wanted to go up into the hills one more time. Just the two of us and maybe some of your friends, if you like."

"I'd love to go. It's been some time. I'd like to try out my new pants." Caroline giggled. "Ten years ago they would've caused a scandal. I must say that they are quite in vogue right now. I'll ask Cathy and Berta right away. We'll make a day of it. But — are you sure it's OK?"

"I feel fine. Truly."

"You must take care. We'll only go to the falls. That's not such a bad hike."

"Is the meeting adjourned or do I have to make a motion?" Alford called from the top of the stairs.

"We're adjourned," Caroline laughed and joined him in the hall.

"Gotta go, love. Vernell needs me and George. Someone spotted smoke near Bear Lake. Don't count on me for the next two days. When's Harms coming?"

"On Saturday."

"I'll be back by then." He gave her a quick kiss and was gone down the stairs.

Emily came out of her room. "Something wrong?"

"No, just a typical day in the Alford household. I guess we'll take the kids. Cory has a pony. Right now, you can freshen up with a hot bath. We have a new water heater for the wood stove. The tub's quite lovely after a day on the train."

Vernell sat on his horse and surveyed the hills with his binoculars. "What's the damage?" he asked Micah.

"About four hundred acres lost, Jack. The wind's died down and the crews have it finally under control."

"No one hurt?"

"Ask Fuller. He turned his ankle."

"Where's Alford?"

"On the line cleaning up. There were some new recruits that didn't square up. He had to show them a thing or two so they wouldn't get burned."

"That's what comes from clearing out a saloon for your crews." Vernell fumbled for his pipe in his coat pocket, then recognizing the irony of smoke rising from the blackened brush, he put it back.

"Still," Micah allowed, "it's a good thing Frazier's the

only thing dry around here. That fire could have gone all the way to Canada."

"Word is the whole state's going dry. Liquor-wise, that is. The saloons could be closed by next year. We'll have to get our men elsewhere."

Micah snorted. "You gonna tell some bull of the woods that?"

Vernell chuckled. "Not the logging bosses I know." He turned his horse around. "Tell Alford to see me when he's done."

Vernell was sitting under a wind-hammered hemlock at the edge of a large, rocky mountain meadow when Alford came over. Waved in, he sat down and joined his boss for lunch. Over the years, they had become close friends. The older man often acted like both a teacher and surrogate father. His expertise was legion and so was his irritation with people that didn't pull their share or finish a job right. Finding no lack of enthusiasm on Alford's part to learn early on, Vernell rewarded him with respect and more responsibility. At fifty-four, white haired and weathered, he still could sit ramrod-straight in his saddle under his broad ranger's hat, a picture of strength and stability.

"Got it mopped up good?"

"Haven't seen a sleeper for hours. We worked it hard down to the mineral layer." Alford rubbed his hands through his hair. He was tired and dirty and his clothes smelled of smoke. "Hanson and Peters are going to stay on an extra day."

"Know what started it?"

"Looks like some citizen from the city. Didn't make a firepit." He took a bite of his sandwich. "Heard the superintendent of the schools was going to talk about that in the city schools. Wouldn't hurt. Two years ago, I counted five motorcars all summer. This year, I've seen that many in three days. Times are changing. Fast."

"You're not referring to citified, unschooled yahoos coming out here to take on the woods, by any chance?"

"Maybe." Alford grinned. "Guess I better ask Caroline to get that hiking club of hers to reorder their handbook for your visitor's hut. Maybe city folks should attend one of their hiking lectures before coming out. By the way, did you get the order for nails for the fence up at the falls?"

Vernell nodded that he did. He looked thoughtful as he sipped his coffee.

"Speaking of yahoos," the older man began, "the donkey engine is scheduled for delivery tomorrow. It'll be brought by freight train from Skagit. That'll mean that Ford and Symington aren't far behind. Your mind easy about that?"

Alford shrugged and expressed concern about the graves and smokehouse.

"I wasn't talking about the graves. There's still time to deal with that. I was talking about Symington. His agent checked into the Hotel today. It was our old friend J. J. Jenkins."

Alford shot a glance to Micah who was adjusting some gear on one of his horses.

"Oh, he knows, but I told him to be polite about it. How about you?"

"I'll be polite as long as he stays away from my family."

"I don't think there'll be any problem. It's no secret about Caroline's relationship to Harold Symington, but as far as we're concerned, you're both one of our own. I think folks will make sure things stay civil."

"I'm honestly not sure why it's taken him so long to come here."

"I suspect," said Vernell in a piqued voice, "that it's been the business climate in the last few years. Things are beginning to pick up and unemployment is down in the woods. Even more, it wasn't until now that things have become pretty heady for the logging and shingle owners, particularly since the end of this legislature year. They got just about what they wanted. With Uncle Sam in a cooperative mood because of the war in Europe, the labor strife will have to end." He paused. "The trees here will be for the taking."

Chapter 35

The morning after Alford took off for the fire, Caroline and her dearest friends — Cathy, Ellie and Berta — gathered with Emily for a hike to Frazier Falls. At first, they planned the outing as a casual affair, but soon other ladies asked and a large party was formed. Emily Harms was no stranger to many of them, having come to the area not only as a guest of Caroline, but as an important member of the hiking club out of Seattle. Her support for a national park here was well known and appreciated. As it turned out, it was a splendid trip for a beautiful July day.

"You mustn't exert yourself," scolded Caroline, worried about her friend's past problems with pregnancy. She then remembered that Emily was more fit than most women of their time because she was an avid hiker and outdoors woman. In the past eight years she had climbed Glacier Peak once and Mount Rainer twice.

What a gorgeous day, Caroline thought. Her heart burst with joy for the chance to be out tramping on a summer day in the North Cascades. She loved her mountains and woods today. They seemed alive from the majesty of the cedars and firs to the tiny twitterings of winter wrens, hidden in the underbrush of salmonberry that guided them along the way. Here and there came the sounds of the creek, its voice an ache of longing. A raven glided through the trees ahead of the party. When Caroline stepped on the dry, dusty maple leaves and cedar twigs scattered across the trail, she felt like she was on an ancient bridal path, leading the way to —

My home.

The women all wore rucksacks and hobnailed boots fit for walking, while Cathy Bladstad's oldest son, thirteen-year-old Peter, rode a pony that held saddlebags of extra food and a bare-legged Cory Alford holding on behind him.

It wasn't a far walk, but encumbered by gossip and story, they took their time going up, sometimes laughing and sometimes singing as they went. For Emily and Caroline, it recalled their first hike ever, a giddy adventure into the unknown, only this time it was Emily who was taking the chance. Somewhere along the trail, the friends linked arms and talked as sisters do.

Below the falls, the sound of the water's rush came to them as it passed below them in a canyon to their right. The trail narrowed here, bound by little hemlocks and cedars that clung precariously to the rocks that lined it.

"You take care with the pony, Peter Bladstad," Berta said as the boys went by.

"It's so beautiful, Caroline," Emily said. "I almost forgot. It's been a couple of years, I think, since I was up here. There's that ledge, though. I hope they put up a fence."

"Bob did. A couple of times. That's why I didn't bring Kate. Oh, she's quite careful, but I thought that this would be too exciting for her. I didn't want to have to watch a four year old."

"Is the cabin still there?"

"Absolutely. We've even fixed it up. Micah only uses it for wintering and curing skins. For summer, it's a good getaway and jumping off spot for some of the newer trails to the top of the mountains."

"But not solely a place for contemplation," teased Cathy as she came up behind them.

Caroline blushed. She and Bob had used it as a getaway place, which was rare.

The trail suddenly widened out and they could see the long slope before them. Considerably more open, the trees stood further back on the hill to the left. Cathy came alongside, her felt ranger hat settled on her dark hair like the most rakish cowgirl.

"Oopf. I'm getting a little out of practice. Or perhaps, it's a refusal to believe I'm practically a matron— heaven forbid!" She waved her hands at her sons rushing on ahead of her, her slim wrists peeking out of her light cotton waist shirt. Dick, the ten year old, waved back as he ran alongside his brother's pony. He was still young enough to want his mother's approval.

Caroline laughed at Cathy Bladstad's remark. At thirty-five, Cathy could hardly be matronly. While chasing after semi-wild boys and a girl could wear a body down, Cathy was fit. She was interested in the family limitation movement and in improving education and workingwomen's conditions at the cannery in the county seat. She was still very much active in the outdoors and often accompanied Charlie and the children on weekend trips to the lakes to fish and camp.

"I will be an example for my daughter," she once said. Marianne was now eight years old and the mirror image of her mother's looks and spirit. Cathy caught Caroline's bemused expression and laughed back.

"Just a moment of weakness, Carrie," she beamed, then moved on ahead. Not long after that, the party saw the old cabin. Pushing themselves a little further, the women arrived at the porch in a heap of rucksacks and baskets.

After giving important rules about the falls to the children, they opened the cabin and took their gear in. Spreading a tablecloth on a small round table in the center of the room, they removed food from rucksacks and set it on the table with bottles of lemonade and tea. Then the women adjourned to the outside where they spread blankets on the hill above the trail.

The afternoon sun threaded its way down through the trees where it laid down large patches of light on the bed of leaves and needles. The women gathered in small groups and visited, glad for this chance to be together.

In front of them, the falls writhed and roared as water poured over the long drop to the pools below. It was an impressive waterfall and one the locals respected. It was possible to walk down closer to it, but the falls had a curious and dangerous approach to a ledge that couldn't be easily seen from the hill. The safest way to come near it was to go to the right where a fence closed off the ledge. To go to the left was to step off into oblivion which some careless soul did once every year or so.

Caroline was glad warning signs had been posted recently on the trees on the slope above it, but there was always some fool who didn't pay attention or ignored signs and climbed over the fence. Since the waterfall wasn't in the national forest, the townsfolk were the ones that fretted over it, equally cursing its dangers and praising its beauty as a fledgling, designated tourist spot.

"What a lovely day," Emily said as she leaned back on her hands as they sat on their blanket. "I'm so glad I could come."

"And so am I," Caroline said. Cathy nodded in agreement. "You've been a ghost this last year."

"Oh, David's been so busy these days and has needed my support. The campus has been a boiling pot of agitation and intrigue lately." She brushed her long khaki skirt. "I'm afraid our progressive days are over. There's such an outcry against change and suspicion of any criticism about business or war preparations. There's quite a push for military preparedness in the Seattle public schools now, though I personally don't know any who'd want to get involved in Europe. David's hated to see it on campus."

"The young men will do it anyway," Cathy said.

"Somehow it's more noble to get your head shot off, than it is to fight for an eight hour day. Far worse to be branded an unpatriotic coward, than a socialist. I fear the day when socialist means traitor." She paused and looked at Caroline. "Do you think your brother Samuel will go? I read that almost fifty boys in one of our county's farming communities wanted to organize. They were quite inspired by Teddy Roosevelt's speeches about being ready."

"I'm not sure. If there should be a draft, God forbid, he would be old enough. He just turned eighteen." The thought made her shiver.

Cathy looked up past the trail to where her sons were playing. "I hope that day never comes. What a waste."

"Oh, let's not get so glum, ladies," Emily said. "There's so much to look forward to." She held her hand lightly on her stomach and smiled at Caroline. When the Bladstad boys roared up into the trees behind the cabin in pursuit of Cory and Karl Olsen, she laughed.

Caroline smiled wistfully. She knew this was what her friend desired most and what she wanted to give David who had been a loving husband and companion for so long.

"You sure you could handle that collection of manhood?" Berta asked.

"Oh, yes. I could die, I'm so happy." Suddenly, Emily shot up. "Oh, dear. Maybe we should eat. My tummy's just taken a spin."

They served lunch at noon and each person took tin plate and cup outside. Cathy and Caroline sat on the porch with Emily, assembling themselves around her feet. Assured that there were no listening underage ears, they talked freely of the politics of home and community and of the latest fashions, including undergarments.

"Did you see that Bien Jolie brassiere in the magazines and papers?" Caroline asked. "Guarantees a good figure."

"Well, it's infinitely better than a corset!" Cathy snorted.

For the friends, one could almost believe that since the woman of Washington State had the vote, freedom of a more personal nature was soon to come. Heads leaned in and this promise assured immediate action.

The afternoon unspooled around them. After finishing their meal, the friends sat back and talked. The outing would have ended peacefully that way, if a sudden shriek had not sent the women rushing desperately in the direction of the falls. Above the stream that rushed toward the drop, they could hear the sound of thrashing, and fearing the worse, each mother sought their own.

Cathy got to the water first. "Peter and Richard Bladstad!" There in the eddying stream her half-grown sons splashed, throwing water at each other with tin cans. Like an angry sow bear, she scrambled over the rocky bank and grabbed them by the ears, pulled them out.

"You're gonna wish you'd died. Don't you ever do that again! You scared us half to death. Someone surely passed on at the first cry. How could you?"

She tugged them up to the trail before she released them to the throng of worried women. The ladies looked scared, the talk of war so frequent now that even these younger specimens of manhood were in mortal danger. But the falls were worse, always the secret nightmare of many a mother that the falls or river would take one of theirs. Cathy squeezed out her knickerbockers. "Now where are Karl and Cory?"

"They're here," Berta announced. The ladies parted to let her son and Cory come down and join the other boys.

"Thank the Lord," Cathy said to Peter and Richard. "Now get on down and clean up the rubbish. There's a potato sack in the cabin." She shooed all the children down, making sure some sentries went along. When she was alone with Emily and Caroline, Cathy sighed. "I love this place, but sometimes it seems haunted. It wouldn't be the first time someone screamed and went over the falls."

"Charlie was on one of the first rescues, wasn't he?" Caroline asked.

"It was hardly a rescue, just a cleanup party. Nor was it

the first. Some say the first one was a woman. Way back in the late 1880s. Micah's Thompson's girl, Hattie Coleman."

Caroline stared at Cathy in shock. A chill went down her arms.

"She was a pretty thing, so they say. The daughter of a homesteader, but she couldn't have Micah because of his mixed blood. Her parents said 'No, never,' so she threw herself over the falls. Some say that's why he built a cabin here. Because of Hattie."

"I never heard that story," Caroline said in voice barely loud enough to be heard over the roaring falls. "Not even from him."

"Few have. Whether it's true or not, I don't know. Micah won't talk about it. Hattie Coleman may not be a real person." Cathy said. "Mary and Jack Vernell might know. Jack's known him since the mid-1880s." She put her arm through Caroline's and gave her hand a squeeze. "Some people find Micah hard to read, so they make up stories about him because they don't understand him. There's the Hattie Coleman story and then there are the stories about how he got in trouble with someone over claim jumping."

"I never heard that story. What was that about?" Caroline asked. Micah meant the world to her.

"Someone tried to cheat Micah's father's out of one of his claims back in 1890. Micah beat the man to death.

Caroline gasped. "Is it true?"

"No. That I do know. But he did give the fellow a thrashing. The man didn't like that one bit. Made a lot of trouble for Angus Thompson, Micah's father. May have led to his early death." Cathy looked at the water rushing to its drop. She patted Caroline's arm.

"Still, the Hattie story makes me sad for Micah, for he has always been a good friend to me and my Charlie." Cathy moved away and laughed softly. "My, you must forgive me for being so morbid. The falls sometimes have that spell over a person but I'm afraid I got quite a scare. I thought it was Peter gone over when he screamed."

Caroline still felt unnerved about Hattie and Micah. *She* had eloped to escape the Can Nots of the world. She wondered if Micah and Hattie had tried to elope. True or not, the image of the young woman going over the falls made her ill.

"Caroline, you're so white," Berta said. "You've taken a legend much to heart."

"Maybe it's the war talk and the unrest in the mills and woods that makes us all unnerved," interjected Emily. "I can feel it. Something's coming. Why don't we go back down now before this lovely day is spoiled?" Without a protest, the women agreed to leave.

It was quiet at the hotel when Caroline came to collect Kate and eight year old Marianne Bladstad. She visited briefly with the new proprietress, Mrs. Jordan from Langley, British Columbia. She had no recent news about the fire, but she told Caroline she thought they had it under control. The amount of smoke drifting down to the ranger station had diminished and changed color.

"Mary Vernell said Jack went up to check and he hadn't left in a cloud of dust to get there, so it mustn't be bad."

Caroline thanked her for watching the girls and promised to bring her some pies for their dining room. Gathering up Kate's belongings, she took her daughter by the hand and walked out to the hotel veranda. Cathy was in front, putting things into her automobile, including her boys and daughter. Cory was already in, showing off a popgun he'd made of an elderberry branch to Emily. Cathy beckoned to the empty seat in the front for Caroline and little Kate.

"Just put your things in the back," she said, then went to the front to crank up the motor.

Kate skipped down and joined the other children in the motorcar. Caroline juggled her things, dropping her hat on the steps. Someone behind her reached down and retrieved it.

"Here you go, Miss."

Caroline turned to thank her helper, then froze. Blood

drained from her face.

It was J. J. Jenkins.

He'd grown thicker over the years, but his drooping mustache and slick hair were as dark as ever. He wore a black pin-striped suit and looked like the businessman she knew he wasn't. A gold watch chain hung out of the fob pocket and the hand that touched it was manicured. His dark eyes looked straight at her, studying her for a moment in a too familiar way that made her feel naked and vulnerable, then he blinked.

She took the hat and thanked him, not wanting to give her feelings away. He nodded at her, then down at the Bladstad automobile now chugging and popping noisily. Kate bounced up and down on the seat next to Emily.

"The years have been gentle on you, Miss Syming — excuse me, Mrs. Alford," he said tipping his derby. "I didn't mean to be rude. Your uncle would be pleased. He always said that his brother's girls were the prettiest and I would agree. You are an exceptionally fine looking woman. Shall I tell him that I saw you?"

The hair at the back of her neck rose. Caroline struggled to keep her fear from consuming her. "Is he here?" Her eyes darted around looking for him.

"No. He's in Seattle. Important conference meeting. Employers' Association." Jenkins nodded his head at the automobile. "Is that your little girl? The redhead?"

Something inside Caroline sparked and surged. Courage came into her voice. "That is none of your affair. Good day."

She walked down to the motorcar, not daring to look back. Cathy seemed to understand Caroline's terror. "Carrie. Oh, dear. Carrie."

"Hmm?" Caroline's voice squeaked.

"You look like you've seen a ghost."

"She has," Emily said from the back. "Please get us out of here." As soon as Caroline was seated in front, Cathy put the car in gear and pulled out onto the main street.

"Who on earth was that *awful* man?" Cathy asked.

"J. J. Jenkins, my uncle's agent for security." Caroline shivered. She put a hand on the dashboard and braced herself. It had been years, but seeing the man triggered a long suppressed memory of the attack at the inn on her wedding night. It made her feel dirty and cheap.

Come along, miss.

Caroline recalled how Jenkins had been so sure of himself as he came into their room at the inn and yanked her away from Bob. How he covered her up with his coat. The nightgown had been light and delicate, not for his eyes. Barefooted, she'd been pushed out into the hallway, while behind her she could hear furniture breaking as Bob struggled, then groaned as blows rained down on him. She was to the stairs in seconds, marshaled between two unshaven men of dubious livelihood. When she fought back, Jenkins had one of the men pick her up and carry her down to the front door like a load of laundry. The last thing she remembered was being put screaming into a closed carriage and the door shut with him and two men inside. As they pulled away, she sought a view of their room, but all she could see were wildly swinging shadows on the lace curtains and then the lights went out.

The car gathered speed, lolling across the deep ruts in the graveled road, putting the distance between Caroline and Jenkins as quickly as possible. Everyone held onto something as Cathy charged down the wooded roadway.

At the house, there was no relief. While the older boys, Peter and Dick, kept the Alford children occupied upstairs, the women tried to get Caroline calmed down, but to no avail. Around the kitchen she paced until finally Cathy couldn't stand it anymore and went to the phone and made a call. Eventually, she came back.

"Bob will be in tomorrow. They're done mopping up, but Mary says Jack called and they went out to look at someone cutting trees in the forest. No permit. Should be back by three. I told her you'd like to see him pronto. She'll relay the message when Jack calls again."

"Thanks," murmured Caroline. She stopped pacing and hugging her arms, went to the window.

"Can we go home, Mother?" A dejected Peter stood at the kitchen door. "We're hungry."

"Yes, you can, Peter," Caroline said. "It's all right, Cathy. We'll manage. Don't let the boys starve on the count of me."

"I'd get Charlie to come, but there's a shinglemen's meeting he's got to go to."

"We'll manage." Opening her arms, Caroline gave her friend a hug and wished her good evening. To make her point, she herded everyone down the hall and outside. The Bladstad kids climbed into the back of the car. The ritual of starting the automobile commenced again and soon they were off in a lurch. Caroline waved and watched them drive off and the forest swallow them up.

They were gone only a few heartbeats, when suddenly, they appeared to have turned around and come back. It took a second glance to see that it was someone else. To Caroline's surprise, it was Billy Howell. She had never been so happy to see him.

"Billy!" she cried, practically running into his automobile on the dirt road.

"Well, ain't this a nice greeting. Evening, Caroline. Bob about?"

"No. He's out fighting a fire." Caroline said. She rubbed her arms to get the trembling under control again.

Billy frowned. "Drat. I really wanted to see him." He peered at her. "You okay?"

"Can you stay?" she asked, hoping that he could.

"Sure, I wasn't planning going back to Twin Forks until tomorrow. That road between us is dark and difficult even in daylight. My missus won't mind anyway. We counted on me putting my head somewhere. You don't mind?" he asked.

"Oh, please do stay. I — the kids will want to see their

Uncle Billy. It's been a month."

Billy scratched his weathered cheek. "All right. Let me park this thing."

Billy Howell hadn't changed much over the years. He was still lanky and looked like he was in a constant state of disarray, yet he was an honest, hardworking man. He was a family man too, having married a local girl the same summer as David and Emily married. They had four children including twin girls and some acreage near Twin Forks.

He made his living as a shingle weaver, working around at the many mills in the valley. It was hard work and fairly steady despite labor unrest or the occasional strike that shut that industry down all over the state. He could make shakes better than anyone and as long as there were the massive cedar bolts from which to make them, there was work.

Caroline was very fond of him. He was as loyal to her as he was to her husband, even when she knew he sometimes suffered from her uncle's policies and practices. Harold Symington and the Employers' Association had little tolerance for the workingman's reforms.

"Now," announced Billy after securing his automobile like he was tying up a horse at the post. "What's up? You're as skitterish as a young filly. Bob OK fighting that fire?"

"It's out, Caroline answered. "It's — I saw J. J. Jenkins. Up here at the Frazier Hotel."

"Do tell." Billy reached for his duffel bag. "Funny. That's why I wanted to see Bob." He put his corduroy jacket over his arm and followed her into the house, wiping his feet before he went in. The screen door whined behind them.

Emily was in the kitchen washing vegetables. She wiped her hands to greet Howell and offered him some coffee. They'd met some years before and were acquaintances.

Billy visited with Emily, nursing his coffee as he sat. Once Caroline was upstairs helping the children take a bath before dinner, he asked what had happened with Jenkins. When she told about Caroline's encounter, Howell shook his head.

"Jenkins has been in and out of Twin Forks for years. I've seen him numerous times out with company timber cruisers or in the mills. Symington, I'm pretty sure, has had a fair amount of interest in the B & E Lumber Mill. There's been a lot of labor unrest over the years, but while the other outfits did get an occasional concession, the labor leaders at the B & E always got canned. What I think now is that there's gonna be a change of things in this county. The shinglemen have joined the West Coast Association. They'll want to be putting a halt on any reforms. And I think they'll get help. The Federal Government's going to want complete loyalty with the threat of war."

"But we aren't at war."

"Aren't doesn't mean won't be. It's a matter of time. With the U-boat attacks, people are getting stirred up. Besides, there's money at stake here. Millions. The government'll want to build ships and airplanes on the west coast because they're way across country from the U-boats. And we got trees. The lumber men will fall all over themselves to get the contracts."

"Caroline said there was going to be a delivery of a donkey engine today to Frazier." Emily began chopping up a carrot, her knife banging down on the cutting board for emphasis.

"There surely is. I saw it loaded on a train this morning in Twin Forks. They plan to cut right across the river."

"Will they cut in the national forest? Bob says there might be more permits than in the past."

"Possibly."

Emily turned around. "I'm glad you came by. Cathy Bladstad and I didn't know what to do. Caroline's afraid that Jenkins will come down here while Bob's away."

"You ever meet Jenkins at any family gatherings? I mean, your husband being related to the Symingtons."

"I've seen him. David and I have been invited to the Symington mansion in Seattle on several occasions. Often Jenkins was there off to the side, talking to Harold

280

Symington."

"Well, Caroline needn't worry. I'll stay the night. Sleep in the living room with a shotgun if I have to." Billy got up.

"I can't imagine Harold Symington hurting Caroline," Emily said. "He's not that callused. There was a time when he had great affection for her. David told me so."

"That's probably true. Jenkins is different, though. You see, I *do* know him. He's ruthless and immoral. He not only orchestrated Caroline's return after her elopement, he's been involved in attacks on labor in the camps east of Seattle and this county as well. I know for a fact at least one man died as a result of his efforts and several have been permanently disabled. He has often acted on his own, free of any constraints."

"I know about the elopement," Emily said softly as she put the last carrot onto the cutting board. "Just horrible. Jenkins came very close to killing Bob. Probably would have if Caroline hadn't been there. So David says." She sighed. "Sometimes I just wonder about people and how their souls get to be so rotten. You wonder what they all gain in the end. My father has answers for that, but I can only puzzle over it."

"That's because you're a nice lady, Emily, and find it hard to accept. Someone like me now, I don't have much. Haven't had much education, but I seen the human soul all right and there's nothing to puzzle. Some folks are born plain nasty. Look, when you're done with that carrot, why don't you show me where Caroline keeps her pillows."

Billy spent the night on the couch. He was at the house when Alford got home at noon. They shared a beer in the kitchen, then went outside to talk by the river's edge. They were gone a long time and the women could see that their conversation was animated. When they came back in, Billy picked up his gear and said he had to get back.

"It's been nice seeing you ladies."

"But the couch," Caroline said. "You deserved

something better."

He gave her a kiss on the cheek. "Any place around here is heaven." He shook Alford's hand again, then nodding to Emily, went out to his motorcar.

Alford said good-bye at the door and came back in. Cory and Kate tagged along behind him into the kitchen. Alford picked his little daughter up and fed her a piece of apple while Caroline rolled out pie dough. Across the river, it looked quiet, but she wondered for how long. The donkey engine was at the station.

"Will you be okay if I go fishing with Cory? Thought I'd go downstream a little ways. Got some new spoons at the general store. I need to unwind before dinner."

"Well, Emily's here, though we might dress up and go into Frazier to meet David at the train. You'll be close?"

"I'll be close by." He gave her a peck on the cheek. "I expect a pie."

"All right, a pie, you'll have. We expect fish for supper."

"Does a Mountie get his man?" he grinned.

The women finished up earlier than expected and had some time to drink a glass of lemonade before changing their clothes. They were both tense, sensing that something was happening they weren't aware of, because of all the time Billy and Alford spent together. They tried to change their moods by putting on their best white dresses and hose, promising themselves a ride to Frazier in the Forest Service truck. Caroline had just learned to drive and she thought it better than a horse and wagon as long as she didn't get stuck. Once she had Kate in a dress, they prepared to go.

Out in the back, the chickens were making a fuss so Caroline suggested that Emily go on out with Kate. Walking down the hall to the kitchen, she heard the screen door creak in the front, then the sound of Emily talking to someone. Kate, she presumed.

She went out the back and over to the cedar trees on the left side of the house where the chicken coop was set. All of her hens, Precious, Sweet Pea and Chloe, were there busily pecking at the sunlit ground. There were no signs of being chased, but something appeared to have passed through them. She looked to the water and hearing voices, walked down to the river's stony edge. If it was Bob and Cory, they were back early. And if they were fishing, it was only to instruct, for there was a better hole a hundred yards downstream.

She came around the alder and vine maple growing under the shadow of the giant cedars upstream from the house and stopped. Two men dressed in high boots and suits of forestry cloth were standing next to the water, engaged in a pointed discussion about something across the water. They were, she thought, total strangers until the larger man turned and stared at her. Like a cat caught at playing with a little bird, he made an absurd attempt to recover his surprise before blurting out jovially, "Good afternoon, sister. You're looking quite fine these days. It's a pleasure to see you again."

James Ford. *What are you doing here?* Caroline came down to the water's edge, careful not to put her white pumps into the muddy gravel. She mustered all the courage and indignation she had. She wasn't pleased to see James Ford.

"What are you doing here?" she said in her strongest voice.

He cocked his head at her. Ford was still a handsome man, but he had put on considerable weight just as Bob had said. It made his once classic features coarse and unrefined. The hint of carelessness about his person belied his expensive outing clothes. Caroline suspected some hidden secret kept under wraps from the public eye. Still, she couldn't ignore his sheer physical presence nor the fact he was from a privileged class. *What was she now?* A simple housewife married to a forest ranger.

"Don't you recognize me, Miss Caroline? Surely the years haven't been so hard on me."

"I know you, James Ford. I'm just surprised to see you

here, disturbing my chickens and staking claims on my river."

"Yours?" He beckoned for the other man to go on up. He was a younger man, a wiry, clerkish-looking fellow with a hairline receding faster than he desired by the way he played with it with his comb. One of the strands of hair was at least ten inches long from another part of his scalp.

"Be up in a moment, Piles," Ford said as the man went up past her and off to the front through the cedar trees.

When Piles was gone, Ford turned back. "I'm sorry that your sister's divorce from me has put a strain between us. So unfortunate when I admire you so much. You're much stronger, Caroline Symington, than poor Sophie and indeed, much finer. *Kla-how-ya* lost its grace when you so abruptly left." He came up closer, causing Caroline's hair to rise at the nape of her neck. "You are definitely more beautiful …in…every…way."

He stopped and gave her a dramatic once-over that made her feel small and vulnerable. "I've always wondered about you up here. Pity, all the years wasted. You're much too refined a woman to be wasting away in such a backwater. What on earth do people do up here in Frazier anyway? Breed trees?"

Caroline flushed, but a rising anger gave her courage. "Stop it. I'm Caroline Alford, not Symington. And when did you become so crude, James Ford? I want you to leave right this instant."

"But I can't. Business. My crews will be arriving tomorrow to commence logging. I'm afraid that I'll be here quite often from now on. I'm looking for a ford to use to get my equipment across." He smiled crookedly at her and again she felt his eyes.

"Does my uncle have the permit?"

"Actually, no. He had second thoughts, but allowed me to proceed." He came up to her and she could smell a sickening mix of cigar and alcohol on his breath. "I have it."

He smiled knowingly again. "Isn't it grand? Now I'm

going to have the pleasure of seeing you every day. Watching you hang up the clothes, feed the chickens, settle down for the night. My — just a pure pleasure." His eyes lit up wickedly as he took her hand like a gallant and kissed it. He pulled her toward him, rubbing the back of her hand with his thumb.

"Let me go at once," Caroline demanded, fear rising in her voice.

"I'll let you go, but first—" he whispered softly, "let me say how happy it makes me to see you again, sister." He pulled her tight against him and kissed her lightly on the forehead. Disgusted, she wrenched away, but he twisted her hand, so she had to come back and stay pinned against him.

"There. That's better," he breathed hotly. "I just want to talk to you."

"Let me go. I won't say a word." Caroline felt like her heart was in her throat. "Just give me some room." *Stay calm. Wait for the right moment.*

Ford eased back from her. "Now that's sensible. We wouldn't want to provoke Mr. Alford, now would we —?"

Before Ford could pull her back in, Caroline stabbed the little heel of her shoe into Ford's shin and dug it in. He howled and lost his grip on her, making her fall against the dirt bank. She was never so glad to be free of him.

"You bitch!" He reached out for her, but Caroline rolled away. "You little prude." he said.

"Stop it right there, Mister!" a voice boomed.

As big as a cedar tree trunk and as earthy, Micah stepped out, his shotgun aimed right at Ford's head. Ford quickly stepped back.

"By God, you help her up or I'll plug you right where you are." Micah motioned with the gun as he walked down. "Then you scat. You come around here again and I'll kill you."

"I'm James Ford. How dare you talk to me like this! I can have you arrested."

"I don't *care* who you are. Don't mean a damn thing up

285

here. Molesting a woman. I'll blow your head off."

Begrudgingly, Ford helped her up, but as soon as she was upright, she hastened to Micah.

"I'll be back," Ford protested. "You can't keep me away from my claim."

"Maybe. But the spirits will. You cut around them graves, you'll answer to another world." Micah offered his hand to Caroline who grabbed it like a lifeline. It was hard not to tremble. He helped her over the bank and up onto the grass. Her soft white dress was only stained on the back with dirt, but she felt dirty all over.

"You go on inside, Miz Caroline and settle yourself. I'll take care of this gnat." Micah's face was fierce and dark with disgust. The braided cedar band moved as his neck throbbed with anger.

She turned back to look at Ford. She wanted to cry, but she maintained her dignity and walked to the house with her head held high. Inside, she turned back to watch, trembling.

Micah waggled the shotgun. "I saw what you did to her. I heard the talk. You're in big trouble, mister."

"You misunderstood. Caroline's my former sister-in-law. It was merely an affectionate welcome. I've the deepest respect for her. Besides, we're neighbors," he said moving a little bit away. "My claim's over there. It's legal. I got a logging permit."

"I bet it's legal." Micah motioned for him to come up. "Ranger Vernell's the law officer around these parts. If you want to talk to the sheriff about this, you'll have to go to the city, but don't look for sympathy. You might have the shinglemen in your pocket, but they're a conservative bunch when it comes to women."

"You're awfully mighty for your breeding," Ford sneered.

"Leastways I got some. Don't see much on your end. Fancy clothes don't cut it here."

Caroline thought Ford looked like he choked on Micah's words, but he was such a fool and continued to act the superior. "Where do you live?"

"Where I can put my head. No place you can reach. But I'll sure know where *you are*," Micah laughed.

Ford's courage folded like a jackknife with a worn blade. "Can I go?"

"Git." Micah backed off, stepping back toward the cedar trees. He began to blend in under the cool flowing branches. "Don't come back here. Ever. If you touch her again, I'll kill you."

On that note, Caroline retreated into the kitchen and remembering Emily and the children on the porch, rushed down the hall in time to see Ford coming around to the front, brushing off his pants. When Emily saw him, she gasped and came into the house with Kate.

"What on earth?" she said to Caroline shaking at the door. "I was wondering who was parked out in front."

"James Ford. And that man with him he called Piles." Caroline shivered. She'd heard that name before. *The inn.* She watched Ford walk through the row of rhododendron bushes way past their blooming season and out the gate toward a truck and driver on the other side of the road. And directly into Bob standing with a fishing pole and a string of fish in his hands. Cory stood next to him.

Caroline stiffened, but Emily put a hand on her arm. Caroline took her friend's hand and clenched it.

"What the hell are you doing here?" Alford bellowed. He was so curt that Cory fled to the house where he watched in safety from the porch.

"Alford. What a surprise," Ford said. "I came to investigate a possible crossing for my equipment. We begin logging next week. As a matter of fact, I've opened an employment office here in town just for that purpose."

"The rumor of your advance was apparently true. You with Symington? Or are you on your own with Jenkins?"

"My business arrangements are none of your concern."

"Point well taken," Alford said noticing Caroline at the screen door for the first time. "If you want a crossing, look upstream. If you want to go hunting, it's out of season until

October 1st. Fishing licenses are at the store. If you need to file a claim with the ranger, that's *my* business." He came past Ford, shifting his pole in his hands. "Good evening. Next time take the trail north of the cedars." With that, he gave Ford no more attention than he did the slug squashed under his boot.

That night, Ford's truck tires were vandalized, David arrived late on the train and Alford had a pale, withdrawn Caroline on his hands. Though she had pleaded with him not to fuss over her, saying that nothing had happened with Ford, not even Harms's cooler head could keep him from wanting to storm Ford's hotel room and beat the hell out of him. Rising before daybreak, Alford saddled up one of his horses and rode into Frazier. At the outskirts of the settlement he came upon Jack Vernell in the pre-dawn light, driving his truck.

"Was wondering when I'd see you," the ranger commented. "Why don't you follow me to Dyson's and get a cup of coffee? You look like you were up all night."

"I have company."

"So I heard, but not the ones you're thinking about. Heard Ford paid a visit."

"How'd you know that?"

"Micah."

Alford scowled. *How did he know?*

Dyson's Saloon opened early for breakfast. Once they were seated, Vernell told him what Micah had said.

"Caroline never said Micah was there." Alford gripped the handle of the ceramic cup until his fingers hurt.

"I can understand why. Micah said she was scared. I'd say she was thinking more of you by not talking just so you wouldn't go get all riled up like you are right now and do something stupid." Vernell smoothed his mustache and continued.

"Ford's no fool, Bob. He's gone over the line and he knows it. But if you call him out, he has the power to get back at you in subtle, even dangerous ways. You're going to have to let it lie, Bob, let it go its course and have faith that in good enough time, the community's going to freeze him out for making an improper advance to a respected woman in the district. They won't trust him and that'll hurt. He needs local men to keep costs down, but I bet he'll have to get outside labor."

Alford made a face. He had intended to confront Ford on his own, not just let it go.

"It'll work, believe me," Vernell said. "In fact, it's probably working right now. Tell me, where were you last night?"

"What makes you ask that? Try entertaining company while calming Caroline."

"Just wondered. Someone sliced up Ford's tires."

"Wasn't me," Alford said, but he had an idea to where Micah had been last night.

Alford came back to the house in time to eat breakfast with his family and their guests. Caroline gave him a worried look when he came in, watching him anxiously from the kitchen door.

"I didn't murder anyone," he reassured her. "You OK?"

"I'm fine, Bob. Truly."

"Then nothing else'll be said." He came through the hall and took her into his arms. He rocked her for a moment and he felt her tension go away. Then he gave her a kiss. "Since you and others wish it, then I'll let it lie."

Later, after breakfast, Harms told Alford he thought Vernell was right. "Let Ford trip himself up." David chewed his lip. "Of course, I could help things along."

"How's that?"

"I could write to my uncle Charles Symington."

"I appreciate that, Harms, but what would writing to Caroline's father do?" They were standing out in the meadow across from the house where the cow had wandered. Alford wanted her back in her pasture before she got out in the thick trees.

"Get his attention. Despite *their* differences, my Uncle Charles still has a say in his brother's business. He can put pressure on him concerning associates, meaning Ford who is still a partner in the Symington company despite the divorce. He won't like Ford's impertinence one bit. And I don't think Uncle Harold would approve of Ford's actions either. He'd agree Ford's gone too far."

"If Charles Syminton's going to be so all fired up to get involved, then why doesn't he take Caroline back?" Alford grumbled.

Harms shrugged. "Pride. Too much pride, I admit, but I haven't given up. Someday there'll be a reconciliation. For everyone."

Alford took the cow's bridle and after clipping on a rope, led her back to the road. The grass was wet with morning dew and signs that the weather might change for once. They needed the rain. David walked along quietly beside him. At the road, they stopped. Up a ways, Cory was attempting to ride a bicycle while Kate skipped along beside him.

"Have some news," David said, clearing his throat. "We're going to have a little one come late winter. Emily says she feels fine. That ever scare you?"

"I was scared the second time because of the miscarriage, but Caroline came through fine with Cory. Kate's birth was even easier. I could have parked the truck and poured myself a cup of coffee and she was born." They watched her hop around in the road, her dress catching the dust on its hem. Alford laughed. "I'm not sure how we ordered that one because she's going to be a beauty *and* a timber beast. I swear Cathy Bladstad switched babies on us, but I'm glad I've got a girl. Girls are fine."

David swallowed. "I agree. I'm married to one of the finest."

That day, Ford opened up his employment office, but by evening no one showed up. When a cruiser went down across the river to look at the forest around the Indian smokehouse, something spooked his horse and he had to struggle back on his own through the dense undergrowth of forest.

Calm was restored to the Alford household over the weekend, although privately Alford's anger toward Ford continued to smolder. Symington's protégé's advances toward Caroline had brought up old wounds from the night Alford had gone to *Kla-how-ya* to see Caroline's father and instead found Harold Symington and James Ford. He had long since forgiven Sophie for her role in undercutting his legitimate bid for her sister's hand. He hadn't forgiven Ford's pompous threats toward him. Now there was a new mark against the bastard. Alford wasn't so sure if he should have let Vernell talk him out of thrashing Ford at the hotel.

David and Emily stayed through Sunday. Having the weekend off, Alford was able to join them for a picnic downriver. There the men could fish and the women visit and watch the children. Charlie Bladstad came by on his way back from the lumber mill he managed and joined them for a time before going on home. He had news of some of the actions of the shinglemen and lumbermen in the county and how that might affect labor conditions in the woods.

"Well, so far," Alford said, "the recent legislation hasn't affected operations in the national forest." He sighed. "But I suppose that by summer's end that will change."

"How's that?" David asked.

"Logging and loyalty will soon go hand in hand since there are profits to be made from the widening war in Europe. Being federal lands, the Frazier District will be the rule, not the exception."

When Charlie asked about news of the new logging operation, Alford could only glower. He expected Charlie to chuckle at his ideals. He noticed that Harms stayed quiet, keeping his thoughts to himself.

After Charlie left, there were plans for a few more hours of visiting, but George Fuller came by and said he and

Alford were needed to help fight a forest fire that had broken out above Twin Forks. "It's already taken out one farmstead and is threatening a mill. They sent the locomotive and tender to Silvern Lake to get water as the train tracks could be threatened next."

"There might be a delay in the train schedule," Fuller told David and Emily. "The telephone lines were down in another fire near the city fifty miles away. Vernell's sending a group of Frazier citizens and Forest Service employees to help out on this one. Best stay in touch with him."

Alford drove the picnickers back to the house and retrieved clothing and a rucksack for fighting fires. Out on the porch, he kissed Caroline good-bye.

"Honey, tell our guests I enjoyed the company. I'd have them pack. The delay shouldn't be too long." He placed his hands on her still slim waist and gave her a squeeze. "I was looking forward to a night alone with you, but dang it, looks like it'll be a while. Maybe, if there's a chance later on, we can go up to Micah's cabin on our own. We've got an anniversary coming up, if you haven't forgotten."

Caroline said she hadn't.

"I love you, babe," he said. He kissed her more thoroughly, then looked out to where Fuller was waiting. "Not sure when I'm going to get back. According to George, the whole county's on fire and it might take several days to control this one. I'm not sure if I want you and the kids alone. Why don't you have Cathy or Ellie come over, just in case."

At six o'clock in the evening, Caroline got word about the train's arrival time. It would be pulling an extra boxcar for additional men to go help fight the fire and wasn't planning to stay long. Hurriedly, she drove her friends to the station and joined the mass of people waiting for word of the fire.

· This wasn't the way she'd wanted to say good-bye. While they had done it many times before, it somehow felt different this time to part from Emily. Over the last two days, they had often talked of the coming confinement and what Emily could expect, but neither knew what the future would hold nor the depth of the risk. All they knew was that this was the last time Emily could visit for several months, so their parting was bittersweet.

"Good-bye dearest friend," Caroline said, her voice thick. "If I can arrange it, I'll try to come and visit this October. We'll look for a layette and all those proper things. Wouldn't it be lovely if it were Valentine's Day baby?"

"Oh, wouldn't it? I wonder if they make little booties that look like climbing boots."

"If it's a girl, she'll wear pants!" Caroline giggled.

They hugged and then Emily was ready. David helped her up. When she was in the coach, David turned to Caroline.

"Thank you so much. It was a good time. As always, you were the thoughtful hostess."

Caroline curtsied. "My pleasure, but such nice company."

He took her hand, gloved in leather for the wagon. "I'll write as soon as I can."

"And I." She smiled softly at him, guessing at his troubled thoughts. "Don't worry," she said, though she *was* worried.

He nodded and then struggling with his emotions, turned away. Caroline squeezed his arm and willingly he came into her embrace. A shudder went through him.

"Lord, I'm afraid," he whispered, his voice cracking.

Caroline hugged him hard, unwilling to let him go even at the train's insistent whistle.

Alford was gone three days. He returned to Frazier on Wednesday, aching, exhausted and stinking of smoke and sweat. It had been a particularly difficult fire, compounded by dry winds. Several homes had been burned and a couple of thousand acres of forest land destroyed, but no lives lost. At one point, the lumber mill that provided jobs for many families in the area was nearly consumed, but eventually, the forest fire was brought under control and extinguished.

There was a great sense of relief. The train had gone through and the telephone lines restored in a few hours, but little did they realize that this was the beginning of a long, late fire season. Before the summer ended, more communities would be threatened and bridges and homes destroyed. When Alford saw Caroline, he fell into her arms and allowed himself to be led like a lamb to the hot bath waiting for him. Within minutes of the bath, he was sound asleep.

Alford woke up in bed at noon the following day to the sound of axes and trees falling.

"What's going on?" he asked Caroline at the edge of the bed. "Did the Ford logging operation start?"

"Yes, they're cutting a road to the river about a half mile upriver from us."

"What else do you know?"

"The fallers are clearing a path for a skid road. Berta heard that lines were to be set up across the river to guide the logs over the water where they could be handed over to oxen teams waiting for them. From there to the train tracks."

And so it went. The noise seemed incessant and it continued for the next few days. Alford was grateful for an assignment building a shelter in the national forest for Vernell. As it wasn't a difficult trip, Caroline and the children came along too in a wagon and camped with him.

There was no getting away from it, though. As the weeks passed, each day when Alford wasn't off fighting fires, he'd have to drive by the road where the logs were brought out. Each evening as summer faltered and the sun spent less time above the mountains, he would walk down to the river and watch the progress of the logging operation across the water. It didn't make him happy to see it work its way back toward the Robber's Bowl and down toward their homestead. The loss of the trees cut into him like a sharp bellyache.

Sometimes debris would float down and he would pull it in, but mostly he watched for silt and any damage to the riverbed. Then he'd take his pole and go to his favorite fishing spots downstream and contemplate the changing world around him. His fish needed those trees. Leaving one seed tree for every forty acres as was the current practice which made the chance of the big trees coming back spotty. With such low numbers of trees to stabilize slopes, the hills washed out and clouded the streams, choking the fish.

Only on two occasions did he see Ford: once on the road from Twin Forks and another at the Frazier Hotel where Bob heard he was holed up with Jenkins. Both encounters turned bellyache to fits of anger. Sometime later Ford disappeared, leaving Piles behind to oversee the work.

Chapter 36

September came, all bright and mellow with a promise of an early fall. The maples changed, their color hardening to reds and browns, but the weather was sunny and warm. At the start of the second week, the Alfords woke to a momentous occasion: Cory Stein Alford was going off to first grade and would be joining playmates in the Olsen and Turner families for the first time at the grade school. Rising two hours before breakfast, he crawled into his parent's bed fully dressed and ready to go, his lard bucket waiting to be filled with the promised lunch. Bleary-eyed, Alford put Cory between himself and Caroline and together, they snuggled until the alarm went off at six-thirty. Rising with his parents, the young scholar stayed close while his father lathered and shaved, then borrowed the razor when Alford wasn't looking. Going to first grade was a grownup affair.

The month continued in glory with high clouds and blue sky. Many couldn't recall better September weather in years. Fires — reminders of the long dry summer — still burned in an area around Twin Forks in some of the logged off lands. Still, hikers and visitors seeking the last of summer came every weekend to Frazier, filling the hotels and main street to overflowing. Even the Mount Kulshan Hiking Club from the city came out for a fall outing, giving Caroline and Cathy a chance to visit with old friends and go on a hike. Excitement grew over the push for a national park, spurred on by the railroads and automobile clubs' interest. The hiking club led its promotion, extolling the area's scenic virtues as well as its resources. The growth in mining claims exploded during the summer. With the increasing popularity of automobiles, there was a push for roads as well.

For Alford, it was a busy time, a last chance to do repairs on Forest Service buildings and shelters in the backcountry before the winter snows came. Often he was gone for days at a time until the month's end. And then the rains came.

October was windy and cold, the frost coming earlier in years, but Alford continued to work out in the field. Left alone with the children, Caroline kept herself busy with sewing and putting up the last of the fall's harvest by canning. There were letters from Emily and other friends which had to be answered. Then, quite unexpectedly, she received a phone call from her sister Sophie.

"May I come up?" she asked. "I'll be in the Northwest for just a little bit and I'm bringing a surprise."

Sophie arrived midweek in October. Stepping down from the train, she was, as usual, dressed in the latest fashion, not the least bit worse in her life as gay divorcée. Her tight slim skirt was accented by her Robin Hood hat and a fox fur draped over her shoulder so that its glass eyes stared out sightless in no particular direction. Her dark hair was bobbed, a daring style for the day. She gave Caroline a warm embrace, then faced the steps behind her. At the top stood a young man still in his teens. Tall and lanky with short cropped cinnamon brown hair, he looked like —

"Oh, my Lord," breathed Caroline. "Not Sammy?"

The youth grinned at her shyly, nervously fingering the leather haversack on his shoulder. "Do you mind? I mean, coming up here unannounced."

Caroline's eyes began to sting. "Mind? I couldn't want

anything more!" She bit back tears, then was overcome. Eight years and she hadn't seen him once. Sophie came to her rescue and led her away from the tracks. Samuel followed close behind with his duffle bag and Sophie's luggage.

"Show us where to go, Caroline."

It was a dreary, dark morning, but Caroline wiped her tears and walked them through the drizzle away from the depot to the privacy of a little waiting shelter for the new auto stage that ran between Twin Forks and other settlements south of Frazier. Once they were out of the weather, the three siblings finally embraced and for a long time said nothing. Eventually, Caroline asked if their parents knew that Samuel was coming here.

"Only Mother has an inkling and I think she approves. I told her that I was taking Samuel to see the state university in Seattle, as he'd like to attend, but if the weather was still good, we might go climbing. I didn't say where, but as you can see, he came prepared." He definitely was. He was wearing the latest gear out of the 1915 Filson catalog and looked the experienced climber he wasn't. Samuel, Caroline recalled, was more inclined toward books than base camps in the mountains.

"So you want to go to the university, Sammy?" Caroline asked.

"Someday, but I've been thinking about the preparedness camps. I believe that it's something I should do."

"You'll do nothing of the sort," admonished Sophie. "Such talk." She linked her arms between both siblings. "Not until the war madness is over. Look at him, Caroline. Isn't he handsome?"

"He truly is," Caroline agreed. *But I missed his growing years.* There was so much to tell him and she wondered if he was adult enough to understand. "Have you eaten?" was all she could think of next to say.

They stepped into the Frazier Hotel restaurant which had expanded over the years. Sophie ordered lunch for them all.

As the meal progressed, Caroline and Samuel began to reclaim their sibling ties. Caroline was interested in all the things that he'd done since she'd left so long ago, even although Sophie had kept her abreast in her letters. Samuel, in turn, wanted to know about Alford and their life in Frazier with his nephew and niece. They both were feeling comfortable with each other when they left for the Alford homestead.

The road was deep and muddy down near the skid road.

"This is awful," Sophie said. "The trees are all gone down to the river." Her face turned white with shock when Caroline told her who was behind the logging operation.

"James Ford. So like him. Uncle Harold too. It doesn't look very practical, but I suppose it's all money they have in mind." She waved Caroline on. "Oh, let's do go. The place depresses me. I hope yours hasn't been scalped." She turned around to her brother in the back seat of the automobile Caroline had borrowed from Cathy. "It's the most wonderful spot, Sammy. So restful. You won't believe the view."

From the kitchen window, the view was obscured by clouds pressing down on the peaks and ridges far below their summits, but Samuel was impressed with the trees wrapped in the grey mist across the river. "Is that an eagle I see there in those alders?" he asked Caroline.

"Oh, there he is. Yes. The salmon can come up this far, though Bob frets about the riverbed now. Not good for spawning with the logging. The eagles like to congregate for that."

Caroline asked if he wanted coffee and prepared a cup for him. She and Sophie would have tea. "Would you like a tour? Or, perhaps, you'd like some introductions. It looks like the natives have arrived." She nodded her head at Kate and Cory standing curiously in the hallway. "Come children and meet your Uncle Samuel." She turned to her brother. "Or would you prefer Uncle Sam?"

"That will do. Sounds patriotic."

Alford came home later that night and was surprised to meet this unknown member of his wife's family. He appeared to like the young man instantly, much to Caroline's delight, and for part of the evening the two spent time together in Alford's tackle room, talking on subjects that interested them both. The following day, Alford took him to headquarters where he introduced Samuel to Vernell and the other Forest Service men, then took him on a ride up to one of the shelters where a hunting party had been camping.

"We've been deserted," laughed Sophie as they walked outside along the riverbank, "but I'm very pleased. Aren't you?"

"Oh, yes. Thank you so much for the surprise. I'll always be so grateful. However, you never said why *you've* come back to the Northwest. How's Mr. Porter?"

"Oh, that. We're divorced. Almost a year now."

"I didn't know you were married. Sophie!"

"Secretly. I didn't think Mother and Father would ever approve of him. I had him sign a pre-nuptial agreement. I have a new man in my life."

"Another Californian?"

"Part of the year. He's from an old monied Oregon family and much more to my liking, though poor Rex did try. I'm afraid he loved his horses and movie starlets more. Simon is quite sweet and more importantly, he can't have children. That makes our relationship much more stable. I do care about him very much." Sophie laughed at Caroline's long face. "Oh, don't take me wrong. I love children. *Your* children. But it's not for me. If James and I had children, it would have been such a mess and with Rex, I was careful. Simon and I have the time to do the things we enjoy and maybe, just maybe I'm a better person with him." She broke the twig she twisted in her gloved hands and threw it out into the rushing river.

"Isn't it odd? Here you were the rebellious one. Defying Father and Uncle Harold and going with the man of your choice. For that you were asked to leave the family. I, on the other hand, married well and performed all my social obligations with James until I couldn't stand the farce with him anymore and left. I still have money and position, yet, you Caroline, have the most wonderful life, even though it hasn't been easy financially. I envy you for your children even though I know it isn't for me. I envy you for Bob, too. I *do* adore him and every time I see him, I regret that Father can't see his way to forgive you. This whole charade should end."

"There are some who probably wouldn't want that to happen. Uncle Harold for one and James Ford." Caroline quickly told her what had happened the previous July when Ford came on her property.

"No! The insipid fool. Lord, what did I ever see in him?" Sophie put her arm through Caroline's and leaned her head against her shoulder. "David's right. Father should be told."

"What'll he say when he learns Sammy came here?"

"Dear heart, I'm not sure if I have the courage to tell him yet, but I will bring news of you for Mother. She always wants to know about her grandchildren. She treasures the little pictures you send to me."

Sophie rubbed her arms. The afternoon was getting chilly and they started to walk back. "One more thing. Do you think you could get away for a few days? I'd love to take you and Sammy to one of the vaudeville shows in your city. He can only stay a few more days, then he has to get back to Portland. Father wants him to take an entrance exam. It may be the last time we can be together for a while. Sammy's taking the test just to please Father and he says he has his heart set on the university, but I fear that there's a greater pull to join one of those preparedness groups. Father doesn't know, but he's been taking flying lessons. His heroes are the English air aces. I'm afraid that he'll run off and join some group and get himself killed."

"Oh, Sophie. That's terrible. At all costs, he must be discouraged. In the meantime, I'll see if I can get away. It has been a long time since I went to the city. You needn't

pay —"
"But I shall insist."

Three days later, they took the train into the city and spent two days there, before Sophie and Samuel boarded a steamer for Seattle. There they would spend the night with Emily and David before going by train to Portland.

"Give Emily my love," said Caroline as they started to board, "and tell her that I hope to see her in November."

"And so I will. And you promise to take care of that lovely man and my niece and nephew. Above all, take heart. If you should ever need me —"

There was a kiss for her and a deep hug from Samuel. After they boarded, Caroline stood alone on the dock in the blustery fall wind, watching for signs of them. Then she walked the two blocks to the train station and her own ride home.

Chapter 37

November came in mild and sunny, but by the second week of the month, the first snows fell. Waking to two inches on the ground and more falling, Caroline and Alford stayed in bed and made love, glad for the heat of their bodies and the pleasure it gave them. Ever vigilant for the sounds of the children, they enjoyed themselves and when they were done, rested in each other's arms.

"Mommy?"

Kate pushed open the bedroom door and stared at her parents snuggled under their quilts. Caroline sat up beside Alford.

"What's wrong?"

"Cory's sick. He spit up."

"Oh, dear." Caroline scrambled out of bed, putting on her flannel robe as she went into the hall. She found Cory at the bottom of the stairs crying. When she touched his forehead, it felt hot. "Let's change your nightshirt," she soothed him.

Snow kept falling until noon. After cleaning Cory up, she consulted her copy of *A Mother's Guide to Illness*. Alford put him to bed. A phone call to Cathy revealed that Marianne and three other children from school were also sick. By afternoon, when more names were added to the list, it looked like the community was not only under snow, but under siege of the grippe. By evening, it closed Ford's logging operation down good for the season.

Alford went to headquarters where he worked until two, then went to the pharmacy to get some medicine. "Dr. Gates and his new partner," the pharmacist said, "are coming up to Frazier late in the afternoon. Write a message and they'll check in on your little ones." Alford left a message.

Back at home, Cory's fever continued to rise. Alford and Caroline stripped down his bedclothes and gave him a sponge bath before lightly covering him again. He was lethargic and cranky, but awake.

To keep him company, Alford read the city newspaper to Cory. Full of unsuitable news about fighting in Brownsville, Texas against Mexican bandits, zeppelins dropping bombs on London and a rabies scare in the Skagit, he chose a story about a bear hunt in the Kulshan district that involved "nine men and fourteen dogs." When Cory asked questions about that, Alford told him about the bear sign he'd seen himself at one of the creeks in the national forest. "Biggest paw tracks I've seen in a while."

"Did you catch the bear?" Cory asked.

"Nope. Too busy looking for poachers. Besides that big old bear should looking for a place to sleep." This led to more stories about going out with some game people to locate a camp just inside Frazier District. Eventually, Cory closed his eyes and went to sleep.

The rest of the family ate the evening meal in the kitchen, but when Kate got cranky Caroline put her to bed too. After a story, she was fast asleep as well.

"I hope she doesn't get sick too," worried Caroline.

Alford put his arms around her. "I'll watch her. Why don't you put your feet up? You'll wear yourself out."

Alford woke at nine that night to the sound of knocking

at the front door. As he started down, Caroline came out of their bedroom fully dressed.

"Who is it?"

"Not sure. The doctor? He's come in time. Cory's sounding wheezy in his chest."

A thin man in his late forties with wire rim glasses waited on the porch. "Bob Alford?" he said with a slight Scandinavian accent. "I am Dr. Svenson, Dr. Gates's new partner. I hear you have a sick little one."

"My son and possibly my daughter. Please come in."

Stamping his snowy boots on the doormat, Dr. Svenson removed his wool cap, revealing a balding pate in the midst of graying brown hair. After hanging the doctor's coat up, Alford led the way upstairs.

Cory stirred when they came in. The doctor sat down beside him. "How do you feel?" Svenson asked Cory as he listened to his heart. "Do you want to cough when you breathe?"

"Uh-huh. My head thumps too."

"Let's see your throat first, then we'll do something about that head. We don't want it to thump."

The doctor spent several minutes with him. Alford and Caroline hovered close by, staying around to answer any questions Svenson might have. Eventually, the doctor covered Cory up. "Pretty soon you'll be feeling better. *God natt,* Cory."

Out in the hall, Svenson turned to them. "He has the grippe all right. Just like the others."

"Is he in danger?" Caroline wrung her hands while Alford kept a hand on her shoulder.

"By golly, not if I can help it, Mrs. Alford." Dr. Svenson smiled encouragingly at them. "You watch him. Make a tent and use steam. That should clear him. He's a healthy little boy, I can see, but this grippe is bad. Now let's look at your daughter."

The snow and grippe raged through Frazier for the next

few days. The day after Dr. Svenson arrived, Fuller called in sick along with two part-time winter employees. By the afternoon, Vernell admitted on the phone he wasn't feeling too wonderful himself.

"I'll come up, then," Alford said. "See you then check on the pump and other machinery at headquarters."

Fearing the bridge that went over the icy Frazier Creek would be too slick for an automobile, Alford took his horse, braving the wind and flurries during the long half hour it took to get there.

"Where's Mary?" he asked when he got into the ranger station.

"In Seattle," Vernell rasped. "Won't be back for another forty-eight hours."

"Need some nursemaiding?"

"Naw. You look after your young 'uns. They deserve two parents to look after them." Vernell patted the side of his rocking chair where he sat before the open fire. In a worn-out saddlebag was a bottle of whisky. "Got my own nurse." He grinned under his grey mustache. "Now normally, I teetotal, but this is one time this sort of medicine is called for. If I really need you, I won't hesitate to phone. I'll be fine." Alford didn't think so, so stayed on a bit longer, then left.

Down in Frazier, he stopped in the general store which was eerily empty. At the back where the fishing equipment was hung, he chatted with Bergstrom by the potbellied stove. There wasn't much business. "Everyone's sick," Bergstrom said. "The hotel's full of sick miners come down to escape the snow only to run into an equally difficult hazard." He shook his head. "It's so slow, I ought to take my pole and go fishing."

"That's not such a bad idea," Alford said. "Down below my place the river's not too low. Got the right color too, but my kids are sick, so I won't linger." Alford fingered one of the lures hanging on a board. "Caught a twenty-two pound steelhead last year about this time. Just about the same conditions."

"Just how many did you catch last year?"

"Now, Karl. You know I don't like to brag on such things. Just say I got my quota without depleting the entire genus." Alford winked. "Even put one or two back because I felt sorry for them."

Bergstrom harrumphed. "You're too modest Alford. You probably put back more than you're saying. You're one hell of the fisherman." The storekeep pounded the counter with the flat of his hand. "Beats me how you get those on your hook."

"We just have a conversation of sorts." Alford grinned. He buttoned up his heavy forestry cloth coat and put on his gloves. "Gotta go. Caroline'll be wondering if I fell into a drift."

Cory and Kate stayed sick for four more days. Kate didn't suffer as much as her brother whose congestion grew worse the second day. Caroline and Alford had several sleepless nights with Cory as he sat under a tent of blankets at the kitchen table with a boiling teakettle or in Caroline's arms as she rocked him when he got too hot.

Eventually, Cory and Kate's fevers went down and their little bodies cooled to a point where both parents could relax. By then the snow stopped and the temperature warmed enough to melt some of the snow during the day. Still, it remained cold and the grippe stayed on in Frazier until most of its citizens were touched. At one point Alford felt sick himself, but neither parent gave themselves the luxury of looking after their own needs until the children were sitting up and asking to be read to or play with toys in their beds.

Alford returned to regular hours at headquarters not long after. During the week-long siege, he'd been the only one there fully upright. Fuller was out and so was Peterson. Vernell had taken to bed not long after Bob saw him and was quite ill with a bad cough when Mary returned. He wouldn't resume work for nearly two weeks, leaving Alford to man the ranger station.

The days turned bright and clear, creating a postcard-perfect picture out of the snowy mountains and dark green forests. People showed up again on the streets and at the general store and hotel, some a little too soon. They would end up in bed for another round, until the sickness was rung out of them or they were rung out. There was one fatality: a miner who drank too much, then wandered out into the snow. He had the grippe, but no one could tell if he had died from the illness or the snow. It appeared they both got him.

On Saturday, Cory got out of bed and wandered into the kitchen on his own for the first time and said he was hungry. Kate came out a little later looking for her rag doll and noticed her brother eating mush at the table. That seemed to put an end to the grippe. When the children were quietly playing on their own in the living room, Caroline and Alford crept back into their own bed and collapsing, slept the morning away.

Sunday came, then Monday but with the illness so recent among them, the grammar school stayed closed one more day while the teacher recuperated. The snow on the ground melted, turning the roads into slushy muds baths or floating gravel pits. With Vernell still laid up and Fuller not up to speed, it fell to Alford to make the rounds. Loading up a packhorse and his own saddlebags, he left that afternoon for Big Fir to check on a hut used by hunters before the grippe hit. Vacated so quickly, Vernell wasn't sure what condition it was in.

Caroline spent the morning cleaning the sick rooms and washing clothes. Cory and Kate stayed in, making a fort in Cory's room with blankets and chairs. Under their cloth roof, they brought in pillows and favorite toys and books. The game was a mixture of the Forest Service and "house," with some cattle thieves thrown in although Kate asked what a cattle thief was.

Not long after they fell asleep under the blanket, the

phone rang. It was Mrs. Purdy, the telephone operator down in Twin Forks alerting all the households on the Frazier line about the death of more citizens of the area, an elderly man and his granddaughter. The line burst with gasps and words of sorrow.

"How's Frazier holding up?" the operator asked.

"The grippe got everyone," Cathy said. "Poor Charlie missed several days of work. He went back to the mill, still coughing and tired."

"It's the worst I've seen," Ellie said. My house, the Turners, even the new proprietress at the Frazier Hotel. The stage hasn't even picked up the kids for junior school."

"Can't believe Thanksgiving's so close," someone else said.

"I've barely given a moment's thought to it." Caroline paused, thinking she'd heard someone at the door. She went on again, then stopped. There *was* someone. She excused herself, then hung up.

"Yes?" Caroline asked.

Standing on the porch was a woman in her early fifties. She was a well-scrubbed woman, dressed in feminine, but practical clothes for the weather and the motocar she was driving. The heavy wool cape she wore gave her the appearance of someone on official business. Yet despite her plain features, she cut a handsome figure offset by large brown eyes and rich brunette hair slightly streaked with gray. When the woman smiled, Caroline instantly liked her.

"Mrs. Alford?"

"Yes."

"I'm Maggie Svenson, Dr. Hans Svenson's wife."

"How do you do." Caroline invited the woman in.

"I won't stay long. I've come for your assistance if I may. You know Micah Thompson?"

"Yes, of course."

"Sometime this morning a young Indian lady caught me on the road. She heard that I was here with my husband to help him on his rounds. Oh, I'm also Dr. Svenson's practical nurse." She undid her wool scarf as she spoke. "She told me Mr. Thompson was quite ill with the grippe. At her urging, I went to confirm his condition. I've seen to him, but he was asking for you."

"Me?" During the entire week when the kids were down, she hadn't been concerned for Micah thinking him safely away working his winter trap lines. "Of course, I'll come. He's close by?" All these years, she'd never been to his cabin before, not sure where he kept permanent winter quarters.

"Yes. Thank goodness. I'll take you there now. He'll need nursing and I can't stay."

"My children are here," Caroline said. "I'll need to call someone. It won't take a moment."

Inviting the woman into the living room where Cory was sleeping, Caroline called Cathy. When she came back she found Mrs. Svenson studying the family pictures on the little spinet piano set against the wall opposite the front window. She turned when Caroline came in.

"Is this your family, Mrs. Alford.?"

"Yes, my children and my in-laws at their home in Swede Hill."

Caroline couldn't be sure, but the woman seemed to stiffen at the name. There was a third family picture of Bob in his ranger uniform with his hat on his lap and Caroline behind him. It had been taken on their third wedding anniversary. Mrs. Svenson stared at Alford intensely.

"Mr. Alford is a forest ranger?"

"Assistant."

"But that's wonderful."

"It makes for an interesting life." Caroline nodded out to the hallway. "I can go as soon as my friend gets here. She'll be along very soon. Should I bring anything?"

"An apron, I should think and maybe some extra warm clothes."

Caroline went up to see the children. By the time she was back down again, Cathy was pulling up at the gate.

"Are you all packed?" she asked Caroline. "Peter can

come over later to relieve me if you should need someone to stay longer, but I'm going to call Mary Vernell. She'll want to help too. The kids'll be fine. Give my love to Micah."

They found Micah's cabin off the road going to Twin Forks. It was back in the hills across the river approachable only by a suspension bridge strung high across a canyon. Below, its narrow sides herded the waters together and squeezed them out on the other end.

"I had no idea he was back here," she said as they swung their way across the rough slats. She wondered if Bob knew. Once on land, they picked their way around patches of mud and still frozen ice pads until they came into a large clearing surrounded by hemlock and alder. There in the center was a low, cedar shake cabin. Next to it was a shed and a small corral for his horses.

The cabin appeared ancient, with a stone chimney and its roof covered with moss. Gray smoke came out of a stovepipe, listlessly rising above the cabin, disappearing into the chilly mist that hung around the fir trees.

"Is he alone?"

"No. I left him with the young woman, Sunny Jack. But she can stay for only a short while. Her mother's very ill. The grippe hit her community quite hard."

"Then I'll have to stay, won't I?"

Mrs. Svenson knocked at the door and Sunny Jack let them in.

Caroline came into the single room cabin behind the other woman and stopped. Nothing prepared her for it. It looked at once like a place taken out of time from the district's fading past, a trapper's lodging, left over from the early Hudson Bay Company days when men passed from the Fraser River in the north down narrow trails through the wetland prairies west of Twin Forks. The single room evoked mystery and a historic past. Its rafters and beams were cedar poles toasted by the occasional smoke, its floors of hand split fir polished by years of use. It had a few windows strategically placed to catch the best light. Animal skins hung on the walls and newspapers placed over the chinks to cut down the draft. The furniture was handmade and the room lit by lantern, but it was the shelves of books that caught her eye.

Here is the heart of Micah, she thought. She thought of all the years he'd been part of their family, how he'd taught Bob the history and the secrets of the district, how he'd been an doting uncle to their children. *I know you,* she thought, *but I don't know you.*

Caroline smiled at Sunny Jack and thanked her for taking her coat, then looked over to the far wall. Underneath an old red, point blanket and a bear skin, Micah lay in his bed and for a moment, she thought he had passed on. She bit her lip, then went to him.

"Micah?"

His eyes were closed and the light mahogany face pale and drawn. Several day's growth of beard covered his chin. For the first time, Caroline noticed gray. Touched, she picked up one of his big hands laying on top of the covers and held it. It made him stir, then cough raggedly.

"How long has he been like this?" she asked.

"Apparently, for several days." Mrs. Svenson came over. "I gave him something for the fever and we made a pot of light soup for him. The main thing is to keep the stove going and not have him get chilled. I think the worst is over. No sign of pneumonia. I gather he's normally a robust man."

"Oh, Micah's very strong." But privately she thought he looked gaunt. A pang of emotion struck her. *What would I do without Micah?* Mrs. Svenson rustled behind her and took his hand away for his pulse. When she was done, she gave it back to Caroline.

"His pulse is good. Wish the cough was better. Would you like some tea? Miss Jack?"

"Yes, please," Caroline and Sunny Jack said together.

Caroline stole a glance at the bookshelf next to the bed. It was crammed full of books, some slim, some massive tomes. Many of the spines looked old. The range of titles amazed her.

"What do... you think of my collection?" Micah's normally big voice was so soft and whispery it startled her, but she felt very relieved at seeing him awake.

"I haven't had time to look," she whispered back. "We can talk about it later."

"You'll stay?"

"Yes, Micah. I'll stay."

His eyes drooped, then closed. A soft smile drifted across his lips. "Good —" He was cut short briefly in a fit of coughing, but finally sagged into his musty pillow and sighed. Caroline took his hand and squeezed it. He squeezed it back, eventually falling asleep.

Mrs. Svenson stayed for an hour visiting with and giving Caroline advice. "I'll go by your home and see if Mary Vernell's been contacted. Maybe she can relieve you later. Or would you be comfortable if you stayed the night?" She nodded at Sunny Jack. "She wants to go back to her mother."

"I can do it. Cathy will understand and look after my children. Micah is special to so many of us."

Mrs. Svenson nodded. "I knew someone like him in the Yukon."

"You were in the Yukon?"

"Oh, yes. I went up there in '07 with my first husband. Stayed there until '10 then moved to Nome. I was widowed by then, but I loved the adventure of Alaska Territory so I sought a position there. That's where I met Dr. Svenson. He was just starting his practice there and in need of an assistant. My father was a doctor. It fell to me naturally."

She looked at Caroline a little embarrassed at her outburst of personal background, but Caroline didn't think the older woman was the sort that embarrassed easily. In fact, Caroline thought she must have an incredibly thick skin. Her face was strong, holding secrets not easily given away, yet Caroline liked her. And trusted her.

"I promise to send reinforcements in the morning, Mrs.

Alford," Mrs. Svenson said. "There's food here and water. He has a straw mattress in the corner. It's clean."

"I'll manage."

Maggie Svenson gathered up her things into a leather physician's bag, then put on her cape. "In the morning then." She held out her hand and shook Caroline's. "Good evening."

The day darkened. Sunny Jack kept the fire going and eventually settled down at Micah's little wood table with some knitting.

"How is your family?" Caroline asked.

"Very bad. My cousin died. Everyone is *hyas sick*"

"Oh, dear. Don't you want to go home?"

"Not yet. I want stay with Micah. He's like my *kahpo*, my big brother." She quickly knitted a row, her needles clicking as if for emphasis. "You are so kind to come, Mrs. Alford."

Caroline smiled. "Well, he's special to me too."

Eventually, Sunny Jack left, leaving Caroline alone to the sound of a mantle clock ticking on one of the shelves and Micah's snoring. *Uncongested,* she thought it a good sign. At six she ladled some soup for herself and ate at the wood table. Later, she went outside in the pitch black night to pump for water and boiled a pot on the stove for dishes. After bringing the room into some order and carrying in wood for the night, she returned to her place by Micah's bed and watched him as he slept. When she touched his forehead, she found only the dregs of fever. Sitting back, she waited for him to stir, but he didn't, so she studied the face she thought she knew so well.

His short, dark hair was matted with sweat, but instead of making him seem younger in his sleep, he appeared older with a world full of cares upon his shoulders. She noticed lines around his eyes and mouth she hadn't seen before. Or maybe being lost in the passing of her own children's lives, she hadn't caught the march of time in his.

I'm older too, she thought, pulling her shawl around her. Thinking of Micah made her think of her parents and how they were getting on in years. She wished she could see her mother, could have her father's forgiveness, but she'd have to be realistic. That might never be possible.

Not wishing to dwell on it, her eyes explored the bookshelves she'd seen earlier. It was an eclectic collection. There was poetry by Robert Burns, Ralph Waldo Emerson, journals and essays by Henry David Thoreau, novels by Sir Walter Scott, Thomas Hardy and Charles Dickens. More recent were *The Four Feathers* and *The Virginian*, books she never would expect him to be interested in reading. There were some old *Century* magazines, too. In fact, the books implied a grand education something not suggested by his life lived so totally out of doors.

Caroline got up and touched one of the covers of the leather bound books. The spine was a little worn, but it was lovingly cared for. Curious, she pulled the thick tome out and discovered poems by Robert Browning and other Romantic poets. Settling down on her chair, she became absorbed in the words of "A Life in Love," something she and Bob liked to read out loud to each other.

> *While I am I, and you are you,*
> *So long as the world contains us both,*
> *Me the loving and you the loth—*

She turned the page and then another, then skipped through a third of the book, coming abruptly to an unexpected sight. The center was bound together like one thick block and the middle of the block was carved out so it made a box. Inside, she discovered an old dark green wallet, the kind used to protect a photograph mounted on cardboard. Underneath was a lock of dark hair and a pair of pearl earrings.

Stunned, she knew she should go no further. There was mystery here. Her hands trembled. The lock of hair was close in color to her own and she guessed it had belonged to a woman. *Hattie Coleman, Micah's woman?* The girl Cathy spoke of on the hike to the falls.

Open it. The voice was very clear in her mind. She bit her lip, torn by indecision, then obeyed the voice.

"Ohhh," Caroline gasped. She stared at the sepia picture of a young woman of about twenty dressed in a plaid dress from the 1880s, stamped with the studio name of Tumwater. Slight and beautiful, she held her pose as she was instructed, but couldn't hold her eyes. They danced before the photographer's glass, like crystal pieces of light, forever captured. A strip of paper lay across the bottom, the words "All My Love, Hattie" written in pencil. Caroline closed the wallet and put it back into the hole in the book. She was trembling all over now, but she made sure the parts were all in place before she closed it up. When she finished, she found she couldn't stand. Her legs felt too weak. She began to weep.

"Don't cry, Miz Caroline."

Caroline jumped, slamming her hand over her mouth. Micah was awake, his big head resting on the pillow. Carefully, she turned her gaze to him. "I'm so sorry. I didn't mean to pry. I'm so ashamed."

"You needn't be. Now you know what no else knows, except for Jack Vernell and George Fuller."

"This is Hattie Coleman?"

"Yes."

"Is it true about her? The story about the falls?"

"Yes and no." He smiled softly at her, then sighed. "It was such a long time ago, back when the forests were so thick and tall you'd have to look up twice to see the sky. There weren't any trails to speak of. You traveled on the water." He cleared his throat. "We wanted to marry but her father said no, so we planned to elope. Just like you two. Only something went wrong. On her way to meet me, her canoe capsized and she drowned in the river down where Twin Forks is today. There were few people here then. The story got all mixed up. She'd never have taken her own life. She was carrying our child."

"Oh, Micah." A strange ache engulfed her. She was full of grief and pity. And love. "Her father was Scots, like my own father. Only he was much more stubborn than I remember mine being. Never did forgive me, never did see his part in the whole affair. I went away after that, pretty much staying in the hills, looking after my claims. After a time, the family left. Homesteading too rough for them. As for Hattie, the story just growed around her, mostly forgotten now. You like them earrings? I was going to give them to her for a wedding gift."

"They're very pretty. Victorian looking."

"You can have them or give them to Kate when she's growed. I don't have any need of them. Silly to hold on."

"I couldn't, Micah."

"Maybe I want you to."

Caroline shook her head, but in fact she trembled all over. She couldn't.

"Don't let that picture spook you. Don't go and get thoughts in your head about it. You're special to me, girl. You surely are."

Caroline began to weep again. She didn't notice he was much stronger now, that the worse of the illness was over and that all he needed was rest. And attention.

"But not for the thing you see in the picture," Micah went on. "It's just an old fool's thoughts. Seeing you growing from girl to lady, seeing you with the young 'uns. Seeing how you come to the land and have become a part of it. Like them timber roses Alford always calls those rhodies."

"But she looks like me!" Caroline thought she almost shouted, but it came out as a sob.

"Aye..." It was strange to hear him hear speak with a brogue. So many sides to him, so strong and powerful. "Don't be troubled. You're the finest lady, Caroline Alford. You and your man are the finest. There isn't a thing I wouldn't do for you, him or the children."

"Because of her — "

"Because of *all* of you and what it means to be a part of

your life and family." He swallowed. "Don't pay me no mind. If I should sometimes mistake you as some soul walking in the woods as if she were here today, just let it pass. I'm just an old romantic who read *Ivanhoe* too many times. It don't mean a thing."

Caroline laughed through her tears, then desperately wiped her cheeks.

Micah chuckled, his strained eyes bright with tears, not fever. "You can have them pearls. You can have any of the books for your family to read. They'll eventually rot here."

"Thank you, Micah." Caroline composed herself, brushing down her straight wool skirt.

He listlessly waved his hand at the bookshelves. "I had a wide and varied education. My father brought all his books from Edinburgh, Scotland and collected what else he could procure. I was taught to read on them and *McGuffey* readers. My mother's people from her Salish side taught me about the salmon streams and the importance of cedar. She finished out the rest with stories from her Hawaiian father he'd told her. We read books on that too. After my mother died, the books were put in storage in town and my father and I went away for a long time into the mountains where I completed my education. I brought them out when I met Hattie. They've stayed out ever since."

There was a large silence, compounded by the mantle clock and the hiss of the lantern.

Caroline was overwhelmed. "You want some soup?" she finally asked.

"I'd be obliged."

Mary Vernell came the next day and found Caroline outside at the pump. "How's Micah?" she asked.

"Resting, but awake. Fever's nearly gone. He's on the mend."

"Good. School started, so Cory's gone. Cathy has Kate. I'm to bring you home, then I'll come back. Micah's got enough friends to watch over him until he's up."

"Did Jack hear from Bob?"

"No, but the weather is holding, though. It's going to be a decent Thanksgiving once everyone is back on their feet." She leaned over and helped Caroline lift the heavy bucket off the pump. "Why don't you get your things together, dear, I'll go in and say hello and then we'll go."

"All right." Caroline hefted the bucket then stopped. "Do you know the story of Hattie Coleman?"

"I know it, but I never knew her. Jack did, though. He's known Micah since they were boys."

"Did you ever see a picture of her?"

"No. That was a long time ago. Why do you ask?"

"Nothing really."

Mary looked at her young friend guiltily. "Why don't you ask him some time? You're family to him and that's a bond forever."

Caroline tugged at the bucket, spilling a little of the water on the cold, hard ground. "I know that now. Didn't realize how much he means to me."

"I'm glad you think that," answered Mary. "God bless you dear, for being his friend. You'll never regret it. I haven't. He's one of the joys of my life."

Mary took hold of the bucket and suggested they take it in together. There were people waiting on them.

Thanksgiving came and was celebrated by the Vernells, Bladstads, Alfords and other close friends at the hotel. After the grippe, no one was in the frame of mind to stay indoors at their own homes and stuff themselves. It was better to do that in the company of friends. So a party was held, much the same along the lines of the other eight years before, but now the children were growing up like weeds and wanting to socialize on their own, so there were games for them and tables of their own. It set the stage for Christmas.

The weather continued to improve and then in typical Pacific Northwest manner, changed its mind, so rain and wind greeted the Alford children on Christmas morning.

They'd been up since six, tumbling into their parent's room after an excursion downstairs to the tree.

"Daddy!" exclaimed Kate as she crawled onto the bed. "There's a big box for me!"

"And what did Santa bring?" Alford asked trying to put his best smile on over a face that'd been up all night trying to put up the tree, then assemble her present.

"I don't kno...ooh," Kate explained.

"Then we'll have to find out." Alford tapped Caroline. "We've been summoned."

"Then we must obey."

"I'll wake up the stove and put some coffee on. See you in a bit."

Downstairs, the children stopped to admire the Douglas fir set up just last night while they were asleep.

"That's the biggest tree I ever saw," Cory said as he danced around in his robe and pajamas. "But what's that string of bulbs going around it? I never saw anything like that before."

Neither had I, Alford thought. Their Aunt Sophie had bought them at great expense just for the children. It had taken some figuring to get them on the tree.

"Shall we try them?" Alford sounded just like a kid himself as he crawled under the tree and plugged the string in.

Hand-blown and hand-painted, the twenty-eight glass lights bloomed to the chorus of childish "ahs." When he was sure they weren't going to explode, he went to the kitchen to get the stove going.

He padded through the chilly house. Outside, the mountains loomed like inky paper silhouettes against a purple sky just barely tinged with lavender to the east. It was one of his favorite times of the day so often connected with rising early to pursue his other passion in life. Out of habit, he glanced at his gut leaders in the bucket in the corner and made a mental note to make up some new ones. He needed new line as well. He got the fire going, then putting on rain

320

gear went out to bring in more wood.

It was quiet outside. Only the cold rush of the water as it worked around the slippery stones in the river and the rain dripping on the ground. Across the way behind a skirt of silver mist, he could see the faint ghost-like lines of the alders and maple stripped bare for winter. Further up river, they disappeared into a dark maw of nothing. Ford had worked his section down as far as he could before the grippe and winter got the best of his men and his equipment. It wouldn't be until spring when he could resume work again because winter was always worse in January and February.

Good, thought Alford. Maybe a nor'easter from Canada would rip through and drop a few trees on their machinery.

Behind him, the telephone rang out their party line number of two longs and two shorts and Alford wondered who in his right mind would be calling this early on Christmas morning. Company in the form of Jack and Mary Vernell and Micah wasn't expected until afternoon. His parents, he knew, would have gone to midnight service the night before. He grabbed what he needed for both stoves and went inside.

Out in the hall, he saw Caroline grip the telephone earpiece tight against her head. She wore a robe over her long flannel nightgown and had her long cinnamon hair tied back in a single, heavy braid. Alford took his time admiring her as he put away the wood into the bin next to the cookstove, missing the frown on her face until he heard her exclaim, "Oh, David. How awful. I'm so sorry."

Alford was alert now and stepped into the hall where Caroline stood on her toes at the mouthpiece. He signaled to her, then moved quickly to her side and put his hand on her shoulder when she began to sag against the wall.

"Caroline! What's wrong?"

"It's Emily," she whispered to him. "She's been ill." She turned her attention to the voice on the other end. "Yes, yes. Of course. You'll let us know if there's any change?" She spoke for a few minutes more, then hung up after final words of love and reassurance. For a long time, she held the earpiece to her cheek, unmindful of Kate tugging at her robe. Alford finally picked up the little girl and took her to the kitchen.

"Mommy's busy, Kate. You want some toast and jam?"

"I want my box," Kate told him.

"In a minute," he told her. He looked back at Caroline, anxious for word of what had happened. Eventually she came into the room.

"How is she?"

"She got a hard case of grippe two weeks ago. She lost the baby earlier this morning. David's quite distraught. He's terrified for her. She hasn't been herself since." She went to the stove and removed the coffeepot on the verge of boiling over. A tear strayed down her face. "The doctors aren't telling him anything, but he thinks they don't expect her to survive."

Alford put Kate down. "Cory, take your sister and go look in your stockings. See what Santa brought." When they were gone, he took Caroline into his arms and rocked the soft sobs out of her.

"What am I'm going to do without Emily? She's been faithful to me from the beginning. If it weren't for her, we wouldn't be together." She sniffed, then wept again. Alford held her close, stroking the hair he loved so much.

Caroline went on. "She thought I was so brazen asking you on the hike, then later said she was glad for it because I was a round peg in a square hole. I just didn't fit into society like society wanted me to." She looked at him with tear-stung eyes. "Why does it have to be Emily?"

He had no answer just as he had no answer when Stein was killed. There was no answer.

He kissed her softly on her lips as if that would make things better. She bunched her fists up and laid them on his chest, crying onto his robe's collar until it was soaked.

"When will you know?" he asked softly.

"David will call again one way or the other."

"Perhaps she's much stronger than any of you believe."

"Perhaps... But why Emily? Why sweet Emily?"

"I don't know, Caroline. It's just life jumping up, like my father used to say. There's no answer for it."

He rocked her gently, deeply moved himself as he remembered his fears when he thought he was going to lose her after her miscarriage. Selfishly, he held her tighter and soothed her with what words he could find.

"Mommy look!" shouted Kate as she ran into the kitchen. She was holding a piece of candy and an orange in each hand. "Cory has some too."

Alford gave Caroline a wistful smile. Grief would have to wait. It was Christmas and sorrow would be banished for the day.

Chapter 38

Emily died the day after New Year's. Growing steadily weaker after an infection set in, she quietly slipped away, leaving behind a grieving David and mountaineering community. When Caroline received the news, she took it as hard as David who kept breaking down on the telephone. When they hung up, she retreated outside to the river where she cried.

She was still there an hour later when Alford got back from headquarters for the day. By then, her tears had been spent and she had settled down quietly on a large boulder to contemplate and collect her thoughts.

"See any fish?" he asked as he sat down next to her on the cold moist boulder. Across the water was a favorite pool he liked to work year round. There were little cedars and winter-bare vine maples behind it and an old log that draped itself over the steep bank. Together, they provided shade and sanctuary for fish below.

"Not a one." She smoothed her wool skirt over her knees, then tucking her hands into her heavy wool jacket, sighed. "Did you hear?"

"Vernell got a call from a friend in the city. Apparently it's in the newspaper. I'm so sorry, sweetheart. I don't know what to say. Except I loved her like the sister I never had. Truly." He put a hand on her knee and rubbed it. "What do you want to do?"

"I want to go to the funeral. David's asked and even though I protested, he has train tickets for us."

"I'm not sure if I can get leave. I'll have to ask Jack, but you can go."

Caroline stifled a sob. "Please, Bob. I can't do this alone. I'm worried for David. He's quite distraught."

Alford grew quiet, maybe for too long. Caroline put a hand on his arm and patted it.

"I doubt we'll see Father," Caroline said. "At least ways, not close enough to talk."

"And what if that should be arranged? Harms has always said he wished it."

"Will you go?"

Alford pulled back. "Only if you want me to, Caroline. I've no desire to see you snubbed any further. But I'm not going to grovel to your father or apologize."

Caroline put a hand over his lips. "Don't. You don't have to say anything. It's all done with and my life is complete." She leaned her head against his shoulder and sighed. "It just goes by so fast. You never really know what you've had until you lost it." She sniffed. "Poor David. He loved her so much. Now she's gone." The tears began to well up again.

"Shhh," was all Alford could muster as he put his arm around her and held her close. He hated to see her so upset, and for that, he'd have to put aside any rancor or discomfort he was sure to encounter in the next few days.

They left two days later, arriving at King Station in Seattle after a long, four hour train trip. Dr. Ellis, David's old mentor at the university and activist in the hiking club, hailed them as they stepped down from their car. Dressed in a long wool coat and black bowler hat, he greeted them each warmly, but with special attention to Alford. Alford was glad for his company. Originally an early patron at his father's store, Dr. Ellis and the elder Alford were close friends. Alford would never forget that it was Ellis who cared for him after his beating.

"So glad you came, Alford. How are you all? David asked me to meet you," Ellis said as he pumped his hand.

"It was a nice trip down. No elk on the track. How are things here?"

"Things have been quite hectic. The response has been overwhelming. The service location had to be changed twice. There are hiking groups coming from all over — even California." He smiled gently at Caroline. "She was a sweet lady, wasn't she?"

"Yes, she was. Such a dear friend to me." Alford squeezed her hand when she choked on her last words.

Dr. Ellis led them across the station floor and out to his Ford touring motorcar. Caroline couldn't help but crane her head up to look at the grand coffered ceilings of the railroad station and its highly ornate details. When they stepped outside, Caroline gasped at the changes since she first arrived in Seattle in 1907. Gone was the chaos of regrading and the scatter-shot building boom around the station. The area was level now, its streets bustling with all forms of motorized transport not seen on the streets of Frazier. In addition to electric trolley cars, she saw a motorbike. But development seem to march away to the north. Towering to the sky was the new L.C. Smith building, the tallest building west of the Mississippi. Caroline never felt so out of place and date. She felt like a country bumpkin. For moment, she hesitated.

Dr. Ellis helped Caroline in, then lifted up the memorial wreath made for Emily by the Frazier Hiking Club and settled it beside her. With a wave of a hand, he invited Alford to get in.

"Where are we staying?" Alford asked. The funeral wasn't until tomorrow.

"You'll be staying with me and the missus. Originally David found a place for you, but he can reach you easier at our place."

"How's he taking it?"

"Oh, he's a good soldier, but when the whole thing's over, I'm sure it'll hit him even harder. They were such a lovely couple. Did everything together. Pure delight to be with."

Ellis pulled out into the evening traffic consisting of automobiles, motorized trucks and horse-drawn freight wagons. He continued talking once they were on their way along the newly asphalted street. "I do wish he'd take off for a while. He could go away for a semester. Others would cover for him. He hasn't been well."

Caroline leaned over to listen. "He's been ill?"

"Nerves, I suppose. Stomach trouble. That sort of thing. It's understandable. The University had all that turmoil with the president and the faculty, you know. Then, there were the anti-socialists looking for dirt which still goes on. Now it's the Student Anti-Drill Society. David hasn't liked the war preparations on campus. Interferes with teaching and learning, he feels. Emily tried hard to keep him distracted. They were going to go back east this summer after the baby was old enough. Now — if I had my way, I'd make him go despite what's happened. It'd do him some good."

Ellis looked at Alford. "How have you been faring with the lumber mill strikes and labor unrest? You get any such pressure in the Frazier District with it so close to the national forest?"

"There've been inroads," Alford said.

The funeral for Emily Harms began at one o'clock at a leading church in the city. Though Caroline knew the outdoor community in Seattle greatly loved her friend and would sorely miss her during the outing next summer in Frazier, she was unprepared for the large turnout. Some of the best-known families in the city attended, as well as friends in the mountaineering clubs in the state and around the Pacific Northwest and the university community. The mourners seemed to have been people from all walks of life.

They were given a seat close to the front of the Gothic-inspired church where David would be sitting, sharing the cushioned pew along with Ellis and his wife and what seemed like university students. As the church filled to overflowing, the service began late, led by Emily's own father. Caroline hadn't seen him in years. He appeared thin and withdrawn, struggling with his belief in God and his deep, personal grief.

Caroline looked for David in the party that slipped into the pews in the front at the last minute and found to her anxiety, her parents and her brother Sammy accompanying him. Feeling her stiffen, Alford looked in the same direction then quietly took her hand and held it throughout the moving service.

Afterwards, there was a private burial in a nearby cemetery, then a reception to be held in a building adjacent to the cathedral. Caroline and Alford became separated from Ellis much to Alford's relief and missed the connection to the cemetery. The press of the crowd pushed them along with David's family and relatives to a cloistered side of the church where mourners rolled the coffin out to a elegant horse-drawn hearse decked with Douglas fir boughs and memorials from various mountaineering clubs. There on the flagstone walkway, they came face-to-face to Caroline's mother and father. Sammy immediately hailed them in greeting, but he was diplomatically restrained by his mother. Her eyes full of regret, she gave Caroline a fleeting smile and a nod of her head before Charles Symington took note. When he saw Caroline, he hesitated. Then he saw Alford. Scowling, he angrily turned his family toward the coffin, looking back only once to give a piercing stare. Separated by only twenty feet in the crowd, it could have been a hundred miles. It left Alford with a dirty, humiliated feeling.

Alford pulled Caroline close to him and turned around to look for Ellis. Going against the flow, they found themselves at the end of the covered cloister where some

French doors were ajar. Stepping in, they stopped to get their bearings. By then, the crowd had dissipated along with the hearse and automobiles, leaving the cloister empty.

"Look's like we're going in circles, babe. They've gone off without us." Alford surveyed the room possibly used for a church library or study. It was full of books from floor to ceiling and had two long windows at the opposite end of the door framed by thick red velvet drapes. Beside them were two ladder-back chairs. "Why don't we camp there."

Caroline sat down, clutching her hands in her lap. She looked numb and confused. Alford reconnoitered the room like a trapped wolf. Opening an interior door, he peered out into a hallway that led back to the main part of the church. It was quiet except for the far off sound of china and silver being prepared for the reception much later. The faint coffee smell made him thirsty, but he quietly closed the door, thinking he'd go investigate later. For now, Caroline needed him.

He sat down beside her and rubbed her shoulders. "I'm truly sorry, Caroline. I'll arrange for us to go and find the gravesite later. Perhaps Dr. Ellis — "

She patted his hand. "It's all right, Bob. I'm more sorry about Father treating you so shabbily. I do want to see David, but knowing him, he'll find the right time to talk to me. If only I could've said something to my mother." She squeezed his hand, tears threatening at the corners of her eyes. "Despite everything, I thought she looked well. She seemed anxious to see me."

Alford squeezed her hand back. He wanted to encourage her, but inwardly he wasn't holding out much hope for an agreeable meeting the next time they encountered the Symingtons.

A clock on the wall ticked the minutes away dully. Minutes stretched out into a half hour, and then to a whole. Caroline leaned against him and fell asleep. When the clock struck a quarter past the hour, activity started quietly, then increased in the hall. Stiffly, Alford got up and went to investigate. Some people were starting to return.

"Shall I find Dr. Ellis? Or would you rather just go down now and get a cup of tea to drink? Avoid the crowd until later."

Caroline straightened up and adjusted her hat. "No, let's go and brave it all at once. Perhaps we'll see Sammy. I do want to see him."

"Then let's get a breath of fresh air and go." He helped her up and putting her hand under his arm, led her to the French doors. He was helping her through when the hallway door suddenly opened into the room.

"Damnation. It's true. You had the balls to come. Come see the bastard, Jenkins, and see what you can make of him."

Alford swung around and came face-to-face with Harold Symington. Dressed in a dark business suit, gray silk tie and these days, bearded, he looked the formidable businessman he was. Discreetly behind him stood Jenkins, dark and sullen. Alford's skin prickled. He steeled himself and turned his attention back to Symington.

You haven't changed much, although you're a little heftier. Alford stared him down, refusing to flinch under Symington's bullying gaze.

"You don't belong here, Alford," Symington sneered. "This is a private family affair and you're not welcome. Go back to your stump farm or whatever it is you do. Rangering?"

He must have thought Alford would either jump or retreat at the insults. When he continued to stand his ground and didn't rise to the bait, Symington's expression changed.

"Hello, uncle," Caroline said. "You are looking well for a man in such a stew." Her eyes not leaving his, she slipped her hand through Alford's arm and stood next to him.

Symington studied them both, then turned to Caroline. "I wish to speak to Alford alone. It's a private matter."

"Family matters are not private matters. You'll speak to us both."

Symington smiled wryly, then beckoned with his head for

Jenkins to go back out into the hall. "Go on, Jim," he ordered. "You might see to my brother and his family. They should be back by now." He turned back to Caroline. "It will only take a moment. I assure you no blood will be spilt."

"And I assure you uncle that we didn't come here on your behalf, but on David's and Emily's." She pushed against Alford to make him move forward, but he patted her arm.

"It's all right, sweetheart. I'm going to give him a chance to talk." When she protested, he played a husband's role and told her to go on out into the church hall. "But not with Jenkins standing out there," he warned Symington. "Call your hound off."

When Symington sputtered, Alford grinned inwardly. He could play their game too.

He bowed slightly to Caroline and let her pass. "We won't take long."

Symington waited for the hall door to close and when it didn't, closed it himself. In front of the French doors, Alford watched him with wary, but amused eyes. Symington didn't impress him anymore. Alford had seen tougher men than Symington in the last eight years. Still, he knew that Symington could be as dangerous as the rough stuff he'd encountered in camps in the mining district near the national forest. The violence at his fingertips would be more discreet and most likely secondhand, but just as deadly. Odd, though, that he would carry a grudge for so long even when it no longer mattered. When it didn't concern him.

"You wanted to say something?" Alford asked. He took a stance that Vernell often took when dealing with trespassers. It had a calming effect while at the same time established a legal authority. As if Harold Symington did anything these days in a legal framework.

Symington removed his dark kid gloves with slow deliberation — like he was skinning a cat. "I don't like you, Alford. I never have and never will. You're rude and insolent in your assumption that by stealing my brother's daughter, you're somehow elevated to new stature. Your presence here — "

Alford laughed. "Where I come from, elevation has more to do with the mountains than any artificially stratified class list."

Symington's dark eyes flashed, then smoldered. "Indeed. But one is more permanently lasting. The machinery of modern times can do anything. Even blow up a mountain. While a name — Tell me, how's the logging operation going?"

"Oh, I can think of several *names* to describe that. But you know more about it than I do. Or maybe not. Ford may not want to divulge all his troubles to his silent partner." When Symington's eyes blinked, Alford knew he'd guessed right. Symington had his hand in it somewhere from the beginning despite what Ford had told Caroline.

"You think you're clever."

"Not clever, Symington. Just not easily hoodwinked. I know what you're up to there in Frazier and down in Twin Forks. You believe you'll get what you want — timber at any human cost."

"You sound like a bleeding Wobbly socialist."

"The words slip easily off your tongue, Symington, but then you've had practice." Alford stepped forward, his disgust at the man growing. "You always want to have the final say, and when you can't get it, you send in your dogs to clear things out. I know what you're doing in those logging camps: breaking men by breaking their backs, then breaking the law to suit yourself."

"I should've broken yours long ago. Had you on morals charges."

Alford snorted. "You're pathetic. Were you in that high-placed bunch from Seattle that got busted by the fish and game officer up in Snohomish? Did I hear a howl when they had their guns taken away — all twenty-two of them — for starting the duck hunting season at 3:45 rather than 6:00 in the morning? You'd thought someone's mother had been murdered. You howl over ducks while men get maimed by work, then beaten when they ask for the eight hour day."

"You *are* a Wobbly."

Alford fingered his watch fob. "I'm a federal employee, Symington. I work for Uncle Sam's trees. That's all." He sighed lightly. "I've no time for this. I'm here to pay my respects, then go. You can stay here and talk to yourself." He crossed the room with purpose and headed out the door.

"Wait," called Symington. "You know Billy Howell?"

Alford turned around. For a moment he was wary, not sure what direction Symington was going.

"But of course, you do. You two go way back to the logging camps down here."

"What's it to you?"

"Nothing, really. He might need watching, though. His being a shingle weaver places him in a bit of a fix. His union's been agitating for months in Twin Forks, goaded on by Wobbly outfits, no doubt, who are urging slowdowns instead of strikes. Perhaps you might visit with him on the wisdom on that."

"He can choose for himself."

"Then he chooses trouble. It won't be tolerated. That and any other labor upset in the woods. The timber will be delivered to the mills and the mills will run. On time."

Alford shook his head. Most of the industries in the state now ran on the eight hour day, but not the lumber mills and the logging camps. The slowdown was a new tactic in the long war to get the hourly condition changed.

"You find this amusing," Symington gloated, "but a man in your position shouldn't be too complacent even in the national forests. The government's going to be wanting to make some changes in timber sales."

"State government?" Alford wondered.

"No, federal. There's a need for spruce for the new airplanes."

"So you think you can get what you want because there's great money to be made off the war preparations." Alford knitted his brows at the thought, then brightened. "Symington," he laughed, "you and all the other timber barons might just end up losing the whole game. Did it ever occur to you the federal government just might want those reforms, just to keep the timber coming?"

He turned away and went out into the dark-paneled hall where Caroline waited at its end. He didn't bother to heed Symington's warning to stay sharp. He just kept walking, keeping his eyes focused on her. When he caught up with her, he slipped an arm around her waist. "Where do we go next?" She pointed to another hallway and a flight of stairs where people were arriving to go downstairs. They started toward it when they were hailed by Emily's older brother from Swede Hill. Franklin Drew greeted them warmly and gratefully took Caroline's offer of condolence.

"Sweet Emily," Drew sighed. "I can't believe she's gone. It seems only a short time ago that she came to our homestead at Swede Hill to care for my wife and our first child. How I'll miss her." His throat caught and he looked away. Caroline took his hand and waited for him to continue. He gave her a weak smile. "Have you had a chance to see David? I believe he just got back."

"No."

"Look, I don't think he's gone down yet. I'll take you to him."

"Bob?"

"Let's go." Alford looked toward the library. The door was still open, but the room was empty. Symington had gone out the French doors.

Drew led them through the church annex to a small lounge room with easy access to the narthex of the stone church next door. Inside, David sat with Emily's father, still in his vestments, on one of the overstuffed chairs set up near an unlit fireplace. Immediately, Caroline went to David as he rose from his place, pale and withdrawn. He accepted her embrace like it was a spiritual balm.

"Caroline," he whispered. "You've come. Thank you."

He rocked her gently in his arms, then looked over to Alford. "Thank you both."

Alford nodded back at him, then to the older gentleman, suddenly feeling out of place. David saw his discomfort and made a quick introduction to his father-in-law.

"Very nice to meet you," Reverend Drew said. "Emily spoke of you often with great affection." He turned to David. "I think Franklin and I will go see how the arrangements are coming along." He patted David on his arm and excusing himself, went out with Franklin.

David gave Caroline a long hug, then released her. He asked about their trip down and their lodgings, but the subject of Emily loomed large between them. At some point, Caroline took her cousin's hand for comfort, keeping his thoughts on good memories. Soon they spoke of family matters.

"Have you spoken to your parents?" David wondered. "Sammy was asking."

"We saw them in the cloister. It wasn't successful."

David winced. "Perhaps I could go and arrange to speak to them all —"

"I don't think so," Alford interrupted. "I don't mean to sound rude, but I don't think this is the time or place, Harms. You've a great many people who want to see you. You should attend to them. As for us, I think we should leave. I'm not about to hide in rooms here, but neither do I want another confrontation. Let's arrange to meet later at our place. We have until tomorrow before we have to go home."

"Bob —" Caroline protested. "Please."

For a moment he hesitated. He wanted to say something strong, but the situation made him choose his words wisely. "Then you stay, honey. You two just visit alone for a while. I'll walk back."

There was a stunned silence. David finally broke the impasse.

"It's not necessary, but very generous, Alford. You

wouldn't mind?"

Alford said he didn't, but he felt the old tension of jealousy flick through him.

David took Caroline's hand. "It won't be for long. And I'll take you up on your offer to meet later." He held out his hand and the men shook.

Alford gave Caroline a peck on her cheek, then nodding at them both, left.

Caroline returned to the Ellis's much later than intended. After visiting with David for a while, she went with him down into the church's fellowship hall and melted into the crowd milling there. Among the mourners, some of whom acting more like visitors at a monthly hiking meeting than a funeral, she found a group of Emily's closest friends reminiscing about some of their outings with her including their first trip to Mount Kulshan. Caroline remembered it well as it was the first time Bob and she had climbed the mountain. She became so absorbed in their stories that she didn't see her brother Sammy snake his way through the tightly bunched groups until he was next to her. Secretly, they slipped away to visit.

"I'm sorry Bob felt he had to go and I know why. Our uncle, the bastard!"

"Sammy. Such language!"

"Sorry, but it's true. I won't take back what I said. Uncle Harold believes he rules everything. Including Father."

"Why do you say that?"

"Father wants to make some policy changes in some of the family business they share, especially some of the logging concerns, but Uncle Harold won't hear of it. Says Father's too sentimental and too bookish to know the real world of men."

"And you know so much about it?"

"I know and hear enough." He looked suddenly grown up to her, especially when he gave her an all-knowing male look. He wasn't her kid brother any more. She forgave him and let him explain himself, then discussed the pros and cons of any action.

It was dark when Caroline and the Ellises returned to home. The lights were already on and a fire burned in the parlor. When the maid came to take her coat, Caroline asked if Alford had retired early.

"Oh, no ma'am. He left in such a hurry. There was a phone call not long after he got here. He was called away to his parent's home. There was some emergency."

Stunned, Caroline stared at Dr. Ellis with uneasy eyes. *How could Bob go at a time like this?* What could have been the emergency?

Chapter 39

Einar Alford's stroke, late in the morning, was the emergency. While he was awake, he wasn't expected to survive. Alford took the nearest trolley to the ferry and traveled across Lake Washington where he was dropped off at Swede Hill.

In the eight years since he had left, the community had grown and even in winter, warranted a ferry. Where there had been trees, there were farms and a busy little lakefront town that serviced them. Shingle mills still persisted, but they were being pushed back to the hills and replaced with farms and other agricultural enterprises. The little settlement had grown into something much more substantial than a real estate office and general store.

In the fading winter light, Alford felt disoriented and confused as he thought of his father. He looked for something familiar and found that the old community hall still stood. It was hard to imagine that here he met Caroline for the second time and where she caught his heart. It was hard to imagine anything at all. Like Papa dying.

His brother Ake waited under the single electric light at

the dock, along with his brother Lars who had moved down from Alaska recently. They greeted him with subdued words. Ake wondered where Caroline was. Alford explained he had left hurriedly without informing her.

"How's Papa?" he asked getting into the waiting automobile.

"Holding," murmured Ake. "He's waiting for you. He keeps asking for you."

"Oh, Lord," Alford choked. He looked away, tears threatening. "I'm not ready."

The Alford home looked like the same, neat place he had known since childhood. Now there was a gravel road passing in front of the house and several runabouts and touring cars parked next to the white picket fence. There was a refined look to it today, even in winter, with its new milled cedar siding and white paint. It looked prosperous while at the same time fully aware of its humble beginnings. Like his father, it had been blessed.

The kitchen was warm and full of relatives and friends talking in whispers. There was a sharp silence when he stepped in, then words of relief he'd gotten the call after all.

Someone took his coat. Another offered him tea. He took it gratefully as the ferry and ride to the house had been freezing. A sister-in-law hugged him, another asked after Caroline. A brother carried the conversation. It all became a blur: the long train ride down from Frazier yesterday, the long funeral today and facing down Harold Symington. Alford, finally overwhelmed, suddenly felt the deepest empathy for David Harms.

There was a rustle from the back and his mother came out. Her face was washed with the shock that comes from bad news, but she still walked with her shoulders back, full of dignity as ever.

"Mama." He gave her a long hug, kissing her on her snowy head. This was the place in life they all came to, but he wished his father could stay forever on this side.

"I'm so sorry, Mama. How are you doing?"

Mama bit her lips. The tears in her eyes said it all.

"Is he awake?"

"*Ja*. He will see you now."

Alford looked miserably over to his brothers. They were all here now. Except Stein and the little sister who'd died long ago.

"Go in, Bob," Olav said. "We've all been with him this afternoon."

Alford followed his mother down to the room he'd once used when he lived at home and where he had recuperated after his beating.

It was as neat as before. Now the room was lit by electric lamps. His father was propped up on a stack of pillows, his white hair blended into the linen pillowcases. Drawn and pale, he looked oddly misshapen with the left side of his mouth slightly drooping. Papa Alford appeared to be asleep, but when Alford came up close to him, he opened his eyes. He gasped and said "You come," in English. Only Alford could barely understand him so thick and tangled were his words.

"Yes, Papa. Don't try to talk."

The quick breath in again. He patted the bed and invited Alford to sit. Alford sat next to him feeling like a little boy again as he recalled the time his father had stayed with him all night when he was sick.

"You look good, Bob. Me, I not so good." He spoke with difficulty, but Alford knew from Olav that the stroke had affected his left side. His speech came and went. "Where Caroline?"

"She's still at the reception for Emily Harms's funeral, Papa."

He nodded. "I see her later. Have you seen Stein?"

Alford hesitated only briefly. Ake had described their father's confusion on the drive over to the house.

"A little while ago, Papa. It's winter, but he's still busy in the woods."

"Foreman. He make good foreman." The old man

looked at Alford suddenly. "You make good ranger. Like Vernell."

Alford brushed the wool coverlet with his hand, then followed the outlines of the colorful panes with a finger. He was trying to be strong, but like a sneeze coming on, didn't feel much in control.

"Don't cry for me, son. I had — a good life." Einar sighed and for a moment closed his eyes. His breathing thinned and a little dribble of spit came out of the corner of his mouth. Alford took out a handkerchief and wiped it away.

"Like a baby, I am," Einar said sleepily. "Like after a good drunk." His eyes popped open. "You know all about that. You were such a drunk. Nearly broke your mother's heart."

"I know — I'm sorry," Alford said weakly.

"It was Stein." With effort, the old man tried to tap his forehead, but the hand fell away. "I know he's dead. I got a little clouds in my noggin, but I know he's gone. And you changed."

"Yes, I changed." Tears welled up in Alford's eyes and began to flow down his cheeks. He didn't care if anyone saw.

"It was Caroline too. You have a fine family. You tell m'… grandchildren…about me. Y' tell them about Stein."

"Yes, Papa."

"I'm going to go to sleep now. Be gone for a little while. You take care of Mama. And… you remember Stein."

"I will, Papa." Alford choked. He bent his head like he had done as a little boy and waited for his father's blessing. The old man raised his hand. The weight of it on his head felt heavy, but Alford took it with all his heart, eventually placing it down on the coverlet again.

"Goodnight, Papa. Sweet dreams."

Einar Alford sighed. He frowned as he collected his thoughts. "You're a good son and I love you. You've done well. Remember who you are and where you came from. Be good to your wife and love her, but above all, love God. That is all I have to say."

He spoke so clearly Bob was encouraged, but a shudder passed through his father's body and he wondered if it was another little stroke like those that the old man apparently experienced all afternoon. The eyes flickered closed and the mouth trembled, then he was still.

"Papa?"

"He's resting, son," Mama said behind him. "Soon he'll sleep forever. You go and get something to eat. I don't think you have eaten all day. Not with the funeral. If you are tired you can lie down in my room."

"I want to stay."

"All right. We both keep him company." She rested a hand on Alford's shoulder and stroked it. He leaned his head into her and wept softly. He hadn't felt so miserable since Caroline lost their baby.

Papa coughed and they both riveted their eyes on the pale face that seemed to droop increasingly more. His eyes were closed, his mouth slightly open. Alford took his handkerchief again and wiped his father's chin, again took his hand and squeezed it. "I love you, Papa." He leaned over and kissed his father's forehead. In his imagination, he thought his father squeezed his hand back.

Einar Alford passed away a few hours later with his family gathered around him. Not long after, Olav helped Alford call to the home of Dr. Ellis where he reached a frantic Caroline. She gasped when he told her the news and from across the telephone line he heard her begin to cry.

"I can't get over until tomorrow," he told her. "The ferry stopped running a couple of hours ago."

"I'll come in the morning. You'll stay, of course."

"I have to call Vernell. My family's making funeral arrangements now. He'll be buried here. Soon, I think."

"I'm so sorry, dear. I loved him so much. I can't believe this has happened. So sudden."

Alford leaned his head against the wall. "Yes, it was. I only talked with him by phone a week ago." He cleared his throat. "Did... did everything work out for you at the church?"

"I saw Sammy. He's grown so. He's all hot for the war preparations and wants to join up with a group who flies. I don't think my father knows."

"Talk with anyone else?"

"Just some of Emily's friends. They're talking about having an outing in Frazier this summer in her honor." Caroline sighed. "It's late. I'd like to retire. I'll call Cathy about the children." In a tired voice, she whispered that she loved him, then after they each said good night, hung up. Alford just stayed at the phone and let it hum. A concerned operator came on and asked if there was a problem. "If not, I'd like to retire too."

Alford and Caroline returned to Frazier four days later. David Harms and Dr. Ellis along with Ake saw them off. When they arrived home in the late afternoon, they were both exhausted. Alford took Caroline to get the children and after seeing them home, drove the truck up to see Vernell.

"Terribly sorry about your father," the ranger said. "This is becoming a hard winter for you, isn't it? Thought 1916 would be better."

"It appears that way."

"I liked the senior Alford very much. Stalwart, upright fellow. I know he'll be missed."

"He was a good father. Taught me everything I know about building and fishing."

Vernell pushed some papers at his desk and cleared his throat. "I'd give you another day, but I need you. There was a big windstorm two days ago. A lot of limbs and a couple of firs down on the upper road. Got folks coming up who want to propose a lodge if the national park idea goes through. Talking about winter doings, not just the summer stuff. The road needs to be cleared. It'll be cold work, but you, Fuller and a few others should be able to get it done by Wednesday."

"Sure, I'll get on it right away. Get the tools together today, go out with one of the horse teams early tomorrow." He stirred sluggishly in his chair.

Vernell went to his wood stove and filled a tin mug with coffee. "Here. This should get the cobwebs out of your eyeballs. Honestly, Alford, you look beat."

"I haven't really stopped since before Thanksgiving when the kids got sick. Then two funerals and the endless line of mourners the last sixty hours." Alford ran a hand through his hair. "When I can, I'm going fishing." He sipped at the mug, then held the hot metal container above his knees. "My father left me his gear."

Vernell waited for him to gather his thoughts and emotions before speaking again. "See any of Caroline's kin?"

Alford looked at his boss curiously. "Saw her parents from a distance, but had words with Harold Symington close up."

"You might encounter him here. There's a new outfit forming south of here. The Hawley Creek area above Twin Forks. Fuller heard about it the other day. The outfit has a big section there and plans to run as much board feet as they can per day. They'll be sent to the B & E Lumber Mill where they're putting up a new building and fancy saw just for that. Symington owns seventy-five percent."

Alford made a face. "That's all fir."

"Some cedar. They'll continue to make bolts for shingles."

"But he wants the fir." Alford whistled. "That's a big area. At one hundred fifty dollars per hundred feet, that's a lot of money for one person."

"Exactly."

"Anything happening here?"

"Some new Forest Service regulations. I think if permits open up for the building expansion already in the shipyards, there might be some changes in the way labor is run."

Alford perked up. "Not an eight hour day?"

Vernell nodded his grey head. "Uh-huh."

Alford flushed, then smiled.

"Thought you'd like that. Another thing. Since the state went dry at this past New Year's there have been two raids on some blind pig operations in the city. One of the fellows had connections down south. Our old friend, Piles. One of my law enforcement friends mentioned it."

Symington again. *He's everywhere*, Alford thought. The idea wore him down. Maybe everything wore him down. With his father's passing, his emotions were raw. He looked out the window and stared into the forest.

"On the second hand," Vernell said. "Think I might reconsider you not taking the day off. Why don't you get yourself organized, then leave an hour early? I'll get Fuller to make a final check."

"Thanks, Jack. I have to say that I'm drained."

Chapter 40

The spring of 1916 came in with a vengeance, bringing rain and wind storms that knocked down trees and caused the river around Frazier to flood. Then a week later, blue skies and sun appeared for a few days before switching back to rain again. It was a weather pattern that continued for the next few weeks. *Unpredictable*, Caroline thought. The weather wasn't much different from the emotions storming through the Alford household since the beginning of January.

Emily Harms's death struck Caroline hard. *How could she die?* She was so sweet and full of life. As a mountaineer, Emily dared to do things most women would find daunting, let alone physically challenging. It didn't make sense she'd died in bed losing her baby. Emily was so healthy. Though common sense told Caroline the grippe did its part in her friend's death, the new "painless childbirth" was supposed to alleviate any such complications of delivery, even if the baby was premature.

Devastated by her friend's passing, Caroline sought out Cathy's companionship frequently. Together, they tried to put Emily's death into rational perspective. Of which, of course, there was none.

"The answer, of course, is reform," Cathy said at a gathering of friends at Ellie's home. "We must work to make such things safer."

All the young women agreed, their heads bobbing over their coffee cups, then in an explosion of chatter, lamented the distance to the hospital in the city.

"To think that our dear friend died with all the best care in Seattle. What on earth can we expect here? We need a clinic just for mothers and children between here and Hawley Creek," Berta said.

Caroline looked up at that. "I wonder, though. With the labor strife going on in the woods and lumber mills in some parts of the district, I think such a clinic would get poor shift unless we took it on ourselves."

"So true, Carrie." Cathy sat more erect, her face aglow. "But a clinic we must have and I hope issues such as family limitation will also be broached as that helps the health of the mother too."

"But not until after the coming summer outing with the Seattle hiking club," Caroline said.

Berta patted Caroline's hand. "Of course, Caroline. It was always a joy for Emily, wasn't it? It will keep her memory alive."

While Caroline dealt with Emily's passing, Alford's grief was just as difficult. It was hard to accept his father's sudden death. Sometimes he felt like a small boy back in his old home, waking up each day to ask his father a question only to remember he was gone. Then he would cry for whatever mystery had been on his mind because it would have to go unanswered. The question would always be hanging there, a piece of life's unfinished business. *How did you lay varnish on that table, Papa? How will I store my flies? How did you and Mama make things work?*

There was still so much for him to say to someone who'd loomed large in his life.

Grief. He was glad Vernell kept him busy, pushing him

hard on projects that kept him occupied and his mind on the present. Once the trees were cleared from the road, there were projects indoors repairing equipment and sharpening tools. The work was endless and for a time it worked. It did him good to be out in the mountains and fighting the contrary early spring elements. When he was with Vernell and Fuller and occasionally, Micah, he was his old self. It couldn't last, though. When he returned home, he was often moody and unreachable.

Little things irritated him: Harms constantly calling to talk with Caroline, the preparations for the opening of the Symington logging operation and the stories of strife in the logging camps and shingle mills down near Twin Forks and the new camp at Hawley Creek. Symington seemed to be everywhere, infiltrating every community including his own. Alford became short-tempered, but he never explained himself to a hurt Caroline. This led to arguments as old hurts festered. Sometimes, he took his pole down to the river and mulled over life there on his own. He began to do it frequently. Then the Ford operation officially resumed.

On that day, Alford rose early to prepare for a trip down toward Hawley Creek where a fish hatchery was being developed by the state. The Forest Service had an interest in it and wanted him to check the stock out. Caroline and he children still slept, but he decided not to disturb them even though he might be gone for more than a day. After making coffee and cutting up some leftover beef for a sandwich, he composed a note. He was about to leave when he remembered his gloves up on the chest of drawers. Quietly climbing upstairs, he crept into the bedroom for the gloves.

Caroline was asleep, her slim body curled up as she rested on her pile of pillows. A glimpse of lace strap and bare shoulder above the top of the coverlet caught his eye. He gazed at her for a moment, then got the gloves. He got halfway across the room toward the door when a floorboard creaked under the large rag rug.

"Are you going, Bob, with no word for me?"

Alford turned. "I didn't want to wake you, honey. That's all."

She sat up against her stack of pillows, smoothing the low cotton bodice across her full breasts. Her cinnamon hair was bound on her neck, but the satin ribbon was slipping and in danger of losing the mass of thick hair to her shoulders. For so early in the morning, she looked fresh and beautiful, but the expression on her face was joyless.

"I'm awake now. Is this the day you go to Hawley Creek?" she asked.

"Yes. I'll see the hatchery manager there. Take in the sights and whatever else Vernell has on the list. Might not get back tonight."

Caroline nodded her head quietly, then stared down at her hands resting on the coverlet. When she stayed silent, he asked if she'd say hello to the kids when they were up.

"Of course."

"Well," he said awkwardly, "I guess I'll be going." He stuffed his gloves into the big pockets of his Forest Service coat.

Caroline slowly brought her head up. There was a glint of hurt in her eyes. It cut right to his heart. *Caroline.*

"I suppose you must. I'll be here for most of the morning, then the ladies mountain club is meeting for lunch. I'm to talk about this summer's outing by the Seattle chapter. David has sent some information for the memorial the ladies planned for Emily."

Something I didn't know about, Alford thought. "I hope that goes well. Say hello to the ladies." He started to back out.

"Bob?" Her voice was a whisper, but never had a voice riveted his attention so strongly. "Have I done something to offend you?"

Alford was dumbstruck. "Why do you say that?"

"You avoid us."

Guilt flushing through him, he walked over to the bed and kissed her.

"You've done nothing. I'm sorry, I'm just not myself

lately. I'll try to get back tonight and then we'll talk. If not, I'll stay at Billy's." He stood up, but didn't move. Caroline reached out and took his hand.

"Is it David? He means no harm. He's so lonely and I'm afraid not well. He just calls to talk."

Alford wasn't sure what to answer. She was right. Harms didn't mean to cause any trouble. He was just lonely. But his closeness to Harold Symington and her father rankled Alford.

"It's not David." He swallowed. "I'm just having a hard time about losing Papa. It's hit me harder than I thought it ever would. If you should speak to David, please say hello. Tell him if he wishes to come to preview the summer outing, he's welcome to stay with us." Caroline leaned against his arm and drew his hand to her cheek.

"Thank you. The mountain air will do him good." She squeezed his hand. "I miss your father too."

A strange feeling went through Alford. He'd been a fool being so standoffish for the past few weeks. He should have explained himself. It wasn't her fault she was related to the Symington-Ford crowd. She couldn't control David Harms's feelings for her. He couldn't change either of those things. He reached down and stroked her head with his free hand. He felt her smile against it and suddenly he wanted to regain her favor very much.

"Caroline —"

She looked up. Her hair was undone now. "Yes?"

"Maybe I won't go just yet."

A little while later, Alford took his gear out to his truck. He paused for a moment, remembering how she had opened her arms to him and taken him in, baring herself to his passion as if there were no clouds between them.

A raven's call cleared his head. It was cool and misty, this last day of March. The fog shrouded the edge of the road and obscured the lower reaches of the big trees going in either direction along the gravel lane. Over in the meadow, he could barely make out their cow. It was the kind of day he liked for fishing along the river, but it wasn't good for driving a truck down a road like the one to Hawley Creek and Twin Forks. The roadbed was unpredictable. In this gloomy light, a vehicle going over ten miles an hour could get into trouble quickly. Mindful, he loaded the truck, then cranked it to life.

Further up the road toward Frazier, the mist lurked like a half drawn curtain across the lane. Alford looked in that direction, then began to turn the truck southward when something caught his eye. A team of oxen lumbered into view, followed by a group of men carrying axes and crosscut saws. In a stream, they seemingly popped through the mist, bright-colored shirts bobbing in the distance, then turned toward the river where the trees had already been reduced to scarecrow-like rubble along the skid road. Alford watched the whole process with resignation. The resumption of logging across the river had been expected for some time, but it still felt like a newly inflicted wound.

Caroline's going to miss those trees on her hills outside the kitchen window. A chill passed through him, a premonition of what could come. Letting the feeling pass, he got the vehicle turned, then headed south. He didn't see the big touring car pop through the mist like the men and stop at the skid road. A figure on the passenger side stood up and stared, then waved the driver over to the side.

The drive down to Hawley Creek took longer than he planned. Though the road was a few years old, it had only recently been re-graveled and graded. Moving through the thick woods, the road rose and fell according to the hollows and hills it passed through. Rough in most places, some portions retained original plank boards, part of an earlier attempt for wagon travel. Others followed a new course high above the river.

About two miles south of their home, the road left the river altogether. It entered a switchback that dropped down to a stream rushing away from a small waterfall. Alford had been down many times so he knew its bad points. In the mist floating up from below, he took the time to stop and light his lamps in the headlights before descending. He'd just take it slow driving down. Jag Martin, the hatchery manager, wasn't expecting him until nine anyway.

The woods were deep and quiet here, the jagged tops and branches of the firs and hemlocks a seaweed grey-green in the thin morning light. From far off, he thought he heard something sputter, but noises tended to get soaked up in the woods, so he ignored it. The bushes next to trees down the steep slope to his right shivered and a deer peered out, then bolted when he put the truck in gear. Other than that, it was still. The truck groaned and he went forward.

At the bottom of the hill, the road followed the stream for a ways until it began to turn back at a bridge built next to the falls. He urged the truck onto the wet boards, then stopped when he discovered recent rains had weakened a section. Testing the boards with his boots, he decided to make some repairs with what tools he had in the back. After gathering what he needed, he went to work. He became so absorbed he didn't hear the car until it was upon him.

"There some problem?" A uniformed driver with cap and over-polished high boots got out of an open touring car. He was a tough looking young man, but one more accustomed to city streets. The man sitting in the car was not. It was J. J. Jenkins.

"Loose boards," Alford said, trying to ignore his nemesis. Of all the people in Symington's crowd, he hated Jenkins the most, yet in the last eight years, he'd only seen him about a half dozen times. Except for the inn and the funeral, it had been mostly from a distance. This was as close as he wanted to get. "I'm almost done."

He went back to hammering. They weren't going anywhere. Not before he moved off the one car bridge. The other car door slammed and he heard Jenkins's boots crunch up toward him, then the driver's.

"Don't have all day," said Jenkins, his mouth down in

disdain.

"I'm sure you don't with business and all. It'll be done in due time."

"This a national forest bridge?" the driver asked.

"No, but it'd be unneighbourly to go off and leave it like it was. Down-right dangerous at night or even in this partial soup." He went back to the section he'd been working on.

"You done socializing?" Jenkins asked, his voice pinched with irritation.

"Sure," answered Alford. "Got somewhere important to go?"

He kept working but listened for where Jenkins positioned himself. Alford didn't trust him.

"Sure is lonely out here," Jenkins said to his driver. "Could really put a man traveling by himself on the spot. Don't you think so, Ranger Alford?"

Alford looked up long enough to get a couple of nails out of a coffee can. "Depends on the man and the weather. How prepared he is." He gave the last couple of boards some attention, then retired his tools to his toolbox. He stood up. If Jenkins was fishing for trouble, he wouldn't get what he wanted. On the other hand, he could get something he wasn't expecting. "Hope you've got the right kind of axle."

"What does that mean?" The driver's face turned dark and sour. Alford didn't think he was very bright.

"Road's kind of rough," Alford responded. He looked Jenkins straight in the eyes. "No telling what you'll encounter." He started to go past them, but Jenkins stepped forward.

"I wasn't talking about the weather or the car. They'll take care of themselves. I was referring to the general nature of a man caught out alone. The vulnerability of it all."

"If you're worried about a dance card," mused Alford, "I'm not available. I've got government work to do, gentlemen. Time to go." He jostled the toolbox handle in his right hand and stepped away, not expecting Jenkins to be foolish enough to threaten him, but he was wrong.

Stumbling, Jenkins jabbed his shoulder into Alford, pushing him back toward the driver. The rush of the falls behind him got loud suddenly. In that instant, Alford became very calm, mentally calculating where each man stood.

"You been drinking?" Alford asked. "Of course, it's kind of hard to get a man's drink in a dry state. Got a blind pig operation near here?"

Jenkins worked his jaw, then his eyes jerked to his driver behind Alford. "You're awfully talky for a man in no position to talk, Alford. I hear there are automobile accidents out here all the time. Bad accidents. Long way for help. Might come too late. Ain't that right, Deevers?" His eyes made a slight signal.

Alford only sensed the driver's muscles tightening behind him, but just as Deevers grabbed him above the elbows. Alford dropped forward to avoid the incoming jab Jenkins swung at his face. The driver took Jenkins's blow in the eye while Alford slammed the toolbox into Jenkins above the groin. With both men yelping and swearing in pain, Alford twisted away.

"Get him, Deevers!" Jenkins yelled. Alford didn't wait for an answer. He swung the toolbox around and into the driver's arm and shoulder. Something snapped and the man went down shrieking in pain. Jenkins roared in fury, then charged.

Alford was faster. Throwing the toolbox at Jenkins, he was back in the truck in seconds and pulled his shotgun out.

"I think that'll be enough," Alford said. "You get your man into the car and sit. Do it now, Jenkins. You're done."

"I *am not* done!" Jenkins bellowed. "This is *not* over. It'll never be over."

"What is it with you? What did I ever do to you?"

"You stole something on my watch. Made a man lose face."

"You care that much? You *must* be Symington's dog."

Jenkins was close to spontaneous combustion, but he was dead to the shotgun's aim. Jenkins's face passed through several shades of red. Breathing heavily, he picked up the groaning driver. He got Deevers to the passenger side of the car and with some effort, on the seat.

"The doctor's just outside of Hawley Creek," Alford said. "You should get him there right away. He's looking a little gray." Alford motioned with the shotgun. "You get in yourself." Alford directed him around, then still training the shotgun, he retrieved the toolbox and put it way, then cranked up his truck.

"I'll go first," he told Jenkins. "You make a move, I'll blow your tires out. It's about twenty miles to the nearest service station."

With that, he got into the truck and drove it across the bridge. On the other side, the road started up a moderate grade. Behind him, the touring car roared to life.

It was no contest going up. Alford's truck performed like it had been fixed up to do: a Huxel axle and other features gave it more power and lower gears to work with. The touring car sputtered and groaned, then immediately fell behind as the grade got steeper. Alford let the truck have its head and made it up to the top where the road widened and flattened out. He put the truck in second and headed down the road as the morning sun fought to break through.

Sometime later, Alford heard a noise behind him. It was the touring car. It gave him an "ah-u-gah" on its horn, then passed him going at a fast clip. Jenkins and Deevers were soon lost in the mist and trees. He shook his head. They knew nothing about the road. It had dried off along here, but ahead were wetlands and they were aptly named. A mile down the road, he found them stuck up to their hubs.

"Got a problem?" he asked as he slowed down and stopped beside them. "I could give you a tow."

"We'll manage," Jenkins spat back.

"All right. The Coleman's stump farm's about a mile from here. If you're not out in forty-five minutes, I'll have someone come and check."

"I said we'll manage," Jenkins growled.

"Ask Deevers that."

"You telling me my business?"

"No, but you're out of your element. This is wilderness country and you don't want to trifle with it. You're not equipped to bash heads with a road like this. In worse weather, you'd be in a hell of a lot of trouble."

He looked at Deevers. His head had slipped off to the side. "I think you better put him in the back of the truck."

"I'll get my own damned medicine for him."

"Suit yourself. People might ask questions, though. It's not in our nature to leave someone hurt stranded out here. Unless, they're trouble. Sheriff might make inquiries. And he's an honest man." *Which means he's not bought off,* implied Alford.

Jenkins started to say something, then clammed up. Fuming, he got Deevers transferred to the back of Alford's truck, then joined him.

Thirty minutes later, Alford pulled into the yard next to Dr. Svenson's home in Hawley Creek. He helped get Deevers out of the truck and to the front door. Their knocking was answered by the doctor's wife. Mrs. Svenson and Alford looked at each other with amused and hidden recognition. "What have we here?" she asked.

"Is the doctor in?"

Once Deevers was settled, Alford excused himself and went outside to the truck where it was parked next to an orchard already beginning to display buds. The screen door on the front porch whined and someone came out. He waited for her to come down. It had been years.

"You're looking fine, Bob Alford."

"You too, Margie Gorham." He said it in jest, but her face turned white.

"Oh, please you mustn't say that. That Margie Gorham was a different life. It's Maggie Svenson now. I'm quite content and don't want to hurt a hair on my husband's head.

He's a dear soul."

Alford smiled. "I promise. Mum's the word. Only I thought you married a miner — Jabrinski — or something like that?"

Margie laughed.

She's still a fine looking woman, he thought. He'd also heard very complimentary things about her during the grippe epidemic. She was an excellent nurse.

"I did," she said. "We went north, where we worked a claim, only he drowned on the way back from the filing office. I didn't want to return stateside, so I went to Nome, Alaska Territory. Met my husband there. He's a sweet man, you know. Very good to me. And I enjoy being a help to him. It was a natural attraction. My father's medical library was my dowry."

"How long you been here at this place?"

"Since this past winter. He still works with Dr. Gates, but we can cover more territory here. Settlements are opening up fast and families as well as men are moving in. There's the road and the train's close by."

She looked her part. She was suitably dressed for a doctor's nurse, plain and uncompromising, but with a dignified beauty a man couldn't ignore. Alford thought there were hints of crow's feet around her eyes, a testament to hard times as she found her grounding over the years.

She moved away from the truck and out into the orchard. Turning, she appraised him with a serious eye. "And you? You seemed to have done what you set out to do. Are you head ranger now?"

"Nope. Jack Vernell's the man and he's got about a century to go. He's indestructible."

"But you have a family now. She's lovely, Caroline Symington. Not what I expected. Has grit."

Alford had forgotten the two women had met during Micah's illness. Now he wondered if Caroline had guessed about Margie's past. "Best thing to ever happen to me. She's special." The words came easily out of his mouth, but he was surprised how guilty he felt.

If she was so special, why hadn't he shown her that? Instead he retreated like a coward to the river whenever Harms called or the thought of her father being alive and not his own galled him to bitterness. His face must have flushed because Margie was looking at him with curiosity.

A voice yelped in the house. Margie shook her head.

"Who's that awful man with our patient? I thought I saw him in one of the camps down near Twin Forks. We went to see an injured logger, but he died before we got there. Some of the men were angry with the owner, but this man—he came out and told them to go away. When they didn't, he came back with some other men with clubs. I thought there'd be a riot."

"That's J. J. Jenkins. One of Harold Symington's security agents. Head one, I think."

"Jenkins. I think he associated with Sheriff Piles in King County on a number of occasions and I know all about Piles. One of the reasons I left."

"Jenkins know about you?"

"I don't think so. I never met him until now."

"Well, there might one or two of your former clients up here, but they won't say anything. As for Sheriff Piles, he got the grippe this winter and died before anyone could investigate him for corruption. I think you're safe, though."

"I heard Billy Howell's here," Maggie said.

"Yes. Has himself a nice little family and a few acres. Works as a shingle weaver. He'll watch out for you too."

"I've been happy, you know."

"I can see. Jenkins or any of the others give you trouble, you let me know."

"You act like you know him well."

"He's dangerous. Don't trust him." He took her hand. "I wish you the best. I won't forget you, Mrs. Svenson. You were kind to a young boy long ago and now people are beginning to appreciate you around here in a different way. They're not likely to forget your care in Frazier this past winter. I suspect that's true everywhere else."

"Why, I thank you for that. And I will take your words of caution."

He took out his watch. "I've got to go. I'm supposed to meet at the new fish hatchery. You might help them get their car towed or maybe rent a wagon. Give them just enough help to get rid of them. I think they're here for a reason. Logging season just opened up again and the way the world's going, so's the trouble." He started up the truck and prepared to get in. "You could do something for me."

Margie said she'd do what she could.

"If you hear about anything in the camps, especially about Billy —"

"You want to be kept posted?"

"Please."

"All right..." She gave his arm a squeeze. "— though I'm wondering what you've gotten yourself into. This is old business, isn't it?"

"Jenkins will always be old business."

Alford's appointment at the hatchery concluded by three, he had some time to call on Billy who was picking up a load of cedar bolts for a shingle mill above Twin Forks. They visited for a time, his friend giving Alford an update of affairs in several of the camps. Though still avoiding Wobbly meetings, Billy knew about conditions in the various camps.

"Symington's camps are the worst," Billy grumbled. "Overcrowded, lice-ridden bunkhouses, no place for a man to dry wet clothes or take a bath for that matter. Ten hour work day, seven day weeks. But if anyone tries to protest conditions, he'll get dismissed just like that." Billy looked down. "Maybe I'm a coward, but I gotta be careful. I got a family now, but I sure try to choose outfits that are clean and more honest in their dealings."

"Can't say I don't blame you. You have to do what's best."

"Well, if there were a chance of an eight hour day," Billy

admitted, "I might think of doing something about it. Speakers have come in, but it's dangerous to be caught listening. Symington's crowd isn't above bashing a few heads when they find out. Frankly, I can't afford that."

At six, Alford said good-bye and hitched a ride with his truck on one of the train's flat cars back to Frazier. The only fee for the truck was to join the brakeman in a game of cribbage. Alford let him win a few coins.

There was no one home when he got back. The house sounded like an empty orange crate as he walked through to the kitchen. He pumped a drink of water, then went outside. On the opposite riverbank, he looked upstream and saw the logging crews going at it. They'd been working since he left in the early morning. It was now seven-thirty, the evening sky turning from pink to lavender to a dusky purple. A couple of lamps bobbed among the black stubby skeletons that were once trees. And the scar was going further up.

Jag Martin, the fisheries manager, had asked him what the logging operation was all about. "Could you build there later?"

"Not likely," Alford told him. "The slope is too steep in most places. The land is low along the riverbank and often floods on that side. I know for a fact old timers stopped building there a long time ago."

"So what do they want?"

"All Ford wants is the trees. No law against that, I suppose, except the silt could hurt the fishing holes because the trees would take a long time to come back.

Caroline's trees. He wondered how far down they'd log.

A sound came from his left and Micah stepped out of the woods.

"Neat, ain't it?" He nodded at the logged-off land across the river.

Alford sighed. "I did that once too. I know it's progress, but when logging's so close to the national forest, it feels different. Nothing's sacred any more. Take away the national forests and the Symingtons of the world would have it all.

Nothing for the people to enjoy any more. All private with gates and fences to keep you out."

"My, you're testy."

"I had a go-to with Jenkins. A little too close for comfort. The man's got a serious problem."

"More than words?"

"He tried to jump me. Wasn't afraid to do it, either." Alford went on to relate what had happened. When he finished, Micah was silent.

Finally, he said, "You say anything to Vernell?"

"Not yet. We're supposed to meet tomorrow afternoon about the hatchery, but this isn't his problem. It's mine and it's personal."

"Don't take it personal. You'll lose focus."

"On what?"

"Jenkins gunning for you." Micah took out his knife and started cleaning his fingernails. "Don't worry. I'll watch your back, but first you tell Vernell. He wouldn't want one of his prized assistants threatened. That's a federal offense."

"That's why Jenkins won't do it up here. He'll just wait till I have to go south."

"Don't go south."

"Billy Howell's south. Symington made a point of that last January. If he wants to start a fight, he'll start there. He's already threatened to."

Micah grunted, then closed the subject by wiping his knife on his pants before putting it away. "If you're wondering where Miz Caroline is, she and the children are at the Bladstad's watching Marianne and the boys. Mrs. Bladstad's father took ill. She went down to the city where he's hospitalized. Be gone a day or two. Charlie will be back at midnight."

"I'll give her a call, then check the larder. You hungry?"

Micah grinned. "I am."

At midnight, Alford met Caroline at the Bladstad's. Bundling the children into the back of the truck, they headed home down the dark road. The truck lights illuminated a path thirty feet ahead, occasionally catching the yellow eyes of creatures in the road or in the brush. A raccoon with her little brood stopped and tried to decide which way to go. When the truck kept advancing, they split in two then doubled back together in front of the truck. Alford put his brakes on so the raccoons could straighten things out.

"Poor things," Caroline said. "They had no idea of what to do." She sighed. "I've felt that way sometimes today."

"Hard day?"

"Yes. One thing after another. Just after lunch, Sophie called. Sammy's joined up with a Canadian air group. He went up to Vancouver, B.C., last night before anyone could intercede. She says Father's furious and Mother is quite beside herself." She shook her head in the dark. "I'd be too if it were Cory. Oh, how could he?"

Alford took her hand.

Caroline sighed. "Cathy's father's dying. It was a heart attack after all. Cathy called to say so. And —— the loggers took out my favorite big leaf maple. The one that leaned out over the bank. I couldn't stand watching it anymore."

"I'm sorry, sweetheart. I couldn't believe it was gone too."

The truck idled, leaving the lights to stare into the black maw of the forest on either side of the lane. He pulled her to him and she came willingly, filling him with an enormous sense of relief from the fear he might have lost something with her. He shouldn't have argued or neglected her all these weeks. They were in this together. He found her lips and kissed her fully, grateful she always responded without fear to his touch. When she melted into him, he put his arms around her and held her tight. "It'll be all right," he whispered. "You'll get through this along with everything else."

"But Sammy... I'm so afraid —"

"I know, babe, but he has to make his own choices. Everyone has to at some point. Then you have to bear the cost."

He didn't add that lately he wondered if his own bill was due for defying her family so long ago.

Chapter 41

The weather improved in April, bringing out the first holiday seekers on the lower trails in the national forest. In Frazier, talk not only surrounded the plans for the hiking club's outing in late July, but of a national park as well, if the damn war in Europe didn't get in the way.

The good weather also brought the resumption of logging operations and within the national forest, several companies secured permits for a particular unit up a canyon. It was Alford's job to check in with the foremen of these outfits and make sure things were up to snuff. By mid-April, many of the operations were pulling out logs on a regular basis. A copper strike back in the mountains started a run on mining equipment at the general store.

The Frazier Hotel got a new paint job near the end of the month of April and the following week, James Ford moved in for an extended stay. Alford heard about it at the ranger barn where Forest Service wagons and trucks were repaired. George Fuller, as usual, had a few choice words to say about Ford, describing his arrival like a grand operatic procession.

"Ford's just the pompous ass he always is, treating us like

the slaves of Pharaoh."

"Heard there were a few around here who court him," Alford said as he oiled one of the saddles.

"Well, that's true. Lumbermen, for sure. He's still a high muckymuck with the power and money he represents. He can afford to be contrary all he wants and to whom he wants."

"Wish he'd get the hell out of here."

Alford saw Ford twice sitting on the top floor balcony of the two story hotel. Fat and lordly, about all he got from there was a view behind the false fronts of the buildings across the street. Alford ignored him. He was more concerned about Jenkins. Until Harold Symington arrived.

"Carrie, are you decent?"

Caroline looked up from the bowl of cookie dough she was mixing. "In the kitchen."

"There you are," Cathy said as she settled down on one of the kitchen chairs.

"Lemonade?"

"Please."

While Caroline got a pitcher from the icebox, Cathy placed a copy of *The Pioneer Register,* the local weekly sheet from Twin Forks, on the table.

"Did you get your dad's estate settled?"

Cathy sighed. "Yes. House is cleaned out and ready to sell. None of the siblings are in a position to take it on."

"I'm sorry, Cathy. It must hurt to lose the family home."

"Oh, bother. I left it long ago." She took the glass of lemonade and beckoned for Caroline to sit down.

"What's up?"

"Thought you should see this."

In the column under "Hawley Creek" listing news about residents in that community, there was an item that Cathy had circled: Mr. Harold Symington, banker, lumberman and leading citizen of Seattle, was coming to Hawley Creek to inspect the new logging mill and operations and to encourage productivity in these trying times.

"That your uncle?"

Caroline glanced at the rest of the story about how the glut of logs on the market was over and there was money to be made with the war in Europe. America could prosper and still stay out of the conflict. The Pacific Northwest would be part of that boom.

"Yes. That's him."

"I asked Mr. Wilkie, the proprietor in Twin Forks, about that. There's going to be some ceremony at the B & E Lumber Mill. A new type of saw is being installed. Then they'll go up to Hawley Creek to see the new mill. There was quite a discussion in the store after I asked. Some grand banquet, I gather. I left. Later, though, I overheard some men at the train depot say that Symington'd be unofficially visiting the camps. There was unrest in Camp Number 3 up near Hawley Creek this past week."

Caroline said nothing, returning instead to stirring a batch of cookie dough. It was getting beyond the creamed stage rapidly.

Cathy cleared her throat. "I heard something else. When I stopped off at the hotel just a while ago, someone said Symington's coming to Frazier with some dignitaries to see the ranger station and take a horseback ride in the forests. Might go up to the falls. There's a dinner-reception in there somewhere."

Caroline stopped mixing and stared out the kitchen window to where the logging operation was seeping down toward their homestead. *Would he come here?*

"Carrie, you're awfully quiet. Are you all right?"

"I'm right as Northwest rain."

"He could be here *this* Friday. There might be a reception for him at the hotel. After all, he *is* an important man."

"Only in his mind. Will you go?"

Cathy laughed, then frowned. "Most likely. With Charlie's position in the mills. You don't mind?"

"Oh, I don't mind if you go, Cathy. In fact, I'd love to

know what it's all about. My cousin David thinks Uncle Harold has political aspirations. With the Republican victories in the legislature, the Employers' Association feels well vindicated. He might run for governor or a senatorial seat." Caroline stabbed the dough with her wooden spoon. "He has the power. Why can't he be expansive? Perhaps you can ask him that. Could you please pass me that bowl of flour?"

"Oh, Carrie. If it weren't for the tone of your voice, you'd give me the chills."

"I give myself the chills." She sighed, then laughing, gave Cathy an amused look. "It sometimes seems all so strange."

"What if you're asked? You're vice-president of the hiking club."

"I'll go. Frazier, after all, is *my* home and this is *my* bailiwick."

Vernell broke the news about the Symington visit to Alford himself.

"Didn't want to get your work list too cluttered," he said, "but there's a party of dignitaries coming to the national forest. Congressman Keenes and a few others. Harold Symington, for one. I believe their wives are coming as well."

"This an official visit?" Alford ran his file across his buck saw in one swoop.

"Definitely. Though we lack in spruce, I'm sure they'll want to check out some of the units being cut now in the Thomas Creek area as well as take in some sights. I've got George Fuller playing host. I'm short so you'll have to go along too if they want to take a look-see around the usual parts of the forest and trails. Word is Mrs. Symington and Mrs. Keenes want to go as well."

Alford stopped filing. "Had to come all the way up here to tell me that?" He'd been at Big Fir working on the corral used for packhorses for the past two days. The weather had let up and had been downright friendly: blue skies under high fleecy clouds and no wind. Warm enough to work without a shirt. He mopped his sweaty neck with his bandana, then took a drink of water from his canteen.

Vernell gave Alford a pointed look. "No, I came to check on those new lean-tos Larson's building with Fuller, but in passing, just thought it'd be for your own good to know." Vernell wiped his moustache with his bandana. "Symington'll be here day after tomorrow. You should be finished here by then."

"All right, I'll be available. What else is new?"

"Talked to Hendrickson down at Camp Two in Twin Forks. There was some trouble there a few days ago. Outside man coming in and addressing some of the men. They started a slowdown right after that."

Alford tested the saw on a piece of cedar post he was cutting, trying to assume a noncommittal air, but he was interested. "Some heads get busted?"

"There was a concerted effort to end the action."

"Any familiar faces?"

"Someone spotted Jenkins, but there's nothing to pin on him, so no outcry. Oh, his driver, Deevers, is out of his sling." Vernell took his ranger hat and ran the wide brim slowly through his fingers. Clearing his throat, he announced that there was something else he wanted to talk about. "Someone got into Ford's outfit the other day — again. Third time this month a piece of equipment was tampered with."

"Didn't know he was having labor troubles."

"Not sure he is." He looked uncomfortably at Alford. "Ford came around to my office yesterday. Was asking some pointed questions."

Alford stopped sawing, sensing that this was directed at him somehow. "In what way?"

"Wanted to know where you were."

Alford's shot straight up, his eyes flashing. "What's the bastard implying?"

"Now, it's only words, Bob. But at the same time, he can

file a complaint if he has a mind."

"Does he *have* a mind?" Swearing under his breath, Alford lay the saw roughly against the sawbuck. "The man's a son of a bitch."

"The man's a piece, I agree, but it's the Fords and Jenkins I find so hard to fight because sometimes when they're doin' something against every moral teaching I know of, they're just so damn legal about it." He gave Alford a look of empathy. "Now you know I don't tolerate his conniving, but at the same time, Ford has political and social influence beyond my control. I don't doubt he wants to cause trouble, but try not to give him any ammunition, Alford. That way I can defend you."

"You think I did it?"

"Now that's an unkind cut, Alford, and you know it." Vernell sighed. "Ever since Jenkins showed up here nine years ago, I've watched out for you. Don't you know you're the best man I got? Don't you forget that. As for Ford, he can sputter all he wants, but I won't let him get away with anything funny." He pounded the top of the corral fence. "I just need you to go with the Symington party and play along. Keep your head on straight. I need you for the things that are to come. Headquarters in Washington's indicating a need to increase timber sales. For a government that's trying to stay out of the war, there's a rash of preparation going on and it's starting to show. Timber's a hot commodity and the government's not going to like the sound of slowdowns and strikes. Something's going to give. Even up here."

"Maybe that's why the congressman's coming," Alford said. "Though I'm not sure where Symington fits in. Makes me a bit uncomfortable."

"I don't like it either, but I guess it only shows to those who have it, more is given. See you around, Alford." Vernell went over to his truck and after cranking it to life, drove off.

The Keenes-Symington party, as the delegation was known, arrived in Frazier by train at noon on Friday. An eight piece band greeted them along with the local chamber of commerce and the Ladies Tea Society. Once the party had disembarked, three touring cars festooned with American flags loaded them up for the short drive to the Frazier Hotel where the reception would be held. Riding in the lead motorcar with Congressman Keenes was Harold Symington. In the back seat behind them, their wives showed off the latest fashions, shining counterpoints to the rugged little town of Frazier and their husbands who desired to dominate it.

Caroline watched the party arrive from a second story room in the Frazier Hotel. She studied Aunt Agatha as she stepped out, feathers floating around her face. Caroline hadn't seen her aunt in over nine years. She was still a pretty woman for her fifty-odd years. *But time has taken a toll on you, Aunt Agatha.* She seemed much older than Caroline thought she ought to be. Maybe she knew more about her husband's dealings than she let on or perhaps it was the secret marriage David said Raymond had entered into last year with a woman a couple years older than he was. It wasn't what Uncle Harold and Aunt Agatha had in mind, but by the time it was found out, the woman was already six months pregnant.

Shades of an earlier time, thought Caroline, *only no attacks at the inn.* The bride was from a well-to-do family, but more radical in their thinking than Harold Symington. Uncle Harold, Sophie wrote her, was forced to swallow his pride and make the best of it. Which apparently he had and as usual, to his advantage. *Like a cat, you always seem to land on your feet.*

There was a knock on the door behind her and Cathy and Ellie came in. The smell of coffee lingered outside in the hallway and the clink of china could be heard from below.

"Are you coming down?" Ellie asked.

"No, I'll wait, thank you. Don't want to cause a scene. Frazier hasn't had such excitement since the first motion picture was shown at the community hall."

Cathy sniffed. "Isn't this the same? What an obscene display of theatrics. You'd think civilization was being introduced to Frazier for the first time."

Both Caroline and Ellie laughed at their friend, but Caroline thought what Cathy had observed was true. There had been big affairs with chambers of commerce, hiking clubs and good roads associations in the past as equally well-attended, but the flurry this time was a bit overblown.

"Isn't Charlie downstairs?" Ellie asked. Cathy had made her point.

"Along with some other lumbermen." Cathy sighed. "He's such a dear, but I can't get him to change the company he keeps."

"His camp is clean. That's what counts," Caroline said.

"He tries so hard. It's difficult managing the mill and still hold the respect of the men. So far, there's been little trouble."

"Well, if *we* don't go down," Ellie said, "we shall have difficulty keeping the tables full with such a press of people. The food's quite extraordinary. You should come, Caroline."

"In a moment. Let me collect my thoughts."

Ellie gave her a kiss on her cheek. "You look wonderful. Your outfit's most becoming."

"Come soon," Cathy said.

Caroline promised she would.

After her friends left, Caroline could hear the drone of voices beneath her and the occasional laugh. The little settlement of Frazier seemed to be relishing in the glamor of the reception. She watched the crowd come and go off the porch under her window and finally decided that Cathy was right. She needn't hide in the room. Her community needed her and it might do *her* some good.

She straightened her hair in the mirror, then smoothed out the long, narrow skirt of her new dress. Turning, she brushed the delicate tucks and lace on her peach-colored bodice until the tunic-top lay properly on her chest. A final setting of her wide-brimmed hat and she went out the door.

At the top of the stairs she hesitated, holding back to listen to the mixed conversations around the corner of the stairwell. The voices of two women became louder, then someone came up. Caroline decided to go down and at the landing came face-to-face with Aunt Agatha.

"Aunt Agatha," she said, then faltered.

"Caroline, dear," exclaimed the older woman. "It *was* you in the window. I could scarcely believe it." She clasped her hands together in amazement and appraised Caroline up and down. "What a beautiful lady you've become."

"Thank you,." Caroline murmured, then stopped short. "Are you alone?"

"Quite. I took a chance to come up."

"You came to see me?" Caroline was incredulous. The last time she'd seen her aunt was the night she eloped. Her aunt hadn't been visible during Emily's funeral.

"Would you mind so terribly? It has, after all, been a long time."

"Oh, I'd love it, but where's Uncle Harold?"

"Downstairs. As always, the center of attention."

"Ah..." Caroline leaned back against the rail. "You're looking well, Aunt Agatha. How's Lisa?" She was careful not to mention Cousin Raymond.

"Well. She's still unmarried." Her aunt went on to tell about some of her social outings.

They made small talk for a bit more, touching on Cory and Kate and Caroline's life here. Then Aunt Agatha ventured to talk about the elopement and the loss of the past nine years.

"Like your mother, I was appalled at first that you had acted so rashly. It seemed that all was lost for you. All your prospects for position and wealth. She was very sad, you know. After your little boy was born, however, she seemed to have a change of heart and I must admit, *I* became interested in the various activities you were involved with up here too. You seemed to have a very sensible life."

Caroline laughed. "You choose your words so carefully,

Aunt Agatha. You haven't said a word about my husband."

"No, I haven't, but I suspect he's a decent man and supports you in your social responsibilities. You don't seem to have lost anything that you were taught. Your dress is appropriate for this gathering. Well done." She made a little sigh. "And such lovely children. Your dear mother has shown me pictures many times."

"My mother?"

"Oh, the things women do behind their husbands' backs. Like little assassins." She played with one of the kid gloves on her delicate hands. "I have a grandchild too. A little girl. I don't believe, though, that I will ever be friends with her mother. Too radical a personality for me, but Grace is a pretty little thing."

"Raymond must love her."

It was apparently the wrong comment because Aunt Agatha sputtered and dabbed the corner of her eyes with a soft linen handkerchief. "Children can be so thoughtless. And time is so short. Lisa has developed an independent streak too."

"Then make amends and enjoy it." Caroline reached over and pressed her aunt's hand.

"You sound like your mother," said Aunt Agatha. "Your elopement was such a dreadful business, but your banishment was even worse. She has wanted for so long to conclude it."

"My mother said that?" Caroline stiffened.

"Most emphatically. With Sophie in California and not likely to come home in any respectable form and Samuel in Canada ready to leave for the continent, she wants it to end and have her grandchildren in her arms."

"Not without their father."

"She wants to conclude *everything*."

Caroline smiled softly. The thought made her very happy.

"How's Father? He wouldn't speak to me at Emily's funeral."

"Oh, he's fine. As stubborn as always in this difficulty, but I believe he does pay attention to David when he calls. Your cousin has pressed for a long time to end your banishment. Perhaps Charles *is* more attentive since David became ill."

"Ill?"

"Oh, I shouldn't say. Nothing's been stated, but he's not taken Emily's death well. It seems to have drained all the energy out of him. He looks so drawn and pale."

"Oh." Caroline became quiet. It hurt to hear the news, but it was something she had long suspected herself.

Aunt Agatha patted her hand. "I'm sure it's nothing serious. Dr. Ellis has been after him to take a leave of absence and I believe he's finally agreed. It'll do him good. His heart will knit in no time."

"I hope so. It was a hard winter for him. Spring doesn't seem to have been any better."

There was an explosion of laughter downstairs from a group of men, then someone chimed on a glass and made an announcement.

Aunt Agatha fiddled with her gloves. "I suppose I should go down. You come too, Caroline. I'd like you to meet Mrs. Keenes and the other women in our party. They're from some of our region's most important and finest families. We've been having such a good time."

Caroline straightened up. "I intend to, even if my uncle doesn't welcome me."

Aunt Agatha sighed. Reaching up, she touched the brim of Caroline's hat as if to brush away a cobweb. "You're too hard on him. Blood is much thicker than politics. In his heart, I think he forgave you long ago."

"And Bob?"

"I can't honestly say that I understand the world of men. They get slighted so easily, especially when a younger man challenges them. That might take a little longer."

"Hasn't it been long enough?"

Aunt Agatha couldn't answer. There didn't seem any

room for that. It made Caroline realize that despite the promise of this polite and open conversation, nothing had really changed. She might be forgiven (for what real offense?) but Bob would always be the interloper and thief. The thought hurt her, but she wasn't about to let her aunt see. Instead, she marched downstairs. Humble as it was, her uncle would know her presence and position in Frazier.

Chapter 42

Alford came in the back door to the hotel kitchen and snatched a roll and a cup of coffee from Fanny Brewster, the head cook. From out in the dining room, there was a bustle of activity and conversation that rose and fell with the opening and closing of the swinging kitchen doors.

"Seen Caroline?"

"About a minute ago," replied the heavyset woman up to her elbows in flour. "She was talking to those fancy folks like she was to the manor born. Right proud of her." She stopped talking long enough to give some directions to the young girls carrying serving dishes to the tables. "They may have come for the logs, but she's in there promoting the national park and trails along with Cathy and Ellie." She gave him an amused look. "What are you doing here? Thought Ranger Vernell couldn't run the forest without you."

"Sent me to catch the general flavor of the crowd. I'm going to take them on a ride tomorrow." He patted his shirt. "Got the mails as well."

"All to see your sweetie." Fanny tossed her head in the direction of the dining room. "Well, they're friendly and with refreshments as dry as August, there's no danger they'll fall out of their saddles tomorrow."

"As long as they stay on the trail. I'm to take them halfway up to the Devil's Hangnail on the mining pack trail."

Fanny laughed, then shook her head as she exchanged her apron for a clean one.

Alford knew what she was thinking. The Kulshan mine trail that punched back through the mountains to the sites of several mining outfits was only partly developed and suitable only for pack trains. The hiking clubs used it as a trail into deeper reaches of the national forest, but it wasn't good as a wagon road nor for the timid. Funds were supposed to be forthcoming in July for grading and widening it, just before Emily's Seattle hiking club came. The Devil's Hangnail was a popular lookout.

"Mind getting Caroline for me?" Alford asked.

"Not at all." After washing her hands, Fanny went out with a tray for the table. Alford held the door open for her and looked across the crowded room. Caroline was standing with a group of women and their husbands near the main window. Poised and attentive, she seemed a different person to him and he felt both pride and unease that she could command the room so well with this crowd. Cathy Bladstad seemed equally impressed, watching her quietly from off to the side of the group, a strange role for her. It reminded him of the letter inside his jacket pocket. It was from Harms and after two months of regular phone calling to Caroline, Alford's feelings of uncertainty increased as he watched her now. After nine years, he still wasn't sure where Harms stood. An uncomfortable spit of anger flashed in his gut. He felt like he was always losing sight of the total picture, only he didn't know what it was.

Someone laughed in the archway leading to dining rooms in the back. It was James Ford holding court with some business types not known to Alford. *Lumbermen*, he thought, then dismissed them as he looked back at Ford. The bastard acted like he owned the place. He leaned back into the shadows and spoke to someone. Bob caught a glimpse of Harold Symington's bearded face, then he was gone from view. Alford wondered if Symington had spoken to Caroline.

"Bob?"

"There you are, sweetheart." Without a word he took Caroline's arm and pulled her into the kitchen.

"How're you holding up?" he asked.

She gave him a soft smile. "Fine. It's not so awful as I thought it would be. My aunt was very clever to introduce me around immediately. My uncle couldn't avoid me after that and I have used that to *my* advantage."

"You looked quite at home."

"It's a combination of practiced skill *and* the desire not to let him get under my skin."

Alford chuckled. "What's Ford doing?"

"Extolling the virtues of logging here. He hasn't come near me."

"Good reason. I'll bust his jaw."

"Shh —"

Fanny Brewster came into the kitchen and resumed shooing the help around. Alford nodded to Caroline and they went outside to the back porch. When they were alone, he told her that she looked beautiful.

"Thank you. Isn't it odd? It feels like dress up, yet I used to do this all the time." She shook her head, then looked away as her eyes suddenly welled up.

"Caroline?"

"I'm all right." She smiled gently at him. "It's not something that I miss outright. It's so light and beautiful, but doesn't really have much to do with *real* life. I much prefer my mountains." She reached over and took his hand. "And you needn't worry that I'm going to become a changeling and go away with them. I wouldn't do that."

"Did I give something away?" His heart picked up steam with her touch.

"Your face, silly." Her laugh sounded forced to him.

"That's why it hurts. Despite appearances, I don't think anything's changed. I'm so sorry, Bob."

He shrugged. "Needn't be. I'll survive."

She sniffed, then laughed genuinely as she wiped her eyes. "Are you done for the day?"

"Almost. I have to get gear set out for tomorrow. Arrange for the horses. I guess it's a party of seven." He reached inside his shirt pocket. "There was mail too." He handed it over and watched her reaction when she recognized Harms's handwriting.

"Do you mind if I read it?" she asked.

He shook his head no and waited patiently while she read the letter.

"How's he doing?" he asked when she finished.

"He's taking a leave of absence. He'd like to come up before he goes back east."

"All right. Give him a call." He tried hard to hide his feelings and must have succeeded. Caroline came over to him and kissed him lightly on his lips, the fingertips of her hand lightly caressing his cheek. He felt himself go hard.

"I love you, Bob Alford. Have I told you that lately?" She stepped back and turned the letter in her hands. "Aunt Agatha says that he's not well. I've suspected it too."

"He hasn't taken Emily's death well."

"I think it's more than that. Dr. Ellis said stomach trouble last January." She sighed and put away the letter. "I wondered if it's worse."

"Well, we'll see what we can do," Alford answered and was surprised he meant it.

Chapter 43

The next day at seven thirty in the morning the riding party gathered at the corrals at the ranger station. George Fuller gave instructions on instructions on where they were going and the equipment they were carrying while Alford took care of last minute details. The party had been up since five, breakfasting at the hotel under glaring electric lights. Bundled now into a variety of outdoor wear, they braved the crisp, spring morning air with the exuberance of a class on a grammar school holiday. Alford found nothing different about this party from any other he had assisted, except for the quality of some of the boots and clothing. As each person was assigned a horse, he checked the gear a final time.

As he corrected the cinch on a gray gelding's saddle, Symington suddenly stepped in front of him.

"It'll do," Symington said and mounted.

"As soon as I finish," Alford growled back. "The strap's not all the way in."

The little party of Symington's male friends hushed behind them.

They know the story between us. They're just waiting for something to happen.

Alford decided to take a firm hand and disappoint them. With little fanfare, he pushed away Symington's boot and put the strap in. He nodded to Fuller that he was done and walked away to get his own horse.

The horses had been selected and saddled earlier, but as he passed Mrs. Symington she announced she'd prefer a sidesaddle, so Alford went back in to look for the most suitable one. A phone call at the ranger's office distracted him for a moment. When he came back into the room used for mending gear, he found Ford hanging around the table where the sidesaddle had been laid out.

"Need something?" he asked.

"No," Ford mumbled and went out.

Alford followed him outside with the sidesaddle and with no further comment put it on the mare chosen for Mrs. Symington. Once she was mounted and her skirt smoothed in place over her boot tops, they were ready to go.

Fuller took the lead, followed by Symington and Keenes. Ford was a close fourth. The middle was taken up by a Mr. Barnes, a photographer from Seattle, and two other gentlemen of business origin. Mrs. Keenes and Mrs. Symington were last. Alford pulled dust detail, but he didn't care. He was already disgusted with the whole business and was happy to stay clear. They moved out and rode past the ranger's cabin where Jack Vernell stood on the porch. He raised his hand as they passed and said he'd have refreshments for them on the way back. He dipped his ranger hat to the ladies as they rode by, but to Alford, he gave a knowing look. Alford dipped his head back to his boss and rode on.

The woods were deep where they entered the trail, the mix of alder and big leaf maple already maturing with solid heads of green and yellow leaves. The salmonberry was up and displayed deep magenta flowers. Alford reached down from his saddle and plucked a couple of red blood shoots still tender enough to bend and showed Mrs. Keenes how the succulent stalks could be peeled, then eaten like skinned celery.

"Oh, my," she said and showed Mrs. Symington.

Ahead of them the men rode on, Fuller pointing out some features as they climbed up through the trees.

"What did he say?" Mrs. Symington asked Alford.

"Probably pointing out the old fir there," he replied. Back in the recesses of the woods, an enormous fir with gnarly bark rose like a repaired leaning tower of Pisa. Somewhere in the heights, its upright branches touched the sky.

"So beautiful," murmured Mrs. Keenes.

"Indeed," Mrs Symington said.

The trail widened enough to go by two's. Alford encouraged the women to move up closer to the men. While Mrs. Keenes went ahead, Mrs. Symington seemed to have trouble following. Alford soon found himself alone with her. Though he remained silent except when spoken to, he was gradually drawn into her one-sided conversation as she sought to engage him in small talk. It only deepened his bad temper. Ahead of him moved two men he detested and his thoughts were often on their motive for being in Frazier and what it meant to the community. *The sooner this day ended, the better.*

"Has Caroline come here?" the woman suddenly asked.

"Sure. She's gone with the hiking clubs, but we've gone out ourselves as well." Alford struggled to keep the growing irritation out of his voice.

"Is it safe?"

"Our children have hiked up here."

"But we're on horseback."

"You'll be all right. Your mare's experienced." He nodded at the group ahead of them. "We best catch up."

Mrs. Symington nudged her horse with her boots and the mare responded, but still the woman seemed reluctant to join the others.

"Mr. Alford?"

"Ma'am?"

"I... so want to talk to you. To discover your frame of mind, so to speak."

"In what way? There's little to discover."

"Ah, but you're a gentleman. I've discovered that already in the way you handled my husband. You avoided the trap."

Alford looked at her sharply, completely surprised. The frivolous-looking woman had more spine than he thought. "I wasn't aware there was a trap." He let his horse walk shoulder to shoulder to hers until the leather in their saddles creaked in unison.

"You have tact as well. Wonderful. I admire a man with character."

Alford frowned. *Was this a game?* He wasn't pleased.

"Do you enjoy your work, Mr. Alford?"

"Do I wish for the comfort of a desk or a station in a sawmill? I think not. I've been outdoors most of my youth and all of my adult life. It suits me."

"You have responsibility. A position of honor." She looked at his Forest Service uniform with its tree badge and ranger hat.

"If you say, ma'am. It's more a position of compromise, a daily encounter with or against nature. Preferably with. The honor comes from being able to do it and get paid for it."

"Your home is provided?"

His horse, Timber, snorted and tossed its head, impatient at being held back. Alford felt the same way. *When would she stop?* "It's my own, ma'am. Bought and paid for."

Mrs. Symington looked away, then grabbed onto the saddle when her horse tripped over a stone on the trail.

"You OK?" Alford asked, reaching out to steady her.

"I'm fine." She sighed. "You must think me terribly rude. So many questions. But you see, I wanted to know for myself."

"Know what, ma'am?"

"That you're perfectly suited for my niece."

Alford came to an abrupt halt, causing Timber to work

furiously on the bit thrust deep into his mouth. *I don't care what you think*, he wanted to say, but what she said next made him flushed and speechless.

"And... I'm so very sorry for all the hurt thrown at you."

They were now entirely alone on the trail, the others having gone on around the bend. They were still amongst the trees, but the landscape was opening up before them where sheer drops fell away from the right side of the trail. He wanted to kick the horse and break away, but courtesy kept him immobilized.

"It's not your concern."

"But it is. Caroline loves you so. I could see it the moment she left us at the reception. You were standing in the kitchen doorway."

Alford shook his head. He knew better than to underestimate the power of a woman when she was on a beeline to something. *Just like Mama.* And in an odd way, he was beginning to like Mrs. Symington.

"Thank you. Now, please, Mrs. Symington, go on and catch up with the others."

"I shall, Mr. Alford, but I hope you take my interest at heart and know I mean well." She urged the mare forward as he requested, then stopped. "The saddle seems to have loosened a bit, but I'm fine for now."

"I'll check when we catch up," he promised.

The rest of the party had stopped up the trail to admire a vista breaking in front of the trees. The sun had come over the high mountains and cut into the mist laying on top of the higher reaches of the forests. The other riders turned when Alford and Mrs. Symington came into view. Harold Symington had dismounted, training an expensive pair of binoculars on the valley opening out below them. Dressed in a brown tweed hiking outfit and tall boots, he embodied an English hunter on a walk with his dogs. He stared at Alford, then asked in a loud voice if Mrs. Symington was all right.

"I'm fine, dear," she called back. "Lovely view."

Alford came up next to Fuller and got down. Below he

could see an eagle clutching the top of a hemlock, balancing perfectly as it adjusted to movement of its perch in the soft wind.

"Everything OK?" Fuller asked.

"Sure. Mrs. Symington thought her saddle was loose. Promised to check it."

"Well, look to that." Capping the top of his canteen, Fuller put it back over his saddle horn. "We'll stay long enough," he told the others in a loud voice, "for Mrs. Symington to get her bearings and perhaps a drink of water, then we'll press on."

Alford adjusted the reins on his horse and told it to stay. Mrs. Symington had dismounted and was next to Mrs. Keenes, watching the raptor. It was an appropriate time to check the saddle girth.

From where he sat astride his horse, Ford watched with veiled curiosity. When Alford noticed, he turned and talked to the photographer who was showing one of Symington's guests how to use his Brownie camera. Alford didn't think it necessarily odd, just a poor attempt to hide the fact that Ford had been staring at him, but he had wondered what was in Ford's craw all morning.

"Steady, girl." Alford checked the mare to make sure she hadn't bloated herself up when he put the saddle on. Finding she had behaved herself, he moved the saddle, but it appeared properly set. He pulled at the saddle blanket and tested the cinch. No problem there. Satisfied, he put down the stirrup.

"We can go, George. Whenever they're ready."

"Looks like right now."

There was a sudden cry and the eagle took flight, its white head emphasizing its magnificent size and strength. Gliding above the tops of the trees, it made its way down the mountain slope and out of sight.

George Fuller mounted his horse and announced details about the next section of their ride.

"Come along, Agatha," Alford heard Symington say.

Alford watched him escort her to her horse, then help her up into the sidesaddle. They chatted for a moment, then he was back in his own saddle. The party left a short time after, each falling into their little groups again, but this time the women stayed up near the front. Alford took the rear again.

The road was steep and as the day warmed, the horses' flanks began to glisten as they plugged along. At the top of a rise where the trail switched back, the party stopped to drink water from a small waterfall flush with melted snow rushing down the sandstone wall that lined the trail. Above it, a large patch of snow could still be seen. Even at this lower altitude, summer came late. Alford led Timber over. He wet his hand and brushed his horse's mouth. When Timber wanted more, he cupped his hands and let him drink.

The party praised the vistas around them — the stands of hemlock and fir, the blue, cloudless sky and Mount Kulshan's mighty white head sparkling in the late spring sun. Barnes retrieved his Brownie camera and took a group picture. Alford stayed by the horses, then helped Mrs. Keenes up when she came back. "You should have joined us," she said. He gave a polite answer why, no.

The ride resumed, the women on the inside of the switchback. It twisted around for about an eighth of a mile, then came out onto another vista even more beautiful than the last. The women were on the outside now, a raw, steep and open descent down to their right. The party stopped again, but stayed on their horses. The ladies' horses went nose to nose as they surveyed the sweeping view in the tree break. Symington was engaged with Mr. Barnes and Mrs. Symington. Ford was with the other gentlemen at the front.

Alford came up to the group and stopped at the edge of riders. They were above an area where a fire had destroyed several dozen acres two years before, leaving behind blackened stumps and snags. Below, in the clear mountain air, a woodpecker tapped a log with the precision of an iceman with icepick. A Steller's jay, disturbed by the arrival of so many, complained loudly, then darted down the mountain to the new growth of brambles and alder. It was a long way down.

Alford wasn't sure what he saw first, but without any warning Mrs. Symington started falling from her sidesaddle as it came undone. For one awful moment, she tried to hold onto the mare's mane, but that only made the mare lose her footing on the edge of the turnout. Rider and the horse screamed at the same time, then separated — the mare falling down backwards on the slope to the right, Mrs. Symington falling into the arms of Alford on the left as he slammed his horse into action and brought it alongside her. He pulled her onto his lap, the saddle finally becoming untangled from her skirt and legs and falling to the ground. He yanked his horse back to the relative safety of the trail, keeping the trembling woman in a firm hold. There was a terrible crashing sound, then a shrill, piercing squeal as the horse rolled and tumbled down the slope until it slammed against a stump. It grunted, then lay still.

"What the devil!" Symington hollered. "Someone help my wife!" Several hands assisted. Soon she was on the ground, a blanket being wrapped around her and spirits offered from a flask. Alford got down and helped until Fuller took over. Stepping back, he picked up the sidesaddle. The cinch had been completely broken, but not at the buckle. It was still intact and holding the two lengths of the cinch together. Near the saddle itself, however, the cinch strap appeared to have torn and come undone. Except—

A cold feeling came over him. This was no accident. Part of the leather was *not* torn. A knife had clearly cut through. Sensing eyes on him, he looked up and made eye contact with Ford who was standing beside the group huddled on the ground.

The barn. The side saddle had been on the table.

Ford's face was ashen, but his eyes were curiously bright. He gave Alford just a hint of a smile.

"What happened?" Fuller asked as he rejoined Alford.

"Saddle gave way." Alford took a pistol out of his

saddlebag and put a couple of bullets into it. "I'll check on the mare. Don't hold much promise. How's Mrs. Symington?"

"Just a few bruises. Good scare, though. We better turn back. Someone will have to ride double."

"I'll walk." Alford shook his head, but couldn't find the words to continue. He scrambled down the rocky slope to where the mare was stopped against a blackened cedar stump. The animal's eyes were opened wide in terror, its nostrils and bared teeth were full of blood. Her head was at an unnatural angle. Broken neck, Alford ascertained, then put a bullet through the mare's head to be sure she was dead. He undid the bridle and climbed back up to the trail. He had a hell of a lot of explaining to do to Vernell.

Word spread quickly through Frazier about the accident. Mr. Barnes had kindly gone on ahead to set up whatever amenities he could for Mrs. Symington at the hotel and Vernell was alerted. He sent a wagon out immediately and met the party coming down about a mile out of the ranger station. Mrs. Symington was loaded onto the wagon for her comfort, then taken to the ranger station where their automobiles were parked. Mary Vernell invited her to warm up by the fire, but Symington would have nothing to do with it and waved everyone into the cars. Keenes gave his apology and went along, leaving Alford and Fuller with the horses.

"I'll take them," Fuller said. "Vernell's going to want to see you when he gets back. Better start writing your report."

"Damn sure, he will. I'll put away the gear." Alford undid his saddle and put it on the corral railing. He helped with two others, then went to the wagon and took out the damaged sidesaddle. "I'll take this in," he said. "Have to get Larson to fix it." He shouldered the saddle and went into the barn where he laid it on the table. Spreading out the strap, he examined it again. It had definitely been cut — just enough to hold off the inevitable. Nothing could prevent it from breaking under the strain of climbing up the Kulshan trail. The question was, why? And at such a risk to life? Control over the accident's timing was impossible.

"Figure out what caused the cinch to break?" Fuller asked as he came into the barn carrying a couple of bridles.

"It was cut."

"You're kidding."

"Wish I was." Alford backed away from the table, deeply troubled as an idea formed in his mind.

"Who'd want to hurt Mrs. Symington?"

"I don't think it was directed at her." Alford suddenly felt very tired at the implication of his words.

"Who then? Symington?"

"No." Alford looked his friend with a subdued expression. "I think it was aimed at me."

Fuller was so shocked that he laughed, then clammed up. "That's crazy."

"Maybe, maybe not." Alford gathered his thoughts carefully. "Jack says Ford thinks I'm behind some sabotage at his logging site. Yeah, he said that. What if Ford wanted to do something about it, but couldn't directly tie me? Why not get me in serious trouble by having me accused of deliberately tampering with the saddle? It's no secret I have no love for Symington."

Fuller still couldn't accept the idea. "That's ridiculous. What makes you so sure it was Ford?"

"Because he was in the barn when the saddle was on the table. I was called out for a few minutes."

"It doesn't make sense. Mrs. Symington could have been seriously hurt and Ford is Symington's man."

"I realize that, but I don't think he thought it through. He looked at me up there — after the accident. He was shaken, but he was also quietly gloating."

Fuller frowned. It was beyond him. "That's a powerful statement you're making, Bob. Makes me uncomfortable."

"I know, but I believe I'm right."

"He's lost his marbles if what you say is true."

"That's why he was shaken. It can all blow up in his face."

Fuller examined the cinch leather closely. "It's cut all right." He frowned. "Could have been a pocketknife or one of them switchblades made this. Easy to hide. But damn, I still don't want to believe it."

"Do you believe that some men will beat a man to death over the eight-hour day?"

Fuller said nothing. He smoothed out the cinch and seemed to chew on his thoughts. "But why you? What's he got to do with your troubles with Symington?"

"Remember that episode last summer when Ford came on my property and frightened the dickens out of Caroline? That was just a continuation of old business. There was similar trouble when she first came to her uncle's home. When I went to ask permission to marry her, I called Ford out about his behavior in front of Symington and he hasn't forgotten." Alford's felt his blood rise dark. "Ford's a lech and a power-hungry, arrogant bastard. He imagines that since he was married to her sister, that he can still speak to Caroline in more familiar tones, but he wouldn't treat a serving girl up at the hotel any different."

George coughed. "Well, he's a fool." He glanced guiltily at Alford. "What are you going to do?"

"I want you to verify the strap as you see it, then we'll put the saddle away in one of the tack boxes. I'll write up a report about what happened and give it to Vernell. In triplicate."

"Think Ford's going to come gunning for you?"

"Possibly. Symington surely will. No denying that."

The phone rang. Fuller went over to the wall and answered it. It was Vernell. He said, "U-uh" and "Yes, sir," then after a long silence hung up. He looked at Bob sheepishly. "Jack wants me to come down into Frazier. Truck got a flat. Wants a spare. I'll take the wagon."

"Say anything about me?"

"Just that local opinion's running in your favor ten to

one. He knows you're cautious and if it was your fault, it was a honest mistake."

"What about the one against?"

"Actually two. Ford and Symington who's voicing his displeasure. Loudly."

"How's Caroline's aunt?"

"Fine, as far as I could see. Leastways, there's no lynching party as of yet."

"Wait 'til sundown." Alford made a face, then picked up the side saddle. "Guess I'll put this away. Tell Jack I'll be ready to see him when he gets back."

Vernell got back an hour later. He wasn't alone. Harold Symington and James Ford followed him in their touring car. Both men had changed out of their riding clothes, but still were dressed for the woods. They parked in front of the corral and walked up in a tight bunch to the barn where Alford was mending rope under a bare light bulb. He looked up when the sound of their high top boots hit the wood floor of the repair room. In unison, the visitors removed their bowler hats.

"Howdy, Bob," Vernell said. "George says you have something to show me."

"For your eyes," Alford answered.

"Maybe Mr. Symington should see," Ford testily interjected behind the ranger.

"Now what do you suppose I have, anyway?" Alford asked. "Or do you already know?"

"Are you implying something?" Ford spat.

"Aren't you?" Alford responded.

"Gentlemen," Vernell said. "This has been a difficult day. Mr. Symington would like to return to his hotel room to be with his wife. Their party leaves early in the morning. What do you have?"

"You ordering me?"

Vernell's face flushed. *Don't give me grief*, his eyes said.

Alford put down the rope he was working on and cleared

his work area of linseed oil cans and wax. He went to an old wooden army trunk used as a tack box and lifted out the sidesaddle. Without a word, he brought it to the table and tossed it flat, spreading out the cinch.

"The saddle gave way because it was cut," he said flatly. He pointed out the end. Everyone around him leaned in. Vernell brought the leather strap up to his face and examined it carefully.

"No doubt about that."

"You did this," snarled Ford.

Alford looked at Symington who was scrutinizing him with quiet, intense eyes. "I did not. The sidesaddle hasn't been used in months. It was taken out from storage when it was requested. I checked it before I put it on."

Ford sputtered and went into a practiced diatribe about Alford's distaste for Symington for past offenses and his logging operations. Alford took it quietly. His eyes never left Symington. When Ford ran out of steam, Alford admitted that it was true, but he wasn't low enough to hurt a woman over it.

"What do you suppose *is* the proper response?" Symington returned Alford's stare.

"An appeal to common decency."

Ford laughed. "Decency. What a pitiful statement."

"I doubt you understand the concept," Alford said.

"How do *you* think it was cut?" Symington broke in.

"Ask Ford. He was here in the barn."

Symington turn his hard gaze on Ford.

"That true?"

For a moment, it looked like Ford would wiggle out of the question, but finally said, "I — yes. I was seeing that it was done properly. The selection of the saddle for Mrs. Symington, that is. What Alford's suggesting is preposterous. He's a damned liar."

Symington picked up the strap, then addressed Alford. "You adjusted the cinch up on the trail."

"Correct. Mrs. Symington asked me to."

"Why?"

"She said it was loose. When I checked it, though, it appeared solid."

"So you say," Ford said. He looked like he wanted to say something else, but he was stared down by his superior.

"How do *you* explain it?" Symington asked Alford.

"The cut was high, not easily seen. It just kept slowly tearing until it broke."

Symington rubbed his beard and looked thoughtfully at the saddle. "I've seen enough, Ranger Vernell."

"Will you be leaving us?" Vernell asked.

"Do you mean, will I be pressing charges?" Symington replied. "That has to be determined. My wife, fortunately, received only a nasty scare and a few bruises. I can see the saddle is old even if the party was negligent. I'll have to think on it."

Ford smiled at this, then was taken aback when Symington asked to speak to Alford alone. "If you will, sir."

Alford shrugged. He didn't think he had anything else to lose besides his job if charges were laid. Which was enough. He didn't doubt the influence of Symington in the courts.

Vernell cleared his throat. "We best go outside," he said to Ford and herded him out.

When they were gone, Symington took out a cigar from inside his coat and lit it, taking his time. Alford ignored him and started to put the saddle back.

"What sort of game is this?" Symington demanded, suddenly pouncing.

"It's no game. That gear's kept in good working shape, even if it's outdated. Someone tampered with it. I think it was Ford."

"Why should I believe you? I've known him for a long time, both personally and professionally."

"Then you know of his abusive nature toward women. Sophie Ford could tell you an earful. Caroline's no exception."

"Caroline? Since when?"

"Last summer."

Symington ripped the cigar from his mouth. "The hell you say."

"Ask Vernell. He knows."

The burly man appraised Alford for a moment, then put his cigar back in his mouth. "You catch him?"

"He was caught. We had words. No more."

"That when his troubles began?"

"Ford makes his own troubles."

"But he thinks you're behind them."

"So I hear."

"What does Ford gain from this?"

"My neck."

Symington smiled wryly. "He underestimated how thick it was. I admit, so have I."

He looked at the side saddle in Alford's hands. "I don't like you, but to my wife you're a hero. She was quite insistent that I come and talk to you when Ford began making his allegations." He clamped down on the cigar with his teeth. "She's worried how this will affect Caroline."

"Give my regards to Mrs. Symington," Alford said, "but my wife's fine. Family interest is a little too late." He opened up the tack box with one hand. "I told you the truth. If you want to do something about it, just keep your hounds off those closest to me and leave me alone."

"Is Ford my hound?"

"He is along with Jenkins and all the others in that pack down in Twin Forks."

Symington's face flushed, then hardened. "You have an overworked imagination. You're also misinformed. Mr. Ford is no longer a partner of mine."

Alford put the saddle in the tack box, then putting the lid down with a measured drop, faced Symington.

"If you say. I don't really give a damn." He looked at his chain watch. "I've got work to do. This interview over?"

Symington first glared at Alford, then laughed.

"By God, you are doggedly consistent and irritatingly

direct. I admire that."

"There's nothing I admire about you, Symington. You command power and authority, yet you stoop to bullies and thugs to do it. Your policies have hurt men in countless camps and in some cases cost them their lives. You're going to lose."

"Maybe, maybe not," Symington said. "What if I were to bow to common decency, as you like to put it?" He put the cigar back into his mouth and took a puff. "Times are changing. Those men I rode with today have a vision. A different view of the future. There are others with similar thinking closer to home. Though a majority disputes it, the writing's on the wall. The reforms will come with the war."

"It won't wipe out what you've done."

"Perhaps. I won't apologize for past efforts. Except for one. I should have interceded long before you took off with my brother's favorite child and had you whipped then."

Alford's cheeks burned, his body bunching to strike, but before the adrenalin could be delivered to act, Symington said, "But... it's over and done with. It's time to put it to rest." He put on his bowler. "I bid you good day. There will be no charges laid." Symington's eyes flashed. He seemed to be enjoying the moment, but without further word, he turned and walked out of the mending room and into the gloom of the barn, leaving behind an astonished Alford. Outside in the sun, Vernell and Ford were watching one of the horses pace in the corral. Symington went toward the bright barn opening, then stopped and abruptly came back.

Alford stepped forward, wondering if Symington had changed his mind about pressing charges.

"David Harms is coming," Symington said in a lowered voice.

Alford didn't ask how Symington knew when an invitation had been sent only last night.

"So?"

Symington moved closer to the barn opening. "Thought you should know something."

"I suppose I have no choice."

Symington acted like he didn't hear him, but he kept a safe distance. "Harms is going away on sabbatical as soon as he leaves from here. So the story goes. I know for a fact that he's going to the Mayo Clinic in the Midwest. He has stomach cancer. It's terminal."

"God..." Alford immediately dropped all posturing, his face betraying shock and disquiet.

"No one else knows, not even my wife. I would suggest that my niece not know as well. I suspect that's what he wishes."

When Alford continued to say nothing, the older man sighed and for the first time ever, Alford saw some hint of decency. "Go soft on him. I know there's tension between you two. I've grown fond of the boy. I want him to leave here in peace." Symington gave him a tight little smile. "You've got sand, Alford. You've got your principles. There's no doubt about it. Now, just give him this day. He has always loved Caroline. It will be hard to say good-bye." Symington put his hat back on. "I bid you good day. I don't believe we'll be seeing each other again." He gave Alford a curt nod, then headed out into the sun.

Alford came to the edge of the room and watched Symington rejoin Vernell and Ford. After a moment, Vernell left. Symington and Ford waited until he was gone, then had a heated discussion. Finally, Ford threw up his hands and marched off, visibly angry. Symington stared after him, then shaking his head, went to his car. It left Alford wondering what Symington told Ford. More importantly, how would he keep Symington's news of Harms's illness from Caroline? Should he?

Chapter 44

Mist stirred on the river when David Harms came to Frazier the following Saturday. The sun played on it for part of the morning, then pushed it apart revealing forests and mountains flush with early summer. Foxglove and goat's beard, even the catkins on the red alder were all full of flowering color along the water's edge.

"I'm glad I came," David said, looking across the river to Caroline's mountains. "This place always restores me. Of the many places we climbed and hiked, Emily and I always remarked how much this was home."

"Well, I'm glad you feel at home." Caroline and David stood on the bank behind the house, watching the river and the woods around it. Upstream, the logging operation had ceased for the weekend, leaving the surrounding area in peace.

She leaned against him, happy her cousin was content, but, oh how hard it was greeting him at the train station. The marked change in his appearance since Emily's funeral shook her. The handsome face and vigorous body had thinned, his cheeks hollowed. His dark eyes burned with the intensity of an oil lamp turned up too high with flicks of dark color laying around them like smudges. He was tired, he explained, from his trip, but Caroline dreaded something worse. She smiled anyway, willing herself to go along with the charade she sensed he wanted desperately to play. What he craved, she found, was someone who would listen to him and help him reach a balance in peace. So they walked and talked along the river's edge, recalling things past: their childhood days in Portland, early hiking trips to the Cascade Mountains in Washington State and the turbulent, exhilarating one summer at *Kla-how-ya*.

Dear cousin, thought Caroline, and wondered why she felt like a storm was coming.

"Will you be back east long?" she asked.

"I want to see the national park in Yellowstone, some libraries in Chicago, then onto Boston and the Atlantic Ocean," he said with enthusiasm. "It's what Emily and I had hoped to do." He sighed. "I'm going to do it for her."

"The air should do you good."

He patted her hand. "I think it will."

At noon, they went back inside where Caroline prepared sandwiches and soup for him and the children.

"Soup's enough for me, if you don't mind," he said, putting a hand on his stomach.

"Soup it is."

They ate outside at a wooden table. While the children alternately fed a chipmunk and ate, the cousins watched the drama of life around them. Eventually, Cory and Kate got down and went off to play by the river's edge, while Caroline kept a watchful eye.

"Isn't it funny? The forests and wilderness around here used to frighten me," Caroline said.

"You? I don't believe it," David said. "You're not the type."

I am, thought Caroline. *I'm frightened right now thinking about you.*

She hugged her arms. "Oh, it was quite true. I had wondered if I had made a mistake."

"A mistake?"

"Oh, you mustn't ever tell, but when I first came to this house, all ramshackle and run-down, I began to believe Father's words that I wouldn't be happy. That I had made a mistake eloping. His words hurt so much, you know." She folded her arms against her breasts and smiled wistfully. "I learned soon enough from Bob's family that it's the home, not the house that counts and when a heart's well fed with love, it can face any kind of adversity." She looked across the water. "I do love my mountains and when summer comes each year — they're so wonderful as they open up to their true selves. And — I love the house."

"Bob Alford's a good man,. I'm proud you stuck to your principles. Your parents will come around." He threw a stick into the river and watched the water take it away.

Caroline sighed. "I don't think they ever will. I've finally accepted that. The only thing I care about is the way Bob's treated. Do you know of Ford and his accusations?"

"Yes, but I assure you, much to my satisfaction, Uncle Harold nipped the talk in the bud. There's something else. Ford has fallen out of favor. I don't think he'll be welcomed at *Kla-how-ya* this summer."

"Bob's not so sure. He feels this episode has blown over, but things will get worse. Ford isn't the kind to let go and Bob's not so sure about Uncle Harold. He doesn't trust either of them."

"Ford's despicable. So's that Jenkins. However, I firmly believe Uncle Harold's finished with Ford."

Caroline sighed and looked down at her hands on the picnic table. For a moment, she gingerly traced a line of grain in the table's boards, avoiding splinters. David reached across and took them. "Be patient. I'm working on it."

"Oh, David," said Caroline. "Don't you do anything else except take care of yourself."

"All right. I promise." He squeezed her hands, then released them. He gave her a quick smile. "Why don't we change the subject? What's happening with the summer's outing?"

Lunch came and went, the afternoon warming further to the sun. By three, it was quite hot. They spent the rest of the day visiting, going for a walk after Kate took a nap. At four she went in to get the evening's meal ready. Once she put a roast into the oven, she cut vegetables for a side dish. David lay down on the sofa and fell asleep. He was roused later when the telephone rang in the hall. After Caroline hung up, she came into the room.

"That was Bob. He's been called up to Big Fir. He won't be back until Sunday evening. I guess it's just us chickens."

The next day broke warm and golden early on. Caroline took David and the children into Frazier where they attended church. Afterwards, they went to lunch with Cathy Bladstad and other members of the hiking club. They had a wonderful time, but the pace of the day seemed to tire David and he asked to go home earlier than planned. When they arrived at the house, he was slow to get down out of the truck.

"David?"

"I'm all right. I didn't want to spoil everything, but my ulcer has been acting up lately. It tires me a bit." He gave her an apologetic smile. "One of the reasons I'm taking the leave of absence. The sea air should do me good."

Caroline put an arm around him and gave him a squeeze. "I wish you weren't going alone."

"I won't be alone. I have a traveling companion, one of my university colleagues. His wife plans to join us midway. Besides, Emily will be in my thoughts the whole time."

He lay down after that. Not wanting to disturb him, Caroline shooed the children out the front door, while she put a pinafore on over her cotton dress and taking a fishing pole, went out to catch the evening meal. Sometime later, he came through the back door, the wire spring screeching his arrival outside.

"There you are. I was going to send for the troops to find you." His voice sounded hoarse to her.

"They're on the front line. Totally absorbed."

"Troops?"

Caroline laughed. "Cory and Kate are out in the front of the house. They've been at soldiers all afternoon." She stood up and rubbed the small of her back. "War seems to be on everyone's mind," she sighed. "As long as it's play and no one is hurt, I'll just have to let it be. Yet, I can't help but think about Samuel all the time now that he's over *there*." She pulled up a line of trout she had been storing in the water at the river's edge. "See? I've been working."

"Beautiful catch. When's dinner?"

"Soon. I just have to clean them."

"Good. I'm afraid I'm so hungry I'll make short work of them."

"I'm glad you're feeling better."

David came down to pull her up on the bank and take the fishing pole she had picked up from the ground. She came naturally into his arms and he gave her a long and tender hug. When he was finished, he let go and sighed.

"Caroline, dear Caroline. Thank you for all your love and concern this past winter and spring. I couldn't have gotten through it all without it."

"That's what's cousins are for." She smiled warmly at him. "Family should stick together," she said, then frowned when she remembered her own situation with her father.

"It's more than family. Before Emily, you were the first to really understand me." He shook his head and Caroline was surprised to see the beginnings of tears. "We're kindred spirits, you and me. Like — twins. And I... I hope you'll always remember me as that." He looked around the woods and the mountains across the river. "This place is about perfect. It'll always be in my mind's eye when I think of you."

His words so moved her, that Caroline reached up and turning his chin toward her, kissed him lightly on his cheek. "Then sibling you'll always be." She began to cry lightly and was relieved when he took her in his arms and hugged her again. For a moment, neither said a word as he rocked her. Suddenly, he stiffened and released her.

"David. What is it?" Caroline asked.

"Damn. It was Alford."

Caroline was shocked. "He was here, then left?"

"Right on that gravel bar. I think he got the wrong impression. He looked rather hurt when he headed upriver."

"I'll go. You take the fish."

"No, I'll go. It's time we talked." He gave her a reassuring smile. "It'll all get worked out." He patted her arm. "We'll be back."

When Alford saw Caroline in Harms's arms, the old hurt struck and twisted in his gut again. Flushing, he turned away and pushed past the willow bushes and alder saplings growing next to the riverbed.

It's nothing, he thought. But truth was, it was *something*. David and Caroline. He knew the man was grieving and now, according to Symington, dying. *Let it go*. Time to grow up and accept love in its many forms. All David took was her time. He had little left. But jealousy stung Alford still.

The stony riverbed petered out, but Alford just circumvented the bank of brush and stone halting him and climbed up on a familiar game trail. Mindless, he just wanted to get away from it all until he calmed down.

The trees around Alford were a mix of tall, old cedar and fir occasionally usurped by new alder and hemlock. He welcomed the silence, his thoughts still hot and confused. *What?* Out of nowhere, he caught a glimpse of a man in a tan shirt making its way through the trees. Curious, he was about to call out when there was a terrible booming noise, followed by yelling and chaotic shouts of rage, all coming from upstream. The man in the tan shirt started to run.

"Hey!" Alford called out, sprinting toward the commotion. When he came upon a split in the wooded trail, he chose the one leading to the increasing noise. Eventually, the branch broke out on small clearing. He barely had his bearings when he heard the sound of men running.

"There he is!" shouted a gruff voice. "Get him!"

A group of angry loggers tumbled into the opening and surrounded him. Though he was wearing his Forest Service uniform, the men were so enraged they did not heed it. As they circled him, some of them shouted, others threatened harm, but Alford stood his ground.

"You boys are sure riled. What happened? Where'd that blast come from?"

"Some damn Wobbly blew up our donkey engine. Maybe it was you." The speaker, a rough-hewn fellow, advanced, pounding an axe handle in his hand.

Alford put his fists up.

"Ah, it's the ranger from Kulshan. Back off, boys." A man identifying himself as Loffman apologized. "You see anyone?"

"Sure did," Alford said, glad things were diffusing. "I practically ran into him. I was just coming from my home when I heard the blast."

"Get a look?"

"Not a good one. His hat was down. About my height, rugged build maybe. Looked like a lot of you fellows here. He went straight for the road. That true about your engine? You got hit again?"

"Damn right we did," Loffman grumbled. "And if we find him —"

"Let the authorities take charge. Anyone hurt?"

"A couple of fellows. One's got burns."

"Well, I'll get you in touch with the doctor in Hawley Creek. You can call from my house."

"I'll take care of that," roared a voice behind the group. To Alford's surprise, James Ford stepped into the clearing, dressed in a suit and bowler, like a banker on the way to a lynching. Even his high-topped riding boots were polished. But he had a day's growth of beard and a prickly gleam in his eyes. "What the hell are you doing here?" Ford strode right up to Alford. "You know something about this?"

"About as much as you apparently do."

"I'll bet," said Ford. "What color was that shirt, boys?"

"It was like tan forestry cloth, boss," Loffman answered.

"Looks like you're wearing such a shirt, Alford. I'm going to have words with Vernell again."

"Haven't you had enough, Ford? Take your troubles elsewhere," Alford shot back.

"Maybe I don't want to," Ford sneered. "You can't hide behind that badge any more. You're gonna get fired."

"*You're* gonna get burned. Look, Ford, you're wasting valuable time. If you want your saboteur, send Loffman and some others out to track him."

"Maybe I got him." Ford leaned in, his sour cigar-liquor breath assaulting Alford's senses. Despite the state going dry, Ford seemed to know where to find alcohol. "You're not on federal land, you know."

"You're not anywhere either," Alford snapped. He looked at the other men. "Go and tend to your injured. If you need help, I'll get a rig." He turned to go, but was yanked back by Ford.

"I'll be damned, if I'll let you!" shouted Ford.

Alford shook off Ford's burly hand with one strong swipe, causing him to fall back. Furious, Ford swung at him wildly, but before the fist landed, Alford blocked it. In one twist, he grabbed Ford's wrist and flipped the heavier man to the ground with a thud.

Swearing with rage, Ford rolled his bulky body and seizing a broken tree branch from the ground, came to his feet in one wild leap. "You bastard! No one does that to me! No one!" His eyes rolling wildly, Ford charged.

Without hesitation, Bob met the onslaught head-on with a branch of his own and he blocked Ford's first blow successfully then a second and third before they separated. Briefly resting, Ford wiped his mouth with the back of his hand and rocked in place for a second, then charged again. This time, he got through Alford's defenses and laid a nasty blow to his shoulder, causing him to grunt.

"That's only the beginning," Ford sneered.

"Maybe." Alford wasted no time with words. One thing he knew: he was outnumbered by sheer weight. The only way to keep healthy was to wear the bastard out or play dirty. Advancing quickly, he clipped Ford on his wrist before spinning away.

Yowling at the pain, Ford shook out his hand, then charged again, only to get hit again. After that, Ford was more careful. For a half minute, they went blow for blow until Alford's branch broke in two, but he dodged the inevitable blow.

"Now you're done for," Ford gloated.

Alford didn't give him the opportunity to prove it. Seizing Ford's makeshift staff, he yanked down with all his strength. Ford's hold on the branch loosened as he was thrown off balance, falling to the ground as he pitched forward toward the small group of onlookers. Loffman caught him and pushed him upright once again. The move surprised Alford, but he now sensed how the loggers felt about Ford. *They want him to get a licking.* Alford wasn't so sure this was in the Forest Service manual.

Livid, Ford charged and slammed Alford against a large cedar at the edge of the clearing. Pain seared down his back and shoulder. Grunting, he fought against the bulk determined to bash him to a pulp. His fingers squeezed Ford's throat below his Adam's apple, but finally, making no progress, he brought his knee up into Ford's crotch.

Howling, Ford staggered back, leaving himself temporarily open. With a powerful blow to the face, Alford smashed his nose. Bone cracked and blood exploded. Ford fell back, with a hand over his bloody nose and mouth.

"Look what you've done! Look what you've done!" Ford screamed, then swore at his men to do something, but as a group, they melted back toward the trees, waiting for the end of the fight. Seeing that it was over, Loffman nodded to some of the men to go and give Ford a hand. To some others, he told them to go on out to the road and look for the saboteur.

Ford shook his helpers off and ripped a handkerchief out of his pants pocket, held it gingerly against his nose. "I'm going to sue you, Alford. You'll be ruined. You'll wish you were dead for attacking me and for destroying my operation."

"You'd be making a big mistake, James," David Harms said as he stepped out from his screen of cedars. "You've got the wrong man. Alford was with me."

Where did you come from? Alford thought. He looked at Harms suspiciously, his body still bunched tightly for defense, but he grudgingly welcomed Harms's arrival.

"You say," Ford spat.

"All afternoon. Do as the ranger says, James. Tend to your men. We'll contact Vernell or the sheriff, if you wish." Harms's voice was cultured, but it carried a tone of real authority the other men recognized. They began to back further away from Ford as if from fear and from a loss of respect. Some started to follow Loffman's earlier orders. In a few, short moments, all dispersed leaving Ford, Harms and Alford alone in the clearing.

"Look what the son of the bitch did to me," Ford yelled. "A vicious, unwarranted attack."

"From what I saw, you deserved it." Harms didn't hide his disgust with the man. "And if you intend to press charges, I'll say that Mr. Alford was defending himself. I believe that I can get a few others to agree."

Ford dusted himself off with his hat and promising to deal with Alford later, staggered off.

For a moment, Alford and Harms stood silently in the clearing, neither one of them saying a thing. The noise from the logging camp had quieted down and once the voices of the men faded away into the dense green cloak of cedar and alder, the forest was left to itself. Cool and inviting in the early summer evening, one by one its little sounds of birds and an irritated chipmunk brought order. After a time, Alford was aware of Harms's heavy breathing.

"What took you so long?" Alford asked.

Surprised at first, David grinned. "Came as fast as I could. Soon as I saw you take off."

Alford looked back up toward Ford's operation. He rubbed the top of his shoulder where he had been pounded against the tree. "Damned nuisance."

"He's quite beyond himself, Ford is. Don't think I've seen him so perturbed."

"That's a high-falutin' word, but I gather its meaning." He gave Harms another sharp look, but it was fleeting. He felt himself softening, like the air leaking out of a tire tube. "What were you going to do? Maul him to death with vocabulary?"

"I normally carry an umbrella."

Alford grinned. "Look, Harms —"

"You're welcome."

Like a river pushing on a logjam, the tension between them broke and simultaneously they laughed, something that caused Harms to wince and abruptly stop.

"You all right?" Alford asked, aware what Symington had told him after the riding accident.

"I'm fine. Just got a little winded. Lack of exercise."

"Maybe the lack of food. You want to go back? Supper appeared to be imminent."

"That sounds like a good idea. Say, that's quite a tear in your uniform."

Alford pulled at the damaged sleeve, then rubbed his shoulder again. It was beginning to stiffen.

Alford jerked his head in the direction of home and together, they started to go back. A short distance further, however, Harms stopped again. "I'm sorry," he said in a tight voice.

"You needn't be. Let me give you a hand."

Harms politely begged him off, so Alford let him be and watched him with growing compassion and guilt. When Harms seemed ready to start again, he again offered to help, but was refused for a second time. A few steps later, Harms stopped with a jerk, his body twisting to the side.

"God," he cried. "This isn't what I wanted." Near tears, he leaned up against the shaggy trunk of a drooping cedar tree and rested, his eyes avoiding Bob.

"How long?" Alford asked in a soft voice.

"How did you know?"

Alford shrugged. "Just wondered."

"A couple of months. Just enough to take a trip and come back. I thought I could come here and just make things right. I seemed to have tipped the apple cart." He smiled ruefully. "You know, you have nothing to worry about me and Caroline. It's not what you think."

"Pay me no mind, Harms. Caroline and I have a peaceful understanding. That includes cousins."

David murmured something under his breath, then spoke out loud. "But not total peace. Nothing will make sense until I tell you a truth no one else knows. *No one.* I think it's owed to you, though I respectfully implore you not to tell a soul, not even Caroline."

Alford hesitated, thinking Harms was going to tell some family secret about the Symingtons and their business dealings. However what Harms said was beyond anything he could imagine.

"Caroline is my sister." Harms said. "Half-sister. Charles Symington is my father."

For a moment Alford was speechless, his mouth open wide.

"I can tell you the particulars if you like," Harms went on. "The story that I was raised by my aunts is true. I didn't know my own history until I was sixteen. It came as quite a shock."

"I don't know what to say, Harms. I'm completely floored."

"No one knows. Only my father and I. He thought it necessary to tell me when I was seeing too much of Caroline. We were always good chums."

Alford cleared his throat a little too loud. "That must

have been difficult."

"Not as hard as having to keep things secret and seeing how he treated you." Harms's voice trembled. Tears thickened it further.

Alford clasped David's hand. In an instant, his perception of Harms had changed, flooding him with a new understanding and respect. And guilt. It saddened him, too, for Harms would not live long enough to enjoy the true, new friendship that would grow between them.

After a time, Alford said they should get back. He nodded at the darkening forest as the sun brushed the tops of the mountains. Harms answered that he thought he could manage.

"Will you tell Caroline about your illness?"

"I think she's guessed as much. I... I just want to go away to the places that Emily and I talked about. I have a colleague going with me, so I won't be without company or assistance. I'd rather not tell her fully. I couldn't stand the pity."

"And the other matter?"

"It's not my place to speak and I ask you not to say anything as I agreed some time ago."

"I believe I can be as good a man as you are, Harms. I'll say nothing."

David smiled. He moved away from the tree and began walking awkwardly. "Do you remember when we first met?"

"A rented buggy and some pouring rain."

"I sometimes believe that things are not by chance, as hard as they can be. I think that I can die now. Everything's been completed."

Alford thought of his brother Stein and wondered if that was true.

When Alford and David came back, Caroline had been terribly afraid to face Alford, thinking only of the storms that would come with him. Instead, she had been greeted by two men who suspiciously acted like they had swallowed something blatantly illegal. Though Alford was supporting Harms, it often seemed the other way around.

When they got up to the front porch, they wavered before they tackled the stairs. Caroline wondered what the joke was when she had been so worried. She had heard the blast and when Berta Olsen called to say that it had been up at Ford's logging operation and a man had been hurt, she had been frantic. *Did Bob know?* He knew and left it at that. David wasn't saying anything either. Happy at the new ease between them, she still wasn't sure what to think of their sudden co-conspiracy.

The trout did wonders for everyone, but David retired early along with the children. Alford helped Caroline clean up. Afterwards, they went out to talk on the back stairs in the mixed twilight air of summer.

"Is everything all right?" she asked.

"Yes. I think it is." *Not everything. David is dying.* He rubbed her shoulders as she sat below him.

"What was the other call tonight?"

"Vernell called to say Ford's man was taken to the city hospital by train. No luck with the saboteur." He didn't mention anything about the fight or about that Ford's nose had been treated and now was heavily bandaged. The story was that he had been injured in the initial blast by flying debris.

"Cathy thinks it was the man who has been preaching strike in the camps down near Twin Forks."

"I can't say, love. It could be one of his own men. That was a ragged lot I saw today."

"You never told me what happened."

"Nothing much. Ford showed up when I offered to help and he got a little feisty. Harms straightened him out."

"David? Did Ford threaten both of you?" Her shoulders stiffened in the gloom.

"Nothing we couldn't handle. Everything's all right. Truly." He found a stray strand of hair near her ear and twisted it around one of his fingers. She leaned back against his knees and closed her eyes to the motion as he caressed her jaw.

"David's terribly sick," she finally said.

"I know," answered Alford, "but he doesn't want you to worry." He bent over and kissed her on her ear, then rested his cheek next to it. "He knows you love him," he added, "and that's what counts."

Caroline turned around and looked at him in the fading light. Even in the gloom, Alford could see the tears slowly rolling down her cheeks. "Does that hurt you so?" she asked.

"No. I finally understand the meaning of the word love." His lips found her mouth and he gently kissed her. Quietly, she came into his arms and they rocked each other silently on the stairs for a while, each in their own thoughts. Then with deliberate tenderness, he nuzzled up against her wet cheek and resumed kissing her. Without a word, she responded. It didn't take long before they slipped down onto the steps, his strong arms cradling her against the hard edges of the stairs. Eventually, they sat up at an owl's hoot in the cedars near them. Caroline leaned her head against Alford's chest.

"The old cherry tree trick," she said.

"Shameful practice," Alford chuckled. He put his arm around her shoulder and gave her squeeze. "The decent thing to do now is to go the shed and finish it."

Caroline straightened out her hair. "Are you suggesting something, Mr. Alford?"

Chapter 45

David Harms left the following day, earlier than planned. He was in pain, he admitted to Caroline and thought it best to go.

"It's been a two good days, hasn't it?" Harms said as he boarded the train.

Caroline gave him a kiss on his cheek and a long hug. "It's been wonderful." *Better than anything I could have hoped for,* she thought.

"You'll send us a postcard?" Alford asked as he handed up Harms's small suitcase.

"Yellowstone's my first stop. It'll be a beaut." He shook Alford's hand warmly. "Thanks." He looked Alford straight in the eye. "I mean it."

"Take care."

The Ford operation closed down indefinitely the week after Harms left. Some in Frazier thought it due to the troubles of the last few months. Others opined it was insolvent and had been for some time. The day after it closed, Alford was called to Vernell's office at the ranger station.

"Got a letter from Congressman Keenes's committee. Wanted me to look into budgetary items for the next fiscal quarter. Despite the call for increased logging in the national forests, he's talking about cutting back personnel. Questions having two assistants." He looked guiltily at Alford. "George does have seniority."

Alford sat down by the wood stove taking away the morning chill. "How close is Keenes to Ford?"

"Can't say, but I think you hit it on the nail. This is purely politics of a personal nature."

Alford frowned. Ford hadn't wasted any time on his threat. "How soon are you to answer?"

"As soon as possible. I'm squaring the paperwork right now." Vernell cleared his throat. "Don't give up. I've got my own troop of supporters too. Your work's exemplary and I need you. Of course, we both know this was expected after the thrashing you gave Ford last week. Fortunately, he couldn't press charges without answering a few questions of his own."

Alford got up. He knew that Vernell was disappointed in him. But Alford also felt that Vernell's displeasure was fleeting. Ford had it coming for some time. "You think I'll be cut completely?" he asked.

"Not if I can help it. Just be patient."

Patient? Alford thought. Odd things happened since the accident at the logging operation: their cow let out of the pasture to wander a mile down the road. A hole knocked into his drift boat and tackle stolen. The phone ringing with no one on the line. He tried to shield Caroline and the children from it as much as possible, but couldn't for long.

"You listening?"

"Yes, sir."

"I said it'll work out. Don't start packing your bags yet. Ford is headed for serious trouble. I heard his operation was broken into the same day that donkey engine was tampered with. Some money was taken. Several thousand dollars' worth, as a matter of fact. Sounds suspicious to me when it's easy to blame radicals for problems that are directly the result of acting illegally."

"Figures." Alford felt drained. "I'll get back to work on the Big Fir report." He picked up his jacket on the coatrack. "Any word on Micah? I know he's had a contract somewhere."

"He's been in Skagit working with one of those scenic photographers. Took the party back into the glacier country for a couple of weeks. He was due back yesterday. I'm sure he'll turn up. Now git."

An hour later, Alford stopped in at the General Store to talk about the summer run of steelhead due in a few weeks. Instead, the talk was about labor agitation. Charlie had come up after some trouble at his mill.

"It's a first for me. The boys know I run it fair and square. They're as upset as I am."

"There's agitation all over," another man standing at the tackle counter said. "No doubt about it. That Symington operation got hit too."

"When was that?" Bob asked.

"Night before. New saw was damaged."

There was a general consensus that the whole world was going to hell in a tin can. There were longshoreman strikes up and down the coast, strikes in Seattle and strife with the lumber and shingle workers. War talk had increased in the last few weeks.

"The papers have been talking about vigilante action down in Centralia and Everett," said Charlie. "I don't think we want that here."

Alford turned a box of hooks in his hands. "No, we don't, but the lumbermen are the last holdouts to the reforms. If they'd give an inch, it'd take the air out of some of the agitators' sails and we could all live in peace." He picked up the package he had purchased and gave a nod to them all. "See you all soon."

Charlie Bladstad followed him out. "Cathy says Caroline's brother is missing in France. Sure sorry to hear that."

"Thanks. She just got word from her sister yesterday."

"He's only a kid, isn't he?"

"Yeah. A kid." Alford got into the truck. "What are you going to do with the troubles at the mill?"

"Mollify them. In the meantime, I'm going to be home for the next day or two. If you want to go fishing, let me know."

"Good evening, Charlie."

The house was eerily quiet when Alford came up on the porch. Seeing no sign of the children in the yard and no one in the front rooms, he listened carefully to the sounds of the house. It felt hollow as a deserted barn. And unusual to be so still.

"Hello?" he called, then stiffened when the phone rang in the hall. He waited for two rings to pass, before he answered it. It immediately went dead on the other end.

He put the receiver back in its cradle and walked to the kitchen. By the sink, he found a note.

"*Be back soon,*" it read. Outside through the windows, the sky looked dark above the mountains, a little too early in the evening. Rain would come for sure. He took a drink of water and jumped when the phone rang again.

He got it on the second ring and was surprised to hear Maggie Svenson on the other end.

"Thank goodness someone's home," she said. "I've been ringing for most of the afternoon."

"Something wrong?"

"I'm afraid I've some rather bad news. It's your friend, Billy Howell. He was beaten quite severely last night. Some of his friends brought him here this morning."

Something stabbed Alford in his chest like a knife of ice. "Know who did it?"

"They had some ideas. Jenkins, for one. There's been some fuss at the B & E, you may have heard."

"Where's Billy's wife, Lucy?

"She was here, but she's worried sick. Was wondering if

he could come up to your place for safekeeping."

"Of course. Is it OK to move him?"

"He's upright. He's got a broken rib and his face is a mess, but he can travel."

Alford looked at his watch. "Be down in an hour, but do something for me. Call someone Billy knows and tell them I'm taking him to Twin Forks."

"But you're not."

"Exactly. You don't have a party line, but someone else might on Billy's end."

After hanging up, he called over to Cathy Bladstad's.

"Caroline around?" he asked.

"Haven't seen her since three, but she was talking about collecting some salmonberries for ice cream. Best ones are down by the Powell's."

"Thanks, Cathy. Look, if I don't find her before I go, could you let her know where I'm going?" Alford paused. *Should I tell her?* He cleared his throat.

"What's going on, Bob?"

"There's been trouble. Billy's been beaten up. I'm going down to get him."

"Good Lord. Be careful."

"I will."

He called George Fuller at the ranger station next. "Going to Hawley Creek," he said and told him why. "I'll let you know when I leave from there. If you don't hear from me, call Vernell. For God's sake, look after Caroline and the kids."

"You sound like you're expecting trouble."

"I am. Something doesn't feel right."

"Maybe the sheriff should be notified."

"Let me check with folks down there first. In the meantime, keep an eye on my family."

Fuller promised he would.

Alford quickly put together a knapsack of clothes and a rain slicker in case he got bogged down in any bad weather and loaded them into the truck. At the last minute, he put in his shotgun, some loaded shotgun shells and a blanket. He left a note for Caroline and he was off.

The sky had darkened in the last ten minutes, thick, gray clouds settling down on the topmost sections of the mountains. A faint breeze was stirring the boughs of the cedars and fir on the edge of the road. He backed the truck out onto the road and headed into the woods that bordered it.

Less than a quarter mile down, he found Cory and Kate carrying baskets along the road's edge. They were laden with berries as bright orange as salmon eggs from the tall, lush bushes around them.

"Where's Mommy?" he asked them.

"Here, Bob," said Caroline coming out of the bushes. "Did you come to pick us up?"

"Wish I could. There's been an emergency. Billy's been hurt. I'm going to go and get him. Bring him home for a few days while things cool off."

Caroline's face paled. Alford suddenly felt bad for scaring her. She squared her shoulders and came up to the car window. She put her hands on the sill. "Will you be gone long?"

"Naw. Make up the bed in the tackle room for him, will you?"

She promised that she would, but he could see her unease as her fingers played on the open window. "Must you go alone?"

He gave her hand a pat. "It'll be OK, honey. I told George what I was up to. He'll let Jack know. I'll call you before I start back." He beckoned to her and kissed her on the side of her mouth. "Don't worry."

He gave Caroline a reassuring smile and drove off. She was still holding onto the children when he looked back in the side mirror further down the road. For a chilling moment, like a knife in his chest, he wondered, *Will I see them again?*

Exactly an hour later, he pulled into the Svenson clinic in

Hawley Creek. Maggie Svenson came out to greet him, prim in her nurse's white pinafore.

"Bob, thank God you're here. I think the house and clinic are being watched."

"Is the doc here?"

"No, I'm alone. He's with a patient. Don't think he'll be back until late at night." She looked over her shoulder. "Did you have trouble coming down? I haven't felt all that safe."

Alford followed her to the clinic door. "Just watching the weather. Where's Billy now?"

"Inside. I called like you asked. A car drove by a little later on. Real slow."

She led the way into the infirmary and down a hall to a simple room with whitewashed walls and lace curtains. A photograph of a couple dancing on an enormous stump was the sole decoration.

Alford found Billy sitting up in bed against a stack of pillows. He appeared to be asleep, but his face was so heavily bruised and swollen it was hard to tell. It made Alford wince, remembering his own beating years ago.

"That you, Alford?" Billy's voice was a hoarse whisper.

"Yeah. I came as quickly as I could."

"Wish you hadn't." He opened his eyes as best he could, but they went barely beyond a squint.

"Now that's an unneighborly thing to say." Alford sat down on a chair next to the iron bed.

"No, I mean it. They're going to get you. I heard them talking. They thought I was out cold, but I was playing dead. They want you to come down."

"Who's they?"

"Ford and Jenkins."

"They do this to you?"

"No. Some of their thugs did, but I saw Jenkins. Ford too. They let it out I'm a Wobbly, but I'm not. I had nothin' to do with that saw being damaged."

"I know you didn't. So does everyone else."

Billy began to get agitated. "Whole town's gone crazy

with wild talk. Some of the camps are arming guards."

"Has the Sheriff been notified?"

"That's the trouble. He's away. Went to Seattle for a sheriff's meeting or something." He grimaced when he moved and grabbed his side. "They'll be waiting for us in Twin Forks."

"We're not going there. I'm taking you up to my house."

"Alford..." Billy grimaced with the effort.

"Quit fussing. Got anything to pack? I brought a change of clothes." Alford looked over at a pile of gear on a bench set against the wall. "This stuff yours?"

Billy painfully nodded yes.

"Good. We're leaving now."

Alford helped him dress, then supported him out to the truck. Maggie put Howell's things into an oil cloth bag and put them in the back while Alford got Billy into the front seat of the truck. At the last minute, she added a couple of pillows from the infirmary to protect him against any jolting.

"Good luck," she said when Alford got in.

"Thanks. By the way, if I were to head toward Twin Forks, would I be able to switch back and come abreast of Hawley Creek without being seen?"

"Yes," she said and told him how. "It's pretty rough."

"We'll give it a whirl. If someone asks, we're going to Twin Forks. In the meantime, call George Fuller at the ranger's station, will you? Let him know I'm leaving now but don't say home. Then call Caroline. Same words. Please."

"Fine. I'll expect a call from *you* when you get there." She peered into the cab. "I'll come and see you tomorrow, Mr. Howell." He raised his hand in thanks and then they were gone, heading south through the settlement.

Hawley Creek wasn't much, with its false fronted buildings barely out of the frontier age, but a couple of the Victorian houses off the main street with their elegant gingerbread scrolling around their verandas gave promise of a more refined future. Alford drove through the muddy dirt street to the edge of the town where Douglas fir and

419

hemlock rose to swallow up the road. As they passed the last house, a man in a dark suit and bowler hat stood up and watched them go by.

"You see that?" asked Billy.

"If *you* saw him, it must be bad," Alford said. "You comfortable?"

"As good as I'm gonna be."

"Well, our cutoff's not too far off. I'll take it as easy as I can."

"You just watch that fellow." Billy gave him a grin. "Just like old times. Remember dodging the police at those girlie shows in Seattle 'cuz we were underaged?"

Alford chuckled. "We were a pair. Still surprised I made it to twenty-one."

"How about forty?" Billy pointed to his side mirror. "That fellow got into a car."

Alford pressed down on the accelerator, hoping not to hurt Billy. They entered the mile long stand of firs crowding close to the narrow one lane road leading south to Twin Forks. Alford welcomed the gloom the huge trunks of the firs and understory below them created, hoping it would buy them some time.

A half-mile down, he spied the entrance to the dirt turn off. He carefully eased the truck onto it. Rolling and lurching, the overgrown brush soon concealed it. Billy groaned.

"Sorry," Alford said. "Did you see anyone enter?"

"Couldn't tell," murmured Billy.

"Well, I'm going to go in a little more and wait. See if he comes by."

The car raced by two minutes later, heading south to Twin Forks. As soon as it passed, Alford put the truck in forward gear and went deeper into the woods.

Alford and Howell hadn't been gone ten minutes when two cars pulled into the medical clinic yard. A group of men got out and came up to the house. As they approached the steps, they pulled bandanas or flour sacks over their faces. Still, Maggie recognized one of them.

"Why, Walt Fryer," Maggie Svenson exclaimed. "How's the toe?"

"Fine," Fryer muttered with awkward embarrassment behind his mask.

"This a medical call?" she said to the rest.

"Now, ma'am, you know we come for the Wobbly," a forceful voice said behind the group. "Step aside boys, so this can be accomplished as quickly as possible."

The men on the steps parted like the Red Sea, revealing a powerful man standing on the ground with an axe handle in his hands. Like the others, his head was covered.

"The only one allowed to come is the sheriff if it's a criminal matter, but I never heard such a thing. This man's no Wobbly." Maggie's voice was clear and strong. *They won't push me around.* She'd seen her fill of rough men and was adept at dealing with them.

"We'll see him and we'll be taking him back to Twin Forks." The man advanced up the stairs, then stopped when she took out a shotgun.

"That's far enough," she said trying to guess at the dark eyes that stared her down. She barely caught the slight nod he gave to someone behind him. Two men slipped away. *Now where are you going?*

"I don't have time to dillydally with you, *madam*." The voice again. Dark eyes in the slits in the cloth. When he put the emphasis on the last word, to let her know that he knew about her past life down south, she had no doubt that it was Jenkins behind the flour sack.

"This clinic is protected by law. You're interfering."

"I'm with security. I can do what I like, *madam*. Now show what a lady you *can* be and let us in."

Maggie raised the shotgun, then was distracted by the breaking of glass in the back of the building. The man jumped and with brute force, bashed the screen door, causing it to break off its hinges. Maggie fell to the fir wood floor underneath it, the shotgun going off and blasting a hole in the ceiling. Plaster rained down on them both as the man scrambled to throw aside the door and rip the shotgun from her hands. From inside of the house, two men came through the broken window and went to search in the back of the clinic. There was the sound of a metal tray falling to the floor and some furniture moving, then they came back.

"No one's there, boss."

All three men stared at Maggie who was sitting up now and nursing the side of her cheek. She crab-walked back from under the broken door.

"Now you tell me where he is and we'll go peaceable-like." The leader leaned into her and whispered into her ear, "If you please, Mrs. Gorham. For old times' sake." The sack pulled against his face. The shadow of a mustache lay underneath it "He's not here, Mr. Jenkins, as you can tell," she answered, still defiant. Her heart pounded.

"You whore." Jenkins raised his hand to strike her, but stopped in midair when Walt Fryer came to open doorway.

"Hey, someone pulled up into the yard," his muffled voice said. "Seen a truck going toward Twin Forks."

By the way he held his shoulders, Fryer looked uncomfortable as he stared at her. Her hair had fallen out of its bun. The white hose underneath her mid-calf length skirt was torn. Maggie just stared back at him.

"Tell Ardell to send one of the cars in that direction. I'll make a call from here." Jenkins stood up and eyed the darkening sky.

It's more like a cool spring night, she thought. The sun was in retreat. *Maybe the rain will hold them back.*

Jenkins looked down at her. "Where's your telephone?"

She nodded toward the tiny office.

"Help her up," he barked to one of the men who came through the window, then stepped around the door. "Put that back too and then get out."

Maggie wobbled to the infirmary counter and dabbed the small cut on her bruised cheek with alcohol on a cotton ball.

She held her terror in check even when Jenkins came back.

"Who's with Howell?"

She didn't answer. "Never mind. Could have been a Forest Service truck. It was Alford, wasn't it?" Again silence. Jenkins shrugged. "Good."

He said something to one of the remaining men outside, then came back in to the infirmary.

"I suppose you won't say where they're going in Twin Forks. Ah, doesn't matter. They'll catch up." He went back to the front and leaned the screen door against the door frame. "It's been a pleasure. Oh, don't get any smart ideas. I'm sure some of the more solid citizens of this community would be interested to know about your other business ventures, but for now that'll be strictly between the two of us."

Maggie straightened up at that, anger overcoming her fear. "They wouldn't believe a word you said, mister, whatever you think my 'other ventures' were. You can bully all you want, but you won't win."

Jenkins took two quick steps toward her and raised his hand. Her heart beating, she stood her ground. The blow never came. When she opened her eyes, Jenkins was gone.

Stiffly, Maggie came over to the door, making sure they were headed in the direction of Twin Forks. Seeing that they were, she went into the back room to survey the damage. Ten minutes later it began to drizzle. Then she heard the car returning and speeding by, heading toward Frazier. As quick as she was able, she went to the telephone.

Chapter 46

Alford found the road through the woods and brush nothing more than a trail, but someone had cut it back recently. Rocking and bouncing over the roots of cedars frequently extending across the pathway, he did his best to keep Billy comfortable as they wove through the trees. Each jolt brought his friend close to passing out. Every time Billy stifled a groan, Alford thought of his own beating. *I'm going to kill you, Jenkins.*

They were both relieved when they made it to the open prairie bordering the edge of the river. The road was smoother here, though Alford had to watch for large rocks hiding in the grass as they passed. To their left, the woods made a screen between them and the Hawley Creek settlement.

"Almost there," he said to Billy. *At least, it appears that way.* The forest closed in again on them, but soon they'd be past the clinic and back on the main road. Billy raised his hand and waved him on. When they came to the woods again, Alford stopped the car and lit the lamps in the headlights.

They went through the forest for the next mile, the road eventually turning up toward what Alford knew was the main road to Frazier. At the road's edge, he slowed down, then let the truck idle as he searched up and down the road for signs of any unusual traffic. To the right the forest closed in on the road; to the left, it broke where trees had been cut for the continuing expansion of Hawley Creek. No traffic. Not even a wagon. The dirt road with its slight veneer of gravel ending at the settlement's limits appeared muddy and deserted.

"Think we're in for a ride?" Billy asked. He listlessly put his hand out the window and rubbed the rain drops he had accumulated in his fingers. "I know we're gonna get wet."

"We'll make it. Caroline's got the tackle room made up and the coffeepot going." He leaned his head out and looked up high at the deepening evening sky pigeonholed between the tops of the giant firs lining the road. With the high mountains around them, the sun already had faded. He figured it would be well beyond dusk by the time they got home. "Besides, I know the road well."

He put the truck into gear, the clutch groaning as the truck moved forward. Once he got down the sharp hill by the creek where he had the run in with Jenkins weeks earlier, they'd be all right. Seven miles distant. He gave Billy a reassuring word and gave the truck some gas.

Soon, Alford thought he was making good time on the single lane road. "How're those pillows holding up?" he asked.

"Fine. Could use a feather bed for the amount of aches I've got, though. Them holes in the road suddenly got bigger."

"And I thought I was driving just fine." Alford gave him a grin, then realized Billy probably couldn't see him all that well out of his swollen face, so turned his attention to the road and weather. And his long-standing friendship.

Billy had always considered Alford superior to him in intellect and character, but Alford never let that be a criteria for their friendship stretching over nearly two decades. Maybe that was the difference between them and all the

Fords and Symingtons of the world. The true model of friendship didn't lie in financial and entrepreneurial alliances, rigidly cemented to class structure. It lay, rather, in respect and a common sense of principles and shared experiences.

The rain increased, making the road not only gummy, but full of dips and ridges. As the rain tapped on the truck's roof, it made talking in the cab difficult.

Still, he began to believe they would get home without the expected attack until they passed a road that cut back into the trees to some homestead. Pulled back against a screen of salmonberry bushes that bordered each side of the lane sat a midnight blue Ford roadster. Alford gave it an initial glance as he passed, then serious appraisal in his side mirror when the car pulled out and began to follow at a discreet, but steady pace.

"What's that?" Billy asked. His swollen eyes squinted even more as he attempted to see through the rain, but his ears hadn't missed the grating noise of the other vehicle's engine as it accelerated.

"Company. You just hold on. The bridge's not too far off."

"Lord," said Billy, his voice cracking. He fumbled around with his hands. "You still got that shotgun here?"

"Yup." Alford gave the roadster another glance, then looked ahead for any traffic in front of them. For the moment, the road was clear.

For two miles they drove on, the blue roadster following in nonchalant pursuit. From time to time, Billy would ask what Alford could see, but there was nothing to report. For the moment, it was just going in the same direction they were going.

The rain continued to splatter; the evening light dimmed, but visibility stayed good. As the road climbed, the forest began to thin and become more open. On the right, Bob knew the terrain steepened, eventually falling away to the river far below, leaving an open vista. Then hugging the forested hill on its left, the road would dive down to the

426

bridge for the drive across and up the other side of the ravine. For now, the truck chugged along, its engine purring when the road leveled out.

"Another minute," Alford announced as he checked the side mirror again, then put the brakes on and stopped suddenly when he came around the corner and came face-to-face with a Packard touring car parked on the road in front of them about two hundred feet distant. A small group of men wearing dark ankle-length touring coats gathered next to it.

"Oh, God. Who the hell is that?" Billy cried.

"By the bandage on the nose, looks like James Ford and some friends." Alford quickly made a head count, then checked the side mirror again. The roadster behind them slowed down and stopped a ways back. He judged the width of the road. Though a single lane, it was wider than most with adequate turnouts. There was one on the left up near the car facing them.

"They're coming toward us." Billy began to panic. "Oh, Lordy, don't let them take me."

"You're not going anywhere. Neither of us are."

Billy swallowed. Even in the dim light of the cab, his face looked as gray as ash in a fire pit. Alford reached for the shotgun and opened it, inserting a couple of shells into the chambers. "Here, try this on for size." He put the shotgun into Billy's hands. "Just aim that-a way. I'm getting out and will be on the left if they get any closer."

Billy sighed heavily, like he was taking in extra air. "Sure." He gasped again, then looked in Alford's direction." Do something for me. Tell Sarah and kids I love them."

"Tell them yourself."

Alford got out of the truck, and standing behind the door, asked Ford in a loud voice what he wanted.

"Isn't it obvious?" Ford shouted back. From under his coat he pulled out an axe handle. "This time, there'll be no messing up."

"Clear the road, Ford. This section is national forest land.

427

You'll be in a heap of trouble if you don't comply."

"You're an ass if you think I believe that. Then again, maybe I don't care." He nodded at a couple of the men at the touring car. When they began to advance, Alford reached inside the truck and honked on the horn.

"Better let them know they're covered with a shotgun."

Abruptly, the men stopped. Satisfied, Alford looked at the roadster behind them. The driver pulled it over a bit, making room for another car that appeared out of nowhere. The new vehicle advanced a few feet around the first car, then idled. On the passenger side of the coal black Chevrolet, someone got out. Jenkins.

"Looks like you're boxed in," Jenkins yelled at Alford.

"Appearances can be deceiving."

"Yeah, that Margie Gorham should know."

Alford stiffened. "You better not have hurt her."

"You're in no position to find out."

"Maybe. You're full of it, Jenkins. You and Ford crossed the line. I wonder if Symington really knows just how far."

Jenkins laughed. "Now that's something else you ain't gonna know." He waved his hand at Ford, then looked at Alford again. "Why don't you say good-bye to your friend," he called. "It's the last chance you'll get." With that, he quickly got back into the car and it suddenly leaped forward.

"Damn!" Alford dove into the truck and grabbing a hammer from the floor at Billy's feet, smashed the window on Billy's side, then put the truck into gear. Jenkins's motorcar came on fast.

"Jesus, what was that about?"

"Shh... Just poke that thing through the hole and keep it aimed. When I tell you to, fire it. I don't care who you hit."

He steered away from the road's edge and the steep plunge downhill and hit the truck's metal accelerator. It was just in time as Jenkins's motorcar tore up behind them in a blur.

Billy tried to turn to see behind them. "He's going to push us off!" he yelled.

Jenkins's Chevrolet roared up to them, its big fenders on a parallel course next to Alford's truck door. It wouldn't take much to knock them over. Worse, both truck and motorcar were on a head-on course with Ford's touring car. Alford's mouth went dry. All Jenkins had to do was bump him, then shoot for the turnout. Faster and faster, Jenkins's Chevrolet roared up, eating up the space between them. Alford could see Jenkins's driver in the mirror. He could almost feel the man's muscles tense in the effort to come alongside and thrust the big motorcar into their track. Shouting, Alford willed his truck to obey.

Then, as fast as the car was coming, everything seemed to slow down. Alford saw the appalled looks on Ford's men as they scrambled to get out of the way. He saw Jenkins's motorcar make one last push, then everything went blank. Flooring the accelerator in one last desperate attempt and with few feet to spare, Alford passed in front of Jenkins's motorcar and crossed safely over to the turnout near Ford's Packard. There was an eerie moment when the only sound he heard was the roaring in his head as all motion seemed suspended.

He didn't hear Billy's scream of fear and pain as the truck was suddenly sent spinning nor did he see the impact of Jenkins's motorcar and Ford's Packard: how the front end of motorcar smashed the touring car so hard that it literally was lifted and thrown over the precipitous side and down; how its tail end rammed into the truck and made both vehicles spin until they hit the road's edge; how for an awful moment they were both impaled on each other before gravity pulled them down. He didn't know anything, except —

Pain. In the dark he thought it would drive him mad. The weight of it all on his legs and hips. The wetness of it. Gradually sound came to him: piercing screams making him wonder if they were his own in Hell and the sound of metal under strain. Smells came next: the smell of oil and flesh burning, like the time the pig house at his grandfather's farm caught on fire and everything was cooked inside.

The smell of fear and dying. He put out his free hand and felt the unforgiving touch of cold metal and grease. Bombarded by his senses, he finally opened his eyes and discovered he was lying against a hill with the truck on top of him. Somehow he had come to lie under the passenger side — the door had been ripped off — the chassis imprisoning him up to his belt line. The only thing keeping the truck from crushing him was an old stump which had caught it coming down. As he used his aching eyes to further locate his position, water rolled into the corner of one. He wiped it away. *Blood.*

"Billy," he called, unaware his voice croaked with spittle and blood. He turned his head seeking the sounds of the injured. A sharp pain stabbed his lower back. He rested against the hill gingerly and discovered something to be grateful for: the rain had stopped.

Down the hill below him, someone screamed louder than the other sounds of misery around him. A harrowing sound of pure agony. He prayed it wasn't Billy. He stared up the hill behind him and was surprised to see that somehow he had been tumbled down toward the creek that ran under the bridge. At least it sounded that way. Water was close by. *Thirsty. I'm so damn thirsty.*

"Billy!" he called out again. The effort hurt his rib cage but he got a groan. "Billy?" He attempted to pull himself up on his elbows, but the pain in his back thwarted him. It hurt almost as much as the increasingly driven torment in his legs. He supposed that was something else to be grateful for. It would be bad if he couldn't feel anything at all.

He laid carefully back down against the muddy earth. It smelled rich and deep with the humus of life. The sky above him was still light, a soft lavender grey as dusk deepened. He brushed a green sword fern out of his way and closed his eyes.

He must have fainted. When he opened them again the sky was darker. The sounds of men crying sounded weaker, though he could hear and smell something still burning down below. The smoke rose above the truck's cab and past the tops of the firs and hemlocks on the hill, sending out a black, oily smoke full of bad omen.

"Billy!" he yelled, then looked upslope. A tattered man stood there, his clothes bloody and torn, his face dark from oil smudges. The black mustaches drooped. The bloodshot eyes were ringed with white. *Jenkins. Back from the dead?* Their eyes locked and Alford knew only a miracle could save him now. The man was going to kill him.

"You're alive," Alford somehow said in a voice as calm as parlor conversation.

"Better than most," Jenkins said. "I jumped." He turned when someone started weeping and screaming at the same time, the words lost in the babble of water nearby. "That's Ford. He's taken a turn for the worse." Jenkins swayed. For the first time, Alford could see he was seriously injured. Underneath his torn shirtfront, a wound oozed blood and matter. When he looked down at Alford again, his movements were slow and mechanical. "Gonna have to say the same about you."

"Why?" asked Alford. "It's never been about Symington, has it? You don't care one iota about him."

"Damn right." Jenkins swayed a bit more, then laughed. The pitch sounded high and giddy. "All those fancy folks with their summer homes the size of mansions. The pretty girls in white playing tennis on the lawns never paying attention to the likes of me. Then you snuck around and soiled one. I had to get her back. Didn't get much for it, though." He closed his eyes for a minute. "Will now." He brought up his right hand. In it he held a large rock. He smiled again, like the grin on a ghoul.

His pain has made him crazy, Alford thought. It didn't seem real when the man put the rock in both bloodstained hands and raised it over his head. If he dropped it or worse threw it down, Alford knew it would split his skull.

"Jenkins!" he warned. "Don't!" But it was useless talk. If he were able to roll away from it the first time, Jenkins could just do it again until it was done right. Bracing himself, he thought, *Caroline! Sweet Cory and Kate.* He prayed they wouldn't be the ones to find him.

He watched Jenkins bring all his strength into his arms to slam the rock down, then suddenly get blown away to the side with part of his head missing. Alford didn't hear the report of the shotgun until it was all over. Stunned, he lay against the hill in disbelief, bringing on new agony to his legs. He began to shiver. Someone scrambled down close to him and hunkered down beside him, but feeling nauseated, Alford suddenly didn't care if it were enemy or foe.

"Lord, what a sight you are."

"Mi-cah?"

"Shush." Micah's big hands brushed the blood-soaked hair off of Alford's forehead as tender as a mother tending her child. Micah gave him a grin and opened a canteen and helped him take a small swallow. When he was done, Micah poured some water onto a bandana and gently cleaned up Alford's bloodied and oil-smeared face. "Just so you look presentable for the ball." He ran his eyes over Alford like he he was making account of his injuries. Then Micah studied the truck.

"How did y — ?" Alford's mouth felt like cotton stuffing was in it. The pain in his legs bore down like a vise. He felt like he would pass out again.

Micah sat back on his haunches. "Saw everything from the hill on the other side of the bridge. Everything. Got here just in time looks like. Help's coming. I sent Sunny Jack on my horse to let the folks in Frazier know."

Alford rolled his head back. The cool earth felt like a balm. Upslope, he could see a shotgun laying on the ground. His shotgun.

"Billy —"

"Don't see him. Leastways he don't appear to be under anything. I'll find him for you."

"Get him — now."

"Hush. Save your strength. I'm going to get this off of

you first, then I'll go get him. You cold?" He pulled apart one of Alford's eyelids and satisfied at the response, felt his pulse. A quick run over his torso and abdomen seemed to put Micah at ease, but it only added to Alford's discomfort.

Finally, Micah stood up. "I'm going to push this thing off now. You're bleeding somewhere. I don't think we should wait." He disappeared around to the other side of the truck, then came back with a large tree limb. "It's all clear now."

He didn't elaborate any further. Setting the limb under the truck's front end, he leaned down onto it with all his tremendous strength. There was a great metallic sound as the truck's battered frame protested against the movement, then the sound of broken glass as it shifted in the cab. The truck groaned, then gave way to a high squeal as it lifted and rolled. Gaining momentum, it rolled and crashed down the hill like a giant iron ball, its path leaving a trail of debris and strange noises. Finally, far down below it stopped abruptly with a final crash of metal.

"That should take care of things," Micah announced. But his audience had passed out.

Chapter 47

Caroline knew something terrible had happened when both Mary Vernell and Cathy Bladstad called on her.

"There's been an accident, dear," Mary said, "right near the bridge at the number four mile post. Several cars were involved, including Bob's."

"Ohh," Caroline promptly sat down on the sofa. "Is Bob... all right?"

Mary took her hand. "He has been hurt, but you understand all will be done for him. Jack's been in touch with the Hawley Creek clinic *and* the train station and they'll send a special engine up here with the doctor on it because we're closer to those that are hurt than the clinic."

"That bad?"

"I can't say, but Sunny Jack who brought the news says he was alive, though there were some dead. She said it was a terrible scene."

Caroline sat quiet for a moment. She felt numb, her heart slowed down to an empty thud.

"There was something else," Mary continued. "That Jenkins fellow may be involved. Jack got a call about him a while ago. Jenkins had been at the clinic looking for Billy

Howell."

"Ohh," Caroline said again, her voice like a little girl's. "Dear Lord. Jenkins." She shuddered, then got control of herself. "If they bring Bob here, I'd best send the children away."

"I would. They might use your house for a first aid clinic until the train is ready. Any of the more seriously injured will be taken into the city to the hospital." Mary patted her shoulder. "You must have hope. Micah's with him. Bob'll be in good hands until the wagons get there."

"How long will that be?"

"Hopefully, an hour's time. Why don't we look for washbasins and clean cloths? A big pot of boiling water should be helpful too. I'd do it now, then I'll take the children to Berta's."

"And I'll stay with you," Cathy said.

Mary squeezed Caroline's hand. "You must be brave, now. Bob will be needing you."

Caroline took a deep breath. "All right. Let's get ready then."

The wagons arrived about two hours later. By then it was dark and lanterns had been set up outside along the fence where some twenty people from town gathered to help. As each wagon pulled up in front of the house, they were directed over the pasture where there would be space to lay out the dead and unload the injured. Soon there were five. When Vernell saw Caroline on the porch he came up the front path to her.

"Where's Bob —?" Caroline asked.

"He's both conscious and complaining which are good signs in any medical book." He took her by the sleeve when she started to rush down the stairs to look for him. "Now, Caroline —" Jack smiled at her gently. "— I want to warn you before you leap in. Bob looks terrible and to tell the truth, he's got some serious injuries, though don't you fret— there's nothing life-threatening at this juncture. He just needs to be calm and lay still. Dr. Svenson may want to do a look see when he gets him inside."

"How bad is he?"

"Bob's got a broken leg that's pretty bad. Two, in fact, and some other injuries when the truck rolled. Doc might set the legs here. When he's stable, the train will take him into the city. In the meantime, he needs to be cleaned up. Just talk to him to keep him alert. He's in quite a lot of pain. Can you do that?"

Caroline nodded yes. She touched him lightly on his arm. "Thank you. You and Mary."

Vernell responded by giving her a hug. "Now, are you ready? We're going to bring him in on a stretcher."

Caroline wasn't ready. Nothing could prepare her for the shock of seeing Alford lying on the canvas stretcher as he was lifted out of the small, canvas-covered wagon. Battered and blood-soaked, he looked like his clothes had burned on him. His scratched face was pale and his eyes and mouth set hard.

Caroline leaned over and kissed him gently on his forehead.

"Sweetheart," she said and stroked his chin. Smiling, she gave him her bravest front.

Alford gave her a tight grin and said through clenched teeth, "It's going to take more than that to turn this frog into a prince, but it was a good start."

Caroline laughed and took his hand. Charlie Bladstad nodded and a host of other friends who were carrying Alford took him inside. After some maneuvering he was put on the dining table and a pillow placed under his head. Every effort was made move him as little as possible and to make him comfortable.

"We put in an extra leaf, Alford," Charlie said to him. "Didn't think you'd want to dangle."

"I don't think I'm capable of dangling. My legs will simply drop off."

"We'll see," Charlie said. He gave Alford a light pat on his shoulder, then left when Caroline came in. She was carrying a ceramic basin of hot water.

For the next few minutes after she removed his upper clothing she washed the blood and mud off of him with a warm, wet flannel cloth while Dr. Svenson cut away his pants and union suit and examined his legs. Both were damaged, but the left one was the worst. Battered and matted with clumps of black and red blood, it had been straightened out, but still lay sickeningly out of line. There was a bad cut on his thigh. On the lower leg, a large slice of skin had been peeled back near the shin. Caroline thought she could see bone sticking out. The doctor worked around it cautiously.

While Caroline washed the blood and grime out of his hair, Alford lay on the table with his eyes closed, trying his hardest not to cry out, but she could tell it was difficult for him not to.

"Keep talking, keep talking, Mrs. Alford," Dr. Svenson said to her at one point. "I want to hear that story about your boy and the bear."

Alford opened his eyes and said through his teeth that he'd like to hear it too as it was news to him, then he groaned. Though she was sure the doctor was being careful, every motion he made around Alford's badly broken leg must have been excruciating. He looked at her, breathing through his mouth like each breath was an effort. Sweat beaded up on his lips and forehead. When she took his hand, he squeezed it hard.

"Are you in a lot of pain?" she asked.

"I'm a little lightheaded. I — " He stopped suddenly and cried out.

"Sorry about that." The doctor looked over his glasses. "Maybe it's best you go, Mrs. Alford. I have some work to do. If you would, call in Vernell or Charlie Bladstad."

"Will you look for Billy?" Alford's voice croaked. His hand grasped hers too tightly. "Micah promised he was being looked after."

"I'll find him," Caroline said. She gently brushed his

cleaned hair back from his forehead.

"Call Sarah. He especially wanted that."

"I will."

"And tell Cory we'll go fishing tomorrow when I'm feeling better." Alford's words came haltingly. His eyes went unfocused.

Dr. Svenson checked Alford's pulse, then after washing his bloodied hands in a basin next to the table, motioned for Caroline to step out into the hall.

"What's wrong?" Caroline asked when they were by the parlor door. "He's not making any sense."

"It's the strain of the accident. I need to work fast and operate. Before I send him down to the city hospital, I have to clean everything to prevent infection. If he gets infection, he could lose the leg. I cannot wait."

"Dr. Svenson," a man said at the front door. "The last wagon came in. The man has a serious leg wound and loss of blood."

"Put him on the front porch and I'll look at him. Please ask Mrs. Bladstad to come in here. We need to set up a clean operating space in the dining room. Do you have sheets, Mrs. Alford?"

"They're in the linen closet. She knows where that is."

"Good. Now, see if you can help outside. I will let you know when you can see him."

"I'll go look for Billy."

"Mrs. Alford — " he lowered his voice — "I'm very sorry. Billy Howell is dead."

Caroline gasped. "Oh, no." She put a hand on her mouth. Tears welled up in her eyes. "Not Billy. He was such a dear friend. Such a good friend." She swallowed. "Were there others?"

"Five from either Jenkins or Ford's motorcars. I don't recognize them. But they just brought in James Ford. He was trapped under a car. It has taken this long to get him out."

"And Jenkins. Jack said something about Jenkins."

"The bastard is in Hell where he belongs. And if Providence so wishes, Ford will join him soon. Forgive me, but Jenkins terrorized my wife. Ford is no better."

Behind her, Caroline could hear Bob stifling a cry. On the porch and beyond came sounds of suffering. She squared her shoulders and took her shawl off the hall rack. "Please help him. When you are done, send someone to get me."

She went out on the porch and into a nightmare lit by lantern light and a weak porch light. Vernell, Fuller and some of the other men had set up an infirmary. James Ford lay on a stretcher, the bandage on his nose soiled and bloody, but everything about him was bloody. One leg was missing, the price of getting him out alive. The remaining one was mangled. She stared at him, not sure of what to say to him if he should look at her, but he was lost in his world of pain, his voice a tattered whisper after hours of involuntary screaming. Besides, her anger at him roared larger than her pity. She was glad to get off the porch, though the scene out in the lantern-lit pasture was no better. Shadows moved in front of bright lights, making strange shapes on the line of trees around the field and the canvas on the wagons. It shifted and wavered like a scene out of Hell.

A tall broad shape caught her eye and she recognized Micah standing by a motorcar. With him was one of the county deputy sheriffs. The two of them were talking to Vernell. Micah got into the back seat of the car. The officer got in the driver's seat, then they drove off toward Frazier. Stunned, Caroline ran down to the gate.

"Jack! Where's he taking Micah?"

Vernell caught her as she came into the lane. "He's going with Pierce. Just a routine matter."

"But why?"

"He shot and killed Jenkins. Sheriff's office just wants him to give a statement."

"Why? Because they think he's Indian?"

Jack told her what Jenkins had tried to do to Alford and Billy. "As far as I'm concerned, Jenkins got off light. Don't worry, Caroline. It's a matter of paperwork. No one's going to hold Micah, but you're right. I'm sure there'll be someone who will point out that Micah isn't white and make trouble for him. Man who does that will hear from me." He gave her a hug, one of many he would dispense over the next few hours.

She stiffened when Alford suddenly screamed. She turned to go back in, but the old ranger caught her arm. "It's best that you stay out here."

"But he needs me. Charlie and Cathy shouldn't be there doing all the work."

"He needs you to be *here*, where he's not going to waste all his strength worrying about you worrying about him. Without you there, he can relax. He knows he won't face it alone. You going to call your folks?"

Caroline shook her head no. "Well, maybe my sister in California. I'll call Bob's mother as soon as I know what hospital he's going to." She stared out across the pasture and watched a wagon drive up with a load of wood coffins. Some men began to hand them down.

"Where's Billy Howell?"

"You're not wanting to see him?"

"Yes. I owe it to Bob — and to him."

"All right. I'll take you to him. He's wrapped up in one of the wagons. When the train goes down to the city, they can drop off his coffin in Twin Forks. His wife has already been notified."

"You've always known he was dead?"

"Since the wagons first went down. Micah didn't want Bob to know. Said it would agitate him and make his injuries worse. He can be told later." They walked through the collection of wagons to one in the back. Taking a lantern, he helped her up. Billy lay wrapped in a sheet of canvas.

"Did he suffer?"

"Micah says Billy's neck was broken. Probably didn't feel

a thing. He wasn't burned or crushed. It happened pretty fast." Vernell pulled back the canvas shroud from the dead man's face. "Don't pay the bruises no mind. Jenkins worked him over the day before. That's why he was at the clinic."

Jenkins. She hated the name and the man. It made her feel guilty because of his connection to her family. Guilty for Billy, guilty for Bob. Guilty for Micah in trouble. She looked down her dead friend's face, surprised to see that it was calm and at rest. Though the bruising around the eyes was obvious, they had been closed by someone and his arms carefully laid out.

"How old was he?" Vernell asked.

"Same age as Bob. Thirty-two."

Vernell started to put the canvas back, but she took it and leaning over, kissed the cold face on the cheek. "Goodbye, Billy," she murmured, then covered him up. Her shoulders began to shake as grief overwhelmed her. She let out a hard sob, but she soon composed herself.

"Can I do anything for you? It's going to be a long night."

"Thanks, Jack. I could use a cup of coffee."

"Well, I'll get Cathy Bladstad to fix something for you. You can't go on like this." Vernell went to the wagon opening and climbed down. Caroline followed. The coffins were all laid out now and by lantern light, the bodies were being removed from the wagons and placed in the boxes one by one.

Vernell led her away. "You don't need to see this, Caroline." They walked back across the lane. Dr. Svenson was on the porch examining Ford. He called to Caroline when he saw her.

"Mr. Alford's been put under. The operation should take about an hour. Another two before he really starts waking up, but you can see him any time after that." He gave her some words of encouragement, then gave some instructions to a man working on Ford. He was about ready to go in, when the front door opened and Cathy called to Caroline.

441

"Telephone," she announced. "Dr. Ellis, I believe." She waved Caroline on into the house, then gave her the phone when she got into the hallway.

"Bob's going to be OK, Carrie. I'll come get you when the doctor's done."

Caroline thanked her. She put the earpiece to her ear and leaned into the wall phone.

"Hello?" It was Dr. Ellis. She listened without saying a word, then burst into tears.

"Carrie, whatever for?" Cathy called from the dining room door. Caroline waved her back in, taking the rest of the news stoically before giving news of her own. She talked for a few minutes more, then hung up. She took a deep breath and leaned into the wall. *How much more?* she thought. Down the hall to the kitchen, moonlight lit up the windows. She pushed away and slipped outside to the cool embrace of night and forest. She found her favorite thinking rock and sat down. Sobbing, she finally let go of all her fear and tensions.

Cathy Bladstad found her about two and half hours later. Everyone had assumed Caroline had gone upstairs to rest, but when they went in search of her, she was gone. Cathy thought to look outside and taking a blanket, went out along the river's edge. Her lantern found Caroline wrapped in her shawl asleep.

"Carrie, you mustn't do this to yourself. Look at you. Come inside and get some coffee. I've made a fresh pot for everyone."

Caroline wiped her cheeks and sniffed. "Is Bob awake?"

"That's why I've come. He's been asking for you."

"Is he all right?"

"The doctor seems pleased. He did both legs. Found a small fracture in Bob's left wrist, so that's set too." He's quite trussed up. Once he's fully awake, they'll take him to the station and down to the city hospital. The doctors there may operate some more." She put the blanket around Caroline and adjusted it as though Caroline was her little daughter Marianne. "Now we just have to worry about infection, but the doctor has a drain for the wound. Wish we had a pill for that."

"Did the doctor say how long it will take until Bob's back to work?"

When Cathy didn't answer right away, Caroline stiffened.

Cathy cleared her throat. "He said that it might take six months to a year for the legs to heal. And — Bob might not be able to work again at the ranger station."

Caroline gasped. She hadn't thought that far ahead. *How would they manage?* The thought of him not working made her ill. She tried to straighten her hair, but had trouble with the pins and about halfway through the arranging stopped and began to weep.

"Oh, Cathy. How can I face him? All this done to him because of me and my family. And the others. They suffered too."

"What are you talking about? You had nothing to do with this. Do you really believe that?"

Caroline shrugged. "It just seems everything is falling apart. I never wanted this to happen. If I'd known — "

"Carrie. You can't control being born into a family any more then you can control the sun rising in the east. But don't ever say it's your fault. This was about the lumberman and their lust for trees and men wanting the eight hour day. Bob got caught in the middle. Forget about the past. Bob loves you and I'd say he walked into making a life with you with his eyes open long ago. The two of you belong together, don't you know? I never told you, but Mary said the night you miscarried, Bob was on the porch sobbing his heart out because he thought it was all his fault. Thought you'd never forgive him for taking you away from your family. You sound just like him now."

"Bob said that?"

"And more."

Cathy reached around and arranged her friend's hair, and gave her further words of encouragement until she was finished.

"Thank you, Cathy, my dearest friend. Better?"

"Honestly, you look like you were sleeping on a rock all night. Oh, never mind, I was teasing." She helped Caroline up and linking an arm through Caroline's, started to pull her along.

"By the way, was that Dr. Ellis?"

"Yes." Caroline sniffed and shook her head in anguish. "My cousin David collapsed at school. He's been sent home to my family in Portland. My Aunt Agatha will look after him."

"I'm so sorry."

Caroline stopped. "Oh, Cathy, if only I could just hold myself together for a little bit longer and then I'll wake up and it will all be over. I *will* wake up, won't I?"

"Yes, but it won't be over. It's going to be hard, Carrie, but you're the strongest person I know."

Alford was awake on the bed in the tackle room. He had been moved there after the surgery and covered up with blankets heated in the oven. He was flat on his back and one of his legs was suspended. An electric lamp was set near his head. When Caroline came in, Dr. Svenson and Maggie stood up. He nodded Caroline over to Alford's side, then left with Maggie, and quietly closed the door behind him.

"Bob?" She dragged a chair over. He turned it at the motion.

"Caroline... sweetheart. You're here. What time is it?" he asked drowsily.

"About two in the morning. How do you feel?"

He closed his eyes briefly. "Tired...pretty battered, actually." He opened his eyes. "Hey, you're crying. Why are you crying?"

"Because I was afraid I was going to lose you. And I hate you being hurt and in pain. My fault."

"Come here," he said in a weary voice.

She came out of her chair and knelt down beside the bed.

"That's my girl, my beautiful wife. It's not your fault. Ford and Jenkins just couldn't stand losing to progress. As for you, blame me for being smitten the first time I ever saw you." He brought one of his hands out from under the covers and she saw the wrist had a plaster cast. He took her hand. "No one's going to drag us apart. And no one's going to regret anything. I'd do it all over again. And again." He pursed his lips.

"I honestly thought I'd never see you and the kids again. When I get back to work, we'll do something special." Alford sighed, his voice a hoarse echo of its normal self. His head sank deeper into the pillow and his eyes began to droop. He turned his head and gazed at her, almost like he was afraid he had to take it in all in or lose it. "Stay with me... just a little bit. I'm kinda sleepy."

Caroline got back on the chair and kissed his hand. His eyes closed, but a smile stayed on his lips long after he fell asleep.

Caroline sat for a long time watching him. His pale face was cut and scratched. His naked body was bandaged throughout and smelling antiseptic, bristled with stitches. She wondered how long before he would feel the pain again. For now, he was safe, but nothing would be the same until the troubles with her family were resolved. As she thought of their uncertain future, she realized she must be the one to take action. She would have compensation.

Chapter 48

Charles Symington looked at the ravaged face once more. It was over. David Harms wouldn't suffer any more. Symington hardly recognized his son. The cancer eroded his flesh to skin and bone. Except for the eyes. Even in death with the light gone out, there was a memory of the spirit that once looked out of them. *David.* He gently closed the eyes.

Overcome with grief, Symington sat down heavily on the chair next to the bed. *Why did this have to happen to the most decent person I've known in my life? Forgive me for abandoning you. What I gave you was such a pittance. What you gave me —*

He put his face in his hands, tears spilled through his manicured fingers. He didn't care if anyone outside heard him through the door. He grieved, for David and for himself.

After a time, he composed himself, knowing that he needed to make arrangements. He wiped his cheeks with his bare hands, then wiped his hands on his pants. Clearing his throat, he brought the blankets on the body up to its chin and stopped. He didn't have the heart to cover David. Not yet. He leaned back in the chair and sighed.

David. David. What was the last thing you said? "Forgive her."

It would be like him to say that. To overlook his own suffering and think of Caroline. David kept his word and had been utterly faithful. Symington looked at the opened letter on the nightstand. It had been written just days before. It must have been painful to write. At least it took extraordinary effort, using strength David didn't have left to spare. Writing it meant that much to him.

Symington took it into his lap and stared at the opening paragraphs. David had written of his last trip to see Caroline and he told of what he saw there:

Go see Caroline and drop the pretense. It's been so long that you don't remember the reason why you disowned her. Sophie is off in California and will never have children. Sammy is in France. There are grandchildren waiting for you. The young boy Cory is the cleverest I've ever met and little Kate is a jewel.

Symington paused. *Samuel. Oh, Samuel.* Word had just come from France this morning. His youngest son had been killed in an airplane accident. His hands shook, rattling the letter.

What should he do now? His wife had left, angry over the whole Symington-Ford mess. The image of her standing in the doorway to their parlor, packed and ready to travel still shocked him. Her lingering words scolded.

"He's our son-in-law, Charles. Caroline needs help. And I just can't sit by and say I don't care for those little ones. I've had enough of this."

Charles looked down at David's letter.

Caroline needs you now. Alford, I'm told, was gravely injured and will have a long convalescence. Give him a chance and the respect he deserves.

Charles knew that this was true, as well. He had sent a man to ask about Alford after he learned of the accident from his brother Harold. But how on God's green earth did David know about the accident? *It didn't matter, He was with the angels.*

He folded the letter and put it back in its envelope. Outside, someone rustled near the door and then gently knocked.

"Mr. Symington?"

"Come in, Harrison."

"If I may inquire — " the butler asked.

"He's passed on. Just moments ago."

"I'm so sorry. What a fine young man. Such a tragedy. Shall I make funeral arrangements?"

"Please. As soon as possible." Charles hesitated for a minute, then went on. "Could you contact that local hiking club? I'd like to see if David's ashes could be scattered on Mount Rainer. I think he would like that. His wife enjoyed the mountain so. And... Harrison, could you book a train to Frazier, Washington? As soon as possible. I'm afraid that any memorial service for David must be delayed."

"Will you need accommodations, sir?"

"I honestly don't know. Make the usual inquiries. I suppose that it's better to plan on it." He cleared his throat, thick with phloem. "Mrs. Symington is with our daughter Caroline. There may not be enough room at their home." *Nor room in my daughter's heart.*

"And Mr. Samuel?"

"I delayed telling his mother long enough. I feel it must be in person."

The butler listened while Symington gave a few more instructions, then left to fulfill them. Charles knew that he would be both efficient and discreet.

Don't.

Symington looked up sharply at the figure lying on the bed. It was as though he had spoken, the words so clear that were now forming in Charles' mind. *Don't continue the pretense.* As usual, David was right. He must stop hiding behind social niceties and let the truth be known.

And I must face my own part in this tragedy. From the beginning, he should have paid more attention to his brother's handling of the elopement and subsequent actions as well as the various business dealings his brother made that concerned the family's larger holdings. His association with

Ford. The ugly accusations surfacing now from the horrific accident bordered on the criminal and embarrassed the Symington name. That Harold said he had no knowledge of the incident beforehand couldn't completely exonerate him. Using J. J. Jenkins, he had ruthlessly attacked many strikers in his logging concerns, including the one in Twin Forks. Just as worse, Harold had done much to encourage the marriage of Sophie to James Ford, a disaster if there ever was one.

Once again, social niceties had been observed and the truth swept under the rug. If action had been taken against Ford early on for his abuse of Sophie, perhaps his other daughter wouldn't be suffering now. For suffering she must be.

Charles took a pen out of his pocket and wrote a list on the back of the envelope: check on Alford's medical bills; compensation; call Harold's lawyers; wire Dr. Ellis in Seattle about David; details about David's will; go see Caroline....

He stood up and put the envelope into his pocket, then leaned down over the dead form of David Harms. "Goodnight, sweet prince" he said and gently kissed Harms on the forehead. He smoothed back the lackluster hair, then taking one final look, covered him up.

Chapter 49

Alford returned to Frazier about two weeks after the accident and was met at the train depot by a small party of well-wishers. Among them were the Vernells, the Bladstads and George Fuller as well as several friends from the Frazier business and mining communities. As his wheelchair was placed on the platform, Cory and Kate came over with bouquets of foxglove and elderberry flowers. When Caroline joined him from the train a cheer and a round of applause went up followed by a crush of folks to greet him and wish him well. In great ceremony comically reminiscent of Harold Symington's arrival in Frazier just a month before, Alford was wheeled up the street to the hotel where a simple, but exuberant reception waited.

"You're looking good, Alford," or "When are you going to attach a fishing pole to that thing?" were some of the comments meant to cheer. Among friends, it carried the medicine of hope, for the truth was that he had a long convalescence ahead of him. Even during the short periods he moved about on crutches, the other injuries he sustained in the accident made things difficult and tiring. With both legs in casts, movement was awkward and in some cases, dangerous. It was enough to get a person down. Some days, he was weary to the bone fighting the future.

As he sat there in the lobby, he thought it odd that after all the years, there was a new figure with them — his mother-in-law, already in love with the children.

After Charlie Bladstad rolled him into the place of honor in the hotel dining room, Alford gave them all a little speech, thanking them for looking after his family and home, for the cards of encouragement and their kind response to Billy Howell's widow and children. When he was through, he thanked the Ladies Tea Society for the food and hoped their sponsorship of the summer's hiking outing would make it the best ever.

"Now, I guess everyone wants those sandwiches, so with your permission," — he nodded at the hotel proprietress — "dive in."

An hour later, Alford whispered that he had enough excitement and should go home. Fuller called Jack Vernell, who brought a truck around to the front. Friends helped lift him into the back where a mattress had been set down. Caroline and the children scrambled in next to him, followed by the wooden wheelchair.

It was a beautiful, warm July day. Leaning back against the truck cab, they watched the world go backwards away from them as they rode down the forest-bordered road. Greens of every hue and color marked their passing, the road disappeared to a light brown ribbon some point beyond. After a while, the speeding lines of fir and cedar trunks next to the road began to make them dizzy, but for Alford, this was the moment he had been waiting two weeks for: to see the river and his home beside it. He endured each bump with the knowledge he was closer. When the truck down-shifted, he knew they were there.

The truck pulled up next to the gate and stopped. Micah, who, as usual, had avoided the crowds, came alongside. He appeared to have put the house in order. A wide board made of fir set up as a ramp for the wheelchair came down the steps from the porch. Cedar boughs tied on the porch posts also greeted them. Vernell and Fuller got out and with Micah's help got Alford on the ground while the wheelchair was unloaded.

"Where do you want to go first?" Vernell asked when he was seated.

"The river," Alford said.

"Mother and I will take the children in," Caroline said. "You boys go look. Call if you need me."

Around in the back, Vernell and Micah brought Alford to a stop and put the brake on. Before him, the river ran, its color clear and cold.

"Height's about right," remarked Jack. "You could fish from here."

"Could. Need to work on some tackle, though." He looked up river. "It true that Ford's operation was bought out?"

"Just yesterday. The new owners have no further plans to cut. Going to build a summer cabin. I think that it'll be the last you hear of Ford. He's been sent to a nursing home in Seattle. With his body all broken up, he'll probably spend the rest of his days there. His mother's too infirm to look after him."

Vernell stuffed his pipe and looked off. "Found the saboteur. Someone in his pay. Ford was losing money on the operations with all his mechanical and labor problems. Tried to make it look like outside agitation was ruining him. His investors were satisfied until they uncovered some dealings that weren't quite up to snuff. Like I thought, that robbery was planned." Vernell paused. He put a hand on Alford's shoulder. "You're looking good, son."

Alford grinned wryly. He never recalled Jack calling him "son" before. "I'm doing OK, though some days I just wish I could get up and run."

"All in due time, all in due time." Vernell drew deep from his pipe, then let it out. "I'll hold a place for you as long as I can, but if in the end you feel you're not up to it, we'll look for other ways to keep you here in Frazier. Community needs you."

"It's not my intention to go. My brothers Ake and Olav are planning to come and visit with their families sometime during the summer and my brother Lars has offered to come and do maintenance around the place while he's looking into a couple of his mining claims, but after that —"

Micah spoke up at that point. "Don't know why you're all worried." He looked up at the back of the roof. "I was thinking of making some shakes for your roof out of an old growth cedar I seen down. Good quality. Time Cory learned how to work a beattle and a froe. You could armchair the whole event."

"Well, you boys figure it out," Vernell said. "You've got all summer. I've got to get back to the station, Alford, but you take care. See you in a day or two." He shook Bob's hand, then wished them good day.

After Vernell left, Micah came over by Alford and hunkered down on the ground. For a long time they said nothing as they watched the river go by. A chipmunk braved a rock at the river's edge, then flicking its tail in indignation, scurried under a snowberry bush at the slightest hint of aerial observation from a hawk flying by. A kingfisher swooped and dived. Fingerling trout paused in the cool pools before they moved to another. Despite water rushing downstream, it was quiet enough to hear insects in the bushes close by. It was the kind of peace Alford knew Micah liked too.

Alford eventually cleared his throat. "Never thanked you for what you did."

Micah shrugged. "Nothing to thank me for. Was glad I was there, though I take no pleasure in killing a man. But it's done and the world's better for it. Don't know what was in Jenkins's craw, but he certainly was bent on killing you for the hell of it." Micah pursed his lips. "I'm glad you come out okay. Didn't say, but I was worried there for a moment." He picked up some pebbles and tossed them around in his hand. "Thought about what you're gonna do?"

"What do you mean?"

"You know what I mean. Jack's all optimistic, but we both know you won't be able to go back. Your leg won't take all that strain packing and fighting fires. Leastways not for a long time. Best to try something different."

"Working the woods is all I know."

"You know fish and you know guiding and you know about running a store because your family did it. You ought to give old Bergstrom a call. He's been thinking about getting a partner. Wouldn't be any loss of face. Folks would pay for what fishing advice you've given away free. Vernell could probably get contracts for you."

"I'll think about it." Alford didn't have much to say. That hollow feeling of falling through the air off the mountain hit him again. How would he be able to do to support Caroline and the kids now?

"You do that." Micah stood up. "Sounds like you got company arriving. I'll take off now, unless you want to get wheeled back in."

Alford said no. "I think I'll just rest for a moment. It was a long train ride. The air feels good. Besides, Caroline wanted to get the kids all settled in."

"Then I'll see you." Micah rested his hand on Alford's shoulder. "Go with the spirits."

Alford leaned back against the high back of the wheelchair and closed his eyes for a moment. "See you in a bit," he murmured, unaware that Micah had left because he could still feel the pressure of the mountaineer's hand on his shoulder. He continued to talk, but felt very tired. He was aware of the river's ripple and a Steller's jay in the cedar next to the house, but soon they were cancelled out as he slumped into a deep sleep.

Caroline heard the car pull up in front of the house. Thinking it Cathy coming to help out for the afternoon, she went out to greet her. Bob was out with Micah and the kids on tour of their bedrooms with Mother upstairs. When she went out onto the porch, she discovered an expensive Locomobile touring car parked near the gate. Wiping her hands on her apron, she stepped down, her heart pounding.

Stepping out of the car on the passenger side was her father.

You've grown old, Father, she thought. His face looked so worn and weary as if all the cares of the world balanced on his shoulders, but could fall off any time. He seemed thinner and his eyes looked bloodshot, like he had been crying.

"Caroline."

"Father." She realized her voice sounded cold and cautious, but she knew no other way to speak to him. And then, a strange epiphany came over her. She didn't need his approval any more. It didn't matter. And that gave her more courage.

Symington cleared his throat a little too loud. "Is... is your mother here?"

"Yes, she's here." Caroline came down the steps.

"Good. Good. I miss her." He came around the car and removed his kid gloves.

"Do you, Father? Or is it because you no longer have someone to lord over?"

"Caroline, dearest girl."

"Please, don't... Not after what happened. Hasn't enough been done to my family?"

Charles put his hand out as if in protest, but he immediately withdrew it. Approaching the gate, he took off his hat and turned the rim a couple of times through his hands. "Of course. I understand perfectly. But I do intend to speak to Alford if he wishes —"

"Really?"

"I thought you could use some financial help. His injuries —"

"We don't want it."

He sighed and it seemed to Caroline that a shudder went through his whole body. "Pride," he said, nodding his head.

"I deserved that. I am so sorry." When he looked up at her, there were tears in his eyes. One rolled down into his graying moustache. He put a hand on the wooden gate. "May I come in?" When Caroline didn't object, he came up the walkway.

"Caroline, I suspect that any forgiveness I might hope for will be a long time coming, but I do need to talk to you and your mother. It's important. I — is there anywhere you and I can talk alone first?"

"Why?" Caroline felt her heart weakening. She was not good at this — denying someone's wishes, especially her father's — but she had to be strong so that her father would understand. To her surprise, her father choked and began to weep.

"Father, what is it?"

"Please, I don't want your mother to hear. Can we go somewhere?"

"Yes, if you have something to say, you must say it in front of Bob. He's down in the back."

She led the way down past the left side of the. porch and around to the river. Above the bank, Bob appeared to be asleep in the wheelchair, his plastered leg in danger of falling off the platform. She gently set it straight, waking him.

"There you are, Caroline. Come to take me away in my chariot?" he said sleepily, then snapped his eyes open when he realized they weren't alone. "You," Alford said when saw it was Charles Symington. "What the hell are you doing here?"

Caroline slipped next to Alford and put a hand on his arm. "He wants to speak to me."

"Now? What about the first time?" he growled. "And later? Did you care so little for her that you couldn't even talk to her at her best friend's funeral? What kind of parent are you?"

Caroline tightened her grip on Alford's arm. She had hoped for a quiet first afternoon home, but it was in danger of devolving into family drama. She worried that it would tire Bob out further.

"Actually," her father said softly, "I have asked myself the very same question lately. I'm deeply sorry for what has happened. You must believe that."

Alford snorted. "I'm sure, in your own way, you are. But it doesn't lessen the loss of a friend nor the hurt for my wife. An overdue visit won't help at all."

Symington murmured something Caroline couldn't hear, then cleared his throat. "I saw wreaths alongside the road above a ravine. Dreadful situation."

"It's one of the worst disasters in the area's history," Alford said.

"Is your friend's widow being cared for?"

"The community is looking after her for now."

"I've filed a lawsuit, Father, on behalf of those injured in the accident." She took Alford's hand. "When Bob is well, we'll see to their day in court."

"Of course."

With some effort, Alford turned his wheelchair around and faced Symington. "How's Harms? You coming clean on that?"

The turn of questioning startled Caroline. Worse was the look Alford gave her father.

"What do you mean?" Symington asked.

"I know your secret. Harms told me."

Symington sighed, a sound that ended in a strange gulp. "I don't know what you are talking about."

"Well, if you fancy yourself coming around here in the future, you're going to have to tell the truth."

"The truth? Of course, I will take full responsibility for what has happened here. Justice will be served for all the victims. I'm having a lawyer look into my brother's affairs —
"

"No, Symington. The truth," Alford shouted.

"Truth...?"

"Bob? What's going on?" Caroline cocked her head at him.

Alford took Caroline's hand. "I'm sorry, Caroline, but I just can't let this lie."

"What do you mean?"

"Your father's a hypocrite. While he opposed your marriage to me, he's been harboring a son by some woman he loved, but didn't have the courage to marry. He adored the son, but faulted the daughter."

Caroline gasped and gripped Alford's hand tight.

"That's preposterous. Where did you hear this?" Symington's face drained.

"Harms told me when he was here for the last time. He said he was your illegitimate son, born before you met Caroline's mother. When his mother died while he was still an infant, he was raised by one of your aunts."

"How dare you!"

"Oh, I dare. All these years, I thought he was one of Caroline's most persistent suitors. And all the time he loved her as a devoted brother. What a waste," Alford spat. "We could have been good friends, but what's worse, it's what you did to him. He sacrificed himself for you and your good family name. I don't know which I hate the most: the way you treated Caroline or the way you treated him."

"Father, is this true? Is this what you wanted to tell me? David's my half-brother?"

Symington opened and closed his mouth. After a long pause, he slowly nodded his head.

"Oh." She felt like she was slipping under the river's cold water as scenes with David from her childhood and as recent as a month ago raced in her head. She suddenly looked up at her father.

"That's why he changed when he was around sixteen. I knew something changed."

"I had to tell him then. First, he was angry, but then sworn to secrecy, he played the role of secret son, much to my joy and consternation. The things he did didn't always please me, such as arranging elopements."

"Does Mother know?" Caroline's head whirled with all

the scenarios the news would create in the Symington family.

"Nobody knows. Not even your Uncle Harold.". His voice lowered. "Your grandfather wouldn't hear of marriage to her. But I did love David's mother and I did look after him when she died."

"But you left her there all because you were afraid of Grandfather?" Caroline was so angry she could barely get the words out.

Symington's voice choked. "Caroline." He looked at her with deep sorrowful eyes. "It's something that I'm not proud of, something that has weighed on me a long time. David was such a joy and absolutely true to me. I didn't deserve him."

Caroline stiffened. "You said was — "

Charles swallowed. "It's one of the reasons I've come. David passed away yesterday at our Portland home. It was his last wish that I come here to make amends."

Caroline didn't hear his words. She slapped a hand to her mouth. "Oh, David," she sobbed. "Oh, I can't bear it. Emily, now him. It's so unfair."

"There's more," Charles said. Then he told her about Samuel.

Chapter 50

There is something about grieving for loved ones you've lost. There is kindness and support from the community at large amid promises of hope and healing.

But grief is quite different when the door is closed and you are alone in your thoughts. Then it feels like a cut to the heart, like an arrow to the bone. A forever cloud that cannot lift.

Caroline felt like that. Grief and sorrow raged in her and in the Alford home as she and her parents grappled with the death of Samuel. Mother was almost inconsolable, her father seemingly defeated by life. David's passing only deepened the pain for everyone. He was that loved, but it was decided that they wouldn't tell Mother quite yet about his true family status.

When Caroline had time to herself, when she was not looking after the children and Bob, she would steal away to her place on the river. Cathy found her there two days after Charles Symington arrived.

"I brought fixings for tonight's meal," Cathy said. "Your mother put it in the icebox." She slid next to Caroline on the wooden slab bench.

"Thank you."

"How are you doing?"

Caroline sighed. "I'll manage. It's just so much to take in. I feel like I went over the falls."

"I'm so sorry, Carrie, but then I've already said that a thousand times. David and Emily were such exceptional people and your brother a real charmer." She patted Caroline's hand, then held it. "Take care of yourself while you take care of others. How is our valiant ranger doing?"

Caroline squeezed Cathy's hand back then released it. "He's uncomfortable as all get out. Can't sleep because it's hot at night and painful when he's awake during the day. The only relief seems to come when he's helped up onto crutches. Yesterday, he asked to be helped down to this bench so he could watch the river. He was so exhausted, he was soon back in the wheelchair, cramped and bedsore."

"Poor dear. Poor you. When are your parents leaving?"

"I think tomorrow. They have to make plans for two separate funerals, but I've already told them I can't attend. Bob needs me."

"Have you made peace with your father?"

Caroline sighed, something she seemed to be doing a lot of lately. "Somewhat. A part of me is having a hard time doing it, but I have to consider the children and I so want my mother to be a part of their lives. Bob's been skirmishing with Father about accepting help from him."

"What do you want?"

Caroline twisted her hands in her lap. "Well, one solution is to accept their help, but only until Bob can literally get back on his feet. Bob was talking about making up some ground rules. They could write to the children as much as they liked and maybe, just maybe, if things between us improve, arrange for them to visit Portland. I'd go along, of course. But that's a bit off."

"Well, that's some sort of progress, isn't it?"

"Yes, but such a cost. I don't know what I feel any more." Caroline turned away. "Isn't it funny? To be

461

reconciled to my parents was something I've wanted for so long, but since the loss of David and Emily, my wonderful father-in-law and Sammy and nearly losing Bob — I just don't hunger for it any more. What I have right here is what I desire the most and always have."

"Well, I'm glad Portland hasn't lured you away. I'd miss you terribly. We all love you, Carrie. Frazier just wouldn't be Frazier without you."

The evening after Caroline's parents left, she went in search of Bob and discovered him missing. As a last resort, she went out the back door. She found him out there staring at the water in the dying light, watching it run over the stones toward the west.

"How on earth did you get off the porch?"

"I slid down on my behind." Alford leaned on the crutches. "I've got to keep moving."

"Be careful. One fall and you're back in bed again."

"I'm tougher than I look."

"You're the embodiment of toughness. That's why I married you. Just don't push yourself."

Alford snorted, then carefully worked his way back to the bench.

"Would you like to be out here during the day? Micah said he might build you a table and a little pavilion to go over it, so you could fish or work on fishing gear." She gave him a slip of paper. "Jack sent this along. Bergstrom got an order for one of your fly rods. He can get the materials to you if you call. Wants to talk to you anyway. About the store. You'll talk to him, won't you?"

Alford nodded. "Sure, if everyone would stop making it their business to look after me, though I know they mean well." He looked across the water to the mountains high above the jagged line of fir and hemlock. Caroline watched his face slowly fall to a distant hurt. For a moment her heart pounded in panic thinking of their way ahead. *I have to be strong, for the both of us.*

Caroline sat down next to him. Very gently, she touched him on his arm, then slipped her hand through. "What is it?"

"Nothing."

"Don't be discouraged. We'll manage."

He smiled wryly. "I know we will. The prospect of working with Bergstrom isn't such a bad alternative to what I've been doing." He looked down at his legs. Caroline thought they stretched out as rigid as forms for concrete pillars. "I'm not discouraged," he continued. "At least ways, not most of the time. I can handle this." He looked up at the tallest peak in the mountain grouping. It was pale pink in the late twilight glow and jagged as a serrated knife edge. "Just hope that you'll get what you want from your folks. Your father. He wanted forgiveness. I gave him a climb as high as Thompson's Glacier. Now I wonder if I won't get stuck down here as well."

"You won't. Dr. Svenson says that you're strong and eventually you'll be able to hike in the mountains again. I know you will. It's just going to take time. Just like my folks will take time."

She paused before she spoke again. "See our cedar tree over there? Micah told me a long time ago about all the things his grandmother's clan made from it: canoes, planks for housing and the posts to support them as well as boxes bent from a single plank, baskets, rain cloaks, hats, ropes and even diapers. I know you know that, but he also said that all of its parts were important to the whole. Like a family."

She briefly leaned her head against his shoulder, then straightened up. "I think he's right. Many parts make up the whole and we often miss the point about the individuals in it. Like the cedar tree, all parts are important. It makes a family strong. I think my father was beginning to realize that. Because of that, I'm going to forgive him."

The back door screeched then banged as Cory and Kate came out onto the stairs.

"Mommy, is Daddy coming in?" Cory asked.

"Soon," Caroline said. "Why don't you and Kate set up the Parcheesi game and play? Mommy and Daddy want to be alone for a bit."

After the children went in, Alford realigned his body to his cumbersome legs. He looked back at Thompson's Glacier, Caroline looked up too and contemplated its cold beauty and what the future held for them. For a while, neither said anything. It was very peaceful, the summer night coming on stronger as each minute passed.

A breeze came up, as though something passed through.

"I dreamt of David last night," Caroline said softly. "He was standing here by the river skipping pebbles with Cory and Kate. He wasn't ill any more. He said, 'Hello, Sister,' and asked me how I was doing. I said that I was fine. That made him smile and before he disappeared over to the forest on the other side, he said, 'Well done.' I think he was speaking to you."

She looked away and started to weep. Alford reached around her waist and drew her to him. They sat there side by side and watched as the twilight faded and the first stars came out above the dark forms of the mountains. They shone like the stars on their honeymoon hike — the night as sharp and clear as she ever remembered. As they watched, the little breeze waxed and waned, bringing the scent of cedar and pine and a powerful sense of peace. As it rushed over them like the water in the river, she knew that no matter what happened, they would be together. Like the mountains, the river and the trees, they were one.

She nestled in closer to him. Alford kissed her on the top of her head. "I love you," he said.

"I love you too."

They watched the stars bloom, then slowly, silently went inside.

ABOUT THE AUTHOR

J. L. Oakley is an award-winning author of novels and personal essays. She won the top prize in non-fiction with her essay "Drywall in the Time of Grief" at the 2006 Surrey International Writers Conference in Canada. Her historical novel, *Tree Soldier*, won the 2012 EPIC ebook Award for historical fiction and the 2013 grand prize for fiction at Chanticleer Book Reviews. *Tree Soldier* was selected as the 2013 Everybody Reads for the Lewis and Clark Valley and neighboring Palouse communities. *Timber Rose* is its prequel.

The daughter of Northwesterners who met over cookies at the University of Michigan, she grew up in Pittsburgh, Pennsylvania. After obtaining her BA degree in history from Kalamazoo College, she made her way west and eventually settled in Hawaii where she met her future husband. They moved to Northwest Washington where they raised three sons. She has never looked back.

History and writing are her passion. She was the curator of education at a county museum for many years and still writes social studies curricula for schools and historical organizations. She loves demonstrating 19th century folkways such as butter making and handspinning, but when not doing that and her writing, you can find in her gardens, tending veggies and flowers alike.

Tree Soldier and *Timber Rose* are available on Amazon and at various indie bookstores. You can find her at http://historyweaver.wordpress.com

Made in the USA
Middletown, DE
06 May 2021